# Dead Eyes in
# Late Summer

**Renée Ebert**

2021 White Bird 1st Edition

Copyright © 2021 by Renée Ebert

Published in the United States by
White Bird Publication, LLC, Texas

ISBN 978-1-63363-548-7
eBook ISBN 978-1-63363-549-4
Library of Congress Control Number 2021947196

Cover design: E. Kusch

PRINTED IN THE UNITED STATES OF AMERICA

## *DEDICATION*

To my Aunt Rose
and to Mrs. Eilenberg

## *ACKNOWLEDGEMENTS*

Thanks to Rebecca Rider, without your incredible talent for first and second edits and for loving the story, this novel would have remained tucked away. Thanks to members of the many writer's groups who expressed support and enthusiasm: writer and friend, Walter Stoffel of Barbara's Writers Group, my dear and gifted compatriot and writer, Madeleine Goldman, and the encouragement of my husband, Louis Wasser. Thanks to the editors at White Bird Publishers.

# TABLE OF CONTENTS

# *Dead Eyes in Late Summer*

*White Bird*
*Publications, LLC*

# *Prologue*

The hammock began to swing; the first sign something was wrong. From a dead stop, a soft movement began, back and forth. Adelyn Crawford told herself she dreamed the whole thing. There stood Innis, handsome as always in summer light linen, swinging the hammock. He came and lay on top of her and it all felt so familiar, so like what had been. Unlike a dream, she felt it when he entered her, rocked her with him, the way he did back then, her only sixteen.

Adelyn came awake with a shudder, finding him gone. Suddenly near noon, the bell from the kitchen summoned the workers from the fields. She cried for Innis and herself and what they had, and sat astride the hammock, straightening her dress, pulling it down before someone walked by.

*That was no dream.* She always knew Innis would come back for her after ten years of being gone. *He came all the way back.* She needed to tell someone; otherwise how would she be able to relive the feelings?

Still drowsy and dizzy, Adelyn got up slowly and walked up the hill to the house, noticing as she did that the hammock hung discreetly just behind two other trees so no one could have seen him on her.

Her thoughts went to her friend. *Delia would listen, like a sister to me, she would understand if I said Innis came back for me. No matter how crazy it sounded.*

# *PART I*

*Renée Ebert*

# *Chapter One*
## *DEAD WALKING AND INNIS*

For a long time, since they came back from France, and since Garnett left in a red-hot huff, Adelyn had felt dead inside. Her heart worked still, but the heart that cared lay withered. Her soul wandered between here and somewhere else as she walked the rough terrain where the unpaved roads cut into deep ruts, and she got her new shoes all dusty. Adelyn passed over onto the greenest grass anyone will ever find outside Savannah. Under the shade of old oaks hung with moss, the dew maintained a sweet wetness that bathed her shoes until they were rid of the dust of Georgia clay.

She thought of her husband, saying aloud, "Garnett's away; he's cut himself out of my life." Propelled to keep on moving, she realized how disheveled she would look to her mother as she climbed one hill after another with no thought to the dirt and mud under her feet. Mama would have a fit, telling her, yelling at her, like she always did.

Missus Jackson grabbed Adelyn long enough to dab the

remaining dew off her shoes with a long handkerchief before Adelyn's wandering began again. June 1931, and everything slowed as the hot, humid air took hold and wouldn't let go again till late fall. All the while, Adelyn stood like a store mannequin, wooden and listless, while her mother fussed about her hair. She could almost cry. At times, her spirit sought out hope, and so, on a Sunday, Adelyn floated into church. The priest laid the thin wafer, *Body and Blood*, on her tongue. She didn't feel it.

Her walking, roaming, riding, and driving took her past the neighbors, with them all lingering on their wide verandas, drinks in hand.

Throughout that summer day on the hammock with Innis, Adelyn took to riding Ramses, him loving the hot days as they galloped and then rested near the creek. With Garnett gone up north, and out west, and anywhere but home, she ran away from his absence on Ramses's back. "Will he finally miss me and come home?"

"Good as dead," she said of her absent husband to Mama at the noonday dinner, after the disturbing visit from Innis. She pictured Garnett with that loose-hipped walk of his, more suited to home than a city. "Always meeting people in harsh places full of pushing crowds and loud-talking men."

Mama pushed at her hand as it rested on the tablecloth. "You hush with all that nonsense." Her mother did not want to think anything bad between Garnett and her daughter, for the sake of their children, for the sake of the inheritance that would be Garnett's, the children's, and yes, Adelyn's. Her mother would wait, the southern country way. "It'll sort itself out." She said this in a nervous whisper.

They all sat at the table for the midday meal, her mother and father, Aunt Grace, Mama's sister, and Uncle Tyree, her husband. And Adelyn's two sons, who looked up from picking at their food, and smiled across the table at their pretty young mother.

Her thoughts flew back as quickly to Innis, how tall and

beautiful he looked for that brief moment in the hammock. She blushed remembering his hands on her. And Garnett, his brother and her husband? Garnett had turned out to be wild. Adelyn's eyes swept the large dining room, her gaze resting on his photo on the mantle over the unlit fireplace. Adelyn could see it clearly, as though she held it in her hand. For a moment, she sensed Garnett's spirit sitting next to her, his eyes that curious amber green, and his hair dusty colored, with highlights of red throughout. She looked around, to see everything in the room near and farther away, clear and sharp. Her eyesight keener now, realizing it sharpened after she woke from the nap and the dream of Innis. *Did I dream of him after all—one moment yes, the other no.*

The photo held Innis's image, in the background, as dark as Garnett was fair. Her boys had a touch of red in their hair, too.

Watching her boys now, she grew sad for neglecting them. Her mother read her thoughts. "All that walking and climbing. Pay some mind to those little ones." She said this while pouring more lemonade for Tyler, the youngest boy. Adelyn defended them running wild all that summer, careless and scraggly, no shoes on them most of the time. "Maybe it didn't hurt them to be so wild, Mama, like their daddy."

Her oldest boy, Trey, asked her, "Mama, when's Daddy coming home?"

"Friday, Sugar. He'll be here Friday afternoon." Yes, her deadened soul had most to do with Garnett's ways. *As it did to the loss of Innis.*

Mama stirred her coffee with a little demitasse spoon and complained mostly to herself and a little to her daughter, "You still set on driving down to the train station for Garnett Friday?"

Adelyn looked up to see the boys sliding off their chairs, ready to escape, "Trey, Tyler. Come on back. You can cool down some in a bath before you run out in that hot weather." She turned back to her mother. "You know I plan to drive down to Savannah." *Will he want to see me?* The family continued with their chicken dinner while Adelyn fell back into her thoughts of Innis, contemplating what would have happened if she had married him, had he lived. *But is he dead?* She felt strongly that he occupied an in-between-place, remembering the hammock and his hands on her body, forcing her to come alive.

Adelyn's friend Delia lived five miles farther west of Savannah and three miles from Tulip Junction. Adelyn smiled to herself. *Delia knows all my secrets, and if she had any, I'd know hers.* Starting out the sun shone through the trees but the sky darkened as Adelyn drove. Rainstorm, she thought, yet no clouds gathered, the sky dead night clear. A wind picked up and the cool breeze offered relief from the dank humidity that settled on everything. Although the car hummed loudly on the hard-paved road, Adelyn's heightened senses picked up sounds of rustling and movement in the back seat.

"You know I taught you how to drive. Remember, Sweet Pea?" The voice crooned, mellow as Uncle Tyree's hundred-year-old Irish whiskey. She should have been startled. Instead, the longing to hear that warm and inviting voice after all this time just made her cry. Adelyn stopped the car on the lonely road no one ever used and looked for Innis. His face peered back to her from the mirror; he seemed to be floating.

"Why did you leave us?" She heard her voice, tense, higher-pitched from the tension.

"Honey, I never left." He settled into the back seat, forcing her to turn full around. He wore the same unwrinkled white shirt and white linen jacket as when he held her just hours earlier. She held out her hand to him, noticing his felt curiously warm. Innis smiled with a shrug.

"No, darlin. Not a vision and ain't no vampire. Yet." And just like before, he magically pulled her over the obstacle of the big front seat, positioning her on top of him, began frankly, expertly to examine the laciness of her frilly light summer dress, tugged on the buttons at the bottom of her shimmy, and released the power of her warmth with his equally warm hand. Adelyn's breathing became uneven and choked as she fought her mind to reach a climax. Somehow, he had moved her under him and placed himself again inside of her, rhythmically thrusting, but gently, as they rocked together and let out a simultaneous sigh.

She knew she only had moments to ask, that he almost fleetingly headed away, as if a spirit greater and more powerful pulled him from her.

"Please wait. Tell me you can stay; tell me you won't leave again. I need to be happy."

Innis flashed his almost translucent smile. "Sugar, I can promise no such thing. Doubt I ever made you that happy. But I can tell you I can't leave you or here altogether, not yet."

Adelyn found herself magically behind the wheel of the car as it continued up the winding drive leading to an expansive front porch where rocking chairs and a long bench all sat in a row.

Delia leaned against a large pillar. A breeze caught her voile dress as it floated on the air before coming to rest against her slim, long legs. Adelyn tapped the horn lightly on the big Hudson sedan so that it emitted a series of short and sharp sounds.

Her car came to a rough stop; gravel flew around its sides.

"I worried to wake those folks that might be taking an afternoon nap." Adelyn straightened her skirt, not for the first time today but for the same reason. Exiting the car, she twisted herself to place her feet on the ground as her mother and her finishing schoolteacher had instructed.

The two friends hugged. "You look a tad frazzled, honey." Delia reached to straighten up a loose curl lying against her friend's cheek. "But no matter, you're always delightful." She picked up a tendril, and smiled. "Maybe this look is just a bit tawdry."

They both laughed and Adelyn felt a blush creep up her face. Delia had soft reddish-blonde curls and a pointed chin in a perfect heart-shaped face. She had her father's longer nose, like his German side, she liked to say. She and Adelyn were the same height.

"Let's go around back to the Florida room. The sun is full on this side of the house so it ought to be cooler there." Delia fanned her moist face and led the way. They sat on plumped-up cushions as a cool breeze flowed through the window.

"Now what did you have to tell me that you must drive all the way over here in this heat?" They sat across from one another and Adelyn tried to think how to tell Delia as she watched the ice cubes melt in a glass of sweet tea.

"Innis Crawford." Adelyn smoothed her dress. "I thought I dreamed it but I had some evidence to the contrary." It all spilled out in a flood of words, the almost dream in the hammock, the encounter just minutes before arriving at Delia's, the lovemaking. Adelyn left nothing to be imagined, not even the hot caresses.

"And he said he is not dead yet. I fell asleep after, it seemed for a bit, and woke up when the wind gusted up and threw some sticks at the car window."

All through the rapid-fire description of a most intimate event, Adelyn noticed her friend's expression change from surprise to deep concentration. Delia took her words seriously; Adelyn knew she could confide in her oldest, dearest friend.

Delia could handle the magic of the mysterious, and never got upset about unclear situations. She'd know what to do.

"Now what has got you so deep in thought?" Adelyn knew that Delia had something exciting to say as she fretted with her bracelet, the one her beau, Lyle St. Lee Spencer, had given her.

"Not a bit surprised at this." Delia worried her bracelet more, as if tapping its bewitching powers. "You remember for a week after Lyle gave it to me, all kinds of happenings went on around here. I told you how I saw two pitchforks flying out the barn. All since this bracelet." Delia liked to tell of mysterious healing of sore mouth, sore foot, and boils that had blighted folks around the little town of Tulip Junction, or those that always loitered about the General Store, and even with people she knew in Savannah. Adelyn saw Delia as a floating spirit and the best one to ask for help. They fell silent as they drank the rest of their sweet tea. Delia straightened her dress and opened the door to the screened-in porch.

## Chapter Two
### MOMMA SORROW

"We must go see Momma Sorrow." Delia took Adelyn by the wrist and headed toward a dirt path packed hard with at least a hundred years of travelers. The path took them near the bottom fields and a small, neat house painted light yellow with dark green shutters. A fence made of wrought iron surrounded the house and its little patch of grass on all sides.

All the while Adelyn's senses of hearing and smell expanded, heightened. She missed not one iota of the route they took nor of the house when they came to it, and all the crops and animals in between. It all looked more, more intense, more magical, yet more real somehow, than the everyday and familiar.

"Now tell me, 'cause I know I'm supposed to remember her. Is she your neighbor?"

Adelyn said it to be polite and maybe somewhat teasing. She knew the Howard family property and farms had no neighbors living within it.

"Don't be foolish. You know Momma and her little store out back where she processes her herbs." Delia swung open the wrought-iron gate and they passed through.

Adelyn swore the gate swung shut of itself. Magic permeated the day and everything in it. She remembered Momma now: though a young girl at the time, Adelyn recalled her mother taking her to Momma for some potion to ease her menstrual cramps. Momma also fixed a tincture of something for her mother, which her mother called her 'headache powder.' Now a woman of twenty-eight, Adelyn knew the potion had eased her mother's hot flashes, and whatever else it could do for her remained unthought-of and unsaid.

Delia's knuckles beat a sharp tap-tap on the door, which looked freshly painted. Adelyn surveyed the front yard of just-cut grass and the tang of it brought back memories of boys and girls, Garnett and her, too, running in summer along the railroad tracks or climbing trees and being shouted at by scolding neighbors for doing so. *Garnett and me as children, I'd forgotten.* She heard some movement inside, light steps, and the door opened. A woman of medium brown skin greeted them. Adelyn reckoned her to be at least sixty or even more, though her skin looked lustrous and young. Momma Sorrow raised one brow high up surveying Adelyn because, of course, she already knew she, not Delia, came to see her, the one with a need to know.

Adelyn stood perfectly still as Momma lightly touched her shoulder to guide her into the cool and darkened room. A single small lamp lit the round table on which it sat and Momma conducted the two young women to the table. Delia finally interrupted the silence.

"Momma, this is Adelyn Jackson from over Tulip Junction." In her haste to move things along, Delia had forgotten to add the Crawford name that stuck to Adelyn like so much honey stuck to her fingers and only hot water and soap washed it off.

"Crawford. My married name is Crawford." Adelyn looked around the room and up close at some of the portraits lining the walls and fireplace, photos next to much older paintings. Even these looked like a camera had caught the solemn or the sad look in the eyes of the man or woman or child. All young people, most in their twenties and a few maybe mid-thirties. Adelyn knew right away they had lived well but had all died. *They were white and black and some looked like Chinese, and a few Indians, mostly sleek, black-haired Seminole.*

"That may be." Momma said, reading Adelyn's thoughts. She settled her cool fingers on Adelyn's pulse. She smiled sweetly, a knowing in her eyes not easily ignored. Adelyn observed this woman surmised more about her than Adelyn supposed about herself. "You have been visited and love came of it."

Adelyn blushed. "How could you know?" To her own surprise, she began to cry. "I wish it to be more than a dream."

"Now, *chère*, don't be wasting wishes on what you already have." Momma Sorrow gently rubbed Adelyn's back, which had gone, all stiff and rigid from nerves. "Sit down now and let me do the telling, not all, mind you, just what you need to know." Momma fussed with a pitcher of sweetened tea and poured three glasses onto ice. The cubes floated up against the sides of the glass.

Adelyn sensed everything in this house carried with it a message of a soothing nature. Smells of fresh bread just baked, cooling in the kitchen, mingled with lavender on pillowcases in, she guessed, an upstairs bedroom. Then she smelled something different but not unknown.

"That is his favorite scent, French cologne, blended with your powder." Momma Sorrow referred to the light lilac-scented dusting powder Adelyn had used after the hasty bath she took after Innis made love to her on the hammock.

"No, he is not here." She answered Adelyn's question before it had fully formed in her own mind. "For now."

"Let's begin." Momma Sorrow sipped her sweet tea with the two young women. She held them with her eyes, and then closed them; her lips began to murmur a soft prayer. "We first acknowledge Him who stands over all, and ask for guidance."

A fan softly whirring in front of a block of ice cooled the otherwise quiet room.

"We ask for one to come forward, or if not in a presence, that he come in spirit and fill me with his thoughts. You have shown yourself to this loved one. Once more, tell us what you want. Tell us how we can help you."

A deeper quiet descended on them. Adelyn could see the white flouncy curtains rustle with the fanning breeze, and then a shadow came across her vision, passing the window, now inside the house and the room. Try as she might, Momma's sultry voice no longer relaxed her. Adelyn felt almost a dread. Something white approached and floated in front of her, not physically, it floated mentally. She could never explain to herself or anyone. Only when she recognized Innis again did her fear leave her.

"Tell us." Momma incanted again.

Words flew into Adelyn's mind, words like images, and they conjured strong emotions. She felt deep sadness, and then she laughed—then smiled. She felt a flirtation; she saw a silly dance in a circle—heard voices in song. In the middle of it she sensed Innis, from as far back as she could remember him. It all went on for so long, like a lifetime, surprising her when she saw Momma and Delia looking intently at her.

Delia took her hand and gently squeezed it.

"Are you all right, Sugar? You had us worried, or maybe just me; Momma's used to having people here with spells on them. Isn't that so, Momma?"

"I went there, went back." Adelyn sipped some of her tea, the ice still solid in the glass. *All this happened in a moment.* "I thought it all took hours. We went back in time. Innis tugging my curls, teasing me at Christmastime when I was sixteen, then whispering to me, what he always did from that time till now."

Delia fanned herself with her open hand. "What did he whisper, can you remember?" Adelyn went back into the images for a second, to prolong the memories.

"He whispered to me, 'I love you, Adelyn. I'm coming back so you'll be mine.'" Adelyn saw Momma's face lighten. *Please tell me what all this means to you. Can you?* Adelyn thought but could not speak.

Momma drew into herself; her face conveyed a bit of the sorrow that gave her her name.

"You can know some things now, others later, when you're ready. Innis Crawford's soul drifts in time. He lives still but in a sideways world, one next to this, not Heaven or Hell. He has unfinished business here. So do you, so do we all, as long as we live." She exhaled slowly and continued. "You have pledged yourself to another, a brother, and there has been some trouble. Innis knows this. It gives him strength to come back and finish, and this part will not be forgotten. He wants to come all the way back."

Adelyn could sense she had more to tell her but decorum dictated that she would share more for her ears only.

Everything got quiet as the séance ended. Momma Sorrow got up from the table to replenish their tea. She reached for a mortar bowl and pestle.

Momma's strength of presence fascinated Adelyn. *She fills the room with herself.* Momma looked up at her as she listened to Adelyn's mind. Adelyn wanted to but could not ask much outright; instead she subtly hinted at her history. "Momma Sorrow, I hear a French lilt in your accent. *Très jolie.*"

Momma stopped in her gathering herbs for a sleeping potion to help Adelyn rest better. Leaning onto the pestle, she crushed the herbs, saying "*Ma chère*, I have forgotten my native tongue of pure French. Comes from living in the Quarter all those years." She rolled up the herbs into a tight square packet and continued, "I learned my English from the servants at my uncle's home as much as from my cousins."

She handed the packet to Adelyn. "Now you take one pinch in a cool glass of water, but let it dissolve first. Do this just before you set your head against your pillow or you will find yourself on the floor."

Adelyn's expression of shock and perhaps some dismay at the potency of the herb caused Momma to rush on to explain. "No need to worry. You will sleep deeply, some say they dream, others complain they do not dream at all, but those that complain have no poetry in their souls and wouldn't know a dream if it snuck up on them in daylight."

Knowing their curiosity, Momma continued to share some of her life.

"My mother taught me medicine passed from her family. She was better at healing than those doctors nosing around with dishes to open veins and bleed people. That procedure only benefits those with thick blood pressure the doctors call hypertension. Then it can save a life. Otherwise, those savages imagine healing begins by opening a vein on someone with a fever. Already weak." She shook her head, and Adelyn admired the perfect shape of it, easily seen as Momma wore her hair cropped in soft curls. Her high cheek bones drew the eye to her finely sculpted bone structure, her beauty undiminished by age.

The two young women listened intently as Momma brought another time and place to life before their eyes.

Later, Delia would say, "She brought her stories to life, almost like watching them on the movie screen down in Savannah."

No one knew for sure Momma Sorrow's age, or how she got her name, except the Howards. Most in Savannah and the Junction preferred wild conjectures about her. Delia's family knew the most about the mysteries surrounding her. Adelyn's friendship with Delia, then, gave her the chance to reach out to Innis through Momma.

Delia told Adelyn that her father, Jacob Montroy

Howard, knew Momma as Monique Du Pré from his connection with her family in New Orleans. The two young women walked back to Delia's house ruminating over their visit with Momma.

"She spoke about her family in Paris." Adelyn noticed Delia's eyes always widened when she had something important to relate.

"Paris?" It was Adelyn's turn to be surprised. "Who would have thought? Yet I heard her speak perfect French, not Cajun brand."

"Her daddy was white, her mother either Creole or from Spanish Moors." Delia had a patina of moist excitement all about her freckled arms and wrists, which she patted to no avail as she continued her story.

"Momma once said she moved with her mother to New Orleans, to live with her father's cousins after her father died. The cousins owned a sugar plantation." Delia stopped to pick up a thin branch and switched it back and forth as they walked.

Adelyn's thoughts strayed again back to Innis, still fresh in her mind; her heart swelled, she loved him. The fires between her and Innis had barely cooled when she took up with Garnett; mixing the two brothers in her mind caused her considerable consternation.

"Penny for those thoughts, Addie." Delia probed her friend's heart.

"Just thinking, Garnett kept me fascinated for such a time that I almost clean forgot my first...." She stopped short of saying it.

"Everyone knows you loved Innis first. That doesn't take away from your feelings for Garnett."

Delia's approval and sage remark comforted Adelyn. She agreed with her friend's sense of her. *The last I saw him, Garnett left for New York, barely said good-bye. I'll see him Friday and make it right again.*

Adelyn's thoughts stalled after meeting Momma. "Thank you for bringing me to her."

"Don't thank me, Addie; I wouldn't have missed hearing what she had to say. She knew Innis. I hoped for her to call Innis all the way back." Delia said. "Course, you brought him back yourself."

Adelyn pushed Delia's comment away as they neared the front porch. "How did she happen up this way?"

"Her mother died when she was eighteen and Momma told how she couldn't abide her boy cousins sniffing around. No one protected her. She met my daddy when he did some business with her uncle Étienne. Daddy heard she could nurse the sick. Thank goodness, too, just think on when the influenza began killing all those young people. She couldn't stop it once it landed on someone, but she kept a lot more people away from the sick ones. You wouldn't remember, but your mother got some of Momma Sorrow's potion when you got so sick."

At the mention of it, a memory of heaviness flooded into Adelyn of barely breathing, and a coffin, her arms pinned to her sides. A chill ran through her and she turned to ask Delia more, but Delia's father stood on the porch as they approached.

Mr. Howard had been a handsome young man; Adelyn could easily see that; his dark hair framed a face that had to be part Indian, his brown eyes flashing a great energy. Delia reached up to peck him a kiss on his cheek.

"Been out seeing Momma Sorrow," she told him now. Mr. Howard blew cigar smoke out and the wind caught it in such a way to prevent it from falling around the two young women.

"She sure has the healing art," he said as he puffed again, "but there's some of the magic in her, too." Neither young woman refuted nor added to his remark.

Mr. Howard continued, "She always has a special way of knowing, turning up at a cottage where a sick child might be coughing from God knows what. And after Momma's brand of nursing, the child's eyes would be back down from burning fever."

He looked closely at her. "Adelyn, you be sure to come over here for a proper visit when Garnett gets home for good. And bring those boys with you. I'll hardly know either of them walking down the square in Tulip Junction." Mr. Howard and Delia hugged her good-bye.

Adelyn turned out onto the two-lane road, past the live oaks and stately elms all dressed up in their Spanish moss wraps, as the sun peeked through them, leaving long shadows across her car's hood this late in the day. Innis didn't grace her with his lovely smile, and so her thoughts moved to Garnett as she turned her fickle heart toward her husband. She had laid out her plan a week ago. She would be standing there on that dusty platform when he stepped off the train that brought him back home from the north. She packed her little bag and tucked it behind the mess in the trunk of the car so no one would find it.

Adelyn saddened, trying to make sense of her marriage. In Garnett's presence, the sun shone down extra hard on their love. No one could make her feel as special as he did. Her life, gone stale, she blamed it on that. *And Paris, no, don't forget Paris.*

A julep or two and she would be blaming him in a hot rage of recriminations for sins she half imagined. Well, she told herself, right now and sober, she had Innis back. She stopped the car at that sudden thought, held her face in her hands, and cried.

"Let me make a list of all the reasons he's not here." She started the car and wiped her eyes, and revisited Momma Sorrow's words about Innis and Adelyn.

"You and Innis share something special. You possess an old soul and so does he."

"But what does that mean?" Adelyn asked the mysterious woman.

"You have been here before, *chère*. Some appear here newly born, never been on the earth before. They shine hard and bright on the world. They can become repeat visitors. But you and your Innis have lived here many times, and the heat coming from you all, well, most likely you both lived here together before, too."

Was Momma talking about reincarnation? Adelyn and Delia both read and shared books on the subject, scary yet enticing all at the same time. But Innis said that he wasn't a vampire, meaning undead. He said 'yet,' like something could come. She shook her head free of all the thoughts swirling like a giant tornado gathering greater and greater power and momentum. She whispered the vampire part to Momma because she didn't want to worry Delia further. Momma assured her she needn't trouble herself on that account. And she believed her.

"Mama, Trey says I have big ugly freckles." Tyler's expression was pouty and contrived when Adelyn took his chin in her hand, and he began to laugh.

"You know perfectly well you don't give a fig about your brother's taunts."

Trey held up one of his mother's dresses, something very white, linen also, with green leaves. Adelyn took the dress and appraised its line, the gored skirt, the whisper-thin cotton fabric.

"Why, thank you, darling, this will be the one." *Trey always knows ahead of me, sometimes, what I want most.* She winked at Trey who smiled and came to hug her as well. "Now, you both move back or you'll crush your old Mama to pieces."

# Chapter Three
## *ADELYN AND GARNETT*

Adelyn heard her mother's voice with the same old annoying message.

"Don't be offering just any ruffian a ride down to Savannah." To which Adelyn smiled back, "Oh, Mama, just nice ruffians with a million in a pillow, or a female ruffian listed in the Savannah Social Registry?"

Her mother swung her damp handkerchief this way and that at pesky flies, real or imagined, and became even more flustered. "Now, missy, you mind yourself. Don't be making fun of my worries. Why do you refuse to take someone with you? Cousin James over the other side of Tulip Junction offered to drive down with you."

Adelyn embraced her soggy mother and straightened the lace collar of her tea dress. "You know I love you, Mama. Don't fret on me, 'cause everything will turn out just fine. Haven't I always been capable of taking care of myself?" She brushed aside the mention of James. How would she stay over in Savannah with James making an awkward third wheel?

Her mother muttered something sweet, saying she knew Adelyn could take care of herself. "But no matter, be careful, these are dangerous times."

Adelyn agreed as much on the surface as in her heart. More bands of rough-looking people congregated along the railroad tracks, more every time she drove down that way, but who wouldn't look rough, living alongside the road? *How long would my hair or clothes look appealing living in a tent beside a creek and railroad track?*

Adelyn hugged Tyler, who skipped away, his new mode of getting around, but Trey stood near her with a pout and a furrowed brow.

"Come to me, sweetheart," she beckoned. "I know you miss your daddy. We'll be back as quick as you can think of bees in the honey." Trey hugged her tighter than usual; so strong, though lanky like his father. Her smile changed to a sad beat in her heart. Garnett's absence made her careless and sad, with her incessant wandering and riding. She'd become a phantom mother with that dead feeling inside ever present these last three months. *But not since Innis.*

She looked everywhere for Innis the whole way to Savannah. At first fearful that her wish to see him yet again would be granted but when he didn't show, not even a whisper on the wind of him, or a flicker of a smile in the mirror, she grew forlorn, then annoyed. If he were watching, she realized, he would be amused. She fervently hoped his fading away visually meant she could keep him out of her thoughts.

The quiet road held no strangers, though a few farm workers she knew exchanged waves with her. Sometimes she'd call out the name of the man, woman, or child if she knew it, in the country way. She felt the power of the big automobile as it thrust itself down the road, shortening the space between her husband and herself. Her heart quickened. Adelyn thought of the little bag tucked inside the boot and then of Momma's little séance when Momma sat upright, eye closed tight, and said, "You love one, you love both."

Adelyn remembered the worried and embarrassed look on Delia's face. "I never thought of that."

Adelyn averted her eyes, pretending not to notice, but yes, both Delia and Momma knew what she and Innis shared. Driving along the dusty road now, she wondered whether Garnett would know.

The ride, without mishap, gave Adelyn time to straighten her hair and dress in the railroad station comfort room. The mirror image looking back showed a young woman, no lines to her beautiful face, her large brown eyes bright with yellow flecks in them, so deep that, as Garnett said more than once, he could drown in their depth. She traced her finger over her lips and felt a tingle of wanting for him that made her blush. Adelyn looked quickly both ways to see if anyone noticed.

A tired old woman sat in a deep chair, waiting on someone, maybe a granddaughter, crocheting a lace collar. Every once in a while, Adelyn heard her call out softly, in a high-pitched and barely audible voice, "Lucianne, have you done fall in?" A girl finally appeared, a thin wisp of a sixteen-year-old at best, wearing her newest dress. Adelyn peered at them through the mirror and the grandmother reached to straighten the girl's hem. "Just look at this dress, all my ironing for nothing, looks like."

The girl seemed to float toward the wash basin and dwelled longer, looking deep into Adelyn's own eyes until she caught Adelyn's gaze in the mirror alongside her.

*I'm really not here; my granny just thinks so hard that I am. You were me, once, you know.*

Startled at reading the girl's thoughts so easily, Adelyn

looked closer; but in the thick haze of the darkened room, she realized she stood alone before the mirror. The old woman, who never raised her head, remained still hunched down, and still crocheting. *Did I imagine this?* She needed to know.

"Excuse me, ma'am, are you waiting for someone?" At first, the woman did not look up; and Adelyn thought she might be hard of hearing. She cleared her voice and opened her mouth to speak again; but the woman raised her eye and looked at her with a weary smile.

"I haven't been waiting on anyone for a very long time, child. Just the train. I'm expecting to ride up this evening to Elizabethtown in North Carolina."

Adelyn collected herself. "I am sorry, didn't mean to intrude." She looked into the mirror again and finished with a strand of hair. A flicker of shadow passed quickly out of her sight; she swore she saw the girl's white day dress.

The woman removed her eyeglasses and settled her shoulders as though she eased a muscle held too long in one position. "Nothing to fuss with. My granddaughter used to ride up with me, guess my thoughts were with her. Dear heart, my Lucianne, been gone since the Spanish flu took her from me. So young."

As the old woman spoke, Adelyn recalled the girl. Her dress with an old-timey look to it, one that she would have worn at the same age. Could she believe what the girl said? A long silence settled between them as the woman, no doubt, thought back to the day she straightened the girl's dress. Adelyn knew that all happened, just in a different time, was all.

"I'm so sorry for your loss." Adelyn's voice came muted.

"It's been a long time, but the sorrow has its own memory." The grandmother looked toward the heavy wooden blinds. "No relief from that heat, is there?"

"Guess it will stay with us till sundown, but tomorrow will bring rain," Adelyn said, then, "have a safe journey, ma'am.

Adelyn picked up her purse and left the room. *First Innis, then this girl. What did she say? I was her once? I'll ask Momma Sorrow.* Her mind swayed like a big palm frond, from Innis and now to this girl.

She settled her thoughts on her husband. Garnett's business, the offer that came from his Yankee partners, to have him move them again, all out of Tulip Junction, and his frequent visits North, the culture sticking to him like rust on an anchor; she'd never gotten used to that. Thinking of him, this very minute, she sensed him, his strong heart beating. *Should I tell him of Innis?* And as quickly she heard herself say, out loud. "No, he cannot know."

Adelyn parked the car alongside the station. Walking back out to it, she tipped a porter to watch the automobile. Out on the platform the big train could be heard a mile away, its whistle wailing its message to scare errant cows off the tracks and warn little boys to move back. It turned its big metal face to meet everyone head on. Steam poured from its stack, the black metal shining in the sun. Adelyn saw the station clock read three-twenty-five. By three-thirty the engine passed her to stop further up the line. The behemoth slowed, and doors began to open, and windows too, for those traveling farther down wanted to see.

The sun, still very high in the sky, lit the dust of the dry day kicked up by the steam as it whooshed out of the train's sides in a quieter stream. The dry air gathered up the steam as quick as it could, and Adelyn felt the skirt of her dress pressed hard against her while the mist hit her legs and mingled with the breeze to cool her down some. All around her women gently fanned themselves to no avail. *Like me, they wait on their husbands.*

She saw Garnett standing three cars down. She knew he'd seen her first, his unmistakable reddish blond hair pushed away from his face. With her eyes made keen by magic from Innis and Momma Sorrow, she saw the dampness settle on his temples. His smile beamed for her alone, and she began to give in to her instinct to run to him. Before she could move, he took long and eager strides to her. All their hurtful words before he last left vanished. When they embraced, they felt an exchanged tremble between them.

"Adelyn, Sugar. Your telegram at the last minute surprised me. So glad you came. And in all this heat?"

Her distrust reared its head again as Adelyn gauged whether he looked for any other female who might be lingering—some other woman hoping that Adelyn was a sister or former school friend on her way to town. She spied a woman hanging back near the car where Garnett stepped down, a tall woman with a heaviness to her hips. She wore a flowered light Alice blue dress, turning her head but not before Adelyn saw her hard smile. Immediately, she searched Garnett's face. The new and heightened powers made it so she could reach into his soul to see her own image.

Discreetly, she pulled away to let some sunshine between them in this public place. She found it mostly curious that the woman's presence did not bother her as much now that she took the time to read into her.

"We missed you. The boys, Mama, all of us."

Garnett's smile grew almost to a laugh. "The boys? Miss me, yet not here?" He pulled her closer to himself again. "How about you, darlin'?" His kiss, light and secret, conformed almost to propriety, always the gentleman. "You know you can always travel with me."

"Well, Garnett, then I wouldn't have the pleasure of surprising you, and that makes all the time apart almost worthwhile."

A porter brought up Garnett's large valise and Garnett tipped him. "Much thanks, Deacon. Let me know after you take that boy of yours to Dr. Parker, 'cause he'll be waiting on you."

Her expression asked a question he answered.

"Deacon has a sixteen-year-old son who hurt his leg playing baseball with his friend. Sprained it and it's not healing properly. I learned about it in Baltimore, and when we stopped there, I rang up Dr. Parker. He'll see the boy." He kept his arm still around her waist. "Now what do you have in mind for us?"

Adelyn thought of the Crawford family, how they were known for quiet acts of kindness for those in need. This simple gesture mollified some of her forced coquetry. With no pretense, she looked one last time for the tall woman; a porter lifted her bags back on the train. *So, traveling a bit farther down the line.*

Smoothly she said, "We can have some light dinner at the Forsythe Hotel then go find us a speakeasy. 'Cause you know I love to dance."

"I have a little surprise of my own. Now, I know you're not fixing to fill me up on watercress sandwiches. When I knew you would come for me, I booked us the night at the hotel. Let's go over, you can buy some lacy thing at the shop next door, to wear just for me." He nuzzled her cheek; she felt his warm breath. "Don't want to be full up with food, like Uncle Tyree. I know he's not getting any loving, these days." Adelyn caught the seasoned edge to his voice, along with an urgency.

Adelyn didn't blush. Instead they both laughed. "I'm thinking something like a gin drink and a long afternoon in one of those rooms full of fans and shadows." His arm surrounded her waist.

She watched him watching her as they left the station in the car with Garnett driving for the short ride to the Forsythe Hotel. He rounded a corner; they paused in the shade of low-hanging moss and he kissed her hand. Stopping, he kissed her cheek. "Something is different, very different." He murmured in her ear.

Adelyn felt the shadows follow them through the lobby, some specters—the wisp of the young girl in white—and others real. Jack Riley, a tall man with broad shoulders and dark hair, walked up to her and tipped his hat. A successful attorney and businessman, prominent in Tulip Junction, and down in Savannah, he knew everyone's business. His eyes just glowed in Adelyn's direction.

"Why, Adelyn, didn't see you at the Church supper two weeks ago. You feeling okay? I almost inquired at the house when I visited with your daddy. How is Captain Jackson?" He tipped his hat at Garnett as an afterthought. Garnett's eyes narrowed, and he had no smile on his face.

"Daddy's fine. We all are. Just didn't have the time to get to the dinner. It did seem promising though. A good turn-out, they told me."

"Well yes, but would have been better with you there." And as an aside, "Of course, we missed your boys." Then he skipped a beat and said, "Hi there; I would guess you're Garnett. I know your daddy and knew your brother. Fine man, Innis."

The men exchanged false sounding pleasantries that fooled no one. *Least of all me,* Adelyn said to herself. She made short work of their dueling. "My, you two are wrapped up in your ole' businesses, aren't you?" She tugged lightly on Garnett's sleeve. "Let's not keep Jack." Then turning to the other man, "Jack, I'll see you next Sunday in church, promise."

The ride up in the elevator remained tense but quiet enough, but the storm bore down on them once they stepped into the room. Garnett tipped the bellboy whose wide-eyed wonder betrayed his generosity. "Get us some ice and Tanqueray." Even with the bottle of gin, she knew Garnett tipped him handsomely.

"Feeling generous?" She removed her wide-brimmed hat and shucked off her shoes, sat on the bed and bent toward her thigh as she pulled up and rolled her stocking, first one long leg and then the other. She found herself suddenly on her feet as he pulled her abruptly to him.

"What game is this? Huh?" He tightened his hold on

her arm and let go when he saw her wince. "Forgive me." His breathing sounded rough and his voice parched. "You're different."

Adelyn straightened her hair as she loosened the pins that held it, and it fell down on her shoulders, all golden brown and red. "You said that before. How am I different?"

"The moment I stepped off that damn train, there too, not just now with that, that..." He gestured with his hand toward the door as if Jack Riley were lying in wait on the other side. "Jack Riley." She finished the sentence for him. He gently embraced her. "What has happened to you?"

"Garnett Foster Crawford, you mind telling me what you mean so I understand?" But all the while she knew. She knew Innis had breathed his own brand of love into her, making her feel whole again in some way she didn't understand.

"You do love me, still?" He sat down with her on the bed and buried his face into her hair, picked it up and caressed it to his cheek. "Because, I swear, I feel like you've been with someone."

Adelyn touched his face while her mind conjured a vision of the woman in the Alice blue dress. "Did you know her? The woman at the far end of the train?" The words belied the caress, and she regretted the words as she spoke them. She tugged on his shirt to keep him near, as he attempted to move away.

She needed him to stay put, not to give in to his temper or, she thought, his guilt about the woman, if he had any. Her tug became a signal that went beyond whatever transgressions they each held close to their respective chests, wanting to covet the memory of unspoken and illicit assignations, and still hold on to one another. Garnett proved all that with the fierce way he grabbed the back of her neck to pull her face and lips to his. His kiss, hard and bruising, forced out of mind the Jack Rileys of the world who might intrude on Garnett's 'home sweet home' sense of Adelyn. Yet secretly he grabbed at her wantonness and celebrated it because it excited him in every way, and she knew this.

In answer to his question of whether she'd been with someone, she asked her own question. "How could you know something like that?" She said this softly, and it became part of the lovemaking song instead of a confrontation.

Clothes came off, her shimmy, his shirt, and trousers; they tore at one another's clothes until their bodies could only feel one another's skin, the sweat, and the sweet smell of it all. And for the time it all took, they both erased thoughts of each other's real or imagined adversaries.

## *Chapter Four*
### *RECONCILING*

Adelyn slept fitfully, tossing covers, pulling them back. Garnett finally laid a hand on her to still the motion. Half-awake, she knew she had been dreaming—her husband lay by her side, in their bed, in their home. She knew she had been dreaming even while it happened. Innis suspended over and around her, a misty collection of clouds sometimes blocking him, making him less substantial. Yet his anger burned her with a physicality that surprised her.

"It constantly pains me. You were with Garnett at my funeral." She couldn't hide that she knew right away what he meant. "Long ago, Innis."

He surrounded her, his image poking into her space first from the left, then above, then the right.

"Long ago?" A phantom hand reached out to touch her cheek and it felt like a soft breeze that ended with a chill. "Just yesterday, Addie."

"I came to Savannah to meet his train." Her thoughts

took over as she felt a world of words coming from Innis to her but not spoken. "What do you mean, just yesterday?"

"Yes, it is." No longer in the white suit he'd worn at each of his visits, Innis now dressed like when they first met. "Countless times I wanted to reach you to let you know. It can't be this way."

The scene changed from nowhere to a permanent place, outside the hotel. "You expect things to change. But they're frozen, Innis. This is forever." He disappeared, and she called him back with a question. "How can you be so angry?"

Adelyn woke from a deep slumber. The room seemed out of proportion to her, hazy and ill-defined, furniture resembling oblong or square objects, no drawer handles on the armoire or pulls on the dresser. Someone shook her; she heard her name.

"Adelyn. Wake up, wake up." Garnett pressed his fingers into her arms and the tightness of his grip finally roused her. "You were dreaming."

His lean jaw accentuated the sternness of his face. Still taking stock of her surroundings, Adelyn drifted half in and half out of the dream. The bed posts, her silk hosiery listlessly draped on one post, the other lingered on the back of a chair. Her mind raced to the progression of each of these things being removed. *Innis, what if he saw us, saw it all?*

"You were dreaming. Of Innis. You called his name."

The sound of her lover's name coming from Garnett woke her fully.

"Blame me for dreams?" She shocked herself with her own cruelty for saying this to Garnett. She had a strong desire to go on dreaming to learn more of what Innis tried to tell her. "He knew we were together in the barn." In the second she said it, she regretted it.

"That's what you dreamt?" He had a hold on her arms still and she wrested herself from him to see the room more clearly. A vision took shape, a woman, behind the opaque curtains. The shape disappeared as soon as she thought of it.

Heat oppressed the room that not even the big ceiling fans could abate. She left the bed and went to the window to find the shape and looked in the direction of the ocean, listening for waves. "No breeze; tide's out."

Garnett watched her. "Seems like your words and motives come from his lips. Wishful thinking, Sugar?" An undeniable acid in his expression. The day faded; he sipped the Tanqueray, ice cubes clinking on the glass.

She chose to ignore the remarks, and climbed onto his lap, brushing his hair off his forehead with her lips. "Sip." She guided his hand holding the glass to her lips. The smooth Tanqueray gin slid down her throat, cooling it, then spilled into her stomach like a small fire. "Not much of this left."

Garnett sat more upright in the rocker. "You shivered just a moment ago, when you were still waking. Why did you shiver, *chère?*"

She ignored his question. "Sometimes I feel half in another world."

Garnett's breath felt hot as he spoke. "That would really be nice for you, 'cause then you'd have us both. Listen, love me, Sugar." His voice low, he wanted confirmation.

"You sure are funny tonight. I can't be hung for a dream." She hugged him but that did not satisfy him.

Adelyn's thoughts returned to the full-figured shadow that passed her eyes. She wondered if Garnett saw it too. *Could he; did he? Yet why would he not say anything? Why call me by a French nickname? And Cajun, it was Cajun French, said 'sha', not 'chère'. Momma Sorrow? Here? Filling Garnett; influencing his speech?*

The phone rang in a loud vibration that stirred her further from her dream and what she just witnessed. Garnett reached and picked up the heavy receiver. "Yes. What time did he call? Did he leave a number in New York?" He turned to her. "John Calloway called from New York. They have the message at the desk. I'll slip down there and be right back." She didn't want him to leave her in this room. She didn't trust the room, and if pressed to explain, she knew she could articulate the reason, which would be all the more disturbing.

He lifted her lithe frame onto the bed, picked up his slacks, pulled on a jersey top, shoving his bare feet into loafers. "I'll be right back, so don't be leaving." And he was gone.

## Chapter Five
### *INNIS CRAWFORD—THE BOY*

A dark-eyed devil, Adelyn's mother had called him back when; yet even she herself smiled and fluttered her eyelashes at him just like all the other women whenever he looked their way. And she meant what she said when he openly courted sixteen-year-old Adelyn. Older by two years than Garnett, Innis worked to be the best at whatever he took a mind to do or be. All the young men on campus held him up as their ideal. His mother would remember and say that he first came to prominence at the age of seven. Innis told the story, and so did his mother, and in their smaller world, Adelyn's family, the Jacksons, all knew about Innis Crawford from back then.

"Innis Crawford, you will be the death of me and you before long." His mother scolded as she took a warm wet cloth to his face and neck.

"Because you'll take sick with some exotic bug bite, for sure." His mother continued to tug at him, straightening his belt, pulling his knickers from just below his knee to where his stockings could be tucked inside of them.

"And what will you die of, Mama?" His grave face showed concern, and though seven years old and perfectly capable of straightening his own clothes, he knew she loved to fuss about him, so he let her continue. Any other boy would worry after someone seeing him being treated like just a young child, but Innis believed that if he were indeed a young boy still, then he felt no shame to be treated as one.

Mrs. Crawford turned him to face her, and he could see she accepted that his neck would pass inspection at the Citadel. He saw her pause and knew he caught her off guard with his question. What would she die of?

"For the love of you, my darling. Just for you." And it would be as she said. From the moment his heart stopped, his mother ceased to draw breath. Long before the sheriff and the town mayor clambered up the front steps on that sad day, with their heavy boots sounding hollow on the veranda, Sarah May Crawford felt a fist reach into her heart, turn it cold, and stop its beat. She lived only two months longer, some said to mother Garnett, but like the husk off corn, she drifted free and left us all in her sleep.

Innis reached around his mother's waist to hold her closer and shivered, and she felt the tremor.

"Did someone walk on your grave just now, darling?" Though only twenty-eight, his mother saw his sparkling eyes and wished, for a moment, to revisit her own youth. Wished to be in a time when her eyes shone as brightly as his.

"Now you go in there to speak with your father and tell him what happened in Mrs. Harper's classroom today." She scooted him toward the door to the living room where his father read the evening newspaper and where his brother, Garnett, lay on his belly quietly flicking his marbles into a cardboard box five feet from him. Innis raised an eyebrow to show his brother he impressed him with the effort and then, when Garnett missed, he snickered.

"Son, you want to talk to me?" His father looked up from his paper.

"Yessir. I'm to tell you about Mrs. Harper at school today." Innis believed his father to be a fair man but one who had high expectations of his sons and how they acted in public.

"Am I to believe that you sassed your teacher today?" Innis heard an even tone, which relaxed him so he could relive the entire event, self-righteous indignation and all.

"All I said was that she was wrong, that Columbus was not the first to land on American soil, that it wasn't even here, but somewhere south and below, in the Caribbean where he first set foot. Why, she was goin' on like he stopped in Plymouth up north before he floated down to South Carolina, or something."

"And you said all this in the same way you're telling me now?" Will Crawford had loosened his tie and rolled his sleeves neatly up to his elbows. A lawyer who mainly worked in wills and trusts, he figured out the property rights of townspeople who had one idea of what they had to bequeath that often didn't match with the city hall and sometimes state records. He loved to research the lands and could see them all stretched out around him as he read from dusty old record books. When Innis did not answer, he lowered his paper to see his son.

"No, sir." Innis's answer came slowly. "I raised my hand, and when she nodded at me, I stood like we're told, and I excused myself and said that I liked the Columbus stories so I read some at the library and then told her what I had read."

Sarah Crawford stood against the door jamb of the high-ceilinged room, drawn by her son's soft and plaintive voice. She did not look at her husband but at Garnett who smiled up at her now and pointed to his marbles, most of which landed inside the Crayola box perched on its side to catch them.

"Well, son, if you spoke politely and presented your

evidence, as you say you did, can you explain why Mrs. Harper might be so upset?" Bill waited, and then offered, "She was embarrassed by your knowing a bit more than she did about the subject. So I want to ask you to hold onto the information until you can tell her with none of the other children there to hear. Okay?"

Innis saw the situation as his father had revealed it, clear and simple. No need to show everyone what he knew, maybe not even tell Mrs. Harper. There would be time to let others know.

"Why don't you just go see your teacher first thing tomorrow, and tell her you're sorry and meant no disrespect? No need to say more."

Innis nodded, having already concluded this was what his father would say. His smile lit up his face and, of course, his mother's.

# Chapter Six
## *GARNETT—HOMECOMING*

The road, rough with stones kicked up under the wheels. A fierce wind blew up suddenly. *Those damn dark clouds again.* Much to Adelyn's relief, Garnett insisted on pulling up the heavy canvas top, lest they and the leather seats get dusty. She remained guilty and unsettled, since only a day ago Innis had made love to her on the back seat of the automobile. *Could that be?* She knew very well that they had.

Garnett reached for her hand. "Your mind on something?

She knew he sensed far more than he was letting on. Especially after the way he shook her when she woke from her dream and cried out Innis's name. She wondered whether Innis had floated between them before now. Suddenly she knew the answer. *He already has. So much to ask Momma Sorrow.*

Halfway home Garnett pulled the car to the side of the

road, his face stern and serious. "Has Jack Riley been hanging around the place? Looking to talk to your daddy while all the time really looking for you?"

He startled her with this question, and it angered her. "Aren't you done with that yet? Beating it to death, are you?" She lashed out at him, surprised at the fury lying deep inside her. Calming herself, she affected nonchalance, examining her nails and saying out loud, "Riding without gloves is just not a good idea." And Garnett breathed heavily for her efforts at such silly tactics.

But then her anger would not be denied. "Besides, I should be the one asking." She left the tone hang in the air and, when he reached for her, she pulled back.

"Who you thinking on now, Sweet Pea?" She heard the sarcasm, gruff, feelings bruised.

"Now whatever could you mean?" She taunted him with coyness, knowing he hated it. "You didn't answer *my* question. Worried about me and Jack Riley? I saw that she-hound at the train station, circling 'round, waiting to see what you might be doing with your time in Savannah."

She continued before she could change her mind. "Don't be putting on any airs with me, Garnett. Jealous of a dead brother in my dream? What next? Phantoms? Vampires?" But those words stopped her as she saw their effect on Garnett. He pulled her to him in a mean and hurtful way. He'd put aside all that passion after his trip to the hotel front desk so there remained her own latent desire, a fire she had banked when he came back from downstairs, all business-like with a 'now-on-to-the-next-deal' attitude.

"I never even sat next to that woman. And what's this? Phantoms, is it? Who's been filling your mind with that?"

Later she would reflect that he didn't mock her—but wary of her, anxious, like he knew more on the subject than just a scary book on vampire lore. The undead. She would wonder if Innis meant that. If so, could he make her pregnant? She thought of the unprotected sex in the hammock and then in the back seat of this very car. Her breathing came faster at the thought. Garnett pulled away from her thoughts.

"You're not going to do this, 'cause it's what you want, you wanton thing." He kissed her long and lovingly and revved the still-running engine. "Just tell me." He pulled the car back onto the paved road. She settled herself, and they drove, not speaking for almost the rest of the trip. As they neared a smaller side road that would lead them to the house and farm, Garnett spoke.

"Tell me first that I have nothing to worry about with the Jack Rileys of the world, and then tell me about Trey." Garnett's voice broke the barrier. She heard his sincerity, and Adelyn loved talking about her boys.

She relented, patted his hand. "Nothing to worry about." She moved on to Trey. "He's first in his class on all subjects. Your old teacher, Mrs. Harper, just loves him." She left unsaid that Trey must remind Mrs. Harper of Innis because he looked so much like him, and Innis had been her favorite. Adelyn sighed, frustrated, and gave up because all roads led to Innis, and she didn't know how to extricate herself from this living dream. When she looked at Garnett, she sensed he had completed the thought for her. He would remember Mrs. Harper and Innis as solidly as she had.

"Mrs. Harper. Innis was a favorite of hers." She heard the wound open in his voice, reached out, and squeezed his hand to reassure him of her love.

The gravel crunched on the long drive up to the house. She saw first the green gables with their narrow windows, high up above the trees, then the long hurricane-proof shutters put up in the late 1800s, now thrown open to reveal tall windows on the first floor, opening into the ballroom. All the windows in the front of the house faced a long veranda shaded by old trees and an occasional awning.

Adelyn hoped the whole family wouldn't converge on Garnett the way they always seemed to do. They had so much unfinished business between them and they needed time.

"I know Trey misses you a lot more these days." She said this in earnest, not to mollify him. The house, once a plantation, conjured a majestic scene with its big veranda of white Grecian pillars. As they wound around the circle driveway they saw movement, and sure enough it looked like a party.

"Damn this congregation," Garnett muttered.

Adelyn reached over and circled his frown line with her index finger. "They'll soon get their fill of you." She smiled at him, and he accepted the olive branch.

She didn't have to look too closely to see her father, whom Garnett and everyone in the world called Cap. Aunt Grace Lee and Uncle Tyree stooped to speak to Adelyn's father, sitting in his chair, and she noticed her aunt twisting this way and that because the wind surprised her and her hairdo. Adelyn's mother stood first along the waiting line of folks, though her father, busy with his drink, sat on his favorite big old chair.

She turned toward Garnett, relieved to see him looking happily at her father as he said, "Cap wouldn't stand up for Jeff Davis."

The car swerved slightly but to Adelyn it felt as if some strong hand reached out to push it. She knew who would do such a spiteful thing, knew the person to blame.

"Mother Jackson." Garnett stepped out of the car and held Adelyn's mother to him while Mary Jackson blushed and smiled softly.

"Now you go on with yourself, Garnett." She made a fake show of pushing him away although she made no more space between them than before. *Mama loves the boys better than the girls.*

And so Garnett moved down the line, away almost a month, even greeting some of the servants and of course, his younger son, Tyler, who held to his father's hand and hugged his waist.

"Trey, honey, where is Trey?" Adelyn embraced the boy best she could with him glued to his father. Garnett released the boy's hand every so often to tousle his hair and finally picked him up and held him while Tyler planted a wet smacking kiss on his father's face, and rubbed his father's chin, saying, "Ooooh, Daddy, you need a shave."

"He doesn't need a shave." Adelyn switched around to see Trey, wearing a tie and white shirt. Though only six and therefore in knickers, she saw the man he would one day be. Adelyn placed her hand on his hair and smoothed it down, and he did not move away.

Garnett let go of Tyler, and the little boy trotted away after a dog and toward one of the barn cats. Trey hugged his father so tight that Adelyn saw the whites of his knuckles. "Missed you, Daddy. Please stay home."

Adelyn could tell Garnett felt some pride to have so poised a child, thankful for his son's wish to have him there. She felt an inch of guilt for not paying more attention to the loss the boys, especially Trey, experienced in Garnett's absence. She admonished herself; maybe she'd not been there for them, noting Trey's loyalty and devotion to his father, feeling blessed to have children who loved that deeply on their own. Pieces of Trey and Garnett's conversation, almost man to man, wafted near, carried by the wind.

"I'll be staying on a while. You can come on with me around town on some of my business visits while I'm here." Garnett smiled into his son's face.

The wind picked up again and they all headed indoors. Mary Jackson called out to them all, "Hurry now, dinner is waiting, before this blessed storm gets us all."

Adelyn's new-found sharpened senses understood the storm as unnatural with hot and cold winds in this early summertime. She set her gaze farther away, over the fields, and saw peaceful white clouds standing still, and knew. *Damn that Innis.*

Inside, the dining room table set with china sparkled as random rays of sun streaked the windows—the glassware, her mother's favorite crystal. The children served, waited politely for the adults, their glasses filled with lemonade. A punch bowl held light wine with fresh juices that made the occasion. It felt like Christmas.

Captain Jackson rose from his chair, held his mint julep up high. "Let's toast to all for good health and to the homecoming of our favorite son-in-law." He smiled around to all and winked conspiratorially at his daughter, Adelyn. "Good to have you back with us, Garnett, and don't be leaving anytime soon. We all missed you."

Garnett nodded thanks to Adelyn's father and squeezed her shoulders. "I am sure going to try to stay home much as possible, Cap." He brushed her hair with his lips, and she felt a hot sting on her other cheek. She pulled away to rub at it. "Something wrong, Addie?" Garnett looked closely at her reddened cheek.

"Just something like a bee sting." She let Garnett inspect her face.

"Sure looks like it." He pressed his finger, wet from his mint julep glass and its cool condensation, to her face. "Now that was fast. Couldn't be much, cause it's all but gone now."

Lively chatter swallowed their conversation about the sting.

"We're going to catch a big fish with Daddy," Tyler said to his grandmother.

Trey looked up from his chicken dinner to add, "Down near Jemadiah Creek, near the river."

Mary Jackson all the while warned them to stay away from the edge because the river flooded from the recent storms upriver. Adelyn reflexively touched where the sting had been, and yes, it had disappeared. *Damn Innis.* Dinner progressed without further interruptions as Adelyn sent mental scoldings to Innis.

"Trey, let me help." Garnett bent to roll up his son's knickers as they exchanged the tie and white shirt for a bathing suit under the cotton pants. Trey stood still, glad for the attention, while Tyler jumped off the back porch, only to climb back up again without resorting to using steps and repeated the jump. "Tyler, be still for just a moment here?" Garnett took hold of the boy's arm. Not used to adult interference, quickly put off by a certain male sternness, he whined at his mother, "Mama, can't I jump?"

"You listen to your Daddy, son." Adelyn rubbed his back to offset the more manful experience of his father's touch. All three left the porch, fishing poles in hand, finally off toward the river and the backwoods. Adelyn waved one more time before they disappeared around the bend. She pulled her linen dress away from her torso and felt the stickiness of it under her arms. She let the heavy screened back door bang closed behind her as she hitched her dress above her knees.

"That you, Adelyn?" Her mother and aunt chatted after their meal and would soon take naps.

"Yes, ma'am. That chicken tasted perfect, Mama. I'm going up for a quick bath to cool down." She took the back stairs two at a time the way she did as a teen-aged tomboy. She smiled contentedly at the thought of her mother once coaxing her not to wear her cousin James's linen trousers. She had taken a shears to them and cut just below the knee. She got past all the objections when she wore jodhpurs, but her mother saw them differently.

A little while later, luxuriating in her bath, she allowed her mind to whirl through the memories of James, their friends, and occasionally Innis and Garnett, all as young people.

The water felt slimy from the soap, so she stood and hosed her body of its stickiness, letting the breeze from the large window dry her. Almost as an afterthought, suddenly, transported in just her shimmy, she stood at the top of the attic stairs, fans in the windows drawing air in and out and the sound, though loud, pleased her.

"Thinking on old times...with me?" She felt his

presence before he spoke.

"I should be thinking about the sting to my cheek this afternoon." She placed her hand on the cheek to feel for swelling. "You doing that before God and everyone."

"God wasn't there, Sugar." He wore a thin, white sweater, his bare throat seemed very suggestive to her, to the point of being drawn to his side. "Everyone, you say?" He shrugged. "Well, let's say the every one of them you care about." He reached for her deliberately, holding her thin wrists out in front of him. "Always loved these." He bent and kissed one and then the other at the place where the small artery pulsed most visibly. His lips felt soft and warm.

"Who are you to come here and do that to me?" She pulled her arms to herself.

"I'm the one who counts, that's who." His dark brown eyes glowed into hers as they always had. "And I had you first."

Willing herself to ignore his remark, she stared at him. "Tell me why you came back. You come and go now; were you here before this?"

Innis sat on an old sofa, and she looked to see his weight move the cushions. "Adelyn, darling, stop reading those silly books about undead. I'm real. I'm here; yet I can leave and move about without being visible as well. I started coming back because he had stopped paying attention to you."

"Garnett? You came back because he was away?" She circled him and stood above the top of his head. She knew if she touched his scalp and hair, they would feel substantial and real. He possessed a physicality she could not understand.

"Stop and sit; will you? Yes, I came back for what was once mine and could be mine again."

"For a spell, yes, I was yours. For a spell." She realized she spoke again more to herself as she had done the last few days when he appeared. "How? Where did you come from? Heaven?"

He shook his head and laughed. "Not heaven, Honey, and sorry to say for all those you would like to consign to hell, not there either."

"I know I'm not afraid of you. You're so real. More solid today than yesterday. Somehow." She finally sat next to him, and he raised his finger to trace where the sting had been and then to her throat and finally to her bare neck and down to her breasts. His voice defiant, he averred, "You don't stop me; know that."

She pushed his hand away. "Is this all you want from me?" She had more to say, but he interrupted her to comment. His face held some sadness.

"Now, you tell me how I can be more than this when I have no child with you, when I have no earthly function? Even if I were idle rich, I would still see to it the farm was run."

"Innis, you despair?" and she thought to say, "Trey looks a lot like you when you were younger. I've seen photographs your mother kept."

His tone changed, his voice now tight. "Don't. Don't speak of her."

"Your mother? Why would you not want…?" She watched his face closely and saw an array of emotions and expressions cross his brow, his lips parting and then tightening as he experienced memories, some sad, some happy.

"So, your boy Trey looks something like me? I guess that's to be, family inherits family traits. Is he smart? Does he do well in school studies?" He showed vulnerability for a moment.

She took his hand, as warm as his lips had been. "Yes, he is good at all things and without much effort. Harvard or maybe Ole Miss. We talk about it. Innis, I'm going down to Momma Sorrow to have her help me understand all this. I lied when I said I wasn't afraid. Right now, I feel that I could lose it all, my life, if I'm not careful. Maybe slip into your world without noticing. You say you're not really dead.

Maybe Momma Sorrow will know what that means."

He stiffened and moved away from her, stood over her. "What makes you think that old woman can answer questions for you and me? Don't be sharing all that you are, what we are to one another." Churlish, defensive, he began to approach her, and she knew he would have her in an instant if she didn't stop him.

"I think going to see Momma makes a lot of sense."

"You're so wrong to do this." And he was gone.

# Chapter Seven
## *ADELYN AND INNIS—THE FIRST TIME*

November 1918 brought harsher winds than usual for Savannah and for Tulip Junction. All through the summer and fall, mountains of grieving grew, every family hit by the influenza, the Spanish flu. Whatever they called it, Adelyn tired of hearing her parents at dinner or late evening telling of this family or that suffering the loss of a child, a sister in her prime. The servants built bigger, more ambitious fires to avoid drafts, because Mama believed that would keep death from their big old house. But it didn't.

One day Adelyn heard her mother's voice change to a deep sob and the words, "oh no, oh no, please God!" And Adelyn knew her mother's favorite brother, Brady, had succumbed, gone like so many others throughout Tulip Junction and Savannah and all the countries of all the world.

Everyone got sick with colds and aching muscles, and then some struggled to breathe, and Mama got out her potions and when they didn't work, she ran down to the far end of Tulip Junction near Delia's home and down the path to the strange woman there who, they said, had powers to heal. They went to her right after Brady and then Old Cap, Adelyn's grandfather, died.

Doctor Fanning swore they had pneumonia, and for some, old age, but Adelyn's mother felt sure doom overshadowed them all. Mary Jackson came home with baskets of elixirs and tonics and rubs to be placed on chests to bring back the warmth. And surprisingly they did, and Adelyn thought differently about the woman down the path from Delia's, and wished for Uncle Brady to be back among the living.

Few students attended classes back then, so many empty seats, and then Delia took sick. Adelyn could not contain herself through the first gray day of her friend's absence until she could run home and call Delia's house— barely able to hear over her mother's pestering voice, as she stood behind Adelyn.

"Adelyn Jackson, you got mud all over the hall rug, traipsing in here without a care to anyone else. Did you wipe your feet? No. Did you shuck off those muddy shoes? No."

"Mama, please, Delia is sick, I am trying to hear Nellie tell me how she is." She kicked off her muddy shoes where she stood and winced, waiting for more to come. With Mama, she always had more.

"Give me those shoes, and let this be a lesson. Come 'round to the side or take them off on the porch. My lands."

"Please, Mama, please." She turned and cupped her ear tighter to the phone. "Nellie, does she have fever?" Her features went from deep scowl to softer relief while she and now her mother listened together.

"Fever some. But she has those potions from Miz Sorrow down yonder, and they's helping a mighty bit."

Adelyn twisted the long cord of the phone box while her mother pulled and straightened it. Adelyn lightly tapped her hand to stop. "When can I come see her? Can I come today?"

Nellie paused, hesitant. "Have to ask her Mama, but she's been having light soup and holding it all down. So, I'm thinking you best come over tomorrow. It'll be Saturday so you can be here early."

Adelyn heard the constant smile in Nellie's voice, there almost all the time. "Thank you, Nellie. Be there tomorrow." She turned to her mother as she hung up. "I can take Pharaoh out for a stretch, he'll like that."

"You know, Miss Thing, you'd think you live alone somewhere without kin. How about you ask your mama what plans she may have for you?" Missus Jackson straightened her daughter's curls, so they fell alongside her face and down her back.

"Oh Mama, you fuss too much, way too much." She kissed her mother's worried brow.

"You just be sure Delia's beyond giving you her illness." But Adelyn knew the woman, Miz Sorrow, and her potions, nursed the entire Howard family often and well, and worried less than she would otherwise if it were any other family in the county.

Pharaoh impatiently moved his hind legs and snorted a mist into the cold morning. The grass, still green under his feet, muffled the sound of his hooves as Adelyn moved him easily forward. She'd decided to run him on as much grass and as little road as possible, preferring the quiet speed to the extra bounce a rough terrain promised. She bent her head close to his mane and breathed his horsy musk, feeling the power of his muscles as they moved up from his legs into his heavy haunches. She dreamed the sweetest of dreams, like life renewed, her dear friend Delia alive, Adelyn alive.

Adelyn and her Pharaoh ascended a hill that looked down onto the cow pasture on the Howard farm, and Adelyn guided her horse to the road. The family knew of her visit, their stable boy wiped down her horse as soon as she jumped down alongside the house. After her mother's harangue, she took special care to clean her riding boots. Her mother's last words admonished, "You don't need to be tracking mud all over Marissa Howard's Persian carpets."

Adelyn contritely answered with, "Mama, you know I'll take care not to injure Delia's mother's rugs."

Inside the house, Adelyn heard loud male voices, recognizing one of them in particular.

"Why, James Jackson, I could hear you a mile away." Thinking her cousin arrived alone to visit with Delia's brother Charles, Adelyn came upon five young men of similar age standing and lying about a large room behind the main hall. Her face blushed hot when she saw both Crawford boys and some others of their college fraternity. They all stood as she appeared in the doorway, her hair all wild from the ride, her shirt open to a décolleté just slightly less delicate or subtle. They quieted down while James went to her side, teasingly whispered something about making grand entrances.

"Miss Jackson." One of them spoke and she turned to look at tall Innis Crawford with dark hair and darker eyes.

James cleared his throat, "Uh, this is Innis, but you know him? Or wait, he was out of school when you came in." Her cousin winked at her.

"I'll just say hi and bye since I'm here to visit with Delia." She looked quickly in the direction of Innis who began to walk toward her. Adelyn experienced an immediate energy in him that surpassed the boyish fooling around the others indulged in. She chalked up his grace and ease to being older, though something about him punched a hole in her senses, and though she may have left the room, she felt him still with her. His long and quick stride brought him toward her, surprising her when she found he suddenly held her hand. The pulse between them grew stronger with his touch and left her silent to his polite introduction.

"I'm pleased to meet you." She called out a quick remark to James about being well acquainted with most of Tulip Junction, company included, and took possession of her hand from Innis before turning to the hall that would put an end to her nervousness.

Adelyn took the stairs two at a time to put distance between herself and the boys, not wanting to overhear any comments. She did note the loud laughing.

Adelyn strode around a circular balcony and down a long hall to the front of the house to Delia's room. Adelyn peeked in to see Delia all plumped up with frothy pillows, her long hair looking a bit tangled.

"My, I think I know what you need." She took the brush from the dresser, sat down on the bed, and put a cool hand on her friend's warm forehead.

"Maybe I came too soon, but you had me worried." She hugged Delia who smelled like rose water. "Did they say it was okay to risk a bath?"

"I'm just fine, don't be fussing with me or I'll throw you out, too."

"Too? Who else was here? Don't tell me that raucous bunch of boys downstairs." She raised a brow in mock surprise and gently brushed the first layer of thick hair. "Not that Innis?" Adelyn suddenly thirsted to hear his name spoken and by herself first.

"They all paid their respects, but from the door, and I'm trying to recall whether Innis was already downstairs…no, he actually said hello and wished me well."

Adelyn applied her energy to the next comb-through. "Now, is he just home from school too?" The comb snagged and Delia yelped "ouch!" and Adelyn stopped and apologized, and the room fell silent as she paid closer attention to the job at hand.

"You're awfully quiet all of a sudden, Addie." Delia's voice got fake syrupy. "So, you'd like to know more about what Mr. Innis has been up to. Seems a mite too old for you, though?"

Adelyn pretended to ignore the taunt, so her interest in him must have been obvious to Delia. *Had she been too obvious? She found Innis handsome, fascinating.* Her sixteen-year-old mind and body warmed with fantasies about older men.

"Everyone who knows you, Addie, claims you are an old spirit, been here before." Delia's remark lingered in the air between them until Adelyn felt coerced to reply.

"What does any of that have to do with Innis Crawford? Besides, you don't believe that nonsense, do you?" She turned Delia's face toward her to measure the effect of all her brushing and combing. Her shiny hair looked angelic.

Delia took the hand mirror from Adelyn to appraise her friend's effort. "Looks less like a sick girl, doesn't it?" She tugged a few curls toward her face and licked her lips. "Honey, my brother Charles says Innis was the man on campus to know. All the girls were crazy for him. Heard tell he may have ruined more than one reputation." She laughed with a sweet lilt. "Old soul, just that you easily sway from the boys at school to that man downstairs, that's all."

Adelyn took the mirror and studied her own face. Some barely visible freckles played over the top of her nose and she reminded herself to wear a hat and gloves when she rode. But she knew the impression she had made when she walked into that room of young men. She held them all in thrall, except maybe her cousin. She certainly had Innis's full attention. A soft knock on the door interrupted her thoughts.

"Delia, your mama wants you to take this soup and some tea and then nap." Nellie nodded to Adelyn.

Before she could protest, Adelyn interjected, "I'll be by tomorrow so we can work on some homework together."

*And maybe I might see him again.*

Outside, Pharaoh moved impatiently, his hooves dug into the red dirt, eager for a run. Adelyn petted his blaze and looked into his intelligent eyes. A mist arose from his nostrils in the colder evening air. He whinnied once and she hugged him before jumping up into the saddle. She felt a hand under her boot, making the movement easier, smoother, and turned to see Innis step back and nod.

"Take care now, little girl."

The remark irritated her, making her nostrils flare much like Pharaoh's had just moments before. She pulled up a little too much on the reins and the horse's head reared. *Who's little?* She saw him laugh and she jerked the reins again and tapped her heels against Pharaoh's flanks. As one, horse and girl, they galloped away over the green and lush pasture.

All the way home Adelyn felt Innis's tone strike her again and again. Had he meant it to be an insult? She worried the thought like a dog would a bone, just not able to let it go until she found herself on her own land in Tulip Junction where she could see the lights on in the house against the gray November day's end. Her heartbeat as though she, instead of her powerful animal, ran the distance.

It would be after Thanksgiving before Adelyn visited Delia again, and a good thing too, Adelyn's mother was quick to say. Mrs. Howard called to say Delia's temperature shot up again.

"She needs her rest," Mary Jackson affirmed, as she watched her daughter's face darken, and noticing, the way older women can, a new energy about Adelyn. And Adelyn waited the days out, dreaming about Innis and feeling a change, a power she possessed that she couldn't name, except someplace in her soul.

The door stood open to the great hall when Adelyn finally arrived back at Delia's. One of the boys might have seen her with two arms full of books as she stepped off the running board of her father's great sedan. Fewer boys relaxed in the hall yet all she saw had been there before.

"I'll get someone to take me back, Daddy," she

promised him. She knew he worried about his wild child.

She slipped through the door sideways and almost lost the barely balanced math and history books and papers. She had printed instructions out neatly so Delia could easily read what her teachers expected next in the lessons.

"Here, let me help." The familiar voice struck every nerve in her. She turned to face him with a saucy smile but was dismayed to see the younger brother, Garnett, broader of shoulder and with a sunnier complexion from all that college freshman football. She tried to erase the disappointment that covered her face instead of a special smile, but Garnett was too fast and maybe too smart for her to fool.

"Expecting someone else?" He chided her gently but with an edge to his voice.

"Can't possibly know what you mean. I'm here to see Delia and that was who I'm expecting to see, or maybe one of the servants."

"Sure you were." He gave a little tug to the books in her right arm and piled them on top of the others. "Where would you be wanting these?" She headed into the living room.

"There." Adelyn pointed to the big divan and the coffee table that sat in front of it. Delia had sent word via Cousin James to Adelyn about working in the front room, saying that since she was well enough to do schoolwork, she was well enough to sit downstairs. Adelyn admired that strawberry blonde hair of Delia's and how it resembled a flame whenever she flew into a snit.

The tall and muscular boy gently laid the books in a pile next to some sandwiches and a pot of coffee that Nellie prepared for the two girls. He stopped long enough to look into Adelyn's eyes and communicated a quiet patience she had not felt from his brother. Almost as though he could read her mind, he spoke softly to her, "I'm the kinder brother, Adelyn. Remember that."

"What's all this whispering in here?" Delia in a dark green wool sweater and pleated skirt looked fully recovered.

Her dimples went deep when she acted tricky, as now.

"I'm helping organize your work for you, Delia." Garnett said to both of them. "That way you two can be assured the best marks in history and whatever else they're throwing at you in Tulip Junction High. Now which of you will be the Salutatorian?"

"Why should either of us be second best?" The color in Adelyn's cheeks rose at the effrontery. "What about Valedictorian?"

Garnett backed off with open palms as if to say *enough of these women*. "I'll be saying goodbye for now, ladies."

The two girls settled themselves in the quiet house and occasionally sipped coffee, nibbling on the excellent sandwiches, and checking one another for spelling or punctuation questions. Delia got up from the sofa and switched on some lamps, as the day got darker. "I'm going to get us some fresh coffee."

Glad for the break from all that history and science, Adelyn scrunched down into the sofa, reading the accounts of Mr. Rochester in her copy of Jane Eyre.

A shadow passed with a voice saying, "What could a young girl be reading these days?"

She knew the voice and her heart beat faster to hear him. Always the Southern girl, not revealing her feelings, Adelyn feigned a casual tone.

"I'm not that young. Besides, I like the Brontë sisters." She held the book out to Innis as he, instead, took hold of her forearm, sliding his hand to her wrist.

The palm of his hand felt cool against her skin. She suddenly felt much older, trifling as she did with a grown man. She stretched out on the sofa where Innis joined her, sitting against her legs. He said nothing; he displayed no nervous physical energy, no uneasy conversation to fill up the silence. They looked into one another's faces, each for particular signs of character. Adelyn saw a serene brow but experienced eyes. *After all, he is older than I am.*

"No, I think you are much, much older than I am." His

smile added a glow to his eyes, which were very warm.

"How did you do that? I feel like that shouldn't be happening."

"That's because you are doing it, reading my thoughts, just as I am yours."

"How can you say that? If I am, I sure am not remembering anything."

"Oh, you know what I am saying; the sound of my thoughts will show up a little later." Innis moved closer as he spoke, and Adelyn wondered how he could. No one, boy or man, had ever sat so close to her.

*You know why I sit this close. I know you, have known you before.* Innis had not spoken a word yet she heard him. She could read his thoughts after all. "Why can't you just speak?"

He laughed. "You read my thoughts, yet ask out loud why I'm not talking? You are precious, to be sure." He straightened his sweater, which she saw as something fastidious in his nature, that he liked things his way and just so. "I don't mean to surprise or frighten you in any way. I want nothing more than to sit here and talk with you. You fascinate me. New and modern."

Adelyn realized he'd been holding her arm all this time, and for decorum's sake decided to pull away, but she did so reluctantly, he felt so much a part of her. "When you say before, when would that be? I went to the same schools, only after you graduated. But I was there with Garnett, two years behind you."

Innis flinched at the mention of his brother's name. "Let's not talk about that. I want to see you again. They're having a holiday dance here for Christmas. Won't you come with me? Or, if that is too obvious, won't you promise to dance every dance with me?" He turned from her and sat straight against the sofa, bending forward and running his hands through his hair. She couldn't see his face but his body told her he felt a sudden despair. "I am sorry. I really have no right to do this, you are, after all, very young, but I really can't help it."

Adelyn felt coveted, desired, glad to know he would pursue her. She thought she understood now what it meant to be loved.

Innis stood and took her hand again and then let go as they both heard Delia and the others joining them. He looked closely at her one more time. "Are you well? I notice your hand, it's very warm. And your eyes. Very shiny as though you have a fever."

Delia came back and stood now by Adelyn's side. "That cough medicine Miz Sorrow gave me has made my mouth dry. Thought I'd have us some tea and lemonade together."

She placed the small tray on the coffee table and poured the elixir into the cup and continued to prattle on. "Looks like you had some time to charm Mr. Innis here?"

Delia's southern coquetry faded when she saw her friend in distress. "Adelyn, sweetheart, you are breathing awful." She turned to Innis, "Isn't she?"

"The room is warm." Adelyn touched her head, and yes, she felt very warm. The drafty old mansion had grown cold, with a fireplace way to the other side of the sofas and chairs warming only the other end of the room. She had ignored feeling warmer throughout the day. She placed her hand to her neck inside her blouse open at the top, and felt her skin burning.

Innis sat down again on the sofa to be near her as she tried to swallow the tea.

"Maybe I might have some of that cough medicine, too." Adelyn spoke to Innis, "What is happening to me? I'm shivering and cold."

Delia's face loomed over Adelyn and she patted Adelyn's hand, "You are worrying me some. I'm gonna call Mama. You *are* shivering."

Innis moved quickly, pulling his sweater off and wrapping Adelyn in it as Delia ran to call her mother. She caressed the sweater, full of his warm smell. He embraced her to pull her up when she wanted nothing more than to lie deeper and sleep.

"I know you want to lie down, but you must sit up some to help your breathing...." He stopped.

*"You forgot, Innis, I can tell your thoughts. Am I dying? It's all gone dark."*

Confinement all around her, Adelyn's arms pinned to her sides, her head elevated for others to see. She begins to float above and look down at a girl dressed in plain white muslin, the best fabric her grandmother could afford. The girl lies in a coffin, her long blonde hair curled to frame her face and placed at the front of each shoulder. All made to look natural, only nothing moves, no eyelids fluttering about to open, no lips pursing and un-pursing, no signs of life, because her life has gone. *I can't be her. I'm not.*

Adelyn called out and pushed the blankets from her burning body. She heard voices and cried out to them. "Don't put me in that box. You promised me I wouldn't die. Please."

"There now, Adelyn, honey. Don't be taking on like that. You're all right. You're all right." Dr. Fanning, placating her, placed his stone-cold stethoscope to her burning chest.

Even in her feverish state her agitation increased. *Comforting the dying?* She heard him saying the same with her uncle and grandfather. Her chest felt heavier again. She called for Innis, but no one admonished her so she knew she called only from inside. *Innis? You promised. Innis!"*

Her lungs fill with the viscous blood, and she chokes. The voices begin again, mumbling over the coffin. A woman wearing a dark flower-patterned dress speaks.

"Granny is all consumed by her going. Lucianne was her prize after a life of hard work. Such a sorrow." A tall country woman in a straw hat says this to a portly woman. Above the casket Adelyn watches now without any emotion, no longer fearful. Her grandmother is helped into the room where they all sit and grieve, and some talk quietly.

"My girl, my dear child." The old woman takes her granddaughter's hand and strokes it. Granny is cried out, feels grief like leaden heaviness in her legs and arms. Adelyn swoops down near the old woman, creating an imperceptible breeze that only Granny can feel. Granny touches her cheek and smiles. She knows Lucianne is nearby.

"You're leaving your old grandma alone, all alone."

*"You'll see me again." Adelyn has Lucianne's dead voice.*

Adelyn is pulled by a great force away from the modest farmhouse where Granny and her family surround the dead girl's casket—a cool hand on her forehead, the scent of her mother's lavender water.

"Mama's here; you're going to be all right. Please sweetheart, can you open your eyes for your mama?"

Adelyn stirred and blinked hard, trying to focus—her mother by her side—behind her chair stood others. Some real, her aunt Grace Lee. But then a girl in white stands next to Adelyn's grandfather and Uncle Brady, some others looking like old photographs, all stand in darkness at the back of the room and begin to fade. She struggled to sit up while Dr. Fanning steadied her head, another pillow placed behind her. "She'll breathe better now, Mary. Let's leave her to sleep just a bit longer."

Adelyn brushed away some crustiness from her eyes and saw him. "Innis?" Reaching out her hand to him while he stepped forward and took hold of hers. A connection made, his energy flowed into her. His voice faltered for a moment, she sensed embarrassment. Had she said more than she should? *Did the others hear?*

"They'll be coming back, your mother and old Doctor Fanning," he stuttered. "They'd be upset if they saw me still here. Adelyn, just hold on, girl. You had us all worried." She felt his lips touch her hand and knew they must be alone. He would not have chanced such an outward display of affection with her family and his friends nearby.

"Was I gone a long time?" The sun crept in through a slit between two heavy drapes. "Those drapes look like they've been hanging there since the War."

Innis gave a short chuckle. "You are a marvel. A sense of humor in all this?" He poured a glass of water. "Something to drink?"

Innis held a glass to her lips as she sipped. The water opened her to a tremendous thirst, and she lifted herself up to drink more ambitiously, until she emptied the glass. "How long was I like this?"

"Two days, Sweet Pea. And you called out at first, my name. You called my name."

"I heard your voice; every time I would get real tired and wanted just to become Lucianne, you would warn me. Do you remember?" But as quickly as she spoke, she saw he was confused and maybe shocked. "Why do you look at me like that?" She sat upright and pushed at her hair; someone had been brushing it all through her crisis because it felt all in place, ringlets and all. *Mama. She would never let Innis into the room with my hair a mess.*

Innis took her hand and laid his cheek on it. "I have something to confess. I contrived a way to stay on when you took sick. Charles was easy enough to trick. Told him I was feeling a mite sickly myself, which, for all the world was true once I saw you were in danger."

He looked at her then away, searching the room, and released her hand to fetch a warmer blanket, spreading it out over her.

"You look like you're about to get chilled again. I was here when all the others, your mother and family, slept. They all came as soon as you began to lose consciousness. I just found a way, and I heard you call me." His look and his voice took a turn toward a wariness. "Tell me how you knew this girl, Lucianne."

Adelyn pulled the cover up, surprised to find her hands

shaking and her body weakening and already very weary. "Who did you say?" She welcomed the blanket, the fever passing made her chill. "I don't know, someone wearing a white dress. She died, Granny was there and a bunch of cousins."

Adelyn's pulse quickened, her own speech and accent changed, like a country girl's drawl. She felt possessed by something she couldn't identify. Innis's face became dreamy again, far away, but she noticed a certain change to his eyes that looked like real terror. Words came out of her mouth, unbidden, "You seen a ghost now, dincha?" The coarse language growled from out of the back of her throat.

Adelyn watched outside herself. Some power took over and drained her of energy. "What is this? Am I her or me?" Then blessed sleep crept in, and she felt herself falling into it, and didn't wake until the sun had left the sky and only her mother and Delia sat with her.

"I had a dream, Mama, Delia." She tossed her head side to side trying to remember it, knowing she needed to remember.

"What is that, darling?" Her mother straightened her bedclothes and helped her change into a fresh nightgown.

"I can't tell. It seemed important, but now it's all gone."

# Chapter Eight
## RECOVERY

Adelyn recovered quickly, though the doctor and her mother prevailed, and she remained at home for a week. Delia took her turn to cart home school assignments and keep her friend up to date on Tulip Junction.

Yet when alone, Adelyn's mind traced through her experience of the girl in white. The girl's name disappeared from her memory; pieces of the girl's funeral fell out of her mind and faded. She had no one to tell. *Who would believe me? No one except maybe Innis.* She recalled Innis felt threatened when she questioned him about the girl, becoming dark and remote. Though the sixteen-year-old her found that exciting, she did not feel an inclination to test his temper's limits.

She took to whispering aloud all she remembered of dropping down into the body of the dead girl. She did it to hear her own words, reinforcing, making it a real, hard fact. As she recovered, she lost more and more of the experience until it had no more substance than a faint shadow on a wall.

"What you doing in my kitchen, Missy?" Aunt May stirred some awful oatmeal.

"Just want some toast and maybe a poached egg."

Aunt May, rotund with bright eyes, flashed Adelyn a look. "You best sit down and out of my way. Don't need no traffic to fuss with in my place of work." She gently guided Adelyn to a spot at the far end of a heavy old deal table, and dropped an egg into a pot, all the while somehow stirring the oatmeal so it wouldn't stick.

"Aunt May, you must hear how so many don't get better. I mean, I feel lucky that I didn't die." She munched on the toast that had miraculously appeared, along with the poached egg.

Aunt May, about thirty but older and wiser than even that age, came to where Adelyn sat, and sat as well, sipping her cup of coffee. She shook her head, and Adelyn could tell she contemplated the long list of mourners in the southern part of the county. "Yes, Lawd, indeed. You know someone down south?"

Adelyn took the empty cup near her and filled it halfway with coffee. "I heard of a family lost a girl my age, can't think of her name. You know that family?" Her voice trembled at bringing the girl's fragile existence into the light of day. *Except for Innis, no one had heard her speak of it.*

"There was one…why, yes, she be Granny Wilkin's grandchild. They's call her Lucy something, spell it like Deep South, Cajun. Seventeen, pretty, and sassy at times." She looked meaningfully at Adelyn. Then, because a sadness had come over Adelyn, Aunt May asked, "You know her, child?"

Adelyn lapsed into that dream again, the confinement of the coffin, the sounds of soft weeping. "I heard tell, don't recall exactly who knew her. Maybe kin to a classmate." She picked at the egg that had gone cold. "Seventeen? So young." Yet inexplicably, all this would fade from the sixteen-year-old Adelyn's memory until it no longer mattered. She would go back to school, to dances; and every so often she would see Innis pass by to talk to her father about some contract or other, the only constant, her heart beating faster each time she saw him.

Sadness, though, draped itself over the students returning to high school. Delia and Adelyn returned to school in a week and waited for their friends to return. After a short while, they saw some had recovered, and slowly, the empty seats and desks filled. But the reality of the pandemic that brought the world to its knees forced them to acknowledge that Mary Sue Jenkins and Bobby Smart and at least ten of their other friends would never again sit at those desks. Adelyn went home weeping almost every day. The lingering thought of Innis became Adelyn's comfort in the midst of all the loss. She played the events over and over in her mind, trying to make sense of them.

*He said something to me about being young, that it was wrong because I was so young.* "That day, before I took sick, he tried to tell me." Deep inside her subconscious, she recognized it as a declaration of love. But in the naivete of her sixteen years, she put it all aside because she had no way of knowing what that meant to him. She continued to be drawn to thinking of him, wanting to speak with him.

Adelyn lost herself in class plays, studying history, and running for class secretary, and often wondered what Innis thought or did. Occasionally her mind's eye would seek images of him. One day as she read her lessons a picture came into mind. She sat very still, and heard Innis as a thought, asking Mr. Pike, in the older man's law office, "Sir, is this date correct on the decision?"

She watched inside, images forming in her head, as Mr. Pike put his book down and pushed his eyeglasses up to see some fine print, all the while tracing the words with his finger, his lips moving. "No, not that date. That was the first date set to hear the defense. Here, here, see this down further, that's the date of the decision, maybe ten days later."

She didn't know what any of that meant. This new gift, when her mind opened a door and she would sense events play out, fascinated her. She had no one to tell, not even Delia, because this special sight couldn't be shared. Adelyn put it all aside, as if waiting for something to happen.

In Tulip Junction, everyone eventually would cross the path of everyone else; no one would be surprised to find Adelyn and her mother meeting Mrs. Crawford while shopping in Savannah. It happened when the Junction's meager shops ran out of the less practical but equally important silk hose or beaded purse. Adelyn's mother saw Sarah Crawford first and immediately called out in a hushed voice, almost a whispering, "Mrs. Crawford. Sarah May."

Adelyn saw the tall and thin woman with heavy dark hair the same as Innis's turn her intense scrutiny from a roll of heavy lace edging toward Adelyn's mother. "Mrs. Jackson, pleasure seeing you."

Adelyn felt the taciturn woman would not enjoy small talk, which her own mother luxuriated in. She inched behind her mother, shy of wanting to intrude on Mrs. Crawford whose chore of choosing lace for pillowcase edging did not include her own mother's overly friendly chattiness; however, Mary Jackson did persist with a comment about the quality of the lace which caused Sarah May Crawford to exhibit an interest in what she had to say.

"Good to have your opinion, Mary. You think this will wash well, then, not bunch up? That would save our housekeeper, Trudie, some time, keep from her toiling over a hot iron."

Mary Jackson's only reply, "Oh."

Adelyn noticed Innis's mother's back straighten at the short remark. Smiling at Mary Jackson, Adelyn could tell she wanted to be understood when she added, "I was thinking more about Trudie with another baby on the way and how one less thing to hot-iron would be welcomed."

Adelyn believed her, that she could be impressed about the world and its poor through her deep feelings, that she felt the toil of one human, suffering for others near her, her children first and maybe even her employer. She also saw that small talk troubled Mrs. Crawford; a stranger to it, yet Adelyn felt grateful Innis' mother made the effort to talk near nonsense with her mother. Sarah May looked directly at Adelyn and caught her eye. *So you are the one, are you?*

Adelyn's eyes widened as she heard the woman's thoughts, saw a smile play on the woman's full lips, her eyebrow lift. *It's not my fault, really.* The thought escaped her before she could stop it, no way of retrieving it. Thankfully, Mrs. Crawford extended her hand instead.

"I believe this is your Adelyn. My, you have grown to such a beautiful young lady." Adelyn mumbled an awkward thank-you and gently shook the woman's hand, her fingers barely grasping, afraid for even that small gesture being appraised and found lacking. And, thankfully, Adelyn's mother took up the slack and filled the tiny shop with exclamations of joy at having a daughter she could dress for the Howard's traditional holiday dance. Until this moment, the dance entirely occupied Adelyn's mind, thinking only of seeing Innis again.

The phone bell clanged as the hall clock chimed eight. "Daddy, Mama, I've got it." Adelyn called to her mother and father not to get up. "This is the Jackson residence, Adelyn speaking." She waited through the connection made by Sally Barnes, their operator, thinking how clumsy she was and then biting her lip at so ungracious a thought. When she heard nothing further, she ventured, "Hello, Adelyn here."

"I know it's you. How are you?" Her memory enlightened her. Not Innis, just sounded like him.

"Who is this?" She felt it safer to let the young man identify himself. Any of the fraternity boys could be prankish for some humor. Cousin James and his crowd would often do this. "It's not Innis, if that's what you mean." Garnett Crawford confirmed his identity. She congratulated herself on her best guess and decided to be difficult.

"Innis? Mr. Crawford? You're with Mr. Pike's law office? Did you want to speak to my daddy?" She barely contained her laughter and tried to wipe the smile out of her voice.

If silence could be temperature, the phone line froze with icicles. Finally, he spoke.

"Adelyn, I'm down at school till mid-week. I know you'll be going to the Howard's Christmas dance. Are you going to save me a dance or two, or are they all taken up?" He could not contain his anger and it had a similar effect on Adelyn.

"I don't see why you can't take a nicer tone, Garnett Crawford. I'm not saving anything for anyone." She felt momentarily ashamed for trampling on his feelings. Begrudgingly she added, "It's promising to be a good time. I'll be looking for you at the Howard's and for that dance." She heard nothing more and thought he had hung up.

"Adelyn, I hope you mean that. I'll be looking for you. You be well now, hear? I'll be waiting on you."

His voice, the longing in it, almost broke her heart. She rang up Delia right away.

"Guess who called?" she blurted, before Delia could even say more than hello. She heard clicking on the line, so she added, "Miss Barnes, we're connected now. Thank you." They heard a loud click as Sally got off the line. "Well, guess, and hurry before that ol' busybody gets on again."

"Hello, and how are you too, Addie?" Delia responded playfully. "Now it can't be that handsome Mister Innis Crawford."

Adelyn refrained from saying anything about Innis, unwilling to make what could just be a schoolgirl's crush into something bigger.

"Garnett Crawford called from way down at the

university. He wants me to save him a dance at the Christmas party."

"Oh, dear. And all I have to look forward to is my second cousin on Daddy's side to fill my dance card." Delia laughed with glee. And Adelyn knew her friend's beauty caught the eye of more than one landowner's son. Both girls let loose their controls and rushed into foolishness, wanting to leave the memory behind them of so many gone from the influenza.

They rang off shortly after these exchanges, and Adelyn wandered into the living room and dropped down onto the overstuffed sofa next to her mother.

"Lands, child, will you plop yourself down like that when you're wearing that new Paris fashion?"

Her father looked up from his newspaper, puffed on his pipe and glanced over at his daughter. "Giving up jodhpurs and brogues for fancy dress? And what did this cost me?"

Adelyn all but ignored both her parents. Her father, she knew, happily paid for a fashionable Parisian dress rather than a flimsy muslin frock for burial. Her mind snapped back to the girl in the south of the county whose name she once knew, alone, arms pinned to her sides. Adelyn coughed reflexively, just to know she still breathed, which set both her parents to react with similar thoughts.

"Perhaps, Missy, that excitement and all those people will be too much for you." Her mother thought out loud. "You do not need to catch cold. You might wear a warmer dress, something wool."

Adelyn did not even glance in her father's direction for any form of agreement with her mother. She thought instead of that silky dress of two thin layers of darker green over emerald green that shimmied onto her hips like a second skin. She thought of the beads of green crystal sewn along each side from under her arms of the sleeveless dress, all the way down her hips. She recollected how the lamp caught all those tiny points of light glistening when she turned this way and that. And the matching slim feather boa and the long gloves that went up to her elbows. She wished she had a long cigarette holder but alas, she did not smoke.

Her father spoke, "That the green thing Uncle Tyree brought back from New York? No one told me that thing came from Paris. Why, Addie, if I'd known that, I'd have thrown it out in the stable for them to use for wiping down Pharaoh."

She went to her father and pushed his paper aside, "Now Daddy, you know I'm your girl. You wouldn't be doing that to make me sad."

He gathered her in a big hug and said, "No, making you sad is far from my thoughts, very far from my thoughts." All the while her mother harrumphed and fussed with her embroidering, and Adelyn felt contented, knowing she lived a blessed life.

## Chapter Nine
### *DRESSING UP*

"You are a true beauty." Uncle Tyree's remarks took Adelyn off guard as she twirled 'round and 'round to watch the beaded dress follow her, sometimes stinging her sides as the beads hit up against her thighs.

"I feel as free as…" She stopped, unable for a moment to conjure any feeling as free as this until her Uncle, followed by her father who came to stand just behind his wife's brother-in-law, threw out suggestions for such a feeling.

"How 'bout you running around in jodhpurs when no girl in Tulip Junction would dare?"

Mr. Jackson offered his own vision of her, "You in your cousin James's swimsuit down by the big pond, swimming just like a tadpole."

Mary Jackson closed the door, but slightly. She wouldn't shut it tight, because that would be impolite, but just enough to finish her handiwork on coaxing her daughter into a pair of silk hose the same color as her dark-green-on-green gown. "I still think it should be worn just above the ankle."

"Oh Mama, it's fine where it is, just on my shin. I can move, I can dance with it this length. And they say this will be all the rage, maybe even shorter soon." She swished again and finally sat down to roll the silken hose carefully up to her thigh.

"I'm not interested in rages, lady." Her mother smoothed the line of the dress with a sad expression on her face.

"Sad? How can you be sad?" Adelyn looked again at her hair. She had compromised with her mother, that she would sweep it up, and not wear it down in that flat look. She noticed some feathery tendrils playing about her face and they looked impish, so she left them there.

"Not sad, dear. Oh, maybe a mite. You're growing up."

"Cicely, love, what do you think?" Adelyn looked toward her baby sister all curled up on the big four-poster bed in the middle of the room.

"I want to be just like you, Addie, just like." She climbed down and walked around her sister, missing nothing. "Maybe wear a dress like this."

Missus Jackson finished with one more quick look at her older daughter, then found herself peering into the same full-length mirror, her hand gently placed under her chin. "Ah, me, you make me feel old, my dear."

"Not true, Mama. You're still young." Adelyn hugged her mother's shoulders as they stood next to one another, Adelyn at least two inches taller than her mother. Her mother hugged her back then began brushing her own long hair, and wound it up, asking Adelyn to help her pin it in place. At only forty, her thick, reddish brown hair still shone. Adelyn knew she would wear a black floor-length chemise. Her mother always looked stunning.

## *Chapter Ten*
### *THE DANCE*

The Jackson family entered the grand foyer of the Howard home amid the large crowd of friends and relatives of everyone in Tulip Junction and beyond, as far down as Savannah. Delia, her brother, and their parents received each group as they entered, her father cupping the elbow of Captain Jackson, and Delia's mother bussing Mary Jackson on each cheek like someone in a European novel. Adelyn's head whirled with the images of fir boughs festooning the white banister, red holly berries peeking in and out. The fir gave off the aroma of Christmas trees and winter and freshness.

"Delia, I am truly pleased. You are ravishing in that dress." Adelyn hugged her friend, who had hinted about her gown but, like all of the girls, revealed it only when she stood up in it. She wore a white beaded dress that grazed her shins, as Adelyn's dress did hers. The beaded fringe of the dress alternated silver and white. "I can't wait to see how those beads move when you dance." As she spoke, she looked along the line of young men in black tuxedos helping young women fill their punch glasses. She also noticed some with little flasks adding something extra to the drinks.

"Don't be craning your neck for him, he's right over there, and he saw you as soon as you walked in." Delia gestured with a shrug to her right shoulder over which Adelyn glanced to see the most burning eyes set in the most handsome face. *He's so dashing; he takes my breath away!*

No sooner had she thought it than she knew he would have heard her thoughts, and her blush covered every inch of her face and slid down her neck.

"It's all so exciting, isn't it, Addie?" Delia took Adelyn's arm and directed her to a young man with curly red hair. "This is Mister Lefebvre. Michael, this is Adelyn, my best friend, ever." And she added hurriedly, "That is, till you came along."

Delia's new beau greeted her graciously, taking Adelyn's hand and gently shaking it. Her long opera-length gloves stopped him from gallantly kissing her hand.

"What do you make of this new decade we're entering? Don't you think the new century should have started now? The excitement, the industry, all of it." He smiled a tricky smile. "The bootleg whiskey, too, of course."

"The new century now? What of everything invented till now?" Adelyn turned to see Garnett standing as close to her as humanly possible. She felt the warmth of his breath on her naked shoulders and turned to look at his fresh, ruddy, outdoors complexion.

"We were just saying how fast everything is changing. Pretty soon, we'll be wearing dresses shorter than these." Delia turned her leg to show off her calf and ankle. She felt daring.

Garnett ignored Delia, spiriting Adelyn away so he could not be overheard. "Will you dance with me? Now?" He had his arm around her waist and moved them both onto the floor of the ballroom. All the rugs had been rolled up and put away. The orchestra sat high up on a bandstand playing something slow.

"My, you're breathing like you just ran a race." She looked up at him, glad she had worn two-inch heels to shorten the distance between her and Garnett and most of the boys who had suddenly grown tall. When he didn't speak, she pressed her arm more firmly on his neck. "Well, did you?"

"Did I what?" Garnett's serious expression looked like someone had just asked him for an overdue assignment.

"Did you just play some football outside with the others before you ran in here to dance?" She giggled so quietly he didn't hear her, and when she saw how much sterner his expression had become, she regretted her remark. *So very sensitive.*

"No, Miss, it's your green dress and green eyes." He stopped his train of thought and started again. "Your mama let you out in that dress?"

"Why, don't you like it?" She pushed the thin strap up that had slid down from her shoulder. "Everyone's wearing these…in Paris."

His voice became impatient. "Paris? Someone sent for this dress all the way there?"

Adelyn straightened her back as their bodies moved with the music. She noticed he maintained a respectable space apart from her, but she also knew he could feel from the position of his hand on her back that she wore no more than a shimmy.

"You didn't answer my question, Garnett Crawford. Don't you like my gown?"

"Gown? Why, it's barely a slip; there's so little of it."

He stuttered the last few words just as the band ended their set. A solo violinist stood to play a sweet old song, and everyone dancing stopped to hear it. Others took the break to get back to the punch bowl. Adelyn did not ponder Garnett's remarks. At sixteen she knew little of men, but almost a woman, she understood his attraction to her and her slip of a dress.

"Thank you for the dance, Mr. Crawford. You certainly took advantage of Mrs. Smiley's tea cotillions as a little one, learning to be graceful."

"I'm happy to know you think so."

The surge of the crowd broke them apart, friends interrupting them to chat, girls about gowns or men about football, and she wandered back toward the grand hallway. Lively conversations began as one boy, then another, stopped by to say hello. Some asked for her health and she had to remind herself that she had only lately been feeling well. These boys remembered she took ill, who had visited Delia's brother and Adelyn's cousin James that day. All but one came forward.

A light touch became a light encircling of her bare arm above her opera-length glove. Her skin tingled to the touch of flesh on flesh and she didn't need to look; she knew him.

"I thought I'd better get hold of you before any more of those Casanovas tried to claim you."

"What a funny thing to say. You think they could own me?" He guided her down the back hall and opened the door to the small porch on the back of the large mansion. With the moon shining high up, they didn't need the porch light to see, yet no one would easily see them.

Innis kissed her, first soft, then probing, and then hard with an anxiety, a longing, almost a sadness. She was sixteen, but she felt it all, mostly the longing making her heart pump faster, feeling blood spilling from one valve to another. He touched her carefully but deliberately as he avoided wrinkling the rich silk dress, yet he felt all along her breasts until he pushed gently on her nipples, sending an electric bolt through her, beckoning as strong a physical wantonness in her as more experienced women would have known. She felt his body push against hers the way she knew it must feel like before she would be entered. "Enough. Adelyn, enough."

Their ragged breathing revealed their passion; thankfully, he stopped them both. Only then did she consider their deepening desires. Yet she shamelessly kissed his face, his lips again, his open mouth.

"Stop now, Sugar." And he took both her hands in his and just held her out and away from him. "My fault, come on. We need to be seen where we should be. We need to dance."

Adelyn opened the little string purse, found her mirror, and brushed her hair back in place, thankful for the loose tendrils she had left undone. No one would suspect then, no one.

Somehow, she followed Innis back, grateful for the lights that had been lowered in the grand chandelier. They moved as one to the music.

And when I told them…

How beautiful you are…

They didn't believe me!

They didn't believe me!

"So much to be sad for, isn't it, Innis? So many young men in the War and all those young people with the influenza."

"Lots of good people gone." He held her tighter than he probably should, and she read his mind when he hesitated and thought he should be more proper.

"Why do you do that? Why do you come to me, only to pull away?" She looked at him fully in the face, his clean jawline, his clear eyes.

"Because you're sixteen." Then a pause, and the song surrounded them. "Because I absolutely love you, in a reckless and wanton way. Because I almost lost you."

His words puzzled Adelyn. "But what is wrong to feel that way? Surely not because I'm young." She hesitated. "I'm not that young."

Innis laughed. "You really don't understand what a drug you are. I could have taken you so easily, so effortlessly, just moments ago."

Renée Ebert

The intimacy of his words, of everything since they first met, hit her. "I didn't…wasn't going to do…that."

Innis smiled at her, "Oh, little girl, yes you were."

"Stop. You called me that the first time I met you. I think we're better off just dancing."

"And I'm inclined to agree."

He whirled her around the floor to a waltz, the beads of her dress and the flow of the silk brushed her legs. She watched some of the other couples, and they seemed to be caught up in the evening and the music. *We're not so different.*

"Yes, we are." He murmured into her hair, careful not to seem as though he kissed her. Reading her thoughts, yet again.

The room looked more crowded than before. Some of the older folk relaxed on comfortable stuffed chairs, others at small tables where two or four could sit and visit. She could see them all in the dimmed lighting. She noticed candles were placed throughout, making it all so romantic. Faces stared back at her as they danced from one place to another.

"I bet I know almost everyone here." She said half to herself and half to Innis.

"Bet not." His smile had changed to a look of conspiracy, and she looked more closely as they came near, then moved away from one group or another. Something *was* different. Shadows masked the people at the back. The chandelier had transformed from lightbulbs to flickering candlelight, and the candles had burned down almost to the end. The room grew darker.

"I know just about everyone in Tulip Junction, Innis. Maybe with the exception of those just born tonight." But she did not know these people. Their faces, worn, not just old, but otherworldly, and them all dressed in finery she'd expect at a laying out, at a funeral. Her skin began to crawl like spiders running along her veins. She felt her palms sweat and forced herself to look away from the people alongside the dance floor. She gazed into his face.

"Please, Innis, make it stop. I don't want to see these people again." Adelyn felt dizzy, shut her eyes, only that made it worse. "Please."

Innis looked into her eyes. "I can't explain, but if I concentrate, I can conjure old and even young who have passed out of this life. It's like they're waiting for me." His voice turned low and haunted, shaking.

"Is that what I'm seeing? First you read my mind; I read yours. Now this?"

The room lightened and the music stopped. Innis took her out to the hall. He dipped a napkin into an ice bowl and pressed it to her forehead.

"Darling, you almost fainted." They walked quietly out to the back porch, then onto the gravel drive to his big sedan parked against the tall bushes. The motor running, he opened the door to the warm inside, helped her into the back seat where a blanket lay spread out. He sat next to her as she straightened her dress around her.

Innis took her chin into his hand and brought her close to him. They kissed. Maybe the drinks she sneaked from some of the boys with flasks produced an urgency in her now, an abandonment. She pulled him close to her and hungrily probed his mouth, touched his tongue with hers. His groan just audible, as he brushed her ear with his lips and he pushed her dress up to open the bottom of her shimmy, his hand maddeningly deft at stroking and petting her until, almost there, he slowly pushed inside her.

She felt the fullness of him, a thrill went up in her all the way to her breathing as he plunged, slowly, slowly, until they both reached their climax. She held him in her a long, long time, stroking his hair, his face. *So that's what it is.*

"Can't I stay here with you? Maybe they'll think you drove me home?" The light from the windows lit the car enough for her to see the crease in his brow and him slowly shaking his head 'no' as she spoke. She wanted to go back to where she had just been.

"I could stay with you all night, but that can't be." Innis stroked her face and felt her breath quicken on his face. "No, sweetheart, stop. I know you're not to blame for any of this. You have to straighten yourself up and get back and mingle with your friends. Hear? Can you think of a way inside?"

Adelyn straightened her dress; the dark silk did not show wrinkles. "I don't know what you're fussing about. I'll just scoot in the back door and straight up the back stairs to Delia's room. All the girls take turns fixing their hair and whatnot. I'll just have more to do." She smiled, and her voice went all sultry.

"You are a wanton creature." He kissed her again, and his lips scalded hers. "But you're my creature." His expression mixed tortured conscience with the desire to keep her with him. "Go."

Adelyn slowly walked away from the car, the better to look and listen for some of the younger high school boys sneaking cigarettes. She saw no sign of anyone in the quiet night. She entered the house and the upstairs without incident. Effortlessly, she went into the bathroom at the top of the stairs and locked the door.

"My hair is a fright."

She found a brush and brought her hair back from the brink of lost respectability. All the while she looked hard at herself in the mirror, looking for the change now that she'd been possessed. Her wanton side smoothed over any guilt she might have felt.

"I love him." She said this aloud to the empty room, a statement of defiance more than a justification. Satisfied with her dress and hair, she opened the door and walked slowly down the grand staircase. Most of Tulip Junction filled the room below. Her eyes sought out Innis, but instead, she saw Garnett at the bottom, waiting for her. Despite her resolve to be collected, her heart felt a strange irregular beat, which she tried to brush away with conversation.

"Well now, Garnett Crawford. You waitin' on me?"

"Expecting someone else?" The coldness in his voice said he knew, that she may not have looked different to herself when she glanced in a mirror, but Garnett saw it all.

*Renée Ebert*

# *PART II*

*Renée Ebert*

## *Chapter Eleven*
### *SOME ANSWERS*

Adelyn dozed again after Garnett left with Trey and Tyler for a trip farther out in the country for 'just us men'. She slept, dreamt, and awakened to the memory of 1918 and her coming of age that Christmas and New Year holiday. Her body thrilled to that first time with Innis all over again. Or maybe she'd actually lived it again. *Is that possible?* She almost answered her own question and bit her lip, not wanting to say it aloud. But the dream had been very real.

The girl in white intruded into her reverie. She hadn't thought of her since that night long ago when she and Innis danced their first dance. She wondered at what magic had erased that event from her memory. She couldn't believe her foolish sixteen-year-old self would have blocked the memory of the magic that had surrounded Innis and her, them each reading one another's thoughts. Were they just in tune, or was it really magic? How could she even ask herself this when Innis had returned to her and made love to her all over again? Her body squirmed in delight at his touch. She shivered at that and then something nagging, a girl in white, entered her thoughts.

"I'm going to see Momma Sorrow, and I'm putting you on notice, Innis Crawford. Don't come by and bother me today." She felt foolish speaking out loud to an empty room, but she felt him nearer to her, more and more, even when she couldn't see him.

Adelyn roused herself out of bed, took a quick shower, and combed her hair into an up-do before pulling out a soft white cotton dress from in the back of her closet. She felt a jolt of recognition. The dress looked like the one the girl in the train station wore when she floated into Adelyn's life through that hazy mirror. It reinforced her decision to seek out Momma Sorrow. She reproached herself for not having done this sooner. Not wanting to answer a dozen questions from her mother about where she planned on going, she left the house from the back stairway that led into the kitchen. Aunt May, still with them and still fussy about people interfering in her kitchen, raised an eyebrow when she saw Adelyn. The look that passed between them told Aunt May not to ask, and so she didn't.

Adelyn walked quickly along the path, but her car was not parked near the front driveway. An old truck stood there instead. Checking to see the truck bed did not hold a payload, Adelyn jumped in quickly to start the truck. Thankfully, the engine was warm, keys in the ignition, and it started up right away. The ride to just beyond Delia's house took fifteen minutes as she gunned the engine to reach its top speed.

Yet her thoughts freely intruded on any peace of mind she may have awakened with this morning. Small pieces of her memories from back then in the winter of 1918 floated in front of her like so many colorful patches for a quilt. She knew Innis wouldn't bother her now, not when her need to know more pressed in on her. *The storm the other day? Kicking up dust because everyone here wished Garnett a welcome back.* She suspected Innis caused it, pleased with herself that she confronted Innis.

*That bee sting near my cheek at dinner yesterday. How truly obvious, and childish.* She reflexively rubbed the place where he must have pricked at her with some intangible pin, robbing her of the enjoyment of her husband's affectionate kiss. *You are a demon, and you know it, Innis.* Her emotion muddled her thinking. How old was Innis? He didn't seem twenty-two. No, he had matured, he even had smile lines. That sideways world Momma Sorrow said he lived in must have plenty of sunshine.

She made the turn onto the dirt road that would take her down and away from Delia's home. The sun raced behind a cloud, setting Adelyn to ponder whether Innis could do that, make the sun race. As she drew closer to her destination, dark clouds began to gather and churn, like a counterpart to the peaceful sky. She stopped the truck and parked it out of the way. No one would guess she'd taken this shambles of a vehicle, one reason she preferred it. She took the key and dropped it into her purse and automatically made the sign of the cross. *I'll need all the help I can get.*

The house looked almost deserted, tall grass grown up over the rose bushes that had been so well tended only a week before. *How could that be?* "Damn, should have called first."

The steps creaked as she walked up and onto the front porch. A curtain fluttered behind an opened screened window. She knew Momma saw her. She'd sensed a body moving away from the window and toward the door. Adelyn raised her hand to press on the doorbell, and the door opened, as if by itself. Momma stood behind it.

"Well, *ma chère*, it is time enough for you to come back for our visit."

Momma wore a riot of red and blue, same colors she wore when she spoke from the mirror of that enchanted room at the Forsythe Hotel.

"You didn't heed my warning about that Innis. Oh, *chère*, he is a pretty one, all tall and thin and sinewy. Yes, and he loves you with an unworldly passion, but it will burn you if you are not careful."

Adelyn opened her mouth to speak, and Momma pressed her finger to her lips.

"Now, one thing at a time. Soon enough, answers will come soon enough."

Momma gestured to the little table set for two. *She knew I was coming?*

Momma waited in silence. Adelyn settled in and spoke in a burst of words and images, living every minute of what she related, at home with the magic of it all.

"You know Innis and I visited yesterday. He warned me not to come to you. He told me he wants to come all the way back. He says I am the only one who can help him do this. I said something about his mother, and he said he didn't want to speak of her. Same with when I said I was coming here today. He almost threatened, I don't know what, if I came. What doesn't he want me to know? I get images as I wake up in the morning, of a girl. Did he know her? Why does he want to come back? Can he be alive in this world, Momma?"

"I knew. I knew it was time. But first, you drink this sweet tea while I tell you more of the history of your beloved. And don't be protesting my calling him that because he is every inch of him absorbed in you. Wasn't always the case, though. But first, tell me what you remember. Do you know how he died?"

Adelyn sipped the sweet tea, tasting of strawberries and some spices. The question hung in the air and held her to this world, not the one Innis came from. *No, I never knew.*

Adelyn found herself reciting in a rush what she had always surmised. "Daddy thought he heard Innis was in a car accident at the University or coming back from some legal case he litigated down near Savannah. Then my mama chimed in and said, no, he suffered a sudden heart attack. My friend Delia swore he was in a car accident where he hit an oil slick, which is what I thought too…"

Momma Sorrow put her hand up like she was stopping traffic in New York City. "What does your husband say?"

A chill went right through Adelyn, like someone had poured ice in her veins. "I don't know."

"Child, have you asked him? Didn't all of you grow up together? You were at his brother's funeral."

Adelyn, face turned burning red, felt the reproach. In her mind she went back there again, eighteen years old, little flapper even in mourning, and then making love with Garnett that very day, in the barn. Tears formed and spilled onto her cheeks.

"I loved Innis and felt so lost that day. When you are that young, you don't even ask how it happened. I just knew he was, and I needed comfort. Garnett felt that way too." She said this because she sensed Momma looked into her crystal ball or tea leaves or whatever and saw what they did in the barn.

"Um hmm." Momma's eyes squinted as if Adelyn sat upon the sun and it hurt to look to directly at her. "Tell me what you remember about it."

Adelyn wiped her eyes with her handkerchief and sighed. "Innis went away; he always went away. After our first time together, he became a drug for me. And it worked the same way for him. I think the world knew we were in love. Garnett knew for sure. And his mama." She stopped to add, "You know, she died not much later, and on that very same day? A Friday. He used to tell me that they had this pact, when he was just a little boy. He would ask her what would she do if he died, and she would always answer, 'then I will too'."

"There are many things that people say; some you can believe; some are not at all true. But this one was." Momma grew contemplative. "I am going to send you back to that time to poke around in that world again for the answers you want from me. Let me tell you this one thing, he didn't die the way you or any of the others say. Only his brother, and his father knew what happened." Momma said again, "Now let's send you back."

Adelyn drew back defensively, and Momma hurriedly said, "Now, child. Don't worry yourself. It will be a little sad and much more interesting than you could think." She stopped and then repeated, "Nothing to worry about." Momma stood up and went around to behind Adelyn's chair. She pressed her cool fingers lightly against Adelyn's temples and spoke softly, in a soothing cadence that sounded like a lullaby. Adelyn sat back and took slow and deep breaths without prompting. Her eyelids began to get heavy and flutter and her body felt light and floating.

A mist covered everything, and suddenly it parted; she could see the day of the funeral. She could see herself and Garnett at the reception back at the Crawford home. Adelyn floated above herself as she and her parents walked up the wide path where all the trees bent and swayed, looking like they grieved as well. The crowds of people, friends of Innis's father and mother, milled about inside, snacking on finger sandwiches. Young Adelyn walked into the house and spoke to Mister Crawford and Garnett, then passed them through the dining room to the kitchen and outside. A few men sat on the steps taking their flasks out of their back pockets and stopped when she arrived. She saw herself nod at some she knew, fathers and uncles to her friends, and younger men with knowing eyes. A voice tugged her away from the scene.

"Tell me what you see. Tell me." Momma's quiet voice, meant to keep her there as the observer, asked her to report.

"I see men I knew, men who knew Innis. Some of them are younger; they seem to know about Innis and me, what we are to one another." Her eyes darted back and forth, drinking deeply of everything she witnessed.

"How can you tell, Adelyn? Are they talking to you?"

Adelyn focused on their faces and watched her young self as she pulled back from them, subtly. They did not see it, but the grown-up Adelyn, the observer, saw it. "No, their eyes betray them. They all knew we were lovers. And I remember knowing that. I...I mean the girl I was should be ashamed, but she is not. I loved him. None of them, no one else mattered."

She watched her young image turn and walk away from them. Terrance Murray, one of the boys she knew in school, speaks to a friend in a low voice.

"They say he died in a car accident. I saw his sedan, and it looked all crushed in front."

Adelyn hovered over the two boys to hear what they say while her image continued away and out of earshot on a path back to the house. The second boy turned, and in a low voice spoke to Terrance, "Yeah, buckshot picked out of his chest may have something to do with his crashing that vehicle."

Adelyn jumped into wakefulness and covered her tear-filled face with her hands, sobbing and saying, "No, no. It could never be. How could it be?"

Momma sat in front of her, pouring some more tea into Adelyn's glass. "Here child; now dry your face, and tell me all, because you sure heard something not meant for your ears. Tell me."

After a few sips of tea and with her mind still whirling over the scene that had just been before her, Adelyn recited all of it for Momma. She ended with, "They say he'd been shot. That was why he crashed."

"And this is the first you know of Innis's death?"

"I can't remember anything. It must have been all covered up, even from his mother, though Garnett knew." She raced down memories all over her mind and images followed many of them. The barn when she and Garnett lay there together, quietly. They only spoke of their mutual loss, and Garnett never volunteered more. "I have to talk to Garnett; I have to ask him."

"Think about this before you confront your husband. If he didn't tell you, he had his reasons."

"I was only eighteen then, maybe too young to tell?" Adelyn twisted the handkerchief that laid in her lap till it was as taut as her nerves. "That may have been true then." *How can I ask him without him somehow knowing that Innis still exists?*

Momma walked over to an alcove where a counter stood, filled with bottles of herbs. She began to mix something that looked like a twig, grinding it in a mortar with a pestle. She pinched a flower from a potted plant and boiled it in some water, siphoning off just enough to add to the ground-up herb. After much mixing and refining she pushed it through some cheesecloth until it came out a light lavender liquid, and she poured that into a small bottle with an eye dropper top.

"You take two drops under your tongue, not more and not less, before you fall asleep tonight."

Adelyn took the bottle and held it up to the light to see it was full all the way up. "What's this supposed to do to me?"

"Not *to* you. *For* you, *chère*."

Momma's face wore an emotionless mask, but her voice conveyed something sad, which Adelyn picked up. She walked to the older woman, who, though she had kept her age well, today looked world-weary.

"Were you always this wise for others? Everyone comes to you with their problems; who do you go to, I wonder?" She dropped the bottle into her pocket and sat again to finish her sweet tea; the ice cubes had melted down and condensation made the glass as wet outside as in. "Tell me your story."

Momma adjusted a turban she had wrapped around her head, all the same deep blues and reds of her clothing. She allowed a sigh to escape and sat at the little table with Adelyn.

"You don't have time for my story, but I will tell you a

piece, just like the pieces we are putting together of your past life and now of this life." She reached across to a bookcase and handed Adelyn a very old photograph, a tintype most like, of a young woman who looked like Momma Sorrow.

"This must be your mother." Adelyn looked closely at the pretty face in the photograph.

"That was taken on her wedding day to my father. All properly done, in the Church." She made the sign of the cross when she said this, and Adelyn followed her. "My family in France you know about from Delia. They all objected to my parents' marriage, most of all my grandmother, who felt that because of her color, my mother did not measure up to her high standards. My grandfather knew otherwise, and he lived long enough for me to hear him say so. Now I take a little of that potion I gave you and meet him when I fall into sleep."

"In your dreams." Adelyn had taken the bottle out and could smell lavender and vanilla emanating from the bottle. Some sweet elixir to help the medicine to work.

"You will not be dreaming. You will gain entry into that sideways world." Momma made the distinction precisely.

"Do you visit your mother there?" Adelyn felt afraid and exhilarated at the same time. Fearful of Innis's hold on her in that place, maybe stronger there than in this world of daylight.

"Sometimes. Though I cannot always see or hear what I want there, any more than in this world, and neither will you. You will learn things. Come back when you have been there, and we will talk about all these strange things."

The two women stood and embraced. Momma whispered as though she feared being overhead by some spirit lurking in the wings. "Don't ask Garnett about Innis. For now. I give you one warning, though: be careful when you enter there. Avoid agreeing to do anything that anyone asks of you there." She thought some more, then said, "…because they will ask you. They all want to connect with this real world. They miss it."

Adelyn retraced her steps back up the path to where she left the truck. The truck started with a twist of the key. She smiled to herself and realized that for the first time in days she felt content with small pleasures.

"Yes, but they don't last long, now, do they, Sugar?" The sound of his voice melted her several resolves to have it out with him.

"Let me just be." She said it aloud, and the cab was as empty again as it had been moments before. A remorse that she chased him away wanted to settle on her but she brushed it off, hurrying now to get back before Garnett and the boys returned. She forced her mind to focus on them because she somehow knew they could keep Innis from stirring her soul.

## Chapter Twelve
### *THE JOURNEY TO SIDEWAYS*

She felt the truck as a friend, helping her, as it brought her home safely. *Is this what I'll find in that other world? Trucks that help me get home on time?*

"Too soon for you to visit, Sugar." He sat beside her. "And you listen to me, not to that woman. She's trouble."

Adelyn's voice came slowly with an edge to it. "As you pointed out, no one ever gave me any trouble, Innis Crawford, except you." She forced herself not to see his face, so sunny, so beautiful, but he tempted her too greatly. She turned to look at him and almost ended up in a ravine of mud and sticks. "That would have done me in."

"Come, Sugar, it's just a little bitty creek." He caressed her bare arm with his finger as she struggled to keep the truck on the rough road.

"Not now, Innis, please." She half spoke, half thought, and it must have been convincing enough because he left her again, as quickly as he had appeared. *Innis has lost the urgency of life and the dangers.* She drove through the red dust and stopped the truck where she had found it. Only a few minutes past noon, the quiet house beckoned her. *All that séance in one short hour of time.* She wondered whether time in the other world moved faster, then briefly remembered the time with the young girl, that it felt more like walking through syrup.

Ramses whinnied; he must have caught her scent. "I'll come see you after dinner." Her senses again enhanced and stronger, she whispered to Ramses, and the words rode on the wind to her beautiful black horse, whose snorts of satisfaction and stomping of the dirt in his stall sounded as close as if she stood right by him.

*After I visited Momma last time, I could see and hear far away.* She knew the powers remained and just grew stronger.

Turning the corner to the back porch, she came upon Garnett and the boys.

"We've been waiting on you, Mama." Tyler squealed in joy that combined with a petulant demand of her total time, her total life force, as small boys will do, while Trey scrutinized her, more than his father did.

She saw all this and thought, *So that's the way it's going to be.* Adelyn cupped Trey's pointed little chin in her warm hand, and he smiled up at her, his fears all chased away, his mother safe and near.

"We asked Aunt May to hold dinner till you got back." Garnett's eyes traced over her body in a wanton way. "And now we got her, don't we, boys?" He playfully swung Adelyn up into his arms, and as quickly plunked her down onto her feet.

"I guess the sun all day out near the water and a hungry stomach haven't taken your energy, Garnett Crawford." She held her hand to his face for just a moment longer than customary, the gesture not lost on Garnett. With the boys in front of them, they all walked up the steps at the back of the house and headed toward the dining room. Adelyn patted the pocket of her dress, feeling the solidity of Momma Sorrow's elixir bottle. The afternoon beckoned for all of them, dinner, the boys reading comics and napping, Garnett and Adelyn visiting cousins down near Delia's, back where she had just come from.

Later, in the evening, the strong smell of citronella oil filled the air, but it kept the bugs away. Adelyn rubbed the oil into the boys, especially their necks.

"Must be your sweet blood that attracts the mosquitos."

"I don't like the smell of it." Trey twitched away from her.

"Be still, or you'll have those great big welts, and you don't like those either."

Garnett had waved her away when she offered to smooth the lotion on him. "Keep that stuff for yourself, woman. Your daddy's cigars are tonic enough for me." They had all congregated on the big veranda. Mama and Aunt Grace spiritedly discussed Adelyn's sister Cicely, due back from her European tour.

"Lands, she'll be back just in time to get fitted up for her last year at Georgia." Adelyn's mother could think of nothing but having Cicely properly attired for her coming out and her last year at the university. Adelyn knew Cicely's thoughts were only for a certain Yankee boyfriend and her desire for a Yankee law degree. She interrupted her thoughts to speak to her father. "Daddy, your cigars come in handy on nights like these." She affectionately hugged her father as he rocked back and forth. "Who would think those ugly Cuban tobacco leaves would be good for anything?" she teased him.

"Now, sister, I had these flown in for such a time as this." Captain Jackson looked over to Adelyn's husband. "You tell your daddy I got some for him, though he takes to them only once in a while."

The quiet deepened the darkness of the night. Adelyn

heard her father remark to her mother about the moonless night, and he teased Trey about hobgoblins in the dark. She looked where the light from citronella torches spread out like a fan and abruptly dropped off where it could no longer venture from its source.

Adelyn's sharpened vision noticed her father adjust his arthritic hip in his chair. He moved restlessly, but she saw what he only guessed at. A ring of light in the dark appears, just like the one the torches had thrown, and in it, old people and young standing amid the trees, all of them in white, summer white, as if going to a lawn party in the middle of August, when the sun blazes in the midday sky.

But these pale spirits all surround Innis and the girl whose name Adelyn could not yet remember. Innis's eyes blaze a hole in Adelyn's heart. He moves slowly but irrefutably as he places a protective arm around the girl's shoulders. A breeze dishevels Lucianne's blonde and streaked hair, no smile on her motionless lips. Adelyn feels an anger rise into her throat. *You do this? Flaunt that poor child in front of me? Do you think you fool me with your manipulations?*

She feels rather than sees a change in his expression as her outburst startles his spirit. Innis moves his arm suggestively down the girl's back. *This world, Adelyn, this world I created, the work of my mind. I do as I please.*

For all his posturing, Adelyn feels a deep resentment coming from him. Something brazen in her taunts him. *Innis, you used to be older and wiser. I think I've caught up with you. Your foolish and immature games tire me. Shame.* She had not reckoned on his powers, that he would not tolerate her chiding. Suddenly, everything happened in a moment. She saw the wrath in his eyes that burns right through her. She catches her breath and quickly camouflages the choking feeling with a light cough. Furtively, she looks first toward her mother who continues in her knitting in the after-supper laziness, then to her father, still puffing on his cigar, oblivious to Innis. And the spirits, unlike Innis, move woodenly like props on a stage, shades of their former beings, no longer possessing the energy and force that Innis somehow summons.

The soft and low voice of Garnett draws Adelyn's attention, talking to Tyler about the types of fish they saw today. "They made a good dinner for us, didn't they?"

Four-year-old Tyler sat at his father's knee and listened intently until he turned and saw the expression on Adelyn's face. He looked where she stared and saw what she saw. "What are those people about, Mama?"

Garnett gazes now on Tyler and Adelyn and then on the trees, where Adelyn senses an immediate change, and a breeze blows the apparitions all away, all except for Innis who pivots on his heel and walks into the deeper darkness.

"That was curious. For just a moment, it looked like…" Garnett shook his head and whispered to himself, "No, no."

Tyler scrambled up to his mother's lap and Garnett, sitting close enough, touched her arm. She feels them, their life energy tugging her to them. All of the electricity that accompanied Innis, his handsomeness, his bold desire of her, all of it ebbs away, and in its place she understands the conflict between Innis, Garnett, and herself for the first time. *Here, life happens here, not where Innis waits. He wants this, and I may be the only one who can give it to him.*

While the others, Aunt Grace, her mother and father, all looked like a picture of tedium that comes from an uneventful evening at home, the night had been explosive for Adelyn, as strong as those little lavender-and-vanilla-laced drops she still kept close to her in the pocket of her dress. The earth around them kept some warmth from the hot sun of the day, infusing the humid evening air. Yet a cooler breeze asserted itself, a harbinger of autumn, something unusual for the deep south of Savannah. *And so, we re-live Innis's life cycle.*

Garnett watched her remove the white dress she'd worn to

Momma Sorrow's séance. Adelyn liked to tease him as a voyeur for his side-long glances whenever she stepped out of a bath or stripped to her shimmy.

"What was all that commotion with Tyler?" He played with the belt she had just removed.

"The wind picked up and startled him, that's all." She found a hanger inside the old chifforobe and neatly adjusted the shoulders of the dress to prevent indentation in the fabric when she wore it again. *Will I wear it or hide it away because of the girl?*

"Adelyn, why must you do that?"

She stared at him for a moment, puzzled by his question, then as quickly knew his full meaning. He'd caught her thinking secrets.

"Whatever do you mean, Garnett Crawford?" She acted coy. And before he could remonstrate, she curled up on his lap where he sat in the comfortable stuffed chair. She fussed with his hair, and he pushed her hand away and held her wrist.

"Tell me what you saw. You and Tyler. And don't tell me nothing 'cause I saw you. Seemed almost like you had a conversation with someone. Your brow shot up at one point." He shifted her to see her eyes. "Tyler closed the deal for me. He saw too. What was it, Adelyn? Was someone you know out near the trees?"

Her mind flew a million miles ahead trying to decide what she could say to assuage him. Some words to satisfy him in this real world he lived in. *There it was*. She realized she lived more in that sideways world, she just said it.

"I thought I saw a ghost." The words leapt out of her before she could bite down hard on them, keep them from opening the door to her soul.

"Enough." He stood up, holding her arm so she wouldn't fall. "I want something, anything, that makes sense."

"Okay." Her words came in a measured tone. How much to say? "But first I want to ask you something, and you need to promise me you won't get angry or impatient."

Silence, then a small nod of assenting.

Adelyn continued, quickly, "'Cause there's a reason for my asking. What do you know about Innis's death?"

She watched his face very closely as she asked, not sure if he'd faint or have a tantrum. She prayed for the one and against the other. His face grew cold, his brow lowered with nowhere a wrinkle like the marble statues at the university, and his expression told her absolutely nothing at all.

"Innis, is it? Mourning for him, are you? All this time?" He grabbed her wrists with such strength that he pinched her skin with his fingers. She ignored the pain.

"Acting like he was still courting me? You promised you would answer me, because what I saw has bearing on all of it. I don't remember how he died. Just that all of a sudden, he was gone." Tears from somewhere deep inside came up and into her eyes. She caught a sob, knowing that if she had given in to it, it would have reduced her to a puddle of emotion. Saying it now, his name to his brother Garnett, sealed their unholy trinity once and for all. She had danced this dance of them all these years, Innis, then her, then Garnett.

He surprised her, buried his face into her hair, kissed her face and neck, moaned her name in both desire and a kind of agony. "He's never left you, has he?" He stopped and wiped his wet eyes with his sleeve.

She saw the half-grown boy, inside the man. His voice came quiet but resolute, a man's voice, not the boy's.

"He'd been killed. Shot. Mike Stevens, the coroner, he kept it quiet, though a few had some knowledge." He unbuttoned his shirt and lit a cigarette. "You know how a lot of people thought about him, they always loved him first though. Yes, he'd made some enemies clerking, there were bound to be enemies." He repeated himself. "You know, someone didn't like the way a lawsuit went."

"Was that it? They found the person who did it?" She guessed at some of the answers but needed to hear what her husband knew. He must have understood, because he stopped her questions.

"Now tell me what you saw." He stood and hovered over her in the chair, close by so she could not wander away in her mind or her body.

Adelyn breathed deeply, her mind full of thoughts sent out to Innis. *I can't tell him all of it, but he needs to have something.* A message flew into her thoughts from Innis. *Tell him little.*

"I saw something move in the trees and remembered him from a long time ago. I remember Innis telling me he'd had angry words." Her lies intertwined with pieces of the truth. "And it occurred to me that my mind worked, my subconscious, they call it that in those psychology books I've been reading, that I've been holding on to some images from back then, and they're coming forward now."

Adelyn could not convince Garnett. He set about sliding the thick suspenders off his tired shoulders, and removing his shirt. His linen slacks had wrinkled, and she thought of having Aunt May fix them for him in the morning. She looked up to see he'd read her mind.

"Stop it, Adelyn, just stop." He came back to her, and leaned down with his arms extended on each side of the chair, barricading her there. "What has any of this to do with what Tyler saw?"

"Tyler thought he saw ghosts. He saw a bunch of them. He said they were all in white. And I'm not sure he was wrong." *A little truth.* She knew Garnett had heard Tyler speak to her, describing some of the old people, but not Innis nor Lucianne.

Garnett moved about the room turning off all but a little lamp in a far corner of the big bedroom. "Most likely some fireflies against the trees, and the wind caused them to move."

Adelyn sighed, grateful to have such a rational husband, far less poetic than his big brother Innis. He'd found his own answer. For the moment.

Garnett came close to her, "Well, Sugar, I'm not a ghost. I'm real. And I'm here."

Their passion soared beyond anything she could remember, more so than her first time with Innis, her husband alternately plunging deeply into her, then stroking her slowly and softly with more languid movements, until she nearly screamed. She reasoned that it had to do with his very corporeal self, his burnished hair and skin, the real earth smell of him, his muscles and vibrancy, his life force.

## Chapter Thirteen
### *SIDEWAYS II*

*Sometimes. Though I cannot always see or hear what I want there, any more than in this world, and neither will you. You will learn things. Come back when you have been there, and we will talk about all these strange things.*

Momma Sorrow's words echoed in her mind as she lay next to Garnett. Adelyn waited until she heard his breathing deep and slow, then shallow, the way real sleep sounds. She found her small bottle of lavender and vanilla tincture, pulled the stopper, and placed two drops under her tongue. Quickly she opened the bedside table drawer, wrapped the bottle in a scarf, and shoved it to the back in the drawer. *I'll find a better place to hide this tomorrow.*

No clouds. No wind. The sky is clear, just blue. As she passed into this other world, she holds on to the image of Lucianne and Innis outside near the trees. At first, she seethes with anger at herself for showing him her jealousy of Lucianne, jealousy of the way Innis fondled and caressed the girl. Adelyn knows she will not remember the girl's name later.

*How could you?* With this thought escaping her, she looks around, no longer lying in her bed next to Garnett but standing in the familiar large foyer of Delia's home where she first saw Innis all those years ago. She moves past the mirror and sees her reflection, the sixteen-year-old Adelyn, long hair down her back, in her riding gear. She doesn't walk, but floats effortlessly from one place to another. She notices the silence until her mind picks up his voice.

Innis stands next to her, holding her hand. *Didn't you know I've been waiting for this, that you would come into this world, be with me? I wanted us to meet here again, as we did that first time.*

She feels disconnected from him, their souls not sufficiently fused together. Still burning with jealousy, she asks him, *Tell me about you and Lucianne. Tell me now. I won't stay here otherwise.*

A vision opens up like a picture show, all black and white, with Innis and Lucianne talking at a church hall down in the girl's county. Adelyn watches them and the connection between them, and sees the girl drawn to the man. Innis the honey, Lucianne the bee. Lucianne wears the white dress that Adelyn first saw when she met the girl in the train station. Adelyn swings back and forth in her reveries, from 1931 to that November day in 1918.

Innis and Lucianne stand as close to one another as propriety will allow with churchgoers leaving the service and passing by them. Adelyn bends close to the images to hear them, seeing the girl's rigid body expressing her anger. The image fades, and Adelyn sees the foyer around her again, Innis there by her. Before her questions can form, he whispers.

*She is nothing to me. It's you.* His sultry voice, his physical presence, lulls her as he bends to her face, his warm breath like a caress on her cheek. She feels his fingers slide up the sleeve of her thin silk shirt. *Innis, Innis.* He kisses her.

*I feel your lips.* The floodgates of her young girl's honest love and desire for him open as she loses any inclination to interrogate him. He embraces her innocently, tentatively, a man checking his passion to match hers, meant not to startle. The other side of Adelyn knows this, the mind's eye that watches, while he lures the woman back to the first blush of youthful love.

The sun painted large streaks over the bed, and Adelyn stretched her body. She still felt his hands on the parts of her he touched, like fire branding without the scars.

"Rise and shine, Sugar." Garnett moved about the room in a hurry—his motions too much for Adelyn, who lingered halfway in that other place.

"Where are you rushing off to?" She sat up slowly and slid to the edge of the bed. Garnett sat next to her, prompting her to wrap her summer robe hastily over her naked body.

"Hiding from me?" He tugged on the robe, exposing her. "That's guilty behavior is all I can say." He dropped his hand from the robe and moved to stand, but she held him back.

"I meant nothing by it." She tried for a conciliatory voice, not wanting to lose what seemed like a new beginning. "Where did you say you were going?"

"Down to take care of some things for my daddy. I thought I'd take the boys; they haven't seen him in a space of time." Wary, he measured her sincerity.

She gathered her hair up and away from her face and let it fall down her back. "If you're not in too big a hurry, we can all have breakfast before you go."

The momentary storm had passed them by once again. He relented, gathered her to him, and pulled on her long hair. "No fancy bobs for you like they wear in Paris, and I thought you were the modern girl."

"Everyone is back to wearing their hair long again." She felt frivolous pointing this out to him as fashion never meant much to Garnett.

He passed his big, warm hands over her shoulders and torso, and stopped. "I'll never get out of this room if I don't move now. Can you be downstairs in thirty minutes?"

Alone, she stepped into a hot bath to soak the night and her journey out of her weary body. A warm washcloth over her face became a veil between the harsh morning light and her need for a mistier, cloudier day. *I really want to be all the way here for you.* She thought this in a private message to her husband, resolving that she will tell him, first chance she gets.

"Oatmeal again? I wanted eggs." Trey wrinkled up his nose at the steaming bowl in front of him.

"Here's something to make it all go down easier." Adelyn sprinkled some brown sugar and raisins on top. "You want some too, little boy?" She glanced at Tyler whom she knew would try to emulate his brother's disdain for the gooey warm cereal. Adelyn privately hated it and never, ever ate any.

"I want what you're doing to Trey's oatmeal, Mama." His eyes shone brightly with the promise of an adventurous day, exuberant, like all small boys in summer.

Adelyn helped him with his napkin, cutting an apple in quarters for him. Garnett in a playful way stayed her hand, asking her to make his meal as nice as theirs. She kissed his forehead. "Who says I don't have three boys to tend?" Their happiness, complete and untrammeled, foreshadowed no storms that she could see.

"Got to get you properly groomed, Ramses." Adelyn stroked her horse's mane. She chose to ride to Momma Sorrow's, knowing Innis would not be near, surmising his hesitancy around the animals, especially her horse. *No matter whatever else you might do, Innis, you'd not spook my horse and kill me.* Joey, the stable boy, tightened the strap under the big horse's underbelly. "Good, my spirits need the rest, and my horse needs riding." Riding slowly at first, she picked up speed over the pastures, arriving sooner than if she had taken her car or the truck.

Momma stood expectantly on the porch, and Adelyn smiled to think their hearts beat like two synchronized clocks. Momma's face again looked tired; her eyes, though, sparkled brightly, alive and deep, missing nothing. They embraced and walked in together. Momma had hot coffee waiting.

"*Chère*, I know you have much to tell." The older woman listened intently as Adelyn told her about her visit to that unusual world, how Innis created an image of Delia's foyer the day that Innis and Adelyn met for the first time. Momma's face showed concern when Adelyn told her of the picture-show image, and Innis and Lucianne's encounter.

"All of these images originated from the same time in the past. He first met you at the same time as he led that child astray." Momma adjusted the bright orange, blue, and pink turban she had wound around her head.

"I never thought of that, but now that you say it, yes. I didn't hear what they said, only saw them. And it seemed, when I think of it, that as soon as I asked about them, the image came, as though he had no real control."

"That may be, child. Innis had control of what you saw, and maybe what you learned from it. Because I don't hear you saying anything we didn't already know." Momma offered Adelyn some just-baked bread and butter, but Adelyn refused.

"It's time for you to visit it again, now, when Mr. Innis cannot exercise all his power." Her voice dropped into the modulation that swayed Adelyn into a light trance. Adelyn relaxed and breathed deeply. With each breath she found it took her farther away and closer to the other world. Momma murmured, "Tell me."

Adelyn's eyes open but at first, they see little, staring into the other world. "It's darker now than it was before. No clouds in the sky this time either, but the air feels heavy.

Two people approach me." Her head swivels in Momma Sorrow's direction, but again, the eyes look inward. "A woman, your mother. I see her and know her. Monique. She hears me call her name."

"What does she sound like?" Momma's voice came from deep in her throat, disembodied as though she wants to join Adelyn.

Adelyn's eyes fill with tears. "Monique wants you to hear this."

Adelyn blinks to a half trance and a voice not her own speaks from her, laced with French and Cajun sounds. "Your father and I walk the promenade as we once did in Paris. Our happiness is great and wholesome. We are free to love the way we were meant to because we have chosen a life together."

Adelyn's head turns one way and then the other, she nods, and her eyes blink open, but she still walks there, in the other world. "Tommy, I knew it was you. We all missed you. I can't Tommy, I am not supposed to, but I will look for you the next time I come here. I will be back, promise." She nods as if to one and then the other spirit and blinks back to the day, to Momma's dining room.

"Momma, I believe I will have that fresh bread and some coffee, too." All her senses revived, enhanced and doubly penetrating. The aroma of the bread and coffee almost hypnotize her as she bolts them down, hungry from time spent where energy seems to be drained. "It was as though I were working hard or had not eaten for a long time," she explains to Momma.

"I woke up today not remembering all the rest. But now I can tell you I saw a world alike but not. Fully aware souls, waiting for visitors from our side. They are very dependent on what we feel and do here, the ones that love us. I don't know how I know this. Tommy was my cousin who died in France near the end of the Great War. Such a sweet young man, only twenty when he died."

"What did he want, *chère*? He wanted you to do

something for him."

"He asked me to take a message to his mother and to take his ribbons from the War." Adelyn paused. "But he looked so disappointed when I said I could not take the ribbons."

"It is good that you did not." Momma's silver bracelets jangled as she leaned on the table closer to Adelyn. "Some of the people you meet there are unfinished. They think they want to complete this life, and then they can go on. They are stuck, *chère*, they don't move on because they want to hold on to what they had." She took hold of Adelyn's hand. "The ribbons would be his bridge here. Best he stay where he is."

"Tommy wants to come back?" Adelyn had a momentary vision. "If he came back he would not be whole, he would be wounded...." Her voice trailed off as she thought whether Innis would carry his wounds.

"You're thinking about your lover. He would be whole. He is not like the boy, your cousin. Innis has special black magic powers, *chère*." Momma fell into her thoughts. "He has already built his bridge here or he could never have visited you all these times."

"Innis wasn't there, Momma. My trip there was meant for me to ask him and see him with the girl, and neither of them were there." Adelyn envisions the girl's face. "I remember now. Her name is Lucianne."

"He's a clever one, that Innis." Momma buttered more of the delicious bread. "He gave you presents, your cousin Tommy, and my mother. He knew I helped you get there, would be listening." Momma shook her head, her bright turban flashing all its colors. "Yes, he's a clever one. But he doesn't know all that you've learned. Did you ask your husband how he died?"

Adelyn stopped pulling the warm bread apart. "Innis was shot by someone. But who that was or why, Garnett doesn't know. But I think I do."

## *Chapter Fourteen*
### *YOUNG GARNETT—THE BEGINNING*

Garnett felt inextricably entangled with Adelyn and Innis. Garnett saw Adelyn the first time at Delia's house on the same day his brother, Innis, 'discovered' her, pursued her, and finally bedded her.

The 1918 November wind blew into the room, leaving Garnett a vision in its midst instead of the red and gold leaves. Delia's brother Charles, the visiting college boys, and Innis, all joking as young men will, about sports first, then about the subject of real and only interest to any of them, a willing female. They displayed none of the chivalry that young women want to dream of and believe in. No, they expressed pure unadulterated male passion, which keeps the world impregnated with the next generation of fresh young faces. Of course, they only sought pleasure. If polled, none of them would have chosen to think in terms of fathering or parenting the next generation, all children still themselves.

When Adelyn rushed into the front room, every young

man automatically stood to attention. Firstly, to see a young woman whose wildly delicious hair proved her energy and health, tresses red and golden brown, much like the leaves the South brings to November. Secondly, her shiny and beautiful dark eyes seized every one of them in mid-sentence. They fell over their own words and one another's. Their guffawing and joking ceased. They became very gentle, solicitous even, and Garnett saw and would forever remember Innis's one step toward her. In that one step he saw it all as though he possessed Momma Sorrow's crystal ball. In that one step he never saw Innis the same again. Always close to one another, that one step separated them. It didn't stop them from talking to one another in the most genuine or caring manner. Two boys always freely sharing their minds about anything or anyone had simply changed about one person: Adelyn.

"Charles, who is she?" Garnett ran his hand nervously through his wavy hair as he whispered to his friend.

"Come now. You don't remember Mrs. Cooperthwaite's tea dances when we were all sophomores in high school? That's Adelyn Jackson, Captain Jackson's older daughter. She was just fourteen back at those dances. But I swear I could tell she'd be the death of all of us some day." Charles looked around and then bent closer to his friend and added, "And I think she already is." He gestured to Garnett to see Innis approach her.

Garnett's eyes rested on her figure; how could they not? She wore jodhpurs and they accentuated her frame admirably. Girls just didn't do that, he told himself. Not good girls, not decent girls. Yet he knew she possessed nothing bad nor indecent about her.

He moved next to his brother in a second, seemingly transported, never having experienced his own walking.

"She's a bit young for you, brother," he said impetuously, all he could find to say.

"Maybe too young for you, brother." Innis spoke so only Garnett could hear the retort, and closed in on his quarry. "It's a pleasure." He cocked his head to one side with a sly smile, "Are you lost, Miss Jackson?"

Adelyn looked closely at Innis then smiled. "Lost? Charles, are your friends from someplace outside of Tulip Junction or Savannah? I think I know you all. No, not lost. I was expecting to see Delia but I guess she'll be upstairs?" She turned with her question to Charles, who nodded like a puppet on a string and pointed to the graceful flight of stairs where Delia waited. "Well then, I'll leave you boys to it."

Garnett watched as his brother followed Adelyn till both had moved out of earshot of the rest. A fire burned in Garnett that surprised even him for its ferocity. *What the hell's the matter with me?* He ached to hear their interchange; he hated to see Innis so close to her, could tell his brother breathed in her perfume, and the clean scent of soap and water from her bath, he somehow knowing she'd bathed before jumping on a horse to ride over here.

He turned toward the stairs and glimpsed Adelyn taking leave of Innis. With a smile she took possession again of her hand, which Innis had continued to hold. Garnett knew Innis's gesture to introduce himself to her would come with a handshake. One riding glove remained, on her left hand. Something resembling resignation engulfed Garnett. *So he touched you first.*

The afternoon grew darker and grayer and the nearest thing to winter asserted itself the way it finally does in the south. Garnett played at backgammon and cards on and off with the rest, all of them practicing at becoming serious men, trying out their unofficial leave-taking from adolescence with cigars and beer. They all felt very comfortable with their alcohol. Though later the county would be dry, as many Catholics as Methodists lived there, and the former more Irish than any other species; thus, Prohibition would be thwarted on all counts. Garnett drank more, being an athlete. He smiled at Jeremy's remarks and braggadocio, nodded in the right places as though listening, and all the time, his ear waiting for Adelyn's footsteps down from Delia's room. His unspoken prayer answered, she passed through the dining room, avoiding all of them, certainly, but then she did a curious thing; she turned in their direction.

Garnett saw Innis move restlessly from their games in the billiard room to the great room the Howard family used for their renowned holiday celebrations, and where the living room of sofas and deep love seats rested in place, for now.

"Garnett is the man among us," chided Jeremy, who knew Garnett too well, suspecting his thoughts dwelled on Adelyn. "You thinking on that young filly that ran in here and changed our lives forever? Sweet Jesus, if I knew her in school before the university, then I am damned for all time. She is…"

"Jeremy, shut your mouth before you say too much." Garnett smacked his cue down hard on the rim of the billiard table. The room grew awkwardly quiet as Jeremy's face went red.

"Come on boys; let's get to the real games; let's see your money down." Charles interrupted what might have been. Jeremy looked over at Garnett who had dropped his gaze to nothing in front of him. They both smiled and shook hands with murmurs of "sorry, sorry."

The tail end of the Thanksgiving holiday found Garnett with the same boys at the same house. A holiday filled with too much food and too little exercise aggravated his restlessness, and desire burned in him to see Adelyn again. He could not deceive himself that Adelyn and all her fire drove his despair. His spirits rose when Delia, now in full health, fussed in the living room with hot coffee and sandwiches.

"You stay away from those." She turned from the ceiling-to-floor window where the sound of tires crunched on the stone drive. "Lord knows, you have enough food in the other room," she joked, "with those gangster friends of yours…and Charles."

Garnett stepped to the window to see the car, recognizing it for Captain Jackson's prized automobile, and prized enough that he would not leave it to his daughter's use, though he'd let her drive and now took the driver's seat. Garnett opened the door as Adelyn struggled with a pile of books and papers.

"Since when did you learn to drive that monster?" Pleased with himself for sounding so casual with a heart rate he'd only ever before experienced from a five-mile run, he reveled in their banter and admired her spirit as she met him point for point on the handling of her books, which he had commandeered, to the driving of a car. But it all ended too soon. Innis appeared and escorted Adelyn in to Delia, and skillfully maintained a connection with the two girls as they studied together. He heard Delia leave for the kitchen, watched Innis take Delia's place in the living room, and heard quiet chatter.

The day wore on tediously for Garnett who ached to join Innis. As evening encroached, Garnett heard sounds from the great room, Innis's voice. Garnett ran in before the others to see what they wouldn't. Tears rimmed Innis's eyes as he stood over a listless Adelyn. "Come on; wake up; hear me?" Innis repeated. He turned to Garnett, "She's burning up. One moment speaking normally and then…" Delia returned, standing on the other side of Adelyn with a wet cloth she applied to her friend's forehead.

"Innis. How did this happen?" Seeing his brother so out of control, clinging to the hand of a young girl he hardly knew, Garnett sensed his brother had tried to engage Adelyn with a goal toward some final intimacy.

"She needs to be moved upstairs." Delia spoke to Garnett whose young muscles effortlessly swept up the girl. Garnett followed Delia up the front stairs to her bedroom. Innis tagged close behind him, helpless, useless as he tried to collect himself.

"Charles, tell Mama, and have her call Mrs. Jackson." Delia called out to her brother.

"It's too warm here." Delirious, Adelyn rambled on about her horse, Pharaoh, and then Innis's name, and though barely above a whisper—still unmistakable. Garnett could feel her body burning through the heavy clothing she wore, could feel her slenderness, and his own heart beating.

"Hush," he whispered, so that she might not be misunderstood by the others if they should hear her say Innis's name. "Hush, sweet girl." And in that, he had declared his heart and his soul to her forever. *And she will never know.*

The flurry of Adelyn's family, the Howards, the servants, and the doctor overcame Garnett. Repeatedly he shot glances at Innis who drooped in the hall outside of Delia's room, waiting to hear more. Garnett watched his brother's demeanor change from a limp corn stalk to a sapling tree whenever the door opened as he bent his tall frame to hear more.

"Innis, let's go. This isn't right. We should leave."

"Speak for yourself, son, I'm staying where I am, till I know."

"Till you know what?" Garnett put a comforting hand on his brother's sagging shoulder.

"That she'll be okay. She must live." Innis shrugged off Garnett's gesture.

Garnett left Innis and joined the other boys. The revelry of minutes ago had turned to a somber church service, the type that had everyone wearing dark colors. The thought unnerved him.

"Adelyn took sick, a fever. Doc Fanning says she should be okay." His words sounded weak and unconvincing, most of all to himself. He no longer trusted his voice and so he stopped speaking. The boys disbanded, Jeremy offering to drive him home. He avoided speaking of

Innis for fear of exposing his brother's motives, or stimulating conjecture about them.

They rode the rough stones down the long drive in Jeremy's big sedan. "Shame if that girl dies." Jeremy spoke as he drove Garnett home.

"Bite your tongue, Jerry." Garnett silently cursed his decision to accept the ride. Jeremy could be tiresome with his inability to keep any thought to himself.

"Still. They won't know for some time, I'm guessing. My cousin, Will, was gone so quick. No time at all." Jeremy shook his head. "Such a terrible death, too."

"Shut your mouth or let me out." Garnett had his hand on the door handle, ready to pull.

Then, mercifully, Jeremy retreated into himself and allowed Garnett the chance to sort out what he witnessed in the turmoil of the day. *Her lungs were clear*. He had heard Mrs. Jackson repeat the doctor's words to her husband through tears and a choked voice. Garnett told himself that meant she would recover. The bad influenza, the one taking its toll on millions, stopping people from breathing, clogging their lungs, had so far eluded Adelyn.

"Will you be going back over for Innis? Suppose he'll stay? Seems like that girl's got a hold on him."

"Charles will probably bring him home. Thanks, Jeremy." Garnett forced a small smile. He looked up to see his mother standing at the door. Joined in their hearts, Sarah Crawford and her first-born, Innis. When one ached, the other felt the pain. Garnett knew she would have sensed this change in Innis. Even if it had happened across the sea, she would have felt it. Still, she looked worried. Garnett reassured her unasked question. "He's all right, Mother. It's Adelyn Jackson. She fell sick visiting Delia." His heart pounded with the uttering of her name. Adelyn Jackson, a girl who wears men's jodhpurs, who must ride a horse like a man, or at least a boy.

He knew he had to tell her about Adelyn because Sarah Crawford did not have the sight when it came to Garnett.

While she adored his strength, and championed his every victory on the playing field, she never entered inside his heart. Garnett didn't mind, it gave him a special private place to live, his father always invited. He turned toward the shadow just inside the door to see his father. "The doctors say she may not have caught the serious influenza." William Crawford returned his son's gaze. Garnett knew, before his father spoke, that he understood the importance of this girl.

"It seems like I'm always taking a back seat to Innis, Dad." They had helped clear the table after a hurried leftover pot roast. Garnett set the fireplace for the long evening. Before his father could speak, he continued. "He's smarter than me, maybe that's it."

Will Crawford folded his newspaper and set it aside. "Innis has a special intelligence, son, but I would never say he's smarter than you are. Fact is, you've always been your own man. Look at you, just eighteen, but I can talk to you as I would an older person. You have wisdom, Garnett, and I don't know a soul who has grasped the economics of our time better than you."

Garnett threw some more kindling under the big logs, and the fire took hold. "Yes, but the women seem to really like him."

"You haven't lacked for girlfriends down there at the university. Didn't I hear you just yesterday say a young woman invited you to her sorority dance?" His father paused. "Unless this Jackson girl is someone special."

Garnett covered his feelings without protesting Adelyn's pre-eminence. "Yes, Mary Lee Spenser invited me. She's one of the few at her sorority interested in more than socials."

"Now, that sounds judgmental, and surprises me, coming from you." Will Crawford's smile lines crinkled as he relented, knowing he touched a nerve.

Garnett finished with the fire, stood, and called out to

his dog. "Colonel!" He looked back at his father. "I'm going out for a walk; the dog could stretch his legs some."

"Stay close to the road, son. Don't want none of those big mountain cats chasing you down, though Colonel would most likely scare them off." Will Crawford clapped a hand on his son's shoulder, a welcomed sign of support. Garnett thought how good it felt to be understood by at least one person, and that one, his father.

The dog waited at his heel, eager for the run. Garnett lifted a heavy jacket off a hook in the kitchen where his mother sat at her little desk, reading. The dog leapt out the door, and Sarah Crawford called out to him, "Keep him away from my tubers."

Garnett followed the slope of the land in the quiet night, Colonel alternately running ahead then back to him, panting, sniffing Garnett's hand, then licking it, and running away again. Thoughts of Adelyn filled Garnett, as he tried to understand Innis. He suspected his mother caught this change in him, probably as it happened, tied to Innis in her prescient way. They would never talk of it. *No need.*

He heard sound in the field and voices. "You there." Garnett called as his dog heeled to his side with a low-sounding growl. More mumbling came. "Identify yourself. Now." His voice sounded more like a man than boy, even to himself.

"Ain't him. Told you." A young man came into the full moonlight, his hair looked to be fair, his clothes old and worn.

"You the other one? Innis Crawford's brother? My name is Kendall Bonet, and this here's my cousin, Louis Bonet." He said the names in the French way. "I'm looking for your brother."

The two appeared to be in their early twenties, perhaps the same age. From their height and weight, he recognized a close resemblance. He turned his direction back toward home, and they walked alongside. "What is it you want with Innis?"

Kendall Bonet stopped in the road where it neared the house. "Don't mean no harm to you, understand. Looking to talk with your brother about my sister, Lucianne. You know her?"

Garnett shook his head no. "You mean harm to my brother?" His muscles tensed while his mind assessed that he outweighed both of them, thin and poorly nourished field workers, who, though strong, had put up bales of hay in the last days and weeks and whose muscles would be all used up.

Kendall moved threateningly but his cousin restrained him. "He don't know nothing about this, cousin. We best let him be." Kendall shook off his cousin's hold, they both stayed in place as Garnett, and the dog continued to the house.

"You best tell him she's dying. If he's any kind of man…" Kendall left off, his voice trembling.

Garnett saw Adelyn in the same struggle against the end and softened, returning to the two young men. "I am sorry that your sister is not well. Innis is not here, he works in Savannah and over at the Tulip Junction Courthouse. He's with a friend right now. I'll tell him as soon as I can."

Kendall and his cousin tipped their caps to him less in the way of equals and more in the manner of those who work the fields instead of own them.

Garnett's mind wandered back to Adelyn, picturing her struggling against the fever. With his mind full of her, he would be derelict in thoughts of Innis or the girl Bonet spoke of, whose name he'd half heard and would not remember.

# *Chapter Fifteen*
## *COURTSHIP*

"Stop being such a pest!" Adelyn shooed Cicely away like a buzzing fly, then felt guilty for being mean to her little sister. She just wanted to look her best for her foray into Savannah, hoping to see Innis. Three months since New Year's and, except for furtive moments in a car, their was only a first intimate encounter. Her hunger for him grew each day. She knew her mother suspected something. Careful as she was, if anyone saw her look at him, her expression would betray her. Adelyn knew he had greater control at hiding emotion. She saw it as his greater maturity. Sincere as she believed him to be in his declaration of love, she also knew his eloquence could sway anyone.

Mama and Adelyn planned to drive down to Savannah and Cicely threatened to complete the picture. Adelyn could just envision the back seat of the sedan, ice cream melting all over her packages after their shopping, with Cicely dreaming out the window at every bluebird she caught sight of.

"Mama!" Adelyn shouted out as she took hold of her sister's wrist.

"Ouch, you know you're hurting me!" Cicely tried to wrench free.

"Oh no, those sticky hands get washed before you touch one damn thing in my room. Mama!" She pulled her sister to her mother's room where Missus Jackson adjusted her earrings. Adelyn's mother looked at the struggling child and the struggling girl and wondered how much a woman Adelyn had become. She pushed that thought out of her head as quickly as it tried to nestle in and take root. She really didn't want to know what happened between her daughter and Innis Crawford. He'd stuck like glue to Adelyn from the time she took sick at the Howard's place, like a specter, sitting day and night outside Delia's bedroom, unseemly, and, as she told her husband, people would talk. It didn't help that the Howard family took pity on his almost schoolboy crush and let him stay, sleep, eat, and live there until Adelyn came out of her coma.

For his part, Captain Jackson dismissed it all, saying, "That little filly could do worse, Mother. Innis Crawford is up and coming in Tulip Junction. Heard tell he may run for office in the next election. Imagine, so much older than his years. Yes, she could do a lot worse." He shook his head when his wife insisted that Adelyn was too young for such things.

"Now, Mother, we all have those wild oats. Can't tell me you don't remember that summer out at the cabin…"

His wife shushed him and ended that conversation. But her mind couldn't let go. Innis had become a fixture in their lives ever since the Howard's New Year's party. He sought out Captain Jackson with excuses and stopped by with this or that legal paper for farms bought up and such, but he always had his eye out for Adelyn and always managed to see her, their heads together talking God knows what, where no one could hear.

Other than dancing at New Year's she had not even seen them hold hands, yet she sensed a wildly physical energy between them. A memory passed through her like a cold wind of once Innis stopping by with yet another legal form for her husband. Through his talk with Captain Jackson and speaking with her, his eyes searched and found Adelyn reading in the living room. She knew they had walked in that direction as they spoke, but she could not remember the actual movement.

It struck her that Adelyn did not immediately look up and her soul told her Adelyn sensed his presence. Innis had spoken softly to Mary Jackson, clearing his throat, asking after her health. And when Missus Jackson looked at him, she saw a glow, almost like a halo surrounding him. She brushed the thought off her mind, telling herself it must have been the sun streaking through the windows, but she strangely felt a warmth and good feelings toward him almost as if he had conjured it all to make her like him, accept him.

Missus Jackson felt relieved every time Innis left Tulip Junction, and whenever Adelyn attended her high school functions. That peculiar light that went on when they came together blinded her.

"Mama, do you know what Adelyn just said? Ooooh, you're going to be so sorry." Ten-year-old Cicely, all long coltish legs and arms, had gotten into full tattletale mode. She studied Adelyn the way most of her friends watched birds. Though she could not put it into words, she knew her sister had somehow crossed a path into a form of adulthood. She just hadn't quite found a way to articulate it so she could threaten to 'tell' on her big, smarty-pants sister. The tattling faded to nothing, without anyone being too sorry.

Somehow both girls and their mother found themselves dressed and ready to drive into town. Adelyn, though not yet seventeen, drove everywhere since her father put her in charge of chauffeuring her mother on her endless errands. Mary Jackson sat in front, and Cicely stretched herself out on the big back seat.

Missus Jackson chatted up a storm of litanies about every neighbor and cousin as they passed by one farm then another and through the Tulip Junction town square. They turned onto the state highway, the only stretch of good road to Savannah, and mercifully, Cicely dozed off because her fidgeting made Adelyn crazy every time she checked the rear-view mirror.

Adelyn looked over at her mother, gauging her mood. "Next week is the Spring dance, and I would like…"

Missus Jackson stopped powdering her nose and snapped the compact shut. "You would like to ask permission to go to the dance with someone?" She straightened her dress and smoothed some of the wrinkles. "Would that be one of the boys from the senior class?"

Adelyn knew from her mother's tone that she would object to Innis taking her daughter anywhere. The thought flew between them as they exchanged glances.

"Don't you see how unseemly that is? He's a man and you're just a girl." Her mother flounced her skirt some and leaned her back into the seat. "Adelyn, what is he doing with one as young as you?"

"Mama, he's gentlemanly," she lied. "He's so much more interesting than those boys at school. All they can think of is…"

Her mother interrupted. "Never you mind, missy. I won't hear such talk." Each of them retreated into her own reverie, her mother thinking on fashionable and proper tea dances of her day and Adelyn thinking of and yearning for Innis's hands all over her.

"We'll see what your daddy has to say about all this." She regretted the words before they escaped her mind and her tongue. Because Mary Love Jackson already knew her husband's mind and it left her indignant that he would chance his daughter's reputation over a man who clearly had gone beyond his own control. "Adelyn, sweetheart, I want to ask you. Have you been seeing Innis Crawford, alone?"

Adelyn kept a steady hand on the wheel, glad her

gloves hid her white knuckles. She cleared her throat, which had gone all dry. "Just when you did, at New Year's." She kept quiet, not asking why. She could tell her mother did not fully accept her words as truth. Quickly, as an afterthought, "Maybe saw him once or twice when he met with Daddy." Her mother remained silent.

Adelyn thought to add, "Garnett Crawford and his friend, Jeremy, came by the other day to visit. Wasn't that kind? They wanted to be sure I was truly well again, though goodness knows I saw them at New Year's." Idle chat, she knew, but her mother jumped in, and Adelyn heaved an inward sigh, relieved she didn't have to pursue the other path their conversation had taken.

"Yes, I do recall seeing them down at the stables with you and your daddy. That Garnett is a nice boy. He's just this year at the University, isn't he?" All of it, the most important part of it, went unsaid, that only two years separated Garnett and Adelyn, that he didn't seek undue attention, that even if he had felt as strongly as Innis, he would never give in to such lavish displays of emotion, of affection. All of it went unsaid, but lay between them, impossible to ignore.

Adelyn didn't mention that Garnett's strong arms lifted her with ease and carried her up all those stairs at the Howard's after she took sick. She didn't mention his conversation with her while they danced at the New Year's party, that he taunted her for her 'slip of a dress.' Instead, the separate truths that each held lingered in a light cloud of concern over both mother and daughter, which neither of them would ever forget.

The doorman at Mrs. Raven's Gowns and Dresses carried the bigger boxes, and Adelyn and her mother took up the rest, with Cicely skipping up the street and around them all.

"Stop circling me." Adelyn spoke in a tight and quiet voice after being bumped twice, which she knew Cicely meant to do. They piled most of the boxes into the trunk with just a few remaining on the seat. Cicely immediately began whining about lunch and her hunger pains.

"We'll lunch at the Forsythe," Mary Jackson told both girls, "and there will be no complaining out of you." She added this hastily before Cicely could protest how the corner luncheonette had the best sandwiches and cokes. Missus Jackson continued, "You'll have a nice, hot lunch and some soup." Cicely pulled a face at her sister, then turned and smiled at her mother.

"Now is that face for the soup or for me?" A familiar voice hit Adelyn's heart so hard, she thought she would stop breathing. Innis stood there, the breeze stirring the dark heavy locks on his forehead. Cicely twisted around him and made an even worse face before Adelyn grabbed her arm and pinched it just enough to hurt but shy of causing her bratty sister to yelp.

"Missus Jackson, you know my mother, Sarah Crawford." Innis's mother extended her hand in greeting to Mary Jackson. Although all of Tulip Junction agreed Missus Crawford had been a beauty in her youth, it seemed to Adelyn that time had no real hold on Sarah Crawford. Her dark hair pulled into a bun at the nape of her neck, she wore a very simple, but well-cut dress that Adelyn knew would cause her mother to go home and search the magazines for its style and cut.

"And it is so good to see you well and thriving." Sarah Crawford gently hugged Adelyn, who heard in her voice a genuine interest for Adelyn's welfare. Sarah held her at arm's length and examined her for a quick moment. "You are better, I can see. At Christmas, I think you still harbored some fatigue."

"Yes, I am well, thank you." Adelyn smiled, knowing that Sarah Crawford approved. As if by a signal, Innis went from standing mutely, hands at his side, to the energetic suitor. He turned away from the two women as they exchanged stories and news of Tulip Junction and all the things that occurred there: a new baby or an old teacher passing.

"I've missed you." Innis whispered so softly that neither the mothers nor Cicely heard, though Adelyn's sister openly watched their body language.

He bent his head to hear her as Adelyn replied, "Well, all you have to do is come visit Daddy."

Innis seemed slightly removed, but only Mary Jackson observed this. She noticed the light shone slightly less brightly around the two young people than on other occasions. Sarah Crawford chatted, her gaze following her son and Adelyn. When she caught Innis's attention, her head nodded down as if giving approval, which Mary Jackson quickly noted. Yet Innis's reaction to this silent communication held and troubled Adelyn's mother. He moved closer to the girl, took her hand, and that strange light got brighter around both of them again. Adelyn saw none of this.

Rubbing her lips with her finger, Adelyn felt that same glow that being near Innis brought to her entire body. Yet the distractions of school, family expectations, visiting with Mrs. Jackson's cousins and elderly aunts, all made the reminders of her experience less intense.

"What are you thinking on?" Delia whispered from her desk next to Adelyn.

Abruptly, Adelyn picked up her pen and looked at her friend. "The holidays and the dance."

"Has Innis called you?" Delia did not stand on ceremony. Looking over at Adelyn's hair, caught up in a fat, yellow ribbon that fell almost to her waist, she asked, "You fixin' to get that hair all bobbed? They say that will be next. Before we even get to the university."

Mr. Perdy looked down his glasses at the direction of their whispering sounds, and both girls sat up straighter, looking more closely at their geometry books. "Let's begin with Delia Howard today," he said, asking her to respond to the one question that, luckily, she could answer. Later the two girls talked at lunch, and Adelyn told her of Innis' quiet pursuit, but not that he'd possessed her, because Adelyn knew no one expected that to have happened.

Innis knew this. Gathering a sense of them through his practiced pursuit of young women, Innis understood Adelyn's memories of that night at the party would fade. A part of him appreciated the holidays and their distractions for Adelyn to get lost in, a safety net for catching her affections. At the same time, her lack of dependency on him caused him to fret. Would he lose her? Would some other young man enjoy her? While clerking in a Tulip Junction law office, being assigned to land acquisitions for Captain Jackson comforted Innis greatly, knowing he would see her often. When he found her walking on the hard, rutted road after school one day in late January, he thanked his luck again. "Adelyn." He rolled the window down as she broke out of a teen girl's reverie and found himself praying her reveries involved him.

She looked up, her eyes still far away, and the fear that she might be thinking of a boy at school stole the smile for her away from his lips. "Adelyn, I'll take you home." Finally, she smiled back in recognition, only partially dispelling his dread. "Is that where you're headed? Home? Or to meet someone?" He lips tightened to keep from saying more.

"Someone? Who?" She straightened her collar, pulling her wool beret over her ears, and opened the door on the sedan.

"I don't know. You were lost somewhere; I thought maybe thinking about people at school." He cleared his throat wishing he'd sounded more casual, but he knew he couldn't.

"You are silly, Innis. People? Do you mean boys or girls?" The lateness of the day darkened the interior of the car, her eyes getting bigger as the pupils dilated.

"No, *you're* the one being silly. You know exactly what I mean." His voice hardened as he reached over, grabbing her hand to stop her from pulling on her beret.

Adelyn smiled at him, opening her palm, and grazing his chin with her hand. "Now, who's being silly, Innis?" And it would have ended like that, her flirtations being just so, but Adelyn felt in that moment a power over him. Though too young to name it, she nevertheless knew her power.

They met in the middle of the seat, him pulling her and she moving toward him, while he covered her face with kisses and forced her mouth open, touching her tongue. The untraveled road protected them from discovery, and again, this second time, he brought her to the highest place she could go. It left them both panting, steaming the windshield with their breath. This time she cried.

"No, no. There's no reason. Is there?" He petted her face, slid his hand down again to where he had just been. "Please tell me."

Between sobs, she swallowed until she could speak. "I feel something and don't understand it." She brought her lips to his ear, and kissed him. "Do you?"

"I think I do." He smiled and hid a tear that had lingered on his lower eyelid. "Yes."

This would be the way of their stolen, furtive moments together; two swimmers treading water, seemingly in one place, while currents carried them inexorably forward. Each time Innis felt sated, and then less so. Each time she swore it would not happen again, and it did the very next time. It strengthened her, at the same time it tore him apart. The adult in Innis knew the morals of it; he also knew he loved her. And he sensed she traveled a different road than he— hers a road of discovery while he wanted permanence, maybe not right away, but after. After she graduated college? Could he wait that long? Yet a mere eighteen months would see Adelyn start at the university.

"I cannot believe you are acting so petty." She whispered into the speaker with the earpiece glued to her, not wanting to miss a word of his response.

"That's how you see me?" Innis forced himself to pull away from his emotions and not play out the game they always seemed to end with. Maddeningly he knew school administrators placed the phones in the main hall to prevent this kind of wanton talk between lovers. "I wanted to come down next weekend. That's petty?"

"Innis, I have examinations to study for. Please wait till I come home. A few weeks." Adelyn fussed with her skirt, and admired her calves and slim ankles, so glad for shorter skirts. She waited, began speaking about each of her subjects, telling him how she loved this history lesson or that paper where she got an "A."

"Okay." He relented. "I'll call you Saturday." A hesitation, then, "you know I love you." This time, he hung up without waiting to hear whether she would say the same.

# October 15

*Darling Innis*

*How could you be so rash? You hurt my feelings with your questions. No, I haven't been <u>seeing</u> anyone on campus. They're all just boys, you know. But how could you question me in such a way? Yes, I am pouting right now, and no, I'm not some dumb dolly, stamping my foot or any of the other nonsense written in those romantic magazines.*

*You saw me almost every day at home, and now I'm at school. You knew this would happen, that I would grow up. But nothing has changed between us, unless it's changed in you. My heart just now thumped at the thought of you finding someone closer to home. Does your heart hurt you like that? I hope it does.*

*I love you.*

*Your Adelyn*

## *Chapter Sixteen*
### *GARNETT IN LOVE*

The rain surrounding them became indistinguishable from the tears that fell from Garnett's eyes and from his father's. Innis and Garnett shared many of the same friends, but for different reasons—Garnett, the teammate, and Innis, the hail fellow, well met. Football buddies of Garnett's, big boys with thick muscles, would be pallbearers. One friend, Brit, a big, husky, farm-bred boy whose thick neck resembled the Georgia University bulldog mascot, felt unabashed grief for a fallen hero, his own face wet with tears. Their mutual friends, all of them there today, had looked on Innis as their model, older, on his way to clerk and study the law, and showing the promise of living life in a grand way.

Brit held up more than his own weight in carrying the coffin up the hill to the plot, to an empty hole that waited for Innis's coffin. Father Mayo had wisely positioned Brit on the same end with Will Crawford, Innis's father, in case he needed Brit's help. Will Crawford, always a giant to Garnett, but now, today, seemed frail and older.

Garnett saw Adelyn, all five foot five inches of her in a dark blue flapper dress showing long and slender legs, shivering in the breeze that accompanied the dark day. They all stood under a canvas tarp to keep the rain off. She straightened her sister's waistband, obviously in charge of her younger sister. Of course, Adelyn came. Garnett knew what went on between Innis and Adelyn though neither of them had confided in him. *You'd have to be blind not to see it.* He took hold of his mind to stop it from wandering to Adelyn. She did not cry yet he knew, like himself, an interior grief made her breathing painful, and he found himself loving her for grieving so sublimely for his brother. *Would she grieve this way for me?*

Garnett gripped the coffin harder, seeing her eyes full and ready to spill and saw his own tears finally fall on his hands as he and the other pallbearers laid the heavy oak coffin down on a very green place. He felt a loss of control of his emotions and worried that they would all see his face open with sadness. *How can grass be so green, be so alive, and not Innis?* He moved closer to his father. His mother had taken to her bed, white as the sheets that covered her. The breeze ruffled Father Mayo's pale hair as he made the sign of the cross and intoned the few words of ceremony, and then added, "We are here too short a time to understand and appreciate what we have. Innis was not one we can say that of. He embraced this life more fully, knowing its value, and was kind to all. He will always remain alive in our hearts. We will all remember him as we all miss him."

Garnett floated through all of it, seeing pieces of it, looking across the grave to Adelyn because, as it turned out, the funeral director led her and her family to that spot. He saw her whisper to her little sister Cicely, who stood a little straighter. And then, just like Innis's bright and shining life force, the ceremony, all of it, ended.

They all trundled down the hill, the younger ones pulled by the steepness, the old ones walking down at angles the way beginners ski on ice-crusted mountains. The Crawfords invited all to their home, a rambling house with one side looking lopsided where a second story had been built on after the War with the North. A reception line grew from the front door to the center of the wide hall that divided the living room from the dining room. Will Crawford stood in the middle, greeting those who mourned with him. Adelyn and Cicely stood behind their mother and father, in line to offer their condolences. Adelyn knew Innis's mother, Sarah, would not appear today.

"We are all praying for her." Mary Jackson said this to Will Crawford as she handed a baked dish to Martha, the housekeeper. "Now, if there's anything we can do… Captain Jackson said to be sure to let you know we can send some folks over to take care of Sarah's late summer garden."

"Thank you, Mary; I know Sarah will be glad to hear this." Garnett's father looked worriedly toward the stairs, waiting for his wife to descend, unsure if she would and equally unsure that she would stay in her room. "Garnett, have you looked in on Mother?" Garnett at his left side, also greeting people as they gathered into the large hallway, whispered into his father's ear, "She'll be down, she said, after most everyone is gone home."

People came and most left and with the thinning crowd, Garnett could finally see Adelyn. He gently maneuvered around this one and that until he stood nearest her. She took his hand and held it.

"Oh, Garnett. How quiet it has all become." Garnett nodded. *Yes, quiet. Forever quiet now.* He held her hand as much as she held his, and both of them, with Cicely leading the way, left for the back porch. The earlier rain cleaned the air, and the sun, though behind a cloud, brightened the edges of the day. Adelyn walked out to the porch, still a girl at eighteen, a freshman at the same university as Garnett, who, at twenty, looking tall and athletic, appeared every inch a man, both home for this sad event.

"You all hungry?" She looked at him and he felt that maybe she saw him for the first time. He wondered how she could be so young and already so in command. Cicely and she stood on the covered back porch looking at some neighbor men with their jars of whiskey.

"I guess I am." He did not want to relinquish the hand he held, nor, it seemed, did she, as she guided them back inside where Martha stood, waiting, and handed them plates already prepared. They let go of one another and all three, Cicely too, went back out to sit on the steps with their plates and glasses of lemonade.

"Martha makes the best turkey stuffing." Adelyn took small forkfuls of her food but, to Garnett's delight, ate like a healthy girl and not like the sorority sisters at Georgia U.

"I could truly enjoy a beer." He looked at her for a reaction but she worried the homemade applesauce with her fork, pushing it this way and that.

"Here." Garnett took a spoon, scooped it up for her, and grinned when she opened her mouth and he fed her. They all fell silent devouring the food on their plates, Garnett listing between a desire to cry for Innis, the person he knew he had loved most, and a fast-beating heart, as he smelled Adelyn's soap-and-water-clean hair and body.

Garnett and Adelyn gathered up their dishes and silverware, placing all in the sudsy basin in the kitchen sink. They walked out to the back porch again, with some working men drinking, glass jars in their fists.

"Let's walk. Cicely?" Adelyn beckoned both of them and they all fell again into a comfortable, maybe even healing, silence. Down toward the back of the property, they walked past the fields, which, though not as vast as the Jacksons' lands, comprised part of the working farm that Will Crawford maintained.

Cicely swished her dark dress as she played with Garnett's dog. In and out of the hedges they all walked until Cicely and the dog ran ahead. "We have a little general store on the property." Garnett nodded toward something that looked more like a still, but it had a porch and some of the older field hand folk sat near the stove inside taking the chill off.

"I know this place, Addie, can we get some Nehi?" Cicely asked, trying to balance on a split-rail fence.

Garnett walked up the stairs pulling Adelyn along. "Beer?" He looked at her for assent and almost knew it would come. A black man, tall and very thin with a small cigar between his fingers, stood waiting. "One Nehi and two beers, Willis, please."

Willis looked at all of them. "Heard about Mr. Innis and your loss, Mr. Garnett." Cicely came up behind and Willis popped all three drinks, handing the Nehi orange drink to the girl and the beers to Garnett who knew Willis tacitly said, 'you, no one else, hand that young lady her beer.'

Garnett would forever admire Adelyn as she coolly, smoothly, removed his hand from the sweating bottle and swigged it like a truck driver. They both thanked Willis for his condolences. Willis looked from one to the other, knowing the relationships: Innis, her dead lover, Garnett the one left behind. They did all live in a small country town after all, and everybody whispered. Out on the porch of the small general store, Cicely emptied the bottle of orange soda, and headed back to the house after a quick and awkward thank-you to Garnett for the Nehi.

Garnett became lost again and so did Adelyn, who sighed to say, "Garnett, honey, he had so much, so much life in one person." She rubbed his bent shoulders, and Garnett wondered how she knew they ached from holding up the world for both his parents and himself. They stepped down from the store and headed back up toward the house. Then, turning into the barn, found themselves holding one another and crying, taking turns sobbing for the love of Innis, until Garnett took her fully in his arms and crushed her to him and kissed her face, her hair, her lips. And Adelyn kissed him back.

They had fallen on a mound of hay just inside the door. Garnett heard his voice outside himself, saying her name repeatedly. He heard no entreaties to please stop; we should be grieving. They felt no traces of recrimination in either of their souls. They had only a great need to fill the emptiness they both had endured from the moment Innis had stopped breathing. Adelyn's mind flew to Innis's image, his secret smile. Garnett's mind shut down because he could only see her, hear her voice, her short and broken gasps as he brought her to where she needed to go. Later they each would trace back but never talk of the steps of their lovemaking.

Now he lay back on the hay and she straightened her dress and then did a curious thing. She buttoned his pants front for him.

"What?" She drew back when she saw a scowl take over from his so recently relaxed features.

"You're so expert. Did he teach you? Did he?" He pushed her hand away as she attempted to touch his face.

"And you judge?" All indignation, she moved to stand when he pulled her down on top of him and wrestled with her to stay put.

"Sorry, please, please, sorry. Stop for a moment, Adelyn, stop."

"What do you want from me? Do you want me to rewrite my history? To say Innis and I...?" He stopped her, put his finger to her lips.

"It's all right, I'm stupid. I don't know why I reacted." He stopped restraining her as he moved the both of them to facing one another again. "Adelyn, it's all such a dream, this, and Innis gone."

She sat up, pulled her stockings up, and rolled them. Her legs looked especially luxurious in dark blue silk hosiery and he understood why Innis had pursued her, because he knew that Innis had made a great effort. He finally asked her, "Can you tell me, and if you don't want to talk about it, it's okay, I just wanted to understand how you and Innis began seeing one another," he bit his lip and quickly added, "but you don't have to say, if you don't want to."

Adelyn had pulled the hay out of her hair and threaded her fingers through it like a comb and pinned it all up again, her eyes wet. "You were there, Garnett. That day at Delia's when I took sick. You have to remember then because I remember you that same day." She hesitated, "Though my mind was full of Innis back then, I remember you." Her thoughts went lovingly through that first time, meeting Innis and Garnett.

"You're such a curious girl. You're shy about it all and yet you're not."

"That's because it's my business and no one else's except Innis." Her sigh marked the totality of it, the finality of the end. "You know when Father Mayo said he still lives? I think I believe that."

Garnett slid his arm underneath her shoulders and moved as close as one human could to another. "Oh, he's just saying things. I think he may have been speaking metaphorically, like instead of saying he lives on in heaven."

She didn't try to move away, instead her breast lay close to his chest where she could feel the rhythm of his heart. "I happen to know what a metaphor is. You know, I came back home from college, same as you." She had a presentiment — *Innis is not dead. I know because I can feel it.*

Garnett thought of Adelyn at the university and conjured bittersweet pictures of her near him on campus, of her coquetry driving him mad, and then, ultimately, of having to ward off the entire football team. He lay silent to avoid saying these things.

# Chapter Seventeen
## ADELYN ON CAMPUS

Innis was gone. Adelyn's heart felt the emptiness in the leaves falling from the trees, autumn looking more pronounced, earlier than any other year she could remember, only late October. Adelyn returned to Savannah, to the university. After the funeral, she blocked her memories except for his gentle love, her feelings of tremendous attraction to him, the flattery of it all.

The first few days, everything at the University of Georgia reminded her of Innis. She wondered aloud whether he would have been difficult with her away at school while he practiced law in Tulip Junction. She recalled his coming down to use the law library and sensed his unhappiness. He disquieted her when he showed his possessive side because he became petulant. She shook her head to erase the one time recently when he purposely flirted outright, a push and pull tug-of-war between them.

In her young girl's heart, part of her played the scenario

through to all the petty arguments and jealousies that distance from home could cause. Then her young mind moved on. She had only a limited time after all, on her way to nineteen on a college campus, and 1922 showed great promise, such a modern time.

Adelyn appreciated the distraction of the university, of everyone rushing to classes after late-night studying, football skirmishes and practice, and all the girls in the bleachers in heavy coats against chilling winds. She found it hard to believe that only a month earlier she had just settled into dorm life; then, immediately rushed by her sorority, she moved yet again, this time to a sorority house and a new room, one with more windows and light.

"When I didn't find you at the library, I knew you would be here." Adelyn's roommate Cara looked down at her, lying on her bed, reading. "Come on, Addie, the girls all went down to the front parlor with Missus Higgins. Drop the books, will you?" Mrs. Higgins, their house mother, a warm and round woman of fifty-five, had freckles on her hands and face and anywhere the sun had cast its rays.

"Just let me finish this one chapter." Adelyn looked at her sorority sister, always fashionable in the newest skirts and blouses. It struck Adelyn odd that Cara's father sent his only daughter to a southern school when she could have attended any of the schools in New England. Cara insisted she chose to come here, and Adelyn, knowing about fathers and daughters, understood the power of a young woman.

"Don't know why you didn't just stay in that musty dorm when you just study, study, study, same as they all do over there. Only they pretend they wouldn't accept an invitation to join us."

"I can do both." Adelyn unrolled her long sleeves and buttoned them at the wrist. "I admire those girls in the dorm. They're planning careers. Besides, I like history, especially when it's about the law." And she embraced it, Innis's final gift to her. Between their furtive meetings and intimacies, Innis talked about the law, sometimes thinking through a case out loud. Adelyn felt proud that he thought her smart enough to grasp its intricacies.

"That boy you know from home, he came around yesterday, calling on you." Cara stretched out on Adelyn's bed, deciding her friend had chosen the better mattress.

"At twenty, I wouldn't call Garnett a boy." Her heartbeat quickened again, and she pushed the feeling away. While younger than Innis, Garnett possessed a certain self-assurance, his way with her, scolding her about her New Year's Eve 'slip of a dress' and other things, bothered her, as though he wanted her under his control.

"How did you say you knew him? He looks some like that young man I saw here once, when we all first got here."

"Cara, please don't play coy with me. Innis has a brother Garnett, that's who he is." She hated saying Innis's name, each time it felt like a sting to her heart, made her heart hold its breath for a moment, made her stop thinking. Made her almost dead. Did she wish that? Was there some place she could join Innis? She hadn't sensed any sign of him. Instead, she felt hopeless, like a giant abyss had opened for them both, and he had fallen first. *Yet, she remembered a small piece of a dream every so often.*

Hearing Garnett's name had a different effect, remembering what happened at home between them at the funeral. She chided herself, trying to make herself feel guilty for their lovemaking in the barn, how they both shed tears, one for her dead lover, and the other for his beloved brother.

"Sorry, I didn't realize." Cara must have seen the change in Adelyn's face, the grief asserting itself all over again. Her friend's voice sounded as sincere as it did contrite. She took Adelyn by the wrist. "Come on. Let's see what Higgins has in store for us this time."

Adelyn put aside her stormy thoughts and followed Cara down the winding stairs of the Victorian-style sorority house into the large sitting room filled with overstuffed chairs and sofas Girls draped on them everywhere, some unseemly with legs over the sides, one girl with her head resting in the lap of another sorority sister. A well-projected sound of 'Ahem' filled the room, snapping them all to attention when they recognized their house mother's voice, making them all sit up, with straight backs and legs crossed at the ankles. Adelyn settled into a love seat only big enough for two small women, and Cara slipped down beside her. All the girls had slim figures, befitting the new era of wearing waist-less, corset-less dresses that skimmed their knees for night-time dances, and pleated skirts and sweaters during the day.

Mrs. Higgins served the girls finger sandwiches and petits fours. She used every opportunity to offer suggestions on proper placement of napkins on the knee, gentle patting of the lips after a sip of tea, and her favorite: "Be certain you bite a small morsel of your cake, that which fits neatly inside your mouth which you widen only enough for such a morsel. And for heaven's sakes, girls, do not open your mouth wide." Her once fiery red hair had faded to a pinkish gray, and she wore a dark blue silk dress with a lace collar that 'the nuns in Ireland had crocheted just for such a dress.'

"If she had her way, we wouldn't eat anything at all." Cara juggled an iced cake on her knee, deftly cutting into it with a little silver fork and popping the dessert into her purposely widened mouth.

"Hush, she'll hear you." Adelyn's eyes opened wide with merriment when only a short while ago, they had begun to fill with tears. Higgins took up the rest of their gray day with tedious lessons of etiquette.

"Miss Adelyn, something for you." Penelope Higgins stood near the doorway as the girls filed out of the living room and left for the upper floors of their sorority house, some for more studies and most for more frivolity.

Adelyn looked at the unfamiliar handwriting on the front of the envelope: her name, printed in capitals, hastily written by someone expecting to have seen her. She thanked

Mrs. Higgins and opened the sealed envelope as she stood against the wall at the back of the grand foyer. She marveled at its many folds; someone wanted to protect the content from curious eyes. The sounds of the girls' voices retreated as they took the lift or ran up the stairs. Adelyn's mind closed to them as she read:

*Where are you? I came by. One of your sisters in my science lab said that you finished your classes by three. Call my House. Tell Central which fraternity. She'll connect you. I must see you. I need to. G.*

Adelyn checked for any stragglers among the girls and then placed the call in the phone booth behind the immense spiral staircase.

"Hi, Garnett?" She hoped her voice didn't sound too expectant, too eager to see him, too obedient. She told herself she just wanted to know what he had to say. She heard noises, feet shuffling, and male voices raised and boisterous.

"Get off, Beardsley. Go dig a ditch." The sound of jostling. Then, "Adelyn? Is that you? You got my note?" Then conferring with a fraternity brother, some mumbling, "Look, I'll be off in a few minutes. Get lost." Then more quickly, "Uh, not you, Adelyn, just these guys acting like monkeys in a zoo here. Can I come over? We can catch some dinner downtown."

She pictured all the fraternity boy ruckus. "I have a test tomorrow. Study tonight. I can see you for a bit before dinner, if you want to come by now." They agreed, and she checked her watch and ran up the stairs to straighten her clothes, change her blouse, pat her hair down, though the expert cut of it allowed it just to fall into place.

She had prepared herself little mental notes about decorum, to put distance between them. He came up the front stairs, and she waited in the vestibule so that they could leave without a lot of people attending. She opened the door as he reached for it; an awkward lunging motion ensued as he pushed and she pulled the door and he fell into her arms, or almost. She noticed first thing that he looked tired, less robust than he did a short time earlier, his face less ruddy from not as much time on the football field.

Awkward apologies spoken by both of them, first from her as she realized what she had done and then from Garnett, as he stumbled into her, face to face, body to body. Finally, "Oh, that's okay, that's all right" as each stood straighter and more subdued than either felt. That would all pass as they fell into the rhythm of their Tulip Junction world. He took her arm as they walked away from the building and began talking nonstop.

"You're thinner." He took her arm, and stopped on the sidewalk, stood in front of her, his eyes tracing her figure.

"Stop that. I feel like a horse being auctioned. You'll be counting my teeth next."

They began walking again, and she stopped. "Besides, you look thinner, too. Have you been well?" This time they stood a long time facing one another, he lightly touching her elbow and she feeling the heat of his fingers burning through her sleeve.

She had hastily thrown her coat around her shoulders when they left the sorority house.

"Here, let me do this." Garnett held her coat sleeves while she scooped her arms into them. He reached absentmindedly to button the top button when she pushed his hand away.

"What do you take me for? A five-year-old? My lord!" She buttoned the other buttons, purposely leaving the top one open, and he began to reflexively reach for it when she pushed past him. "Come on; it's cold." She looped her arm through his, while they crossed the street to the little restaurant that students didn't frequent. The waiter nodded a hello to Garnett, and she surmised Garnett must be a regular there. He guided her to the back of the bar to a secluded booth.

"I have been calling and leaving messages, haven't you received any of them?" His voice got tight. "Or are you just ignoring me, to drive me crazy? Is that it?"

"Garnett, I just today got your note from Missus Higgins and called you as soon as I saw it. What do you mean, ignoring you? Why should I do that?" She sat against the back of the booth and sipped her coke, the room warm and dark in their corner. She purposely skirted the "driving me crazy" part but when she saw the torment forming in his eyes, she took his hand that had been tapping on the table. "Stop that. It's distracting." They both fell silent. "What did you want to tell me?"

His gaze would not stay fixed. One moment his glare burned into her, the next, he averted his eyes to something above and beyond her head. He sipped his coffee laced with something from his flask. "Just that I can't live on campus, knowing you live so close."

Puzzled by this, she blurted before he could say anything further, "Now what does that mean? I should go home?" She sped on, oblivious, making all the wrong turns. "Just 'cause of what happened at the funeral? Honestly, Garnett, I thought we both agreed about that."

"We never agreed to anything. Do you make this all up in your head?" He rubbed his eyes, which looked bloodshot. "I don't want you to leave. I want to see you, I have to be with you." Adelyn's lips parted to speak, but he stopped her. "Please don't tell me not to say these things. Thinner? You think I look thinner? I haven't lived since that day."

"Garnett, honey. What we did was necessary for both of us. I thought of it as the beginning of a healing. Everything back there happened so fast. I haven't even had time to make sense of it." She dropped her straw into the coke bottle. "Do you know about it? Did someone hurt Innis? An accident?" She pressed his fingers.

"I don't know. I heard some talk from down in the south part of the county that I have to look into." He lied to her, not telling her of the men who visited him about Lucianne. "Mother has taken ill, from that day to this. I've been back and forth to try and help out."

They spent the waning day and the evening there, ordered a supper and talked about school as two young people might, drifting from the reality of Innis's passing to the actual and physical world that surrounded them. As they walked back to the school, he veered off the lighted path to a bench behind one of the buildings and held and kissed her, and she kissed him back. He murmured her name, brushed her temple with his hot lips, pressed them to her eyes. She remained clothed, yet felt him taking ownership of every part of her body.

She stopped him. "Garnett, what I did in that barn…" She wavered.

"Don't tell me you held me out of some misguided mercy, that you only pitied me." He shook with rage.

Someone walking toward them interrupted their conversation.

"How convenient." She could not believe he was laying blame on her for someone arbitrarily walking by. She could hear Garnett's smirk and wondered whether he thought her a magician, able to conjure people to block his path to her.

Adelyn pulled him closer to her and kissed him full on the mouth as the person, teacher, student, priest, and ghost, walked by. "Now don't try to tell me I planned this any more than I planned that time in the barn."

The set of his shoulders told her he was mollified for the moment. As they walked back to her sorority house, he told her about his classes, how he had been watching the stock market with its own science to it, telling her he would one day explain it all to her. She told him about her history classes and her professors, most of whom he knew. She could tell that, in fairness, he did not pass judgment on any of them, wanting her to form her own opinion. And for a while they simply became two young people with a tremendous affection for one another, who one day might plan a life together.

Yet something twitched in the wind, and the bare tree branches rubbed against one another, setting her teeth on edge. Deep inside her she felt a growing sense of something with an ability to interfere with their physical world. That sense would lay dormant for now and a long time after. So they had this peace, which they both experienced as a salve on sore wounds.

Some day in the future, she would pull this all out, examine it again, and call it by its name. For now, they had mid-terms and soon, the holidays. Another year had passed.

## *LETTER HOME*

*November 1922*

*Dear Mama and Daddy (and Cicely),*

*I hope you remembered that we had our finals as soon as we returned, and I was busy studying for exams and writing papers. Because I wouldn't want you to think I forgot everyone there.*

*The ride back to school was easy, not too many people on either side of the road. I guess everyone is staying close to home, getting ready for holidays. Mama and I will do some shopping when I get back to the Junction. Some of my sorority sisters are planning a trip into Savannah next weekend, which will give me a chance to see what the stores have. Mama, write back if you have anything special you want me to find for Aunt Grace.*

*It's almost lights out now. I am sad as both of you are. I miss Innis.*

*Love to you all. See you for Thanksgiving*

*Addie*

*P.S. Saw Garnett last night, and he said Hey to all of you and best wishes.*

## Chapter Eighteen
### *THANKSGIVING 1922*

"There you are." Captain Jackson watched Adelyn as she jumped off the train. "Careful now, girl. I know you're homesick, but you can at least wait till the engine comes to a stop."

"Who says I'm homesick?" She hugged her father tight, realizing the truth to what he said. A strong tug of nostalgia and childhood memories engulfed her and she fought a desire to weep.

"What you looking for, Addie?" Her father squeezed her hard.

Adelyn stared down the track of the little station at Waycross, trying to fix on what she sought. *I'm looking for you, Innis.*

"Nothing, Daddy, just taking it all in. Everything seems so small."

"Yes, that's the way of it. Makes me sad and happy all at the same time." He kissed her cheek, and she felt self-conscious, not wanting anyone to see her as a young girl.

"You know, sometimes you make no sense." She

rubbed the stubble on his chin, noticing some white among the red.

"You are moving on and the first thing is seeing home as smaller than the bigger world you're living in." Adelyn felt the pulse of the world she inhabited, accepting her father's insight. She participated in something bigger now. Home and even this big stretch of paved road from Waycross to Tulip Junction seemed smaller by comparison.

"Everyone at home feeling good, Daddy?" She looked over and thankfully observed a father still very much in his prime, his big hands lightly gripping the steering wheel, not the bony and gnarled hands of an older man.

"Mister Norris down back of the lower fields was off of work for a spell, but everyone else, I hear tell, is doing fine." How like her father to think that home included everyone within his farm's reach and then some. "I know it's only been a short time still, but you leaning in any special way with your studies?"

"I like history. My roommate teases me about the time I spend studying instead of attending silly tea parties in the front parlor."

"History, huh? Any special time or place?"

"American history especially, and the law. I like it best studying history when they tell of how laws were made and laws were changed. My professor gave me some other books to read. Different ways of seeing things I didn't even know existed. I guess I know why Innis loved…." Her words froze on her lips. Innis loved the law and succeeded so well at his first try in court. No need to share with her father what he already knew; Innis's first case involved land rights for Captain Jackson.

Adelyn noticed the speedometer and saw the needle pushing sixty miles per hour. "Daddy, you had Billy fix this car to go faster, didn't you?"

"Now honey, you know I keep my Stutz Bearcat very up-to-date." He lifted his foot from the accelerator as the courthouse steeple came into view on his right. They turned into the town of Tulip Junction, rounding the courthouse plaza and exiting onto the road that would take them home.

"You tell me if I'm poking where I ought not, but little girl, I've been worried about you, and I believe you know why."

"I sleep less, Daddy. It's so much and all at once. Going away, then Innis." She didn't tell him that a weight hung from her, a weight of guilt for any time she began to laugh at friends' jokes, or if a boy smiled at her in the dining hall, or if she received a high mark on her history tests. The awful guilt weighed her down for being alive and almost nineteen and Innis gone.

In the silence, Adelyn felt her father embrace her wounded soul. She reached over to squeeze his hand as if to say, 'I'm okay.' She pulled a mirror and a little comb from inside her bag to smooth down the little curls popping up around her face. Her soul lifted up as she surveyed the physical world around her. The naked maples stretched out their old arms as if wishing for leaves. Ahead lay the farm, the land, and the house.

"It all takes time, sweet girl." She barely heard his whispered words. He stopped the car and she jumped out. Then the ruckus of family surrounded her, and she noticed how everyone had changed—Aunt Grace looked heavier, Uncle Tyree thinner, her mother a bit older, and Cicely, tall, very tall and slim, and, yes, quite sophisticated. *When did all this happen?*

"Adelyn, someone to see you." Uncle Tyree bent down his tall frame to tell her as he glided by her on the way to the dining room. His eyes shifted toward the back hall. The family congregated for leftovers from the Thanksgiving meal, the bowls as full as on the holiday. Adelyn pushed back her chair, momentarily pre-occupied by all the food. *Did we not eat at all?*

"What's that?" Hard of hearing and always worried she

would miss something, Aunt Grace Lee sat upright at the table, trying to hear her husband's conversation with Adelyn.

Adelyn hurried out as she thanked her uncle for his discretion. The family all gathered in the dining room, distracted with savoring Thanksgiving leftovers, and Aunt Grace thankfully succumbed to the festivity.

She saw him, tall with broad shoulders, as a shadow against the opaque glass pane. Her heart jumped though he would never know it as she swung open the door. "Thought you'd be down there in Savannah whooping and hollering after the big win."

"No need, they won it without me. I came home yesterday morning."

"Well come on in, no point in heating the outdoors." She secretly congratulated herself for washing her hair earlier that day and brushing the curls to frame her face. She noticed Garnett noticing, his hand suspended, reaching out to feel the softness of it as she turned to walk back in. She felt his hand and it warmed her.

Garnett took one of the curls near her cheek. "Quite the flapper, are we?"

He took two steps inside, brushing against her as she held the door open. For the briefest moment they felt the warm air breathed from each other, could almost hear the throb of the blood coursing in one another's veins. He pressed slightly against her and she didn't move back.

"So, it's just your mama's kin?"

She knew he made polite conversation. Adelyn took his coat and hung it on one of the hooks inside the back hall.

"You know Aunt Grace is Mama's sister. She and Uncle Tyree have been with us since he came back from the Great War. He was doing more administrative stuff, certainly no soldiering. But claims he was mustard gassed, though I could never tell." Her chattering on just barely covered her own unease. *Why does he always make me so?*

The lights glowed against the gray day, and the family

talked busily and passed dishes to one another. Another chair had appeared next to Adelyn's when she came into the room to tell them. *Uncle Tyree had played Cupid.* "Garnett is here, and I asked him to dinner with us."

"Of course, dear boy." Mrs. Jackson, nearest Garnett, stood and briefly hugged his shoulder. All others including Captain Jackson said hello, the men in full voice and hearty. Garnett sat, and he helped himself from all dishes passed to him, waiting until the initial polite questions had been asked before biting into his food.

"Well son, heard the Bulldogs done it again!" Uncle Tyree shouted from his end of the table.

"He does that because he thinks everyone's as deaf as his wife." Adelyn whispered to Garnett whose smile broadened.

And he whispered back. "Adelyn, I know your family stories almost as well as my own." He looked to Uncle Tyree to answer him. "Yes, sir, I heard that too. I've been home since before the game." His voice dropped, "My mother is not well."

"Garnett, I am so sorry." Soft murmurs throughout the room duplicated Adelyn's wishes of genuine concern for Sarah Crawford. Even Cicely expressed concern, recalling Sarah Crawford's absence from the funeral. The Jacksons each held some memory of the time after Innis's passing when Sarah walked about town shopping and took part in the Altar Society looking like a specter, wan and weak. She faded from those events until no one saw her any longer in church or town, and as people will do, most ceased to look for her. A collective guilt permeated them all, most of all Mary Jackson for not visiting Sarah more.

"Doctor Spencer, the new young doctor in town, he trained up north in New York City, and my daddy took her to see him." Adelyn could tell that talking to them gave Garnett a release from his silent fears for his mother's welfare. Garnett had held out hope that his mother would get past the grief and live fully, but she began to fade as they entered the holidays.

Mrs. Jackson, who sat on the other side of Garnett, spoke softly, and Adelyn alone heard her saying, "I spoke with your mother last I saw her; she told me of her childhood illness that weakened her heart."

That was what it was. But she's been resting a lot, and they expect her back to normal, soon. Soon." He repeated himself without even knowing it, a wish more than a belief.

Adelyn studied them, her family, the way Garnett acted with her father and uncle; far more deferential than his older brother though her male kin had been fond of Innis. Innis's cunning, beating out the world under the law of those northerners, the natural enemy of the men of the south, earned their admiration. Instead, Garnett belonged to the greater world; he belonged, and no one held it against him. They all settled in and traded stories of one another's kin, shared old experiences, and new ones. Adelyn touched his hand that lay in his lap, wanting him to know through her touch that he belonged with them, with her.

Adelyn and the rest all knew that Edna had a thing about Jeremy, fidgeting or otherwise.

"Jeremy, kindly stay put, your shifting about drives me crazy." Edna Gray fidgeted with the fur collar of her fashionable coat. The car held them all comfortably, William, a Georgia U senior and Edna's brother, Garnett, and Adelyn in front next to William, Edna and Jeremy in the back. Missus Jackson had consented to Adelyn returning to school with Garnett because the Grays went along on this road trip. Adelyn thought how ridiculous that her mother trusted Innis and never questioned her daughter about the relationship, yet would not allow Garnett to drive alone with Adelyn back to the university.

"But Mama, I don't understand the difference." Adelyn threw her things into her suitcase while her mother took them out again and neatly folded sweaters, skirts, underwear.

Her mother went into a huff, but finally got the words out, "It's because Innis was already well on his way to a profession. Garnett is a junior in college." The rest of the implications fell around them like petals off a late-blooming rose. Adelyn caught them all.

The ride quickly settled in with short conversations above the roar of the large-engine car. They encountered almost no traffic the entire trip to Savannah, with one or two cars passing on the opposite side. The monotonous motion of the car and a full stomach of dinner to 'keep her from starving' as her mother had said, now lulled Adelyn into sleep, her dreams fractured with the heavy automobile sounds and occasional twitters from the back seat. She almost smiled at them.

*Did we behave the same way? Did everyone know?* Back came the answer. *Does it matter?*

Abruptly awake. Undeniably, she had heard Innis. *You returned here.* And then a curiously sad lament from him in some other place, *No, Sugar, I haven't.*

"Did I put you to sleep with all my chatter?" Garnett leaned over to be heard.

Adelyn feigned sleep to collect her thoughts, trying to remember, finally deciding that it couldn't have been a dream because she saw no images. *Then it's my own mind.*

She opened her eyes, "Must have dozed off. Dinner filled me up; I'll be lucky to fit into any of my clothes."

Garnett took advantage of her remark to flirt as he squeezed her hand, "You'll be fine in all those skirts."

A half hour later, they arrived at the university's big front gate. Edna and Jeremy dispersed after Garnett thanked William. Jeremy, intent on Edna, barely stayed long enough to say good-bye. Garnett picked up Adelyn's bag, and they walked together back to her sorority house.

Curious, she asked, "I heard you saying to Jeremy you planned to go up to New York City for some special program next year."

"You don't see why I should, do you?"

His presumption rattled her. "Try asking me when I'm a sophomore. I'm sure I'll have plenty of wisdom then." She exhaled in exasperation then thought better of it all. "I'm not who you think I am, Garnett. Not the little southern belle with cotton candy for brains, here at the university to snag a husband."

"Never thought that for a second. You've proved your maturity to me." Immediately, he wished he could take back the words that fell around them with the thud of lead. He spoke quickly to cover up the *faux pas*, "I'm going up there to New York to learn more about finance. New York is more than just geography. Not just north, but central to the financial world and growing that way more and more."

They stood awkwardly, now facing one another, having spent the best part of the holiday together. Adelyn sensed a thread, though thin, still very strong, that tied one to the other.

"When will you leave for New York?" She emphasized the last word in two southern syllables instead of one and watched a smile break over his face. She gazed at his full lips while he passionately urged her toward him. She kissed him slowly on the mouth, her lips just slightly parted. He appeared neither surprised nor expecting her move. His affectionate return met hers. Garnett took hold of the front of her coat to keep her there with him.

"Thank you, Adelyn."

"Why are you thanking me?" She stayed still, wanting to prolong this closeness.

He began to walk away and turned before she disappeared inside, "All this." He gestured to her and then pointed to himself as if to say 'we.' "This is everything I want. But I'll be up there in that frozen place come January." He walked back to her and retrieved her from the open door, shutting it. "Thank you while I'm here, though not so when I leave."

## *Chapter Nineteen*
### *SARAH'S PASSING*

Sarah's hands twitched as she pushed the covers away from her. She felt more than heard her husband Will's light movements in the room, meant to disturb as little as possible. But soon she would leave, so it didn't matter. She would take as much of this world with her to remember when she went to that other side. Innis. Innis would be there. Even now she heard his voice more strongly. From the start, from the moment his eyes blinked at the bright light that would be his journey away, Sarah felt a fading of physical energy into a vaporous ether. His intact spirit nevertheless moved further away and lacked something she could hold in her hand. That pained her the most, not being able to hold his two-year-old hand crossing a street, grasp his seven-year-old fingers as she prepared a bandage for some childhood injury, feel the teenaged muscles of his arms when he hugged her, sweaty after a game of baseball. From this she understood the loss of the physical Innis.

"Hold still, Sarah. I'm trying to fix your blanket."

She found comfort in Will Crawford's cool hand on her forehead and blinked open her eyes to focus on his gentle face.

Tears stood in his eyes. "The fever's passed."

"Oh yes, Will. It's fine now. Fine." Her heart near broke for him. He knew what she meant. She would leave but would wait till he looked away. Better that way, less pain watching; the almost dead sought to ease the sorrow of their loved ones.

Sarah floated back to her dreams where she lived more than here. Her first dance and Will swinging her gently into a waltz. Her brothers and their young wives came home, all the kin celebrating her engagement to this wonderful man, this honest man who would be father to her beloved sons that she would carry and give birth to. She dreamt of Garnett, always the serious one, bringing her daffodils in spring in time for her birthday. He would miss her, and she regretted only not giving enough of her time to him. Her last words exhaled, "so sorry my son, but I loved you just the same."

"Hey Garnett. Phone for you; sounds like your Dad." A senior, Martin Blake, came to his room, tapping lightly on the door.

The closed doors of his fraternity brothers' rooms lined the dark hall as Garnett walked barefoot on the cold floor. He took the earpiece and spoke into the receiver.

"Is that you, Dad?" Garnett knew why his father called and his mind raced to find words he might say to make it easier for his father. "Are you okay?"

"Yes, son. Your mother…." Will Crawford stopped. The spoken words solidified the reality. If he didn't say it, then it didn't have to be true.

"Your mother was peaceful at the end, son. Very peaceful. Her words were for you."

Garnett heard his father's voice break, no other words

followed. He rushed to fill the space, the great clock standing in the hall measured time like a metronome between his desire to comfort his father and his ability to stutter out a few meaningless sentences.

"I'll leave right away."

"No, Garnett, that's why I called. Wait, wait till your finals tomorrow. Soon enough for you to be here."

Garnett knew what he meant; he'd be home, soon enough for a Christmas that would be anything but a holiday. No cheer, no warmth of a fireplace. Gone, all gone. The wind blew cold through the old fraternity house as he said his good-byes and took the stairs, like an old man, one, then the next, then another. He stopped toward the top and sat on the step, holding onto the bannister, and cried for the memory of his beautiful mother. *I hope you found rest. Both of you.*

The dining hall was quiet for a Friday morning before a holiday. Heavy mugs of coffee propped open textbook pages, preventing them from turning. Last-minute note-takers jotted down things to remember. Garnett's final exam pushed his mind and heart away from the things that really mattered. Somewhere in his psyche he knew he reacted to the inevitable news of his mother's passing, that all of this would matter again, someday. Garnett read through the remaining notes, hastily gathering the last-minute facts he needed, picked up his books, and swallowed the scalding coffee. Doctor Stanton was punctual, and Garnett wanted to arrive on time.

"Mr. Crawford." Garnett entered at the end of the study hall to see Professor Stanton removing his eyeglasses as he waited. Garnett took long strides to the front of the room. They shook hands more as colleagues now instead of teacher and student.

"I would expect you have everything in order for your trip up to New York." He spoke in a singularly Yankee and unmistakable New York accent.

"It will be a change, but I wonder whether this fellowship is such a good thing for me."

He knew as soon as he spoke that Stanton would roundly disagree and almost allowed a smile to form on his lips, settling instead for a twinkle in his eye because he could so accurately predict his professor's response.

"Sometimes, Mr. Crawford, one new step is a step into the future. This is one of them."

"I'm truly grateful that you considered me." He wanted to say more about how much the mentorship of this very intelligent man meant; tell him he guessed this help would put him squarely on a path toward something significant. Still, at only twenty-one, he had only a glimpse of the magnitude of this gift.

"Just show them what I've seen here and you'll be fine." Stanton straightened and cleared his throat. "I know this is a very difficult time for you. But don't abandon hope, my boy."

Garnett left Dr. Stanton and the warm building, pulling his heavy jacket closer to him against the cold wind as he climbed the hill to the Quad. The sun slid away west, away from Savannah. He saw silhouettes of a man and woman standing far away up yet another bleak and frozen hill, their backs facing him. Automatically, Garnett's hand shot up to greet them, call them to him. He knew them, the way they stood. But he froze in that moment because he swore to himself then and always afterward, that he saw Innis and his mother.

The wind carried a voice, and Garnett turned and looked back toward the library. The fading rays of sunshine illuminated a girl with long reddish hair wearing a beret, walking fast. Adelyn raised her hand as she hurried. He hesitated, not mentioning what he just saw.

Adelyn embraced him before he could speak. "I know, I know. I am so sorry, Garnett." Mindlessly, she kissed him on either cheek. "Your mother was an inspiration for me for a long time now. She's at peace..." She stopped, her next words, "at peace with Innis." Adelyn somehow knew.

He felt the cold air caught and melting between them and looked down and smiled at her heavy mittens, almost childlike; someone, no doubt her mother, had embroidered red roses on them. He mumbled an awkward "Thanks, Addie," and hugged her back.

"Let's get out of the cold." He took her hand, and she walked with him toward the bar and grill. "You remember this place, don't you?" He wanted to reassure her that it was okay to be here with him. "All done with your finals?" He helped her off with her coat at the booth at the back of the bar.

"Six o'clock must be the witching hour for this place." She shook her arms out of the coat sleeves. His raised eyebrow questioned her remark so she hurried to explain. "Last time here it was mighty quiet, too."

Garnett checked his first impulse, to tell her he had no agenda bringing her here. While he arranged his thoughts into sweet words, she took his hands in hers from across the table, her eyes shining in the light from the low-hanging lamp.

"Daddy called this morning to tell me. But I just got the message." Her voice lowered and held a grieving emotion. "Your mother was very beautiful, and gracious."

Adelyn could not tell him. He would never believe how she knew his mother had passed, how certain she felt about what she saw just before she called out to him as he stood on the Quad. Adelyn recognized Innis and Sarah at the crest of the hill. She told herself their images formed in her mind, because no words solidified the mystery of the apparitions. Instead, they floated in her mind intact, the two people she knew who left the earth for someplace else.

"You knew my mother?" When she nodded, he asked, "You spent time with her?"

"Living in Tulip Junction, I guess we all saw one another in passing. I met your mother almost two years ago, just before the Howard's Christmas Party. We bumped into her down here in Savannah shopping." Her heart skipped a beat as that day opened up in front of her, finding gloves in the dry goods store that would suit her green dress. She still held his hands and sensed an unusual communication between them, as though she sent him pictures just like the movies, and he saw them. Innis had been with his mother that day she met Sarah. He held Adelyn's hands. The thought must have passed from her to Garnett because he let go.

"Stop with this, will you." She knew he meant her sending thoughts to him.

Adelyn could not summon anger, not with him so wounded. "Stop what, Garnett?" She wanted him to tell her what she knew, that he had connected with the images through her thoughts.

"With this witchery of yours, whatever you want to call it." He suddenly lost the energy for anger, drained of all rancor toward his brother, who more than ever dwelt with their mother now, never to change. He wanted this, with Adelyn, this life with her. "I am so sorry; I always seem to be angry with you, and I don't mean to."

"I know, I know." She stood and went around to his side of the booth and sat next to him. He felt her body insinuate itself so completely against his that they melted together. "You know what you do to me." He stammered out the words, just short of a declaration. *So easy for my brother, so easy for Innis to profess love.*

Adelyn held his hand, turning the palm open. She told herself she needed to have his solid and corporeal hand in hers, to ground her, to keep her from escaping into that other place. How would she ever explain that since Innis died, she'd felt this strong pull from him, to follow him? "Yes, I know and I feel the same. I need things to be solid, to not float away, because Garnett, I'm afraid I'll float away myself."

Joy and happiness fill the holidays for young people unless tragedy strikes. In quick succession, Garnett lost his brother and then his mother. Sometimes they remained with him. He'd turn a corner and swear his eyes played tricks, as a fleeting vision would move just out of his sight. If asked about these happenings, though, no one except Adelyn would understand, he couldn't define them. And the darkest kept secret of all, somewhere in that dark place in his soul, he hid a mild jubilance. After all, Adelyn now drew close to him, more than he'd ever hoped. Did he think it would be this way? He asked himself that question at the end of each day when he laid his head on the pillow, and before he lost reason or consciousness. Awake, his guilt grew insurmountable.

He would rationalize, always the same way. *Yes, I can be happy with Adelyn, because, inevitably, we belong to each other. Yes, God has granted this gift to me. The loss of Innis grieves me. He has his own special place in my heart. I love him and always will. But if he were here, and she were his, would I love him? Yes, but differently, bitterly, despite my efforts not to.* This last thought would come much later, to the older, wiser Garnett in 1931, thinking back. For now he would finish a special internship in New York, and then go on to Harvard for yet another business program, an international venture. At Harvard, he would find he could easily learn French and Italian to converse with his colleagues in those countries. But he learned that every final negotiation always expressed itself in one's own language, the *lingua franca* of the mind. And much later, he'd learn the *lingua franca* of the heart that finally told him he had only half of Adelyn's heart.

# LETTER TO WILL CRAWFORD

## December 15th

*Dear Mr. Crawford,*

*Garnett and I spoke today, and Daddy called with the sad news of Mrs. Crawford's passing. My wishes and those of my mother and father are for you and for Garnett. I'll be riding back with some of the others and most likely will see Garnett when we come back to the Junction.*

*I have fond memories of Mrs. Crawford as I came to know her some in the last two years. She was a beautiful person and a wonderful mother.*

*Every girl seeks a model, someone they can try to be like. From the first time we met, I knew I wanted to be like Mrs. Crawford. I always felt very special when she spoke to me. I know how she loved you all.*

*May she rest in peace.*

*Adelyn Jackson*

*PS*

*Mama said you should come to Christmas dinner with our family.*

# Chapter Twenty
## *FAMILY CHRISTMAS*

Mary Jackson fluffed the ruffle at her neck while she perched on tiptoes in front of the hall mirror. "Mr. Jackson, I've asked a dozen times to have this mirror lowered. I can barely see anything in it. Adelyn, why don't you call Garnett and his daddy?"

Missus Jackson spoke to both her husband and Adelyn from the different vantage points of her thoughts, her personal needs alongside those of the two grieving members of the Crawford family. "I've thought of nothing else since Sarah passed. It would be criminal, not to mention unchristian, for them to be alone for Christmas dinner."

"Now, mother, all you have to do is slide over just a bit and look into that big old long mirror I had placed there just for such a thing as fixing ruffles and whatnot."

Captain Jackson projected his booming voice from inside the cavernous living room, big enough and frequently used as a ballroom on fancy occasions. He never addressed his wife's comments or suggestions directly because, after twenty and more years with her, he knew the decision had already been made. If she wanted the Crawfords to join them, she would have them, though the mirror might not be moved down so easily.

Adelyn headed to the back hall to phone Garnett. She had mixed feelings long before her mother uttered her last words about inviting the Crawfords to dinner. Her feelings jumbled together when it came to Garnett. Right now, and for no good reason, she felt they had left each other at the campus in frustrated instead of cordial circumstances. Uneasy about her affections for him and how easily everyone could see, she didn't relish sitting next to him all through a long dinner with everyone watching. Cicely would be watching for sure.

Anxiously she waited for the clicking to connect her to the operator, Sally Barnes. "Good morning, Sally." She waited. "Yes, Mother is fine. Yes, Daddy is too. Yes, we just got home last night for winter break."

Her anxiety at calling Garnett propelled her past the niceties and she got to the point.

"Please connect me to Mr. William Crawford's residence." She did not want to say "Garnett Crawford" because she feared Sally would fashion something between Adelyn and Garnett. She knew Sally had already made the connection to Innis. Almost two years of Innis courting her covertly, and at times not so quietly, she felt the constraints of small-town gossips. Mercifully, the loud buzzing ring began and drowned out her half-felt 'thank you.'

The line opened and his voice answered, "Hello."

"Garnett?" She fidgeted with the phone wire and almost dropped the earpiece, jumping in without waiting for his reply.

"Mama said we should have you and your daddy here with us for Christmas dinner. It will be just us, none of the other relatives." She didn't mention the letter she'd sent to Will Crawford.

"So, you got back okay?" Garnett always sounded like he'd just had a good run on the track at school.

"We had car trouble. The big car had a cold engine or something." She heard her voice sounding irritable. Not knowing what to say, she pushed on. "Of course, if you have other plans, you wouldn't be in any way obligated."

"So you got back to the Junction late?" He plowed through and wondered whether he grounded himself this way whenever he spoke with her. He admitted to himself that he needed that to keep his breathing and his heartbeat regulated.

"Garnett Crawford, Mama wanted me to call to ask if you would like to come to Christmas dinner here. Or are you otherwise committed?"

"Yes."

She heard mumbling, and she knew he was speaking to his father, but he had covered the mouthpiece with his hand.

"Yes what, Garnett?" She had had enough.

"I was just passing your family's invitation on to my father, and he appreciates your having us to dinner." Some more mumbling.

"Dinner is usually early so that Aunt May can get home for her own family holiday. Why don't you come on over after church? Mass is at ten...."

"I know what time Mass is, and I'll see you at church just like I have all of your life." He bit his tongue at saying more than he meant. It would never do to let Adelyn know how, over the years, she had been observed, though he marveled at this realization. *I never knew how much and how often she was just out of my focus.*

"Fine. Tell your daddy we're looking to see him."

"How about me?" Silence. "Adelyn."

"Yes." She looked at herself in the mirror near the phone, suddenly realizing mirrors hung all over her home. "Yes, we're looking to see you as well."

"It's nice of your folks to invite us, Adelyn. I'll take that as 'Yes, Garnett, I just can't wait to see you again.'"

Adelyn smiled as they each hung up the receivers of their old box phones. She knew Garnett smiled too, and she took comfort in knowing that she could help him through this sad time.

No Currier and Ives snow draped on fir trees here. It had been twenty years or more here in the deeper south since any real snow had fallen on the Jackson homestead. In the living room, tissue erupted out of gift boxes and spread from one end to the other of the cozy arrangement of overstuffed sofas and love seats. Midday in Tulip Junction would warm up considerably, so Captain Jackson banked the fireplace to a safe and moderate flame off several logs.

"As it is, I'm just glad the kitchen is far enough away from the dining room." Mary Jackson held up a new silk shawl. "A cooler place is always better when it comes to dining." She spoke to her family and no one, as she looked around the room. Her husband smoked his pipe, reading the papers, Aunt Grace with a cup of coffee, wide awake, yet with a dreamy look on her face. Cicely trying on new shoes that she'd outgrow before she'd wear them out. And Adelyn sat snugly next to her on the roomy love seat.

"Momma, that green is just delightful against your hair and lights up the color of your eyes." Adelyn reached over to her mother and surprised her with a kiss on the cheek. Her mother surmised that Garnett's coming to Christmas dinner brought out her thoughtfulness as much as her growing up to appreciate her mother.

A chill passed over Mary Love Jackson as she thought how the loss of Innis and then his mother may have forced maturity on her daughter faster than she, herself, would like to see. She sighed, as she thought how she could not protect her children from this sadder part of life. "We best start picking up. Cicely, help Adelyn. Wind up those ribbons, child, so I might use them again."

The sisters, still in their robes and slippers, made short

work of the boxes, stacking them in a neat pile, and Uncle Tyree took them all out to the back pantry. "Good kindling, when we need it," he said to no one in particular. Both girls ran up the back stairs to their rooms, now aware of the lateness of the day. Enticing aromas proclaimed the turkey and ham were well on their way to doneness, and Adelyn actually heard her stomach gurgle in anticipation, though she'd eat like a bird in front of Garnett. She opened her closet, searched for her green dress with the gored skirt, and thought how it made her slim body and waist look even thinner. She could swear she'd left it, just to the left of the front of the closet, but her school skirts and sweaters hung in front. Painstakingly, she pushed each successive hanger from left to right, as she dug deeper into the closet. At the very back hung her green dress.

"Damn." She pulled it to the front, her hair now a fright when she turned and looked into the mirror. She turned quickly, thinking she saw something fly past her vision. "Nothing." She shrugged her shoulders, slipped the dress over her head and straightened it as it fell against her body. Something scooted past again as she reached for her brush. Her heart jumped and then she saw her sister. "Cicely! Lands, you'll scare the soul right out of me."

Like a sapling that knew it would be a tall oak someday, Cicely moved her supple body with a natural grace, arms and legs longer still than they had been in early fall. "I didn't do nothin' to scare you," she insisted as she fell onto the little chaise lounge.

"Try sitting instead of jumping onto furniture, you gawky thing, you." Adelyn took her sister's chin in her hand and then hugged her.

"Stop, Addie, stop. What's the matter with you today, anyway? Pecking Mama's cheeks, kissing Daddy?" She stilled for a moment, then said in a slow drawl, "Maybe you're practicing on us till Garnett gets here." She jumped just out of Adelyn's reach and giggled all the way back to her room.

Adelyn brushed her hair back into place, glad for her decision to have it trimmed to a 'long cut' so that her curls could play off her face and fall to just above her shoulder. She thought it more dramatic. Looking closer, she examined her smooth skin, some color in the cheeks, and heard the clock chime in the hall downstairs. "Mama, it's nine. I'm ready if you are." By some miracle she hadn't discovered yet, she knew they would somehow get to church and back before twelve.

And Garnett and Mister Crawford would be coming back with them.

# Chapter Twenty-One
## *ADELYN IN THE WORLD*

Garnett sent photos of himself with his friends, all young men who, like him, had distinguished themselves at their respective alma maters, unexpectedly sedate, almost somber and wooden, posing for the picture. Adelyn would spy a little turn of the lip on one or a glint in the eye of another, hinting at the joyous and rambunctious times had by all with plenty of beer and heavy food. When Adelyn could, she did the same, but it wasn't the same, it was terribly different because she and Garnett had experienced a different and sometimes magical world, had seen the spirits of loved ones, traveling over the hill, Innis and his mother, hand in hand, leaving for some other place. She would write Garnett, but refrain from saying she dated other boys because he already knew.

Jeremy called on her first, whom she turned away at the door saying, "Someday you'll want to be friends with Garnett again, and you will have thrown it all away for a chance to say we went out on a date together to some silly football game." Besides, she counted Jeremy's girlfriend as her friend; she wouldn't endanger their friendship.

Adelyn had a definite moral code, and though occasionally flighty, she remained steadfastly loyal. More than anything else, she would never betray a friend. Innis had not been married, nor Garnett—loving one and then the other did not constitute a betrayal. Deep inside her soul lay a forgotten memory of being inside the body of Lucianne. Lucianne had not appeared to her in her dreams. That would come in time. For now, if anyone asked Adelyn about Innis and the girl from South County, she would not have an answer; in fact, she would not have understood at all. Adelyn basked in the luxury of ignorance through innocence. She had no way of knowing Lucianne's story back then, even with the many intimations.

## Chapter Twenty-Two
### *JANUARY 1923*

*"I'll never leave you like he does."* The soft, engaging voice coaxes her to feel stirrings of sensuous thrills flowing through her body. Adelyn looks into the mist that clouds her vision. *"You did. You left me all alone."* Her thoughts unerringly transmit her sarcasm, anger.

*"I'm still here, Sugar."* His voice carries the notion of a smile that she hears and imagines. *"You haven't looked for me hard enough."* She tries to follow his voice and moves toward a dress, white and floating.

"I wore that dress." She reaches out for it, and a face takes form and disappears almost as quickly. But not before she sees it.

"You have your Granny's look about you," Adelyn calls after the image. She wakes mumbling 'no,' and hears him once more.

*"Never mind her, forget her. She'll be nothing but trouble for you."*

The shock of Innis's voice comes after the dream. Her arms, straight and pinned to her sides, remind her of something but she wakes too abruptly to remember what that means. Six o'clock in the morning, the sun only dimly lighting the room—she springs up with energy when she realizes she leaves today for New York and for Garnett.

All dreams fade with the light of a living world.

"Hurry now, Adelyn. Trains wait for no one, not even you." Her mother's shrill call from the bottom of the stairs ripped her out of a reverie, a mood she often visited since she agreed to meet Garnett in New York City. The sound of her mother's voice tugged her away from the haze and into the focused image of herself in the mirror, her brush still in her hand.

"Coming, Mama." She hastily threw the brush into the opened valise that sat on her bed. Looking around the room, she spied her silk hosiery and a plain cotton pair of stockings, side by side, her mother's hint that it would be cold in New York. She should choose practical, not pretty.

"Because a red nose and a bad cold won't make you pretty. And that's what will happen if you insist on showing off those legs of yours." *Nothing gets past Mama.*

She and Mama had already packed her dresses into a steamer trunk, which she thought unnecessary for three days up north. A bead of moisture formed above her lip as she struggled with the zipper that stuck on her dress. One gentle tug and the slider loosened, letting her zip herself up. Her watch said ten o'clock. She'd been packing since six, and it just seemed that each time she remembered to pack one thing, another went missing. Sometimes her room possessed a magic about it—a scarf would be caught by a strong breeze and float just that moment longer to signify that spirits moved it as much as the air coming in through a window. All her life she had experienced this type of magic, with spirits who did not harm.

"After all, Tulip Jackson's ghost lives upstairs. We've all seen her. And the mirrors, I'm always catching one or the other of this family's ancestors peeking at me from the mirrors. Mama has noticed them, and she is the last one to put much stock in spirits."

"One more thorough look." She swirled in a long and slow circle; something caught her eye. A fog entered the room, neither wet, nor warm, nor cold, almost taking shape. A sharp ray of the sun glinting off metal distracted her, and she thought it was a silver coin on the rug. Bending to it she saw a silver pin shaped like an arrow, small and elegant. She plucked it up and slipped it into her purse. "Just what I needed for our dinner alone tomorrow." Her heart skipped when she thought that tonight Garnett would be holding her hand, making sweet conversation with her and polite chat with her mother. Her mother's shrill call brought her back. Adelyn rushed down the stairs and outside while Mr. Edward toted the heavy trunk into the back of the big sedan.

"You'll be the death of me yet. What were you fussing with that took you so long?" Mary Jackson sat up front in the shiny new sedan with Mr. Edward all decked out in his livery. Captain Jackson had hired him away from a race car driver after he observed his mechanical ability, tired of paying locals for less-than-adequate work. "Besides, mother, ain't that many mechanics worth their salt anywhere outside a city."

Adelyn happily sprawled out on the comfortable bench seat, wool plaid blanket draped over legs that wore silk hose and not plain cotton. She admitted only to herself that her mother had been right. She would just have to purchase a long new coat in New York to protect her against all that wind and cold air. She sighed thinking that, at almost twenty-one, she had to force herself to be more responsible. For a moment, she felt guilty about the long new coat. It had been a long hard eighteen months since Garnett left.

Leaning over the front seat, she responded to her mother, "I was looking for just the right piece of jewelry to wear when we dine out tomorrow night."

She pulled a silk scarf out of her pocket and unwrapped the silver arrow. Turning it over she saw that it had tiny diamond chips along each point. Though small and delicate, the stones sparkled brightly, and you couldn't help but notice the pin, even in a dark room. She decided to wear it in her hair. "Look, Mama, I know I've seen this before."

She dropped the jewelry into her mother's hand who adjusted her eyeglasses to see it more clearly. Adelyn felt memory creeping up with the answer, but her youthful impatience moved it back to a safe place.

"It is old, Adelyn, from an earlier time. You found this in your room? Must be it was in that valise or the steamer trunk. Might have been Aunt Grace's, though I don't recall ever seeing Grace wear anything this fine." Handing it back over the seat, she voiced what her daughter had been thinking: "I'm sure Garnett will find it very lovely if you wear it to decorate your hair."

The rhythmic clump-clump of the wheels wherever they ran over the protruding seam of the road to Savannah settled her mind. Adelyn pulled a briefcase to her lap, one of her father's oldest, and took out her American history book and read several eye-witness accounts of the Great War. She read the footnotes and wrote the names of the references, then flipped to the end of the chapter to read the list of books, diaries, speeches, and newspaper clipping dates. She would go to the archives at the New York World-Telegram & Sun building tomorrow, Garnett arranged to take her, while her mother visited a cousin, *the one who defected and became a Yankee.*

"Did you notice those azaleas already out, down on the front walk?" Her mother wore a hat with netting that protected her face better than Adelyn's cloche helped her. They stood near the tracks when a dusty wind kicked up, blowing particles of sandy soil into Adelyn's eyes. She shielded her face and mouth best she could and turned her back to the wind.

"Honestly Mama, I didn't really see the flowers. Seems like no time to be admiring the first signs of spring." She groaned in annoyance and impatience to be out of Savannah and on their way. Everything impeded them. They finally made their way onto the train, following a porter to their pullman car.

"Thank you." Adelyn handed the porter a dollar coin for helping her up the steps and into the train. They settled into seats facing one another in the luxurious compartment. A small table placed between them held individual tea and coffee pots. A whistle blew outside, and bells clanged, followed by the "all aboard" shouted down the length of the train station. The train pitched forward with a start and then began to pick up speed from a halting rhythm to one that resembled a regular beat.

"Now, did Garnett say he would be there when we arrived?" Missus Jackson straightened her slim skirt, and Adelyn noticed she was wearing navy blue silk hose. *So much for warning me to err on the side of comfort and not fashion.* "I imagine those are going to keep your legs warm enough." She couldn't resist the tease.

"No such thing, little girl. Your mother is old enough to make her own decisions, and my long coat will do just fine." She smoothed out her stockings, and Adelyn smiled, knowing her mother wore a garter belt *or worse yet, a corset,* and not rolling her hose.

Adelyn poured some tea for her mother. "Garnett called long distance early this morning to say he'll see us tonight and then early tomorrow." She glanced out the window at the land and early budding trees as they blurred past her vision. "This ride is making me sleepy, Mama. I think I'll just stretch out on this seat and sleep a bit. I didn't sleep well last night, dreaming and restless about the trip."

"What were you dreaming?" Missus Jackson believed in dreams as reality, and never bothered about putting any barrier between the two.

"Now Mama, everyone knows you love to interpret dreams. But I am curious about one thing. I never actually heard you relate any dream of yours."

Her mother took Adelyn's remarks at face value and sighed, "No darling. Your mama has had dreams. My brother, Brady, when he passed or just before, I can't remember which it was. But he came to me and said to not grieve too deeply, he was going to be okay. I thought that to mean he would heal and recover. Poor dear, he was telling me he was leaving us."

"I want to nap some." Adelyn knew she sounded cross or cranky, something to do with her mother's remarks about Uncle Brady. She couldn't remember the coma and how spirits visited her when she lay in Lucianne's white dress, arms tight by her sides in that coffin. She pulled a light blanket over her legs and dropped into sleep immediately.

She walks out of the compartment and into the hallway, for a moment standing in the hall and seeing Innis at the other end. He stands near someone, a girl, the white dress that looks so very familiar to Adelyn.

"What are you doing here?" She calls down the hall to Innis and he immediately appears by her side. She knows she should be afraid of all this, Innis appearing, the strange girl in white.

"Sugar, you know. You should not be leaving Savannah and Tulip Junction. I can't follow you up there; I can't have you feel my love for you there."

"You mean Garnett, don't you?" Her voice not fully her own, a blend of some other voice that sounds familiar to her. The girl at the end of the hall vanished, but Innis, so flesh-and-blood real, Adelyn can't help but reach out and touch him.

"Clever girl, solving a problem that you won't remember when you wake up. Yes, my power isn't so great when my brother is near." Innis let her touch his sleeve so full of his arm and muscle.

The train lurched to a stop. Adelyn woke with a start. This time, in this dream, she held onto the memory of it, and heard Innis. She rubbed her eyes hard, aware that she was trying to get out of his world and into this one. The thought alarmed her, the thought of another world. She sat up and forced a smile because her mother's face registered real concern. "What, what, Mama?"

"Adelyn, honey, you've slept for hours. You were talking in your sleep, again. It sounded like a nightmare." Mrs. Jackson arranged her hair and began to pull on her coat. "No time to talk now, let's settle in at the hotel."

"I slept all the way from Georgia?" A whisper of many dreams passes through Adelyn. She stiffens like a cat, stretching the fatigue out of her system, and feels her blood flow through her. *Innis, I dreamt of him and a girl in white.*

"Gracious, Adelyn. You have me worried. First sleeping as much as you did, and now not remembering the sandwiches that you gulped down with hot tea when we got to Baltimore. I'd call a doctor if it hadn't been for that appetite. Lands!"

Energy surged in the night air as they emerged from the overheated railway car into the Grand Central Station: the excitement of the city, people rushing about even late at night, all around Adelyn. Still close to her heart and mind lingered the dream of Innis she could not ignore. The string, so taut, had momentarily but unmistakably sprung, and she had moved beyond Innis's powers to hold her, even as she felt his pull. She could not say what any of this actually meant. She let it blend into the other excitement, the real and tangible New York City. "You best put on that coat. It's a cold night."

"No more nightmares." She muttered an assertion to herself and pulled her coat closely around her, though it barely covered her knees. All the while she remembered pieces of conversation with Innis, wondering whether they happened before he died or as part of the dreams now. She shook her head against the question of whether dreams have their own separate reality.

And then she saw him, his broad shoulders and a bowler hat, which she deduced all the young men must be wearing in New York. She smiled at the crease in his brow from frustration at the crowds of people blocking his way to her. Garnett's arm shot up in a salute. Then he pressed the hat more securely on his head and used his arms and hands like a plow in soft earth, slicing through people on either side, parting them and reaching her. For just a moment, he forgot his future mother-in-law's presence, grabbing Adelyn to swing her around in uproarious glee. *Yes, and I love him as much.* Adelyn squeezed his arms and flung hers around his neck, leaning into it and smelling the warm and earthy Garnett against some expensive and subtle cologne. She registered his new sophistication and smiled to herself.

Then came the bustle as they all followed the porter with her steamer trunk, placed into a cab with very little confusion. Mary Jackson recorded all of this in the back of her mind, pleased that the more proper brother *except for a short public display of affection,* would have her daughter. *If he hadn't already.*

Garnett opened the door to the cab in front of their hotel. Adelyn watched him assess her mother's fatigue, and her own. "I thought a hot drink might be a good idea, here in the bar," he gestured from the immense lobby, "but I think I'll just escort you up to your rooms and see you early tomorrow morning."

She smiled, grateful for his thoughtfulness. Sarah Crawford had taught him well. In a more sedate manner, they briefly hugged, and he took her mother's hand for a space of a moment.

"Well, Mama, you sure thought of everything." Adelyn

surveyed the suite while her mother tipped the bellhop. They stood in a common sitting room separating two bedrooms off at angles from one another. Adelyn dropped her gloves on the coffee table and entered the room where the bellhop placed her trunk. The double doors to the bedrooms swung inward, turning into discreet screens blocking the view of the bed and any dressing gowns or shimmy from view. *Or my silk stockings from Garnett's view.*

Her mother called her from the sitting room. "This is very airy, roomy."

Adelyn noticed the opaque glass set into the maple frames of the bedroom doors, to keep prying eyes from seeing what they ought not. *If mother could, she would have ordered them just so.*

"I'm soaking, Mama," Adelyn responded to her mother's shrill call. Moments after her mother tipped the bellhop, Adelyn stripped down in her room, turning on the faucets to fill the giant tub in her own bathroom. She slowly slipped into the steamy water and reduced the tap to a thin trickle to keep the bath hot.

Mary Jackson, a great believer in personal privacy, would not interrupt Adelyn luxuriating in her tub. Adelyn sipped some Bombay gin from a little flask, thinking how college had taught her more than history. The fiery gin washed over her knotted mind the way the hot water soothed and cleansed her body. Startled, she'd fallen asleep momentarily, almost submerging. She tightened the screw top of the flask and laid it on a chair near the tub.

"Adelyn. Did you see where my I left my brush?"

"No, Mama." *She cannot seem to leave me in peace.* Adelyn pulled the plug on the tub and watched the water rapidly swirl as she rubbed her skin, first with a towel and then with some fragrant lotion. She looked at her naked self in the mirror with a frank and honest appraisal of her thin, almost hipless body with small breasts, remembering Innis's hands. *Stop.* She pulled back from this natural tendency to think of her body in terms of Innis and their intimacy. *Just a child, even only yesterday.*

Her mother did her own appraising as Adelyn floated into the sitting room in a short nightgown opened at the neck. The room felt like a sauna.

"Lands, child. Where is your dressing gown? You'll catch your death." Mary Jackson made room for her daughter on the large sofa, and Adelyn curled up with a couch pillow, legs to one side. She pulled a throw shawl over her bare arms and neck, more for propriety, her mother clearly not comfortable with so much flesh showing.

"Mama, this room feels like Savannah in June. That hissing sound coming from those radiators is heat rising from the rooms below." Adelyn dismissed her light clothing with this excuse. Ignoring her, Missus Jackson held up the brush that no doubt had not gone missing—her mother's way of getting her daughter out of the tub to join her. Mary Jackson hated being alone, her family doting on her to make certain she always had someone with her, most of the time, anyway.

"I heard you one night, thought you were talking to your sister or someone." For Mary Jackson, she saw it as a momentary break when Adelyn awoke at the train station till now, sitting in their hotel room; the same being true with the thread of her conversation. She simply picked up where, several hours ago, she'd left off about Adelyn talking in her sleep.

It took Adelyn a few minutes to make sense of her mother's patter. Years of her mother's pieced-together conversations lasting over an entire day forced Adelyn to remember what topic her mother now settled on, and prepared Adelyn for the break between the train station and now. Adelyn credited her ability to recall pieces of information for tests taken at school with this disjointed and ongoing conversation with her mother.

"I told your father, I did. That you were troubled. No one goes talking in such long conversations with someone in their sleep unless they're troubled." Mary Jackson held up her exquisitely manicured hand. She addressed her daughter's unspoken remarks with, "I know, I know. And your father would agree with you. You were pouring yourself into your studies. I told him, it was too much and so short a time, from when you lost Innis."

"What did I say?" Adelyn looked at her own nails, aware that a good manicure should be an early morning task. "In my sleep. Who was I talking to?"

"Well, truth be told, you were talking to…it had to be… Innis." She went on to avoid interruption. "You were asking him who he loved most, then there was talk about someone he knew at church." She rushed on. "It is unseemly for you, now almost two years past, and you and Garnett…"

Adelyn prided herself on a mind capable of keeping two dialogs going at once, that special talent never called into play more than at this moment. She responded to her mother's musings with short remarks as her thoughts whirled around images of Garnett and all the intervening days, from the funeral until this night, and experienced all the missing of him. The other side of her repeated an old refrain, Innis loving her, whispering to her of her sweetness, of his impossible attraction to her. She got close to her mother and cuddled near, the way she did as a child. But recognizing this, she said goodbye to any facet of a lingering childhood.

"I dream but don't seem to remember, so I'm not troubled. I feel something different, more grown-up, with Garnett." She thought how her parents saw him, so steadfast, holding his father's business interests up in such family turmoil. She knew they thought him the better choice for her, but she also knew they would have rallied around Innis as much.

Her remarks must have been what her mother needed to hear, not to mention her daughter's closeness on the sofa. Her mother could hold her, just one more time, and recall all of Adelyn's babyhood and childhood when she could dote on her.

"There was one thing I do remember hearing because it wasn't just one night. There were many. You were asking him why did he leave you and when was he coming back. You were planning on marrying?" Adelyn heard some dread and a good measure of embarrassment. "Only last week I asked your daddy whether you should take a year off from school after Innis was gone."

"I felt stronger connections to Innis in Tulip Junction than on campus." She tried to placate her mother's real concern. "I guess my studies were a godsend." Convinced her mother had heard more, their intimacy somehow revealed, Adelyn's real concern lay in her fear that Mary Jackson and her father thought she should take time off from her studies.

To ward off any further possibility of this happening, she lightened their mood. "No one can be faulted for a dream, now can they, Mama?" She stood and wrapped the blanket around her, and kissed her mother's soft cheek, hoping her tone would set her mother at ease.

Adelyn tossed one hot pillow after another to the foot of the bed. She slid out of the lavender-scented sheets and heaved the heavy window up to let in some air. The hissing steam from the radiators muffled the sound of her movements. She sat on a chair near the window looking out at the cityscape of lights twinkling like so many stars. She thought of the black sky at home and breathed deeply of the night air. The clock on the dresser said 2:30 a.m. yet cars moved, and trolleys skirted past them as if the sun shone at high noon.

Her pulse quickened with so much activity, and she wondered about Garnett. Would he be with his friends at some saloon in the Bowery? Surely he didn't have his nose in a book in his room in a hotel further downtown. She fussed in her daytime purse to find a cigarette, feeling sure the smell of smoke would be drawn out of the window as it pulled the heat away from her bed. Maybe she'd get to sleep.

*What holds me?* She blew the smoke out and rubbed

her temple where it ached from thinking. The answer met her question: *all these dreams.* She didn't have to say his name because Innis permeated her dreams. On many sleepless nights like this she pondered how different her life would be if Innis lived still. She focused on details: she would have been on campus with Garnett, and Innis would have risen in his law practice. From two years of his courtship, she knew Innis would never have brooked his brother's interference with her. And Garnett? His respect for his brother had limits, she knew that with certainty. His passion ran too deep.

The smoke unfurled from her cigarette as she thought of Garnett—how well she knew him and how much time they spent together. A chill came on her, a momentary spasm, as she realized she loved Garnett now, deeply and more fully than she did Innis. *I have matured, and this love has matured from a sixteen-year-old's childhood infatuation into something real.* It was late as Adelyn pushed the window closed and jumped back into the bed, which had finally lost all the body heat she had generated earlier.

Early the next day after her manicure, Adelyn stepped out of the hotel's revolving doors and surveyed the trollies, taxis, and horse-driven surreys. Turning toward the south, she could see Garnett walking down the broad Fifth Avenue, his coat open, flapping against the wind whenever he crossed one of the streets. His smile told Adelyn he saw her.

Her mother absently waved her silk scarf, as he got closer.

"Mama, please quit that. Goodness, we're not back home in Tulip Junction, out on our lawn." The brisk wind somehow magnified his masculinity; she decided he looked outstanding. His white shirt against his serious dark suit made him look every inch the captain of the financial world he hoped to be. She offered him her hand when she really wanted to embrace him.

"Garnett, you're looking very healthy. This Yankee weather must appeal to you."

Mary Jackson gave him a short hug and stood back to appreciate how handsome he looked. "My, my. Your daddy must be very proud of you. Adelyn is right, the Yankee environment is a tonic for you. I spoke to your daddy just yesterday, and he sends his best wishes."

Garnett spoke directly to Mrs. Jackson, though when she looked away distractedly, his eyes drank in Adelyn. She sensed an almost animal-like covetousness in him. Neither of them trusted their eyes not to betray all that lay between them.

"Now Garnett, I know you will take good care of Adelyn while I visit with my cousin Candace. She's my first cousin on the Love side of the family and married to that banker from the Middle West after he established himself here in New York." She prattled on while snaking her fingers into her kid-skin gloves. "Adelyn said she had some research for a history class."

"Don't you worry, Mrs. Jackson. I have a friend at the World-Telegram & Sun archives, and he expects us at ten-thirty. He can help her find the editions she wants." Garnett nodded to the hotel's doorman to flag a taxi and within a few moments would have Mary Jackson conveyed to an address on the Upper East Side.

"We'll be here in the lobby waitin' on your return." The doorman swung around in surprise to hear such country-sounding remarks. Garnett cursed his down-home inflections that took hold when he spent too much time with Adelyn's mother. The cab whisked her away, a plume of smoke pouring out of the taxi's exhaust on this cold day.

The floors in the old World-Telegram & Sun building creaked as Adelyn's heels tapped along sharply behind Garnett's friend, Mitchell Weinberg. His fuzzy red hair and piercing dark green eyes blinking behind large eyeglasses fascinated her.

"You'll have to excuse me for rushing you like this, Miss Jackson. I'm used to running behind long-legged creatures like your friend here." He gestured toward Garnett who walked alongside Adelyn. "Oh, here we are."

Mitchell consulted some notes he took when Adelyn described her interest in infantry staging camps in 1918. Foot-high lettering on high signs marked the contents of shelves that stretched for several rooms. Each shelf had layers of newspapers in long sheaves separated by wooden slats. Mitchell pulled a heavy tome onto a table on wheels, and he and Garnett moved it into a large room that looked more like a barn for newspaper. There, Adelyn lost herself in reading while Garnett and Mitchell stepped outside the room and talked quietly. She had taken her notebook with her and wrote dates and figures down; she immersed herself in the pages of splendid journalistic reporting of young men returning from war. Her excitement grew as she saw the connection between their weariness and then the flu symptoms doing what the war had not, killing them, hundreds of young men, one cousin and Uncle Brady included. She heard Garnett clearing his throat, pulling her from her concentration. Mitchell and Garnett had grown quiet, waiting for her. Looking up and at her wristwatch, she saw it was one o'clock already. Adelyn closed her notebook, sure that she could have stayed there for hours and hours.

"Mitchell, please forgive me for taking so much of your time. Your work here fascinates me, researching and finding important information. Didn't you say you had a request from a member of Congress?"

"More than once. Yes, fascinating." He looked about the room, lost for a moment himself in the annals of history, then turned to Adelyn. "I hope you found what you needed."

How many steps do we retrace when we seek to unlock a secret, one that we kept from ourselves, a fact there all along but somehow we ignored it? Adelyn would count this evening as the first misstep and a secret that got away from her.

She never would have guessed as they held each other's hands and felt the electricity between them that interruptions, an unraveling, approached. Garnett lost himself in her presence; she felt loved, she felt treasured, coveted, almost a prisoner, captured. Lunch in the Central Park, the French restaurant where their fingers entwined, the food they barely tasted for love of each other, all impossibly perfect.

"This will sound crazy, but from the first day, I knew you would be with me." His face blushed while he said this, even above a ruddy outdoors complexion. He fidgeted with his spoon instead of stirring his coffee. He repeatedly pulled her hand across the table. "I want you to be mine, alone. I want you to marry me." Adelyn paused; his face grew dark and he scowled. "Don't break my heart. You haven't said anything. Why?"

Adelyn covered his face with her eyes, each glance another layer of affection. Her voice wouldn't come because she pictured it all again. His strong arms lifting her from the sofa that day at Delia's when she was only sixteen. His voice always in command even in mutual grief. "I'm not saying anything because you're not leaving me much space." She, too, fidgeted but not with a coffee spoon. Her nervous energy found its way into a flutter of her heart, and a racing of her pulse.

He motioned to the waiter and moments later they walked a narrow and desolate path that would lead them back to the hotel. He stopped near a bench and pulled off his gloves. "Here." He handed her a ring, rubies, emeralds, and two diamonds on either side. "Christmas colors." They both said it at the same time. *That Christmas. He had to know Innis knew me by then. He had to.* But she could only say, over and over, as he kissed her eyes, her mouth, her neck, "Yes, yes."

"I had a dickens of a time to get to see your papa. I met him at Waycross, at the station. I couldn't chance you would be home. I had to have that part of it out of the way."

"What do you mean?" Her eyebrows arched. "Asking Daddy before me?" She wanted to feel insulted but knew he did the right thing. Garnett grabbed her arm, afraid she would leave.

"I had to ask him. What if he said no?" Garnett kissed her again and they finally made their way to the hotel.

And then it almost all fell away. They had no preparation, no clarion calls from large trumpets to signal the direction it all had to take.

"Adelyn, I hope you're not dawdling in there." Missus Jackson found herself once again waiting on her daughter and the last-minute adjustment of her wardrobe. She wondered how a dress without any corset, like the one Adelyn wore, could possibly take that long to put on. Ready to call out once more, and this time with authority, her daughter's appearance in the doorway appeased Missus Jackson, Adelyn a vision in navy blue silk with jet-beaded beribboned streamers to below her knee, though the hems seemed to be climbing every year. Missus Jackson wanted to blush, yet found a way to quell the emotion. After all, the girls all wore them that way.

"At least you're wearing dark hose." Having made what might sound like a slight toward the wardrobe choice, she quickly covered with, "And such a good decision." She gestured, "Turn around; let me see."

Adelyn obliged as she pirouetted in a circle and then back again, the glint of the diamond pin catching the light. She saw her mother's expression. "I know; I saw it in the mirror. It does look good, doesn't it?" She began to pull on her gloves. "I want to get to the lobby before Garnett arrives."

"I am certainly not the one detaining us, my dear." Her

mother held the door open for Adelyn. "Besides, it's not always good to be on time."

"I think I've made him wait long enough, Mama." She glanced once more in the mirror and realized how, at home, she avoided ever looking too directly at her own image. A chill caught her shoulders, but she shook it off. Her mind moved quickly in an attempt to resolve this phenomenon of shunning mirrors at home. *As though someone stands behind me, always just out of sight, and my body hides them from me.*

Adelyn sensed her mother contemplated her remark about Garnett's waiting.

They left for Delmonicos where friends of Garnett would attend with their wives or girlfriends. Mary Jackson spoke to each of the young people in turn, about careers or the girls completing college like Adelyn, and about babies to the few already married. They enjoyed a festive dinner, full of sparklers placed on a celebratory cake. Her mother's eyes filled with tears at the Christmas engagement ring, and quietly remarked how Sarah Crawford would be proud to see her son accomplishing so much. At Garnett's insistence, the three of them drank two bottles of wine, one of them champagne. Her mother would sleep soundly.

They dislodged themselves from the taxi onto one of the side streets downtown. Garnett took her hand and led her to a door that looked like an apartment. Two sharp knocks and a peep hole opened; a man nodded, waited for the password. "Carnival season," Garnett mumbled.

"Where did you tell that taxi driver to take us?" Adelyn adjusted her rolled-up stockings and straightened her slinky dress. "I thought you said 'back room'." Garnett put his finger to his lips to signal her to whisper.

The peephole closed, and the door opened. Garnett entered first with Adelyn trailing behind him as he held her in a tight grip. People packed the sweaty, smoky room, sipping drinks with ice cubes out of coffee mugs. One table held at least ten men in evening formal wear who openly sipped from glasses of bubbling champagne, and the subdued lighting made it all romantic. Garnett joined a younger crowd of men in suits with young women wearing glittering dresses. Adelyn, Garnett, and his friends took turns toasting one another and soon drank their way to an alcoholic haze. The orchestra played racy, hot Dixieland jazz, then would switch to swarthy and dark slow music.

"It's new, isn't it? C'mon. Let's dance this one." Garnett pulled her to her feet and surrounded her with his body. "It's a tango." He breathed heavily. "I heard that Valentino danced the tango here just last week."

Adelyn never knew a more exciting evening and began to think of reasons to leave Georgia for good. Garnett's face scowled some form of disapproval, and she whispered in his ear to further tantalize him. "You're not the only one who keeps up with fashion." She followed his movements; his body signaled her left and right legs as he kept no space between them. The dance lasted long and ended with her body curved down and his almost laying on top. "And, no, I wasn't dancing with Valentino last week." She teased him, and he let her.

Garnett led her back to the tiny table in front of the dance floor and wiped his face with a handkerchief. "I'll be right back." As he left, the band went into a spirited "Clap Hands Here Comes Charlie" and the dancers crowded the floor, all the young women dancing the Charleston. Adelyn jumped to her feet and danced with them, relishing the attention of a few old, portly financial titans. At least, she thought that's what they might be.

Garnett came back at the finish, and she settled at their table, next to him. "Don't you know those women are mostly prostitutes? You can't be up there, dancing with them."

For the space of a moment, she lowered her head, surprised and chastened, but then the wild something in her took possession. "I'm in New York City. I don't see any kin, do you, Garnett? I think we're safe from Savannah Society News."

She coaxed a semi-smile, and the band drew them up from their table into a slow dance. She hummed to the song, "What'll I do when you are far away…." The words struck something deep in both of them as they danced closer, Adelyn's imminent departure the next day, the long winter without one another.

They didn't speak as the song ended, but hastily threw on their coats and left for Garnett's hotel. They tacitly felt their movements more than spoke their intentions, as she lingered near the door of the lobby and he got his key from the night attendant. Long years of hotel work had taught the solitary man to look otherwise and not at Adelyn as the two young people took the lift to his floor.

She thought of the times they had been together, but this time they were engaged, and she turned the pretty ring around and around her finger, watching the diamonds sparkle and savoring the true red and green of the other stones. They made love tenderly and quietly, two people who cared for each other. They fell asleep and woke to a phone call.

"Good morning, sir. This is your three o'clock morning call." The night attendant's voice informed Garnett. "Okay." He had thought to ask for a call in case this very thing had happened. Adelyn stirred and miraculously plumped up her hair to where it had been hours before.

"Don't worry, Garnett. Mama will be fast asleep when I get back. She has these potions she takes to sleep soundly. That, and the extra bottles of wine." Adelyn pulled the hose up and then rolled them down to her thigh.

He watched her sultry moves and listened to her sultry voice. "We should hurry, or I won't be able to let you go." He crossed in front of her where the light sparkled against something in her hair. Bending close he touched the diamond pin, asking, "What's this?" Looking more closely, he saw the diamonds shaped like an arrow. "He gave you this. You wore it only a week after…," but he didn't finish, then, "a week after he had you."

She felt the painful tug as he plucked the pin and strands of hair from her head. "Ouch. What on earth are you doing?" She held her hand to the place where he pulled. "Are you crazy? I have no idea in heaven what you mean." But then her mind filled with lost memories of a time when Innis had gently pinned the diamond arrow in her hair, saying to her, "Adelyn, you've pierced my heart." At sixteen she had giggled self-consciously, now all of it came flooding back.

"Four years? You expect me to remember something that happened four years ago? I was barely a woman. How dare you?" She tore at her hand and wrung her fingers till they swelled, trying to pry off the engagement ring. "I won't do this. I won't be a part of this." She flung the ring at him and her coat over her shoulders.

All the while Garnett took stock of everything, experienced it all as if he floated above it as it all happened below him. "Don't." He pulled her to him as he realized what had just happened. "Please, don't."

"You go to hell." She slammed the hotel door.

*Renée Ebert*

# *PART III*

*Renée Ebert*

## Chapter Twenty-Three
### *THE BREAK-UP AND BEYOND*

Rain turned to sleet, and Adelyn cursed the entire night as the cab took her back to her hotel. *Garnett, this weather, the world.* She fumbled with her gloves, thankful they covered her bare arms as she wrapped her coat around herself more firmly. The doorman rushed to her with his circus tent of an umbrella, another reason to be thankful. She steeled herself against the possibility of her mother waking as she returned, which kept her clearheaded and forced the discipline on her of dropping her emotions somewhere between Garnett's hotel room door and the one that she now carefully opened into her hotel suite. She turned the key in the door with a shaky hand.

A small lamp emitted a dim light, enough to negotiate the room without bumping into anything large or noisy. *Please God, let her sleep on, for now.* Adelyn rushed to strip out of her clothes and into her nightgown; this time she hastily tied the ribbons in a bow and she did the same with her dressing gown. She eased between the silky sheets, faintly aware of the lavender scent coming from sprigs that some maid had taken the time to spread out between the sheets. The aroma had a softening effect on her jangled nerves as she lay on her back breathing the cool air from the window left open to stave off the suffocating heat of the radiators.

Though she welcomed sleep, she struggled to make sense of the evening, from beginning to end, because she could not believe that one small thing, a silver and diamond pin, would cause that explosive change in Garnett. Her mind flitted from one scene to another, dinner, dancing, the gin. Could it have been tainted liquor? Bootleg gin or Champagne in fancy bottles? Something in her said no to bad gin or bad champagne. She left all the evening behind her and somehow, gratefully, fell asleep.

Across town, Garnett sat in hazy confusion. He moved in fits and starts every time his mind came back to the two or three short events in the room that ended the evening. As each thought played out he moved rapidly toward following her. His mind would not stay on point, however, and he sat down again on the bed to contemplate fragmented memories of the evening. Finally, he dressed, his coat on, his white silk bow tie dangling, hatless and gloveless. He rushed down in the lift, waved away the cab, and walked in the direction of Adelyn's hotel.

The deliberate, well-planned part of him wanted to make sense of it. He pictured her face, her body, the length of her shoulders to her back. He tried to conjure a common-sense answer to her actions, to his own. He finally hailed a lonely cab on the lonely avenue and listened to the tires on the paved road of lower Manhattan, all plans thrown out the window like so much smoke from his cigarette. He threw that out as well along with the idea to confront her again. *With my ridiculous jealousy of Innis?* He thought further back to the morning and how stolidly she had researched, took notes, became enthralled with the subject of the influenza and how it infected all those young soldiers. These thoughts just made him more furious with his own stupid lack of control, because now he recalled his jealousy-tinged remarks at lunch. He painfully recalled how he forced her to justify her actions, her feelings. *Does she love me, then?* And he knew she did.

No one milled about the lobby of her hotel, but a few remained in the coffee shop where he gravitated. He thought he recognized a man sitting alone at a table. Though his hair had turned mostly gray, he saw evidence of a young man's face that looked familiar.

"Can I sit with you?" Garnett waved to the waiter who bustled over, even at four o'clock in the morning. "I'll have what he's having." He gestured to the man who raised his cup of coffee. The man paused until the waiter set down the cup and saucer and returned to the kitchen, then pulled a flask out of his coat pocket, dragging Garnett's cup to himself and pouring liquor into it. "That'll be some fine brandy, son, for that coffee." He pushed the cup back in front of Garnett, the brandy's aroma warm and sweet as it mingled with the hot coffee.

"Do we know one another? I could swear...." Garnett sipped the coffee and brandy, appreciating its warmth as it rolled down his throat. The urge to drink it all filled him, and he drained the cup. Another appeared before him, and the stranger fortified it with more brandy.

"Sure do, son." He looked kindly at Garnett and shook his head in a sad way.

"You feel sorry for me. Why?" Garnett quaffed his refill, and he felt light-headed. "'Cause you can't possibly know. Can you? That I so thoroughly threw away my own happiness tonight?"

"Listen, son. It's not too late. Give in to your feelings for her. She's yours, not your brother's."

Startled that this stranger should know so much about

him, Garnett sat up straighter, glancing into the mirror that lined the wall near their booth. He looked closely at his heavy-lidded and weary eyes and ran his hand along the red stubble of a beard. Looking over toward the man, he saw no image of him in the mirror. Only his own.

"Who are you?" He framed the words as he quickly looked back at the man.

"You'll see my face in your mirror when you are much older and hopefully somewhat wiser, son."

A hard knock woke him as someone poked him in the shoulder.

"I don't know why I came down here. But I am certainly glad I did." Adelyn stood over him, looking as bright as the rising sun.

"What?" he looked around the empty coffee shop.

"The front desk recognized you and called and thank God, Mama was still asleep. It's almost seven o'clock."

Garnett stood up. "Please, please."

"I don't want a scene here." Adelyn had looked to see the coffee shop deserted and allowed his embrace. Her body stiffened, a signal against anything that might be considered questionable behavior. They took the elevator up.

"Five, please." He spoke to the elevator operator. He prayed she would not contradict him, and she didn't. They got off two flights below her own. The hallway as deserted as the coffee shop had been, he embraced her again, and she let him. His lips touched her face and hovered over her lips until she tipped her head up and accepted his mouth open and on hers.

"Just let me hold you. Don't ever leave me. Promise." His voice came in short sobs from a deep, deep place. He had grasped her to him and hugged and hugged. No passion, no sex, only love, and a desire to be forgiven.

Adelyn did a curious thing—she took his face in both her hands and studied him. Her eyes scanned his brow, his cheeks, his chin, then his eyes again, for a long time, and then his lips, where she kissed him fully, this time her mouth open and sultry but loving, too. "I love you, Garnett. And I know how much you love me." She smiled. "Let's not waste time. Let's have babies and a home and a wonderful life."

# Chapter Twenty-Four
## *LIFE TOGETHER*

Listless in the heat, Adelyn walked from veranda to back porch and then down the path to the stables. She didn't go in to see her beautiful thoroughbred, but instead walked alongside the long wall, her hand trailing along its rough surface. She stopped and looked at her dirty palm.

"Damnation." She opened the faucet to run water over the dusty smudge on her palm and fingers, admired the sparkle the diamonds and gems in her ring gave off when the water fell over them, delightfully cool as it ran down her wrists. Troubling thoughts came as her mind circled back to cool compresses meant to suck the fever out of her sixteen-year-old body, long ago. *The days I met them both, Garnett and Innis.*

"Hello there!" Delia's voice flung away in the breeze, her skirt billowing out from her as she hurried up the hill to Adelyn, who waved back.

"You're breathless, Sugar." Adelyn shaded her eyes to

see her friend's face.

"Not as breathless as you should be." Delia unraveled her skirt from around her legs. "This weather should hold, and that breeze is gonna come in handy tomorrow. Now look at you! Why are you not going crazy today? One day away from a wedding? I cannot wait to see everyone tomorrow and Garnett…"

"Oh, he'll be here." Adelyn picked up on the hesitation and the question not asked. She understood how the Tulip Junction folks viewed her less-than-normal life, her running to New York for research on college work none of them could make sense of, and all that travel that Garnett did.

Delia tidied her hair and adjusted her wide-brimmed hat meant to keep her freckles from springing up everywhere. "Your new husband has been to London and then Belgium and then home again. It's no surprise that even my daddy has asked."

Adelyn patted her hand and tried to reassure her. "I know, I know. It will all be fine. You'll see. You want to come up and look at the dress again?" She knew the answer as they walked back to the house, but not before Adelyn walked back into the barn and gave her horse an apple.

Delia huffed to keep up with Adelyn's long strides and smiled at how riding boots and jodhpurs must be infinitely more comfortable for walking than dresses with heeled shoes. Delia asked, "You still working with that Yankee fellow at the newspaper? I'd think you would be spending your free time on planning a family."

"You mean Mitchell Weinberg at the Sun? He called me just yesterday. We're working together, seems my story caught fire for him, no wonder though, Mitchell lost a brother to that awful disease." She turned to face her friend. "He was one of the young men at a staging area, coming back from the war, and he died before he was mustered out." Adelyn's mind conjured a vision of thousands at the front, surviving the war only to come home and die, drowning in their own blood. She grimaced at the thought, and picked up the fragment of Delia's question.

"So, caught you dreaming, could that be about family?" Delia patted her neck as they walked. The humidity rose, even in the shade.

Reflexively Adelyn touched her abdomen and let her hand fall casually to her side. "Family soon enough. I'm just hedging my bets, Delia darling. I have this final paper for my history professor and then I am free." She whirled around to face her friend again. "Tomorrow, I don't care what the weather is. Tomorrow I'll dance and dance and dance. All night."

"Well, Sugar, not *all* night." Delia's eyes lit up in humor at the raciness of their conversation. The two friends would both agree that the Jazz Age had thoroughly infused their morals, and both of them would say for the better. They had read books on the body and the subject of how to please a woman fully like thirsty people drink cool water. Both knew of the new-fangled ways to prevent unwanted pregnancy.

They climbed the back steps of the old plantation that led to the long hall of bedrooms, some, like her parents' room, the consolidation of three smaller rooms, forming a suite. Delia's heels clicked along the hallway, along with Adelyn's booted footfalls, that fell again on rugs that quieted the sounds. Adelyn's room sat at the farthest end of the hall, facing the broad expanse of green lawn with trees draped in moss.

Her wedding dress hung from the door. Stylishly, some might say scandalously, short, it featured a long tulle train that could be wrapped around the bride several times. The jeweled headpiece sat on a dressing table, the crystals glinting in rays of the sun, the creamy white pearls glowing. Adelyn took it up and perched it on her head. "Better with my hair pushed back?" She modeled the little crown and fluffed the silk veil to cover her face.

Delia made a face that said no. "Try it the way they show the model in the magazine."

Adelyn brought curls to the sides of her face and perched the crown farther back so that her reddish-golden and auburn hair framed her face.

"Much better. Let's look at the gown against you."

Adelyn obliged, quickly undressing, stepping into the gown, pressing the bright white fabric against her. The suggestion of a bulge made its impression on the dress's material, and on Delia, who feigned a look away. *Just how much does it show?* Adelyn adjusted the long mirror to be sure the cut of the dress would hide it. She hated the idea of any kind of girdle.

Staring at herself in the mirror, Adelyn looked down a long corridor, past many images of herself. Then she saw an end to infinite images and peeked around herself to see a long sleeve, unlike the bare shoulders of her gown. A familiar sense of cold crept into her, as she spied blonde hair at the end of the line of her images. *What was her name?*

"Addie, Addie." Delia tugged on her. "Wake up. Lands, you went into a trance."

"I was. I was. I saw her. The girl. I saw her again. So long ago, I was inside, became her."

"You are sure enough scaring me. Please Addie." She tugged on her friend's arm. "Wake up. Please."

Adelyn moved away from the mirror and forced herself to stay with Delia or she knew she would stray into some other world. "Strangest thing," she told Delia. "I remember her better now than before. She wasn't a dream, Delia, she was real."

Delia held her friend's hand tightly. "You're cold as ice, Adelyn. What did you see?"

"I was adjusting the dress and looking straight into the mirror and then I tilted away because my image repeated, like it does, you know, infinitely. Except when I leaned to my right, and my image leaned too, I saw one image that was not me, and not moving with me. When I looked closer, I saw that one image was someone different."

"Different? You mean, not you?" Delia's patted her

perspiring face with a hankie.

"She wore long sleeves; that was the first thing I saw. And then her dress came to her ankles, not her knees, and her hair was long and blonde." Adelyn shivered when she said this last part.

"You said you knew her? Who was she?" Delia's face lost color.

"My God, my God. She was the girl who died instead of me." Adelyn repeated the words over to herself while Delia sat her down gently on the bed, at first worried about wrinkling the fabric of the wedding dress, then quickly brushing the frivolous thought away, sensing her friend's experience held far more import.

"Addie, you are truly scaring me, child. But I feel the need to understand. You have always been the unusual one, flamboyant, loveable, and strong all at the same time. Right now, it's like someone got inside you and you are some little insecure farm girl with her first pair of new-bought shoes."

"Because that's who she was." Adelyn turned to her friend and hugged her and then stood and stripped out of the wedding dress to her shimmy and sat down again.

Delia took the dress and hung it back on the door. They would iron out the tiny wrinkles, but no one would iron out what they said here today. Delia sat down again. "Now tell me slowly all that you remember."

"You'll think me a fool." Adelyn's color had drained from her face, but with the oppressive heat of the day, it quickly returned.

Delia settled her friend with a look. "Sweet pea, I visit this woman down on the lower road of our property and she says much stranger things than you, and they are as real as the sweat on my face right now."

Adelyn found the little flask and sipped the gin to revive herself.

"I got sick at your house. It was the day I met Innis. He sat next to me and said some things that a man should never suggest to a sixteen-year-old girl. But there he was. Then I began to feel horribly sick, a fever came on me. I didn't remember anything but one thing, and that was Garnett came and carried me upstairs. It was all very dark and a sick room where I couldn't breathe and it was then that I sank deeper and away from all of you in the room. And heard crying and felt my arms pinned to my sides and I couldn't move. And I saw Granny and she cried because the girl had died; only the girl was me." She saw Delia's face gone all white again, and serious. "It was me; for a very short while, I became that girl. Listen to me, I was in a coffin."

Delia seemed recovered and collected herself. Adelyn knew her friend recognized the magic; after all, she would say, she visited the lady down the road with her mother too many times. The woman could always interpret dreams where anything could and did happen. She was the first one to talk of conjuring wild happenings. And for Delia? Magic infused everything. Delia believed some fussy dead person "kicking up dust" caused storms. Adelyn thought of Delia's sense of the magical that informed her now when she circled Adelyn's waist and told her, "Don't try to understand. Just let it be. You have a wedding to think on."

And because they lived in a magical place where ghosts or spirits enhanced reality, they turned away from the images in a mirror.

# *Chapter Twenty-Five*
## *JOINED*

"Let no man put asunder." Father Dolan intoned the familiar words and raised his arm, punctuating the sky with his two fingers, "In the name of the Father and of the Son and of the Holy Ghost. Amen."

Adelyn and Garnett grinned, trying to suppress laughter as they and a healthy number of the Roman Catholic folk crossed themselves. Adelyn knew ahead of time that Father Dolan would not suggest they seal their vows with a kiss. He said as much and made it clear at the Pre-Cana conference meetings. With a little of the gin from the flask giving her false courage, she seized the lapels on her new husband's morning coat and planted a very wet and somewhat chaste kiss on his sweet lips.

"I love you, Adelyn, and will until the day I die." He kissed her back. "Or you kill me. Whichever comes first." He grabbed her ferociously to him as though he would devour her spirit and returned the kiss twofold. Applause went up from the audience, filling the cathedral-sized Catholic Church established in Tulip Junction for all the Irish Catholic who had settled here, whether indentured to start with, or plantation owners: villains, one and all.

"Enough of that!" Father Dolan began to restrain them and they both broke the bond to explode with laughter. All the while deep in her heart's quiet place she sensed another beat, and her mind knew of it. Innis lived there and had stayed away. Adelyn knew only in the dead silent instant because it blinked away, she felt and heard it, and it disappeared. The horrors of the dead girl's image and the time she spent in Lucianne's body fled, too, in the face of too many new things to do, too many people to see, too many smiles and too much laughter, and a little wine.

The beautiful young people turned to their family and friends—Adelyn with her slight rounded belly completely hidden by her Flapper waist less dress and Garnett wishing to place his palm there in excited anticipation of another generation of Crawfords. He looked down at the front pews and saw his father and the meager Crawford family smiling back at him. Garnett thought more on Innis's absence than Adelyn, all day and into the evening. He would not be able to explain it, but he felt a waiting, a biding of time until some other day. He didn't question it; after all, this magical time, his wedding, and magical place, Tulip Junction, celebrated an even more magical woman he had now inextricably bound himself to, Adelyn Crawford. Her new name tumbled from his lips and stirred his passion. He wished they were on their way to New York in their own private car on the train.

"Did Mama say it was okay for you to be sipping the wine punch?" Adelyn held onto her sister's hand.

Cicely giggled and tried to ignore Adelyn. "You're not the only one who can have a good time." Adelyn attempted to pull the wine glass away but feared the wine would spill on either or both of them. Garnett steadied both their hands and embraced Cicely's wrist.

"Now you all are flirting with me?" The thin and gangly Cicely batted her dark eyelashes at her new brother-in-law. "You see him, don't you, Addie? Look, he's a reckless one."

Adelyn didn't like the direction of her sister's remark, about to compare him with Innis. She'd skulked around enough, young as she was, when Innis visited Adelyn, and learned more than she should.

Adelyn's voice whispered close to Cicely's ear. "Let's go and freshen up a bit, Cicely. Come on, we can have some more wine later."

Cicely's eyes filled with tears. "You're always getting everything. When's it my turn?" She became a puddle of emotion yet relented and let her sister take her away toward the kitchen, so they could climb the back stairs to Adelyn's bedroom. Talking nonstop all the way, Adelyn comforted her sister. "Your figure is quite exquisite."

Adelyn had strewn clothes in every direction; face powder lay in a film on the tops of dressers and hung in the air. The fragrance of orange blossoms and sweet yellow tea roses lingered in the room.

"Geez, you could get a headache in here." Cicely picked her way around the opened suitcases to examine herself in the full-length mirror. "You know, I used to come in here to scare myself."

Adelyn smoothed cream into her hands and looked up from her dressing table to admire her sister, the naïveté of her youth. "What scared you in here?"

Cicely continued to study her lithe figure and the blush orange color of her gown. "I would sometimes stare into your mirror. I'd see me and then, if I looked hard enough, almost crossed-eyed, I'd begin to see a whole bunch of other figures behind me. It was just for a moment, my imagination getting away from me." She stopped when she heard a small valise fall to the floor, spilling little bottles and jewelry onto the carpet, and heard a strange sound in Adelyn's voice.

"When was this? When did this happen?" Adelyn felt like ice flowed through her veins.

"A long time ago. Maybe when I was twelve." Distracted already, Cicely spread her sister's balm on her full lips.

"A long time ago? Four years?" Adelyn stopped to calculate the death of Innis, the one person she had sworn she wouldn't think of today. Her hand trembled as she smoothed the chemise-styled gown, pulling short of examining her figure in the mirror, this object that saw more than reflections that seemed to generate them from some other side.

Cicely chatted on. "Once, I thought I saw Innis Crawford, but it was dark in here that day. I got so scared; I just froze and then lit out and promised myself to stay away from such thoughts." She turned toward Adelyn. "Did you love him better than Garnett?"

"You do let you tongue take over your mind, sister. Foolish thing to say, little girl. No, I don't."

"I'm not asking about now; I'm asking about then." She paused and examined Adelyn. "Unless you still love him." Cicely looked up from playing with her sister's cosmetics, her eyes widening. "Your face looks frozen, like a painting or something. Now *you're* scaring me." Cicely dropped her sister's rouge.

"Darlin', why don't you tell me what your fussing was all about downstairs? Seems it was just a tempest over nothing." Adelyn questioned, eager to keep her sister off the topic.

"Nothing. Maybe, like you said, too much wine. But I was just wondering which one you loved most, like I said. I would choose Garnett over Innis. He was too stuffy, always drooping along everywhere you went. Though I wouldn't say as much in front of Garnett." She flounced her skirt and pouted. "Only you're always the wild one, and Mama and Papa have sworn to keep me on some straight and narrow. Adelyn, I want to have adventure, too."

"It's impolite to speak ill of the dead, Cicely. I'm just glad you kept some of your thoughts to yourself, instead of spilling them everywhere, and Garnett might be hearing them." She looked again at her little bulge of a tummy and put a gentle hand to her sister's head. "Don't worry, Cicely, you'll have your turn. Then you can tell me all about it."

## *Chapter Twenty-Six*
### *CHANGE OF HEART—GARNETT AND ADELYN*

She could hear his footsteps down the hall, a clip-clipping sound of the leather heels and soles on the linoleum floors, an echo ringing out against barren walls and windows with no curtains.

"Curtains, that's what they need." Adelyn repeated the thought out loud, her voice sounding as blurry as her vision. The nitrous oxide gas buffered the labor pains but made her light-headed and nauseated.

"What's that you said, Miz Crawford?" The disembodied voice reverberated in echoes, and Adelyn turned her head left and right to fix a face with the voice, but no faces appeared.

"Missus." Her blurry voice said back to the phantom nurse or nurse's attendant or sprite. "I'm having a baby and I am Missus Crawford." She smiled and tried to turn over on her side, but a strong and sharp pain gripped her, and she remembered all over again. She was having a baby. "Why's it taking so long? Where's Garnett?"

A cool hand clasped hers in the middle of her contraction. "He's just outside, but you're in labor and no one but the staff can be here." The nurse's serene face proved her experience, and Adelyn thanked God for her because no one wants neophyte student nurses in attendance, telling you that you would be fine, when they didn't know a fig about birthing a baby.

Adelyn turned toward the voice and finally settled on a face. "He can be anywhere he wants, Sugar. You wait." She listened for him, his voice. His footsteps had stopped so he was, indeed, nearby.

A stronger hand, one she knew so well and in so many ways, one that had traveled the length of her body and which she welcomed, held her hand. "See?" she said to the onlookers. "You all may be staff, but he's the only other person here with a legitimate reason." Her doctor chuckled at that.

"Hush baby, I'm here. I'm here." She heard the tremble in his voice and loved him for it, for the fragile state that her discomfort caused him to be in. She began to compare, to wonder about Innis, whether he would be so fragile toward her pain. As quickly, she chastised herself for bringing Innis here tonight, and then for being so unfair. After all, Innis had once, long ago, been beside himself to see her sick with fever. Still, she scolded herself for these random thoughts.

"So good of you to come, Mister Crawford." She smiled as she affected a proper British tone. Garnett kissed her forehead. She tried not to show him the pain of the next contraction, but he leaned too close, would always be too close, not to notice.

"Give her something. Now." He spoke quietly, in control, but firm—although very young, a man whom people listened to, one used to getting his way.

"She's almost there, Mister Crawford. It wouldn't do her any good now, anyway." The nurse said to her, "Just breathe the gas deeply. Missus Crawford, Adelyn, do you hear?"

Her roiling belly felt like jelly, moving this way and that as she lifted her head to see. At least six people in gowns and masks stood in a wide circle. Automatically, and without any instruction, she began to bear down, and in one-two-three, she delivered the baby. "Trey." She sighed his name as they held him up already squalling that loud entrance call to the world.

"He's here."

Any danger to mother and baby past, a festive feeling pervaded, with congratulations to her and to Garnett from the doctor, the anesthesiologist, and the nurses.

Later, alone together, Garnett rested his head on her pillow, almost lying on the narrow bed with her. "Can I love you more than in this moment?" He held her wrist tightly in his grasp, his eyes wet. "Never again. Never." His remorse at her suffering brought a smile to her face.

"Never? What?" She saw the tears and anguish in his eyes. "You want this child to grow up alone? Hush, now, Mister. You'll wake your son. I am fine. Really." Content to lie on her side, she wanted not to move for at least another twenty-four hours. The clock ticked in the quiet room, and she dozed and woke; each time he squeezed her hand.

Marianne, her nurse, came into the room. "Time for you to let her sleep."

Adelyn looked to see Garnett relinquish her hand. "When can we take her home? And the baby?"

"Mr. Crawford, that will be something for the doctors to decide, but you can bet it will be a week, at least. Now let her rest."

Adelyn floats out of consciousness into somewhere else.

"It's so misty I can barely see." Adelyn carries Trey in his swaddling, picking her way carefully. She saw the path ahead, dirt on the road, yet nothing moved, no leaf on a tree flutters; no breeze carries the fragrance of a flower or the aroma from a kitchen. She looks down at her new son as he sleeps contentedly, breathing that alternate fast-then-slow breath that new babies do. The mist begins to dissipate. "Looks like Tulip Junction." She gazes down a long expanse of green pasture.

"You must have just fed him, Adelyn." She hears the voice but cannot see through the fog.

"I know you." Adelyn feels no fear, just curiosity, her soul as calm as the airless place she walks through.

"Yes, my dearest girl, you do know me." The person takes shape: Sarah Crawford, a bright illumination about her face, as if a light glowed inside of her. "Let me see this wonderful grandchild." Sarah draws near, and Adelyn instinctively draws back from her.

"Ah, you are a wise and good mother to your son, and careful and observant. You're right to pull away because I must not touch him." She sees Sarah holds her arms at her sides. "Sadly, I cannot touch you, my dear and beloved daughter. We live in this place where we can only look at real life. You will learn about us much later, at a time when Trey is older and can speak and read and know his father."

Adelyn's thoughts run rampant, assessing and making sense of all this. *Have I dreamed this, then?*

"No, my dear, this is all true. Right now, you appear asleep to the nurse in your hospital room. Though, if she were to take your pulse, she would be alarmed because it is racing. Not at all at rest."

Sarah looks around her. She clasps her hands now and Adelyn senses her tension. "I must hurry now and say all this before we are interrupted. We here cannot touch you unless you allow it but you must not. Later there will be a time when someone here comes to your world again, and he can and will touch you. But remember here for that later time, never to let him touch you when you visit with us. You would create a physical bridge between the two places, which is not good."

"Sarah, Sarah." Adelyn hears herself calling out. The mist had begun to deepen but another form comes her way and divides it.

"It's just me and you." Innis speaks to her.

"And my baby, Innis. My Trey." Adelyn holds the baby tighter to her and backs away.

"Don't draw away from me, love." At first, he doesn't acknowledge the child.

"Come, there are a host of loved ones who want to wish you good luck. They want to see your boy." Innis watches her, sees her hesitation. He transmits his thoughts to her. *I would never hurt you.*

Adelyn stops herself from mentioning Sarah. Innis gathers people near him to see her and Trey. She sees her dear young cousin, Tommy, who died in the Great War, and some friends she knew who had succumbed to the influenza. Her grandmothers come near; they both have calm faces as they gaze down at the baby. They all stand with their arms at their sides. Adelyn begins to feel protected by them all.

"You are all so gentle, so beautiful." In saying this, Adelyn knows the singular difference in the two worlds: no sharpness, no feelings, no anxiety, no energy, and no life force. The houses far down the lane look like a memory placed there. Some of the houses, she knows, date from an earlier time and have been torn down or built onto since. Since? Since the person whose memory of it had passed on to this place.

One person after another swirls away, replaced by someone else, equally dear, and Adelyn calls out to each by name and tells each how much she loved this one and that.

*I know you wouldn't hurt either of us, Innis.* She comes back to him confident in her safety with him. A moment moves by like a soft wind and she renews her love for him, but from the past. An attendant guilt comes along with it. "I loved you honestly." Her reasoning dissipates the guilt.

She looks around now as the spirits have all disappeared and the mist parts, creating a way for her to travel back to the real world. Innis has moved a distance from her, though in this world she can hear and see him as if he stood next to her.

He holds out a hand. *Perhaps one day I will come back to you, and your love will truly be tested.* This remark puzzles Adelyn. She begins to feel light-headed and dizzy. The baby stirs, turning his head toward her breast, eager again to feed. She looks up to see Innis dissolve and hears Sarah's voice again.

"Adelyn, you will not remember any of this. Adelyn." Sarah's voice repeats, calling to her. "You will not remember."

"Look, Missus Crawford. These are really lovely." Adelyn opened her eyes to see flowers wrapped in green waxed paper carried into the room by a nurse. "There's a card."

Adelyn tore through the flap of the little envelope. "Best health and all the beauty you can and do muster. Love, Delia." Sweet friend. She felt momentary disappointment. *Who did I think sent them?*

"I had a dream." Adelyn stretched out and felt a dull pain in her side. "Ouch."

With a rapid motion, the nurse lifted the covers, carefully examining Adelyn's bandages. Adelyn heard rebuke and concern, and felt wetness, knew she bled. "Have you been out of bed?"

"I don't think so. I started to tell you, I had a dream...." Garnett at the door to her room interrupted her words.

"Mister Crawford. Can you wait outside for just a moment? Missus Crawford is having her bandages readjusted." The nurse whispered to Adelyn, "You must have gotten out of bed. You're bleeding more than you should be. It's not an emergency, but it's more like how a farmer's wife would flow. Up too soon, cooking the men's dinner." She didn't add, but Adelyn could guess, "And not the way a lady should be."

"I'm trying to tell you, I was dreaming that I took my son..." Her voice trailed off, as images came into her mind and quickly faded to nothing. Adelyn felt irritable, frustrated. "I was standing a long time." She tried to see what the nurse did and felt heaviness, like packing bandages. "That is, in the dream. It was a dream, but it was so real."

The nurse exchanged the old bandaging for new, but not before Adelyn saw the bright red suggesting new blood. "It's like a wound, isn't it?" Her curiosity overcame any squeamishness she might have had. "It all seemed so natural, having a baby. "

"Well, at least you were spared stitches." The nurse kept her eyes round and without emotion, *deliberately so I won't know that she judges me as having the stamina of a field hand and as being less like some delicate, fainting lady of leisure.*

"Garnett, honey. We're all through in here. Nothing to worry on. You can come on in."

"My, you look natty, rep tie and everything. If I didn't know better, I'd say you were a man on the make." Adelyn ran a distracted hand through her hair, wondering whether it had become tangled somehow, yet not aware that the trip to the Sideways World caused this concern.

"You look fine, right down to that little blue bow tied up in your hair." He caressed the curls surrounding the bow.

"Mama brought in some blue fineries she'd been holding onto until she knew for sure. 'Cause she said all along how I carried a boy." She kissed him back and took the top off of one of the dishes on her tray. "Our nurse, Mrs. Wright, said the restaurant in town cooked all this food, so it's bound to be good. Hope you're hungry."

"Wasn't till I smelled all that roast beef and saw that mess of greens. I think I can help you with this." He munched absentmindedly, and they took turns feeding one another from their plates. "Now the big question of the hour is who gets the ice cream."

Adelyn sat back after just a few bites, glancing out the window at the gray day. "Looks like sleet out there." Her thoughts flew to the New Year coming around again and to the first New Year they ever shared, though more to the point, she'd been with Innis then. She cursed her mental ramblings, afraid they would play out on her face. *Why think of him just now?* Something told her in that second that if she continued this interior dialogue she would hear Innis and Garnett would know. *Know what?*

"Tell me something funny and full of color to make this gray day brighter." She spooned the last of the ice cream and turned the spoon toward her husband. "My, you are a child. You looked absolutely about to cry for not having the last of this homemade ice cream." Garnett took hold of her hand and helped her deliver the dessert to his eager mouth.

"We're going to Paris." He scraped the plate for the last vestige of ice cream. "Maybe we can ask for another helping?" He moved from the chair so he could sit beside her on the bed.

"Did I hear you? When? With the baby?" He promised a mixture of adventure and fear of a city far away, of a baby, maybe too small for such a journey. "Garnett Crawford, you know there's more to tell, so stop your teasing and finish what you started."

"Honey, I've been trying to do that for some time now. Finish what I started, and I'm not sure I will ever find an end to it." His merriment, his love of her, his contentment at finding his place, his family, his life, all mingled too enormous an emotion to contain. Joking, for the time, saved him.

## Chapter Twenty-Seven
### CHANGE OF HEART—LETTING GO

"Oh, baby, Trey, please don't cry. Mama's got to finish this one last thing, and then she'll pick you up. Honest." Perspiration clung to Adelyn's hairline and brow on this unusually warm and humid May afternoon. She continued to type, slowly, carefully, not wanting to mess up one more time and then resort to erasing the original and two carbon copies of her paper. "Why the History Department and Professor Stanley each need a copy is beyond me."

The baby continued to fuss as Adelyn framed the words for her paper that would describe the effect the influenza had on the town of Tulip Junction. She skillfully placed it in context with the wider world, first Georgia, then the country and on to the pandemic that the disease had been. The little bell rang on her typewriter when she pressed the key to end the sentence. Trey wailed in unison.

"Coming, I am here, baby." She swooped him up and felt his wet diaper. "So, it's not supper time, then, making you fuss so."

"What is this mess in here, child?" Her mother stood in the doorway and rushed to hand her a clean diaper. "I don't know why you persist."

"Really, Mama, I had an obligation to complete this last course. The history department didn't mind that I'm a married lady." She resisted the words *old married lady* and frowned at the thought.

"If you wanted to keep on with your studies, you should have stayed single. All those young girls on campus down there, and you walking from one building to another, and in that state." Her mother stopped.

"What state would that have been, Mama? Pregnant?" Adelyn noticed her mother flinch when she said 'the' word. *So old-fashioned. It's a wonder she doesn't wear boots with buttons up the front of them.*

"Never you mind, Missy. It wasn't appropriate for you to be on campus in that condition. Whatever would Innis have said?"

The silence passed between them for a second yet encompassed them with images and memories of him. Adelyn felt her heart stop at the mention of his name, the wind in the trees outside the opened window even stirred differently. *Innis made Mama remember him.*

"I don't know what came over me, honey. I've been four sheets all day long, woke from a dream I couldn't remember though I could swear it wasn't a true dream, more like real, and have been crazy ever since." Her mother sounded nervous and a little embarrassed at mentioning Innis. Her devotion to Garnett had shifted her allegiance away from Innis, and now toward the baby.

*Or so I thought.* Missus Jackson had long ago accepted her daughter's intimate relationship with Innis. She wanted to believe they came to that arrangement after Adelyn turned eighteen, and Adelyn tacitly allowed her to continue believing that.

Mary Jackson now took out her lace hankie, patting her

moist face and bosom, speaking all the time in her fluttery tone. The practical and unpoetic of the world would think her ready for a straitjacket. Adelyn, and the woman who lived down the road from Delia, considered Missus Jackson transfused with magic from another world, a seer, a visionary, and to Adelyn she embodied all of these. And a little craziness too.

Adelyn looked archly at her mother. "How could you, Mama? Invoke Innis? Thank God this baby has no chance of remembering this day." As she looked at her son, a smile, his first, played across his baby lips, and she noted his peaceful state. In an instant Adelyn knew the smile had more to do with some otherworldly presence of his dead uncle than his dry diaper.

Trey looked almost too serene and still. "Trey, baby. Mama, this room never has enough air." Shaking him gently, he breathed a little deeper, and so did his mother. She reached for his bottle with one hand, and with the other flounced her light dress away from her sticky legs.

She considered the dead of winter when she came home with Trey, before Garnett left them for business in New York and Europe. She wished now for such a cooler day, less like summer, but knew the heat would continue unabated. The baby suckled contentedly. "Mama, why don't we go down to the ocean or maybe even up to Cape Cod? Anything to get away from this heat."

"Could Garnett take some time?" Missus Jackson fanned herself with one hand and continued to dab at the perspiration with the other.

"We can meet him up there—take the train. I'm sure he'd rather be up north than down here in this oven." She gently patted Trey's back, waiting for that little bubble of air to surface, glad she remembered a clean cloth for her shoulder when he finally did burp. "I'll send Garnett a telegram after I get back from the university tomorrow."

"There you go, always running off, now down there to that school, and what then? To the post office? You have got to settle into a more matronly way, my dear, or you'll be the talk of Tulip Junction."

"Me, matronly?" Adelyn lay her baby on his side, propping him with a small blanket, leaving his legs uncovered. "You know that will never happen. Lord, I'll go to my grave in a short skirt."

Missus Jackson smiled in spite of herself. "You will be the death of me yet, sister. With all your prancing about like a flapper and then wearing those trousers like a man."

Adelyn bit her tongue against sharing a secret about to tumble out. Garnett's telegram, neatly folded over many times and tucked into her pocket, told of their plan to free the both of them and their baby from their serious, adult life, lacking in fun. He had written to say they would board the ship in a month's time for France and Paris, then in fall travel to the French Riviera, and by winter farther south to Italy. "We will follow the sun," he had written. She felt lucky to be married to someone who liked to meet new people and go to parties. After all, at twenty-two, her life had only just begun.

"I've got a penny for your thoughts." Her mother had picked up on Adelyn's deep musings, wanting her to share all. And given Mary Jackson's propensity for a just barely hazy second sight, she sensed a secret.

"Just that I miss Garnett. All this talk about going up north to Cape Cod and such makes me want to break out even more." Bursting to tell, she thought about how much she could reveal, maybe hint at.

Missus Jackson half-listened, and started up with her habitual meanderings, picking up stockings off the floor, hanging a dress inside the chifforobe, folding some of Garnett's shirts to place in the laundry basket for ironing.

Adelyn stopped her mother's folding and fixing and scolded herself for all the distractions. "Stop now and tell me what you were thinking that you should throw out Innis's name."

Missus Jackson placed the last of the shirts to be ironed

neatly on top of a big stack. "Aunt May's friend will be mighty busy, working on all these."

Adelyn marveled how her eyes worked, how, every once in a while, she would see things more clearly, like now, seeing the younger woman, her mother, fiery red hair pulled into a soft bun at the top of her head, tendrils of curls still holding most of their color falling on either side of her pretty face. Adelyn impulsively pulled her mother to herself and hugged her. "I know it must be hard to see Cicely growing, and me and Garnett...."

"You and Garnett, what?" Her mother hugged her back and circled her arm around her daughter's waist.

She held only curiosity in her voice, and a deep trust that she would know all in due time. If her daughter told of their plans, it might shock the system of her world and life.

Adelyn paused. *Garnett and I need to break free of here, of something here.* "I mean, Garnett and I...he'll be expected to make a greater commitment to the Shockley & Shockley Company. They're paying for his law degree and he's been doing more of that international work for them. Now, tell me why you spoke of Innis that way, as though you just saw him yesterday."

"Come, sit down with me." Her mother had released her hold on Adelyn and sat next to the baby's crib. Missus Jackson patted the empty spot on the love seat. "Darling, don't you never mind about what this all means to me or your daddy. We know you two have to live your lives."

Adelyn observed a note of hesitancy before she spoke. "I dreamt of Innis last night. I see him a lot, while I'm out walking. Why, just the other day near the pasture. But I know it's my heart that sees him and not much else. So I don't pay much mind to any of it. He might just be telling me and maybe you that things are okay where he is." She sighed. "Truth be told, I mourn his youth and life taken from him so soon."

Adelyn tensed like a railroad tie as her mother described her experience of Innis in her dreams, but most of all, out walking. "You saw him? How could that be?" She breathed slowly to get her heart to match her breath.

"I sometimes see something out of the corner of my eye and often it looks like that lean young man. Always in white, and usually it's in summer, or near enough to summer." The baby stirred, and Missus Jackson turned her head. "It's really nothing." She started to say something more and stopped and whispered. "I better run this basket downstairs before I wake our angel."

Adelyn peeked at Trey, touched his naked tiny leg. He looked comfortable, and his body was dry now and not all sweaty. She leaned against the comfortable love seat, resting her back, thinking that she had a magical life. "A little magic, that's what it all is." Then the memory came back, of the pretty silver and diamond hair pin, the unmistakable havoc it brought them all. "Mostly the pain for Garnett." Innis had done it; she knew that, and she knew he meant to hurt Garnett.

"Trey's bottles are in the ice box. I'll be back late tonight."

"That sure is a lot of driving." Aunt May walked out of the pantry wiping her hands on her apron. "Here's your lunch basket. Should be enough for you and Miss Delia, the way the two of you all pick at food."

Adelyn gave her a quick hug. "Now how do you expect me to keep my figure if I eat as much as the men in this house?" She felt a hollow tone to the question, thinking how little she saw of her Garnett. "I hear Mr. Hamilton's car coming up the drive now. Delia is a good driver, and fast. She'll get us there in no time. Thank you for helping out, Aunt May."

Settling into the front seat of Delia's big roadster, Adelyn felt a cold tug on her heart. She had never left Trey for more than an hour since his birth five months earlier. Her mind flooded with apprehensive messages and what-ifs. What if Aunt May positions the fan directly on him and he catches a chill? What if Mama forgets and feeds him twice? He might choke. Along with the words came the ghastly mental pictures she conjured.

"Your mama and Aunt May kept you alive, didn't they?" Delia glanced over at Adelyn and away from the rear-view mirror where she primped with her hair and her lipstick.

"That was different, they were younger." Adelyn fussed with her straw cloche hat to keep her hair from flying wildly, expecting Delia to keep the car cool with all windows opened on this very warm day.

"And they weren't Trey Crawford. Which makes all the difference. To you, anyway. Now quit your worrying or this car will not ever leave Tulip Junction." Delia pressed on the pedal of the souped-up car, and it sprang forward like a cat in heat. "Besides, you could use a day away from baby and bottles and such."

The sun had climbed high but would soon dip just behind them as they headed east toward Savannah. Yet another month of not enough rain made the clear road dusty.

"Daddy says that he's ready to pull water from the deeper wells in the south fields. I know we're all feeling it, but there's a part of this world you and I skirt ever so carefully." Delia shook her head with worry, always keenly aware of the very poor among them.

"Delia, honey, my folks give out more than they can afford to the people who have the least. There's not much going to be left other than the house and land when they're done. I know it's the same for your family. It's a good thing that your brother Charles has been such a caring son, and that we have Garnett." Adelyn paused. She marveled at how well Delia drove her car, as well as Adelyn rode her horse. "And I'm headed to Europe." Naturally Delia should know of Adelyn's plans, like sisters would.

"Your mama any the wiser yet?"

"We were just talking about all that yesterday. I didn't tell her because I haven't even seen Garnett. He'll be home tomorrow, and then I'll have something solid to tell her and Daddy."

"You having some second thoughts?" Delia stopped in a small town for gas, then parked under a shady tree for the perfect lunch Aunt May had put together for them. Delia looked up from her sandwich with a wicked smile, "'Cause if you're not going, I am." Her dimples deepened as she smiled.

"The hell you will, you hussy." Adelyn settled back against the seat, enjoying the cool breeze, and a chicken sandwich that only Aunt May could make. She looked to the east, facing into the wind. "Must be coming off the ocean, now that we're closer. Mama told me she saw Innis the other day."

"Your mama! She sure surprises me. What was he doing? Looking for you?"

"Oh, stop. She said she saw him out of the corner of her eye. Passing by."

"Making trouble, more like." Delia knew her quarry well.

"I guess I dream of him, more when Garnett's away, but not since Trey was born."

"Must be he didn't want to get caught up in all that baby mess of bottles and late-night feedings." Delia wrapped half of the unfinished sandwich in its waxed paper and placed it back in the lunch box.

"He's never really left me, Delia. There's always been this tenuous feeling that he wanted something from this side."

"This side of what?"

"I don't know. Maybe this side of the world. The living world." Adelyn became engaged in the concepts she was forming "It's like I know I'm going to see him again."

"Yeah, when you die."

"No, no. I'm going to see him here or someplace else, and we'll talk."

"As long as that's all you two do." Delia pinched

Adelyn's soft upper arm, something the two young women had always done, even as girls, a reminder to bring one or the other of them back to earth.

## *Chapter Twenty-Eight*
### *CHANGE OF HEART—INNIS IN A DREAM*

"How much time do you need for your research?" Delia left the motor running as she dropped Adelyn at the steps of the library.

"Couple of hours." Then Adelyn added, "Hope this is not an inconvenience to you. You must tell me, Delia, honey."

Delia shook her head emphatically, "Nope. I have to spend some time with Miss Ferguson. This scholarship needs more than just my daddy's money. Lots of fine points to settle."

"Such a great service for young girls—you helping them." Adelyn had seen girls on campus, serving dinner to the sorority sisters, knowing they would never have seen the inside of a university if not for Delia and the Howard family's generosity.

"Oh hell, if they got this far with good grades and fell on bad times, and the money they thought they could depend on melted away, then they deserve some help."

Adelyn smiled, feeling lucky to know so generous a young woman. "I'm off and looking forward to it. I'd spend my life on a campus if I had no family to care for, a spinster. Maybe in another life?" She exhaled, smiled at her own nonsense, and then, worried about finding documents she needed to finish her work, she stepped into the cool dark hall of the library. Fans whirred everywhere against the high humidity. She knew from four years of living in Savannah that the rising tide would bring a brisk and cooling breeze.

Dropping her books, she settled her sweater on the back of the chair, a way of claiming some space, though, looking around at the almost empty room, she doubted she'd have much competition for a chair. It all reminded her of something…a long time ago. *I was eighteen and here with Innis.*

She sat for a moment while she reviewed her notes on some first-source, eyewitness histories, the best ways of getting at the accurate facts, according to her professor, finding the records of what really happened. Several accounts had dates and some even mentioned several book titles. "Good luck for me." She wrote down the titles.

She picked up the list and waved to the librarian at the front desk who knew her as she headed to the stacks. Once in back, she sneezed right away. "Damn dust." She took out her handkerchief to cover her mouth and nose from the motes floating down around her like a snowstorm. Using the letters and numbers assigned to the books, she quickly read through the table of contents and found three accounts.

Back at the table, she leafed through the pages and read of medical doctors who took different paths to study influenza. One looked for the origin, another studied the sheer numbers of infected young people who died, and another went on to work in educating the public about preventing disease. She piled these and others together and made her way back to the main hall. Adelyn place-marked the books with slips of paper where she would read more thoroughly later. One slim volume with a red cover caught her eye, and she pulled it over to her and skimmed the first-person account of a young physician who published his own work. His prose mixed science and personal experience as he described the futility of trying to save young men from the awful disease.

"His name seems familiar." She whispered the words as she flipped the book to the end and pulled out the checkout card to see handwriting she instantly knew. A dash of a scrawl, his signature: *Innis Crawford had checked out this book.* Her heart wanted to stop. Later she would recall that it felt like it did stop.

Now, instead of the library, a scene appeared before her eyes, of Innis in another place, familiar.

*"No more hiding from me." He extends his hand, and when she touches him, it electrifies and excites her. They walk up a hill, and she finds her face wet with tears...* wet for the lost love of him, of the young man he had been, and she a girl of eighteen.

"Innis, I still love you." She feels no remorse of the heart, no nagging conscience constricting her into blame for a wicked turn of mind, of her leaving her husband and son behind and pursuing this illicit love affair. He kisses her passionately, deeply, the kind of kiss he used to seduce her, a seduction without hesitation.

"I've lost myself in you again. I want you, Innis."

"And I need your physical heart and soul to be with mine. Now, at least for now."

In front of her she sees the green otherworldly grass never bored into by an insect, an earth without an earthy smell. She lies on it as does Innis, and they slowly, languidly, know one another all over again as they had the day she visited this campus with him.

After they find that deepest place in one another, time stretches as though they alone live here on this earth. Adelyn drags her fingers over the perfect grass and turns to look more closely at Innis, touching the fine smile lines at the corners of his eyes. "How is it that you have these?"

He pulls her hand to his lips and kisses her fingers. "We get older here, differently, more slowly, but definitely." He has an edge to his voice.

"How can that be? Do you live ordinary lives, work, play? And how about the old ones? Do they live out a shorter life and then get to die again?" As she speaks, she looks around to see some movement beyond the hilly slope they lie on and notices a girl in white watching them from another hill much farther away. The girl, faintly familiar, wearing an old-fashioned dress, continues to walk toward a small farmhouse, and then disappears inside. Adelyn does not ask Innis about the girl.

She could see him thinking and measuring what she should know about this magical place where that feels neither hot nor cold. "Some of us, like me, came here too early, with life still to live. We're looking for a way back."

"You look so sad, Innis." She kisses him again, and the mist begins to rise around him and her, quietly separating them. She suddenly recalls this familiar way of leave-taking. *This happened before. In my dreams.*

"Oh. Don't go." Innis's voice.

Abruptly Adelyn felt a tug on the cap sleeve of her dress. The grass, the scene, evaporated from her mind.

"Sorry, miss, but you looked faint. I thought you might fall." A young man, a student, now held her hand, which she withdrew, mistaking his hold on her as a flirtation. She shook the dream out of her head, and realized he kept her from falling out of her chair.

"I'll be fine. It must be the heat," she apologized. Standing, she began to stack her books then stopped to open the back of the book with the red cover again, and again brushed her fingers over the fading ink of Innis's signature as though it were his body.

She would keep this little secret to herself. No one, not Delia either, could know. She felt that if she kept the dream to herself it would not fade, would not go away, would be retrievable again, when, on some dull day, she could pull it out once more, and maybe, she prayed, maybe relive the passion, and yes, the love.

Quiet on the way home, Adelyn reflected on her dream until Delia asked, "Your thoughts all over the place, honey? You thinking on moving away to Paris? First you best break the news to your mother and daddy."

"I fell dead asleep in the library today. I must be tired with all those nights of waking up with Trey." She pushed her hair under her cloche hat and looked over at Delia's carrot-top hair all curly and wild. "I dreamt of Innis," she blurted, unable to keep the information from her friend. "Just for a second, mind, but it was him, for sure."

"Now why did you want to go ahead and do that, Miss Thing?"

"As though I have any control over what I dream."

"Well, you had to be thinking on him for you to dream about him. Besides, what did you dream about?" Delia almost bit her tongue, but she had to know.

"Funniest thing, I'm pretty good at remembering, but I swear I cannot tell you anything. Only a feeling." Adelyn adjusted her watch and saw that six o'clock had already come and gone. The late spring sun would set soon, and she wanted desperately to see her baby and her husband. She wondered whether she rushed toward life or away from that other world.

"You're not saying anything, leastways to me."

"Just that Innis and I talked, and he seemed happy. But I really don't remember much else."

Delia said nothing further, and Adelyn wondered whether Delia sensed Adelyn held back. A surge of emotion flowed over her, and with it pieces of her dream, of the place, the hill they sat on. She remembered the reason for the dream. "I was eighteen and Innis took me down to the university. You remember, don't you?"

"I remember you being so excited and what to wear and everything. We were foolish little girls, weren't we?" Delia laughed.

"Innis checked out a book." Adelyn recited the events of that day from memory. "And it was the same book I was reading today. A doctor from near Tulip Junction wrote about influenza. Today, I was reading that book and checked the card in back and saw Innis's name, the ink all brown from then to now."

"How did you happen to see his signature?

"No one else had checked it out since. I guess I fell asleep reading, that's when I had the dream." Adelyn could barely breathe as a deep sadness set in, for the innocence of the girl she had been then, for the heat between her body and his, of how he died only a short time later.

"You say something, Sugar?" Delia heard her mumble as she drove past the courthouse, only minutes from home.

"Just thinking some nonsense out loud."

Delia turned up the drive to the Jackson's place. Adelyn could see the usual crowd with Garnett enjoying the last rays of sun from the shade of the long veranda.

"Guess everyone's home."

"Thank you for taking good care of my girl." Garnett kissed Delia on the cheek and held so tightly to Adelyn's hand that he fairly shook.

"Now, you come on by to our place before you take her away." Delia whispered to both of them and raised her eyebrow at her friend, a knowing eyebrow that meant, *I know your love for him and for Innis are inextricably entwined, and I do not question you nor pass judgment. You are my friend.*

But Garnett missed nothing of the exchange, and Adelyn saw his mood heighten. *My love, he relishes a race.*

"Mama, let me take him from you. I hope he wasn't too much of a problem today." Adelyn reached for Trey whose head swiveled and who erupted in smiles when he heard her voice. "There you are, my bundled boy. You been good to your grandmama?"

"He's been no burden and you know that. Supper's almost ready." Her mother looked at her. "That hat sure crushes your hair-do." She relinquished Trey, named so, in the Southern tradition, as trey, the third William Garnett Crawford after his grandfather and great-grandfather. "He sure doesn't mind being passed from one to the next, does he?"

"No, he doesn't seem to, Mother Jackson, but he sure knows his mama." Garnett hugged Missus Jackson, and the affection that had grown up between them comforted Adelyn. He turned to her as they walked inside. "Didn't know you planned on being down in Savannah today."

"Didn't know you would be back so soon. Delia had that meeting for the scholarship, and I had my last bit of research." She gestured to the books her mother now carried for her.

"Here. I'll take those." Garnett leafed through the several histories and then to the slim history book. "Doctor Merrifield, my daddy knew him. He moved up to Baltimore and works at Johns Hopkins. A researcher." He thumbed through the book and saw something on a page. "Look here. Innis read this book. See that pencil check next to the page number? Innis always did that. Mother would scold him about defacing books, and he'd have his ready answer, that he'd erase the pencil mark later. But he never did."

Garnett talked more to himself than to Adelyn, who tended to her baby, pretending to half listen to him. A nervous energy mounted in her that she did not want to acknowledge, fearing her husband would read her emotions. She saw him drop the books onto the hall table along with the keys to his car. "Can't wait to get you upstairs, lady."

Somewhere earlier she recalled feeling her blood had chilled, like white wine. Her reverie of Innis and her fear of being discovered for it had passed to the warm, very real blood pulsing through her husband, and through her. She wrapped her hands around his upper arm and felt the strong, young muscle.

"You know, Addie? When I come back here, I feel closer to Innis and my mother."

"Of course you would. You shared your life with them here in Tulip Junction."

"True enough, Sugar. But there's something else, like they're actually living down the road. I expect to turn a corner of my father's land and find Innis with a book in his hands."

For a brief moment, they looked into one another's souls and saw what neither said, that Garnett turned a corner and found her with Innis. As long as they lived here, she would feel that Innis could always be found, just around a corner.

*Renée Ebert*

# Chapter Twenty-Nine
## PARIS AND FLAPPERS

She would be surprised at how mature she sometimes had acted, one day when she looked back on all this. She gazed around the spacious old apartment, seeing the romance of this Parisian world. Adelyn took note amid all the bustling, the coquettish petite maids pulling her things out of steamer trunks and exclaiming at the colors or the fabric, and equally expressive, with little pursed lips when something struck them as quaint or country.

*"Voilà, madame. Les jolies robes sont rangées dans la garde-robe."*

Adelyn understood most of what the little maid said and thanked God for her mother's insistence on choosing the French language for her in high school and college. The maids' impeccable fashion sense led them to refer to this or that frock as being the loveliest. And she smiled and said nothing as the girls took the least pretty dresses and neatly folded them as if they should be used to clean the windows.

"*Merci*, Angelique." Adelyn asked her to hang the maids' choices in the spacious closet and felt sure it would be full again with new clothes before the fashion season concluded. The new nurse came near, carrying Trey, and Adelyn kissed his sweet head. Still very much a baby at six months, yet he singled out his father and mother amid any crowd. Now he glowed and smiled his wet grin, one tooth peeking out of his lower gum. She swept him up out of the nurse's hold, alarming her with the suddenness of the movement, and took him to the tall open window to see better the busy street. The baby's eyes darted back and forth. "Hold on now, little boy." She held him tighter as he lurched to reach the filmy white drape and would have pulled it all down if he had grabbed it.

A gentle breeze blew against his face and he closed his eyes at the sensation. To Adelyn the breeze reminded her of their recent voyage to this magical place. It had been a languid pre-summer voyage and they stopped at many ports of call. Garnett seemed to change with each nautical mile of ocean. If she had to explain the difference she would say, of course, he seemed happier away from Tulip Junction.

But that didn't explain it all. He seemed stronger, more resolved. Had Garnett matured? Quickly, she knew he had not, not if you weigh in the raucous, almost fraternity-house events they attended. No, that didn't explain it either. He asserted himself more strongly, when he pulled her close as they danced, gone the tentative gestures he had made when they lived with Mama and Daddy. *I guess he's his own man now. In charge of his destiny?* But then she wondered, did that put him in charge of hers as well, and did that mean she had lost ownership?

"I'd pay a half dollar for those thoughts, lady." Garnett made her blush when he nuzzled against her cheek. "Your color runs high there, Madame."

"There's all these people running back and forth in here and you wonder that I am shy and not wanting to share my personal life with them?"

"Oh, Addie, they are used to it. You think you're the first young thing to be staying in these apartments? Why just last week, Henry Boonster brought his young bride here to Paris."

She pretended to dust off something from the baby's clothes, and Trey thanked her with a big and wet mouth on her face. "You trying to devour your mama?"

Garnett took his boy from her. "When you going to invest in some pants for this child? These dresses make *me* blush."

"He's a mite too young for trousers, if that's where you're heading. Besides, all genteel babies wear these dresses. Otherwise someone might think they should be squatting down in the Georgia red dirt, picking beans."

"Nothing wrong with beans, is there, Trey?" Garnett hugged his son. "Nothing wrong with red dirt, either."

"Homesick already?" Adelyn threw the comment over her shoulder as she helped Angelique hang the remaining dresses. She sensed that even the most fashionable of them would be criticized by these overly fashion-conscious young women. She looked back at her husband who all this time had been studying her.

"No. Not homesick. There's something about being away from Tulip Junction. I always feel you belong to me more solidly away than when we're back home." He watched her, and she knew it, for some sign of her recognition of what he meant. Adelyn always knew more than he did about their personal world. He only knew it as her afterthought. *But that may have changed too.*

"My sweet men. What would I do without one or the other of you?" With the maid gone, she pressed her body to Garnett. "Maybe it's time for the nurse to bathe our boy." She had come away from Tulip Junction yet her powers of almost reading his mind had stayed intact. Now she mentally shook her head to clear it of these thoughts of enhanced powers and settled, instead, for the fact that she had known him, and therefore his mind, for many years. She knew she had wielded her physical presence against his questioning. *Why face the things that get in the way when we were back there in the Junction? We're here now and I am free of....* But she would not go that far, not say what or who she freed herself of, not today, maybe not at all.

"Wild! This is absolutely wild!" Adelyn grew breathless from one Charleston after another. The band's brass section played exceptionally well. Confetti and streamers draped over everything in the grand hall, transforming it from a regal room in an equally regal estate to a bawdy, loud, common room filled with an exuberant group of young men and women and not-so-young men and women, all dancing, twirling, as the women's shorter skirts, barely covering their thighs, threw off sequined light.

"Where are we, Garnett? I forgot where this is." She hung on him like a rope and he held her up.

"South of Paris, in the countryside. How much champagne have you actually drunk?"

"Mmmmm. Enough, I'd say." A slow song began with a tentative clarinet piercing the air, yet mellow as though wrapped in heavy gauze. "Who's that playing?" She gestured to the heavy black man who stood, swaying to the feel of his music. "He's magic."

"I believe that's Sydney Bechet. Yes, darlin', he's the best."

Garnett swirled her around and pulled her tight and Adelyn noticed that, wine or not, he always kept a part of him in check, a part that did not give in to total abandon. She told him as much. "Is it your boss over there that makes you wary?"

"Why? Don't I look like I'm having fun?" The slow song ended, and the band took a much-deserved break. "Let's go out to the terrace. They say the gardens here are something. We'll come down with Trey some Saturday."

Tiny lights in the trees helped them see their way. A

tall, thin man walked past them as they settled on a stone bench. Garnett's expression changed as the man blatantly stared at Adelyn. "Something I can do for you, sir?" Garnett's voice cut with sarcasm.

The man smiled, but focused even more on Adelyn's face first, and then his eyes ran down to her exposed knees and the length of her slim legs.

"What's that you say?" he asked in his Texas drawl, slow, languid, and full of meaning. His face became visible to them as he turned. His handsome eyes struck her, and as did his languid gaze, first at her, then at Garnett.

Garnett sprang from the bench. "Hush now, Garnett, he's drunk. Can't you see?" Adelyn took hold of his arm and felt the muscles ready to spring into action toward the man's well-defined jaw. "Besides, darling, he's just a kid. Look closer," she whispered, and Garnett's jaw relaxed.

"Well, so you are, you big hulk." Garnett grabbed the young man's arm with one hand and shook his hand with the other. "How did you crash this party, son?" Garnett turned to Adelyn with some relief in his face. "Sugar, this is my friend Howard, just up from Texas, that dirty, dusty place."

Garnett meant this last remark in jest, and Howard seemed to take it just that way. Or perhaps, as Adelyn surmised, he didn't really have much love for his home state. But he did persist in looking at her not altogether chastely. She decided he feigned drunkenness to give his behavior more leverage. She wondered how many wives he'd seduced just tonight. *Am I being seduced?*

"I'm pleased to meet you, Ma'am." Howard bent to kiss her hand and Garnett stopped him with a hard pat on the back, which sent his friend off balance, making him sit down hard on the stone bench. "Yow! You'd think they'd put some cushions and stuff out here, wouldn't you?"

"Aren't you going to tell me your friend's name, darlin'?" Adelyn looked down into Howard's mischievous eyes. *Yes, you could get lost in them.*

"This is Howard Hughes and he's a friend of Jeremy."

Garnett turned toward Howard and helped him up. "You all took that engineering course together, ain't that right?" Adelyn smiled at her husband's Georgia twang reasserting itself.

"Yup. Jeremy is fine people, now, isn't he?" Howard stood up on his feet again where Garnett had planted him firmly, between the bench and himself. *My husband, nobody's fool.*

"You see that little Jeannie I met last week? I've been looking for her in this crowd."

"And I've been looking for you, devil that you are." Adelyn and Garnett turned to see a pretty blonde girl, hair in a bob, feathers coming out of her headpiece. Howard made the introductions, seeming soberer than just moments before and finishing with, "How 'bout we all find some strong coffee?"

The big sedan slid along the road back home. *Already thinking of Paris as home. Home is where my baby sleeps.* Adelyn felt Garnett's body slump further; he, too, had fallen into a dead sleep in the car. She took stock of the evening, and of Howard, of his electric sensuality and relaxed southern charm, and of his flirtation. She knew he persisted, though more subtly, after Garnett introduced them, and understood she had caught some of his fire. *Just innocent foolery.* She told herself that.

Their evening ended near dawn as the big, black limousine slid along the empty streets, past the Louvre, and finally to the side street that looked insignificant and tiny until you opened the tall door into the wide expanse of the courtyard and heard the quiet spill of water from the fountain that rose two stories high.

They stripped off their clothes as they walked through the apartment, laying all but their most intimate clothing on the enormous sofa, and falling onto the perfumed scented sheets and into one another's arms as they half-consciously made love and finally fell deeply asleep.

Their Parisian life encompassed all this, along with espresso and *apéritifs* on warm weekend days, because they were young and life was strong in them. They never tired of the round of parties, followed with walks on weekends in the parks, Trey in a stroller.

# *LETTER HOME*

*Dear Mama and Daddy,*

*It was such a treat to have you meet us in London. You both looked so well. I am sorry Cicely couldn't be there with you. It isn't easy to coordinate all those schedules, and the high school Spring Ball is not something a girl should miss. I know I wouldn't leave town even to buy a pair of opera gloves to wear with my gown for fear of an accident coming back from Savannah and not make it back in time for the dance!*

*Isn't our Trey getting big? Can you believe he is actually saying 'Grandmama'? It's a year already! Life is on roller skates, Mama. And Daddy, we tried to get Trey to say 'Grandad,' but it's coming out 'Papa'. Thank goodness the Channel is such a little crossing. I can't imagine traveling with the baby any greater a distance just now.*

*Nothing else has changed much here except Garnett gets busier every day. They're giving him more work than the others, if you ask me. Guess that's as it should be if they are grooming him for partner. At least, that's what he's saying.*

*I've been busy with our little one, but sometimes the days do drag, and no wonder without kin to distract me, and my lovely horse. Be sure to kiss him for me, and to kiss Aunt Grace and Uncle Tyree for me. Give my sister a special hug and say Hey to Aunt May. All my love,*

*Adelyn*

## *Chapter Thirty*
### *HOWARD*

The perambulator rolled along on its sturdy chrome axles, the wheels thicker than a car's tires. The nurse stopped to check the light blanket that lay across Trey's chubby legs, his new shorts Adelyn's concession, finally, to her husband's demand to find the boy some pants. Glad to see her baby still deep in his own dream world, Adelyn had time to think, and to window shop, gazing at the clothes laid lightly on the mannequin's arms and shoulders. Unmoving and stiff, how could they not look beautiful? But the shop where Coco Chanel's skirts and jersey sweaters hung comfortably on wooden frames most attracted her. She'd come back another day with Suzie Arkins from Baton Rouge, and they would spend a fortune on clothes for their trip in the fall to the French Riviera.

Adelyn and the nurse turned a corner onto the Champs-Élysées and faced into a mild wind, Adelyn catching her breath once again, and every time, she came upon l'Arc de

Triomphe. *All those books, novels, and histories…* remembering the grainy photographs of this beautiful monument. *They don't compare to the real place.* The nurse mumbled something in French as she claimed a park bench and Adelyn walked away to look in shop windows.

Her thoughts quickly turned again to the explosion of dancing, music, and general revelry at the quaint and beautiful château, which had become a kind of speak-easy for them all. She didn't shy away from remembering Howard there again. Her thoughts wandered back relentlessly to the young man with dark eyes. She tried to push other thoughts in the place of the memory of Howard's warm hand on her back when neither his new girlfriend, Françoise, nor Garnett watched. Most of all she wanted to stop the memory of her letting him touch her. She could hear Delia's practical voice scolding her, "Missy, you are in danger of losing too much of a good thing."

"Lost in thought on a day like this?" A voice warm as the sun caught her dreaming. She shaded her eyes as she looked up at the tall man with his back to the sun and she swore he wore its rays. "So pleased to see you again, and so soon, Mrs. Crawford." The long and slow drawl suggested to Adelyn his long and slow lovemaking.

"Why hello, Mr. Hughes. You following me?" She blushed at her thoughts and at the words that spilled out of her mouth. *Delia's right. I'll be damned for all time. I must be insane, flirting with this man.*

"Looks like we'll be thrown together once again, if you can stand it." He smiled and began to reach out for her chin to push a strand of hair away, when he stopped. "Well, just look at me, taking liberties."

"I should say. Besides, I have to take Trey home. It's his lunch time."

Hughes looked around. "That your nurse and baby over there?" He gestured his rolled newspaper toward the nurse sitting forward on the bench while arranging the blanket in the carriage.

"You can send them on home, can't you? I saw Garnett this morning and he's invited us all to the *Théâtre des Champs-Élysées* Friday night. Josephine Baker will be dancing. I'm licking my lips in anticipation of that."

"No doubt." Adelyn pulled her little leather gloves tighter, pushing between each finger.

"Careful. You'll stop all your circulation." He hesitated. "Now, if Garnett is coming Friday, so are you."

"Why would you be that sure?" She felt like she rode a carousel, getting dizzier by the minute.

"Oh, I figure you two for an everlasting love, always together," his voice serious now, "something I am mighty jealous of. Can't seem to find that."

They had walked to the bench where the small early spring leaves did little to shade the unforgiving sun. She spoke up so the nurse could hear her, in perfect French, "Madeleine, *veuillez amener le bébé à la maison pour son dîner. J'y serai bientôt.*"

*Yes, take the baby home.*

Howard stood back as Adelyn walked over to the nurse with some additional instructions for Trey's bath and his lunch of puréed foods. She turned back and smiled to find this slim and extremely handsome young man standing next to her, his timing perfect in joining her after the nurse had disappeared around the corner.

They sat where the nurse had vacated, the bench roomy enough for three. Yet Howard leaned closer to her, though still discreet, so if seen from a distance he would look respectful. *Was it decorum or restraint?* But his action fueled a speeding up of her heartbeat. In anticipation of what? She couldn't name it but knew she waited to see what he would do.

"See, that's what attracts me to you, your audacity. I want to know your secret." He slapped his newspaper on his knee. "Come on now, girl. Help a man out. Come with Garnett so we can all have a good time. You'll meet Josephine, we'll dance. 'Sides, Garnett is all for it."

"My secret?" Instantly she knew they spoke a special language, one that left incomplete thoughts where the heart filled in the rest. *Is my secret lusting after life experiences with no thought to the consequences?*

Howard moved closer now, discarding decorum after all, and though she knew he did, she did not move away. She felt his warm breath on her face. "Your guile to draw me in without it seeming so. How do you do that? Is it those lovely eyes?" She couldn't believe his words.

"Audacity, Mr. Hughes? I believe mine pales in comparison to yours." She said it without disdain, her voice, as her feelings, suddenly very full. *I sound like a Jane Austen novel.*

A thousand responses filled her; she checked each one, as she considered the fact that he spoke to her in so casual a manner that he referred to her as 'girl', his obvious and undisguised flirting. Adelyn struggled with her deep need to put him in his place and with her peculiar desire to be near him. Howard telegraphed not just his charm but the strong message of his own need. She stood up abruptly, startling him to do the same. She bit her tongue against the cutting remarks she would have spit out, because if she were honest, they cut into her as well, deserved accusations for her emotions, which she knew he read very easily. She tried for propriety.

"Until I've talked with Garnett, I'm not really aware of any plans for Friday night." As she turned to walk away, she saw his hand reaching again toward her, not for her chin, this time, but for her hand.

"Then I will wait, of course, until you talk with Garnett." He had taken her hand in both of his, now released one, and gently shook hers with the other.

As she walked back to the apartment, the day grew colder and the breeze freshened, the sun now hiding behind a stubborn cloud. Relieved that the nurse had already taken Trey home and tucked him safe and warm in his crib, Adelyn shivered and put her handkerchief to her face, blocking the dust away from her nose.

Garnett fumbled at the door. He finally learned not to call out when he arrived home, after a few occasions of waking an irritable baby who then would stay awake and cranky while they tried to have a decent supper. Adelyn pulled the shawl around her shoulders, feeling shivery all over again.

"What's this?" Garnett came to her side, cool hand on her warm brow. "You look pale, too."

"I must have caught a chill today when I took Trey to the park. The weather turned very quickly."

"The Atlantic chills the air much faster at this latitude." He took hold of her fingers as she traced his concerned face with her hand.

"Sugar, even your hand burns like a branding iron." He kissed her fingers. "Guess an early night and no going over to the theater for you." She heard a thin trail of disappointment in his voice that he couldn't hide.

"I clean forgot. Why don't you go? Your boss expects you there, won't he? I know the rest will have me back on my feet by the weekend." She fought with herself back and forth, whether she should mention Howard. Something said no.

"But what will you do for supper, darlin'?" He had loosened his tie in preparation for his tux. She found it amazing that men took as much pride with their attire as women. *In Paris.*

"Sophie will warm a stew for me." This subtle hint said, *Yes, do go. I prepared for it.* And his unspoken, *Yes, I can have some time, some freedom.*

"I had Michelle lay out your things."

She fell asleep on the sofa in a pile of pillows as soon as he left, and awoke near midnight. A dim little lamp in the hall sent gray shadows across the parquet floors. Adelyn's head felt like lead, like she had swallowed all the champagne Paris had to offer in one night. Still drowsy, she got up, slid on her silk mules, and clip-clopped across the floor, finally shucking them off for fear of waking Trey. The chimes in the hall rang twelve as she entered their bedroom, where she fully expected to see Garnett's clothes in disarray on the floor and chair, and him fast asleep, pillow over his head. But the vacant bed remained made up, with one side turned down. She shrugged off concern; *these parties last longer than midnight.* She lay down, covering her shoulders against the cool air filtering in from the window.

"Trey, sweetie, now don't pout. Here, here, some nice warm oatmeal and look! Your mama has a surprise! Yes, taste this, what's this? Applesauce for my baby boy!" She laughed at his frown turned to delight as he wrapped his baby tongue around his spoon and then puckered with the sweet and tart combinations.

Garnett walked slowly behind her, gliding his hand along her back as she shrugged him away. "Now don't be cross, Sugar." He nuzzled her cheek, which began to lean into his chin. "Come on. You know these things run late."

"Two o'clock." She avoided his eyes, wanting him off balance, nervous.

"That late? No. I can't believe it ran until two. Not really." They both played at the game, neither of them serious.

Adelyn wiped her baby's face, raised the sides to his highchair, and lifted him to her. "Michelle, please have Nurse begin his bath." She said this in the most Parisian of accents. She could tell by Michelle's raised brow.

"Good God." Garnett heard the chimes on the clock ring out nine times and gulped some hot espresso followed by some juice. "You feeling better now, Sugar? I'd better hurry. See you tonight."

"Yes, time seems to be eluding you." Her smile played at the corners of her mouth as he kissed her loudly and left. She hadn't replied to his question about her health. The deep and restful sleep had renewed her youthful verve. The phone rang in the bedroom as she lounged for a moment before a leisurely bath. Her friend Suzie called her to make plans to meet for lunch.

"Let's meet at the Café de Fleur at one. I have some writing to take care of first."

Suzie insisted they meet. "Just as long as you promise to be there."

"Late lunch sounds delightful, Suzie." Adelyn's bathwater ran into the porcelain tub, and she pulled the phone cord to follow her, answering yes as she poured a jasmine scent into the water. "See you then," she said, replacing the phone on the receiver.

Walking back, she automatically picked up Garnett's shirt from off the floor. Later she would ask herself what startled her when she saw smudges of lipstick and rouge on the front and near the collar of the white starched formal shirt. *After all, he danced with someone.* But her troubled and pounding heart signaled what she believed he had done—from the mingling of perfume on all of the outer clothes as she went from one to the next, then his undershirt, the thing that changed her life forever. She dismissed the outrageous notion, but some of it stuck to her like the perfume.

She raged, she wanted to cry, but her heart choked on the sob that engulfed a space in her and stayed there. Finally, she talked aloud to herself. "Will I just ask him? Why not? We danced with others at the château."

"Howard." She said his name, bringing up guilty images of him holding her too close, and yesterday in the park. *How was that different than this?*

"This speaks of intimacy." She quickly looked to see Michelle and Mathilde, the maids, who continued with their tasks, and who didn't understand her words. Still, she reasoned, her dalliance differed from this. *Someone had been a part of Garnett's life, if even for a moment.* Luxuriating in a bath no longer appealed to her; she quickly sat, splashing in her tub, scrubbing the hurt away with the sponge, erasing the get-even thoughts that wanted to consume her. She slid further down until she submerged her head. The whoosh of the water above her shut out the world.

"Damn." Her hands shook as she buttoned the front of her dress. Michelle rushed to help her. *"Non, merci."* She gently shrugged off the girl's attempts to help. Besides, the gossamer-light linen and silk blend would wrinkle beyond help if one more person put their hands to the effort. Inside she scolded herself to keep a cool head.

"Call Suzie, and cancel?" She said this aloud while adjusting her pale silk hose and looked at her image in the mirror. *Does a jilted woman look like this?* She laughed out loud for being studiously melodramatic. The young woman in the mirror looked back at Adelyn, reflecting a dark bonnet of soft curls that moved when she did and then fell into place again. *Free, like me.* Her eyes looked larger and more luminous and it occurred to her that a certain electricity surged in her jumping pulse, almost an animal energy, though for the moment she would not admit how she envisioned the need to be desired would play out. Briefly, she thought of Innis, seeing herself though his eyes, the long line of her thin body, her legs up to her knee exposed and slender. She turned one way and then the next, no longer feeling like a victim. *Haven't thought of Innis for a while.*

Adelyn allowed Suzie's chattering about all the latest gossip among the naughty ex-patriots, and a perfect coq au vin, to assuage the pain she felt from the morning's revelations. Adelyn tried to mollify her stronger emotions with snippets in her memory of her own transgressions, flirting with one or another of the men she had met since they got to Paris. And Garnett's even-tempered, good-natured acceptance of all this flirtatious behavior made her uneasy. She pushed it away like so much salt that falls from the plate as she seasons her dinner: seemingly small and insignificant, but glaringly obvious against a black dress.

Half listening to her friend go on about the latest corporate gossip, Adelyn shook her head, refusing to make it all her fault. They both liked to tease one another, whip up a lather of passion with a small and spicy bit of jealousy; she told herself this. Secretly, she admitted it started that way with Howard. His tall, dark good looks just became more than flirtation, and she knew it.

"I liked the apricot hosiery best; they'll look perfect with that peach-colored silk. How do they get the colors so subtle?" She woke out of her reveries as Suzie gazed at Adelyn's long and skinny legs as she reached over for her third glass of wine.

"Darlin', you sure you'll be in any condition to walk home after this?" Suzie looked slyly at Adelyn, who laughed. Suzie, so unchanged, both of them, from little girls in kindergarten.

"I can't say it enough; it is sure good to have you here." Adelyn sipped the wine a shade more slowly. Wouldn't want to be out of control when she got home, when Garnett got home.

"Honest, I wasn't all that convinced earlier, but wine is helping, now, isn't it?" Suzie peeked at her freckles in the little compact, patting some powder on them as camouflage.

Adelyn paused, hearing her friend's remarks. Suzie could have been referring to Adelyn's hurt after Garnett's indiscretion, but she hadn't told Suzie, and therefore she couldn't know; yet Suzie's remark that Adelyn didn't look all that happy did plague her as though her face mirrored her heart's pain for the entire world to see.

With more than one too many glasses of wine, Adelyn convinced Suzie to share a cab. "Now isn't this better than trusting our judgment to balance on these impossible shoes all the way home?"

On the ride home, Suzie comically held on to the straps as they turned tight corners, her legs up in the air in a most unladylike way, Adelyn laughing aloud at her friend's craziness. Suzie giggled back at Adelyn, "Balancing. Are we at the circus on a tight rope in tutus and white tights?" Then something closed up inside of Adelyn, and she quickly covered her emotions, pretending to be inside of the merriment with Suzie. Adelyn stepped outside herself for a moment, looking at herself and judging. *Do I want to be like this? So unsubstantial?*

"Well, Sugar, we're here." Adelyn paid the cab driver and assisted Suzie to the doorman who seemed used to her friend's lunches lasting longer than she thought and, more often than not, filled with wine.

"What, Addie, are you not taking the cab home? Why not come up, then?"

The doorman gently but firmly kept Suzie upright as Adelyn pecked her friend on her powdered cheek. "Sweet of you, Suzie, see you tomorrow night. Trey waits for me."

She pulled her light coat around her and walked up the avenue, her mind muddled with contradictions. She muttered to herself in a whisper, fearing that the sound of the words, if too loudly spoken, would become like marble, and whole, and more real than she wanted them to be.

Adelyn chided herself: "He didn't do anything." Then, "Yes, and how do you know, and why won't you ask?" This banter took her over with whole scenes of dialogue between her and Garnett and lasted for the entire twenty minutes. Thankfully, the rain only began as she entered the ornate lift to the apartment. She closed the gate, sensing movement behind her.

"Garnett. How foolish to startle me." She turned away, not wanting him to see the confusion of anger and sorrow that had stayed in her mind and, she knew, on her face as well. As quickly as she spoke he reached to embrace her, but she pulled back. "We're in a public place, after all."

"That never stopped you before." He gently tilted her chin up to see her eyes, which darted back and forth trying to gather up his face, read his feelings.

Pulling away from his slight hold, "Who was she?" she

blurted, before the accusation had time to fill her mind.

Adelyn knew the change in Garnett. He tensed, and she felt his grasp on her arm tighten, she felt it for the boldness of it, that she did not intimidate him by her arch remark, nor did that surprise her. She felt him taking control and it caused her to tremble, as though he pulled her strength into himself.

Garnett's lips parted to speak as the lift opened onto their floor. She walked out and the moment ended, only the closeness of their bodies as they walked down the hall to their door. She entered the apartment hall ahead of him, opened the closet door, deposited her lightweight spring coat and her gloves, and he his hat. The conversation had ended in the lift. This mundane exercise of taking off outdoors clothes and hats became an occasion for communication of a different sort. He could see her face, feel her arm with its short sleeve. His nearness thwarted Adelyn's attempt to distance herself from him and thus from her feelings. She could not escape the current always between them.

Adelyn heard Trey's baby laugh coming from his room and pushed back the angry words, instead following his sound. "There's my boy!" The evening rituals ensued— Trey's supper, his bath with both parents playing with him, absorbed in his smiles, his grabbing their faces. Adelyn's arms ached with tension of needing Garnett's hands on her. At Trey's dinner, she watched Garnett smile at Trey's tasting his ice cream. They caught one another watching, studying one another for reactions. Trey's day finally ended as they put him to bed, where he fell fast asleep. Their supper waited on the table for them though Adelyn's stomach hurt as they sat over their uncomfortable meal. She stopped picking at her food, put down her fork and knife, rested her napkin on her plate, and left the table.

"How long, Adelyn?" Garnett finally broke the silence. Before she had chance to speak, he continued, "I was drunk, baby, that's all. Nothing really happened."

But it happened again, this cosmic shift of strength. Always and before, Garnett sought her out. Adelyn reasoned that a woman had to maintain the balance, be loved more than loving. It gave her a spoonful more strength. At one of their late-night young college-girl chats, Delia once said that men chased women and women let them think they chased, the natural order of things. In her alone time since she had discovered the traces of his betrayal on his clothes, she heard Delia's wise summing up: "Sugar, if he doesn't feel unsure, then he owns you for certain, and there'll be hell to pay."

For now, she responded to his remark that nothing happened with a woman whose perfume pervaded his clothes. "I'll have to trust you on that." Her small smile belied the tears she held back.

They lay together in bed. He reached for her, and she received the healing gratefully. Afterwards she studied his quiet peace. Though sleepless, Adelyn used the time to reflect on the many ways her life had changed. She discounted taking impulsive actions that would hurt their little family. *I won't leave him; there's Trey. And I do love him.* Finally she decided. *I need distance between us, for now.* Settled, she finally fell asleep.

She drank the strong espresso to wake out of her reverie while Garnett buttered his brioche.

"Addie." Shaking, he pulled her out of her chair and held her tightly. "I'll prove it to you. We all stayed late together, drank more wine than we should have. And Mr. Callaghan and the other bigwigs had already gone home. Just a lot of dancing and singing and such."

She let Garnett hold her to him tightly, needing to feel his warm body, his love for her. He finally looked into her eyes, and she gave him an unfurrowed brow and a smile she meant, her hand caressing his face. "Howard and a few others were there…" he began to explain.

"It's better to leave it there, then, isn't it?" Her fingers to his lips kept him from saying more. Of all her sleepless thinking, she knew this one thing for sure. *Don't re-examine the deception.* Somehow, she knew if he began to tell her the woman's name and what they did together, she, Adelyn, would become the victim. *We'll set his sins in a deep, deep grave.*

## Chapter Thirty-One
### A REASONABLE FORGIVENESS

Garnett found Adelyn's love-making aggressive, and mistakenly took it for forgiveness, or desperation. His dalliance gave him a new way of seeing himself. He walked in a swarthy fashion, cocking his straw boater over one eye like Chevalier as he cavorted with his friends. He contemplated the night, with that little thing named Marianne, saying to himself that it meant nothing. Still young, in his late twenties, he had worked so hard, first at the University of Georgia, then at Harvard, and then at the law and international business. At some point, all of it had to deflate this balloon he kept punching to keep aloft.

So, he forgave himself for fondling Marianne, as he told himself that Adelyn had forgiven him, and he swam in his complacency through the remaining days of the week. He enjoyed her desire for him. He had almost forgotten his need of her. Silently, though, his need grew.

"Hold on, baby, let me catch my breath." He stopped

her hands from wandering over his body, awakening his senses again.

"Why Garnett, honey, you can't be tired already." She let him hold her and she pressed her breasts to his chest and watched as his breathing changed yet again and felt him move. "You have my hands, so I'm not touching you." She blew a stream of air on his chest.

"Somehow, Sugar, you overpower me without using your hands."

"Do I?" She did not ask the way she might have back in Tulip Junction, no little-girl coquetry. Instead, she spoke low and smoky, far more woman than girl. She twirled his remark around her tongue, *overpower me.* Adelyn liked that. He rolled almost on top of her and began all over again.

The next morning brought with it a blanket of quiet thrown over her emotions. Watching Garnett dress, she lay under covers, pillows propping her up to see him in front of the mirrored armoire, tightening the knot in his tie. His hushed voice matched the mood of the early day, just past dawn.

"I'll be straight home tonight," he whispered, bending now to catch her eyes for a response. He smiled as she stretched her arms. She smiled back, "Good. I'll tell cook to prepare something French." They both enjoyed the joke.

"Just some espresso this morning" his way of saying 'don't get up'. He bent down to kiss her and suddenly pulled her up into his arms. "You know I love you." She pulled herself away from his chest to see his face. "Yes, I know." And she felt it again, that small change, the one that shook their world. Adelyn's sense that he withheld a part of himself, whether business kept him preoccupied and she might not understand, so why explain, or a subtle shutting her out of his being. He no longer gave himself fully to her. Not right now.

Adelyn found her solitary noontime walk took her to the Champs-Élysées, to the front of a bistro with an impossible name. Sitting at a small table, the officious waiter came to her. "*Un café, s'il vous plaît.*" She stopped the waiter, hesitated, and ordered amaretto instead.

A shadow draped over her. Howard arched his brow. "A mite early for that, *n'est-ce pas?*" His hand covered hers.

"Is it? Too early?" Tears stood in her eyes as she offered him a genuine and warm smile. She swiveled her head toward the large awning above them. "What does that mean? Translate to? *Café Trieunaux?*"

"Is that really what you want to know? Come on, sweet lady, tell me." Standing discreetly behind Howard, the *garçon* waited until he finished his remark. "*Monsieur?*" Howard waved his hand away as if to dismiss the man, thought better of it, and immediately beckoned him back. "*La même chose pour moi, s'il vous plaît.*"

"I thought I could keep up this awful ruse."

"So strong and willful, honey, we all need to share, maybe you more than others."

"Why do you say that? Am I a lump of feathers, no center, nothing substantial?"

Howard's metal chair screeched on the concrete as he moved closer, where they sat side by side. In a natural and graceful move, he gathered her shoulders to himself. "I've been alone for a long time. Father dead, mother dead to me. I know you bask in your family's love for you, and it strengthens you. You're stronger than you know." The question he posed earlier remained unanswered, but now hung in the air between them. "Adelyn, what can I do?" He tugged her to him, and she told him.

"I think I could say all this because of your obvious fondness for Garnett." She had not moved; in fact, she enjoyed the gentle pressure of his arm on her shoulders, his chest close by.

"And you. I've been chasing you from the night we shook hands. You're a vixen; sometimes you seem more like me than I care to admit *I* am."

The week passed. Friday, sitting in her bath, popping the bubbles surrounding her, she thought about the nights of Garnett and her together. *Tuesday and on through Thursday.* Adelyn stayed her first desires to kick and bite and hate, and replaced them, instead, with sex and with a plan. She acknowledged that a space grew between them now.

Tuesday morning brought the worst of it. She woke early and weary. She wanted to weep, but the sun through the heavy drapes brightened her. She vowed the space between them could be fashioned for her benefit. It bestowed personal freedom. Then Howard became her confidant the way that no woman, not even Delia, could. He did not judge her. Garnett's sea change did not make her the pathetic little wife that girlfriends would have fashioned. Howard made her aware of this freedom and how it could work for and not against her. Garnett's eagerness for the nightclub and carousing tonight hurt her less than it might have earlier.

"You daydreaming in there?" Garnett's head poked around the corner. "Coming tonight? We're over in Montmartre and then the *Théâtre des Champs-Élysées.*"

Adelyn stood in the bath, rinsed the jasmine bubbles off. "Who's we?" She turned fully toward him and pretended not to hear the sharp intake of breath as he watched her nakedness. She moved her towel around her body slowly.

"All the gang, all of them you know. Maybe some others. About nine. I'll come straight from the office. You can meet us, just take a cab?" He'd entered the bathroom more to see her than to adjust his tie.

"I'll be there, maybe 9:30. That way I can be sure you all have arrived." She leaned near him covered in a large bath towel. He kissed the curls she had tied with a ribbon to keep them up and dry. She knew he wanted it this way, her meeting him at the club. She shivered with the despondency that wanted to creep in and possess her.

"You cold, Sugar?" He stepped toward her and, as she had done in the lift, she instinctively stepped back.

Rifling through her closet, she finally found it, a sleeveless top of silver and black sequins that shimmered when the light caught them. She slid into a tight-fitting black satin skirt, just above the knee. *Chanel.* The phone rang. "*Bonjour? C'est* Adelyn?" she answered, her voice ending in a question.

"Now, are you askin' or tellin'?" Howard's gravelly Texas drawl filled her ear and most of the room. "'Cause I know who I'm speakin' to, and sure as hell hope you know who you are. You comin' tonight?" He paused, and before she could reply with some remark equally clever, he continued, "I'm not even askin', cause I'm comin' to get you now, so be ready. Ten minutes."

Her heart lifted not from his outrageous flirtation, but from the solidness of his affection for her, a salve on her wounded heart. "*Merci, mon ami.* Of course, I wouldn't miss Josephine Baker for anything."

"Now, darlin', you better say you wouldn't miss the opportunity to be with me."

"Is there any doubt?" Her face flushed, and she sensed he could hear her voice quaver.

"None." He hung up. She knew he lived nearby in an apartment on the Champs-Élysées, and hurried to be ready, feeling the blood surge through her and her pulse quicken.

When Howard arrived, Adelyn saw the more sedate, polite Howard, the tall figure in white shirt and tails entering the living room. She stood outside his vision to watch him with Trey, the toddler wrapping his hand around the big man's finger. He looked up in his handsomeness as she walked in slowly so that he might prolong his connection with her baby.

"Little soldier." He cooed at Trey who slobbered all

over his hand.

"Howard, let me wipe that up." Adelyn hastily grabbed one of the clean diapers piled high on a credenza. "This apartment looks more like a nursery every day. I apologize." She blushed at the disarray that a baby brings to any living quarter.

"Nonsense, Miss. I almost said 'Ariel', because you are a creature more than human and seem to float more than walk." Howard took her hand as she wiped and she felt a tremor of shakiness. *He's in love with me; this young man loves me.*

"Why, as a matter of fact I do." He pulled her close. "Your eyes betray you, and you are magical, because I've had a straight line into your thinking from the start."

Unhinged, Adelyn bent her head as she continued to wipe the baby's spittle from Howard's hand, and feared he would see her entire and senseless situation, the bruised heart her husband had left her with.

"Let's go." He whispered in her ear and caressed her face with his own cheek as he moved away. Trey continued to gurgle his appreciation for all the tactile connections that flowed from them to him and to one another.

## *Chapter Thirty-Two*
### *JOSEPHINE BAKER*

The darkened room shed no light on the stage swathed in shadows, until a spotlight illuminated the dangerous and beautifully dark creature who stood there magnificently in front of them, in command. She moved across the stage, first one way, then the other, her hips swaying seductively to the music. The audience whooped, clapped, some stomped their feet in this tiny smoke-filled theater. Josephine's barely-there costume enhanced the appeal of her sensuous body, her breasts naked, their fullness revealed. Her smooth body glowed each time her dance brought her into the spotlights.

The woman enchanted Adelyn. *Maybe these men see this and more at some burlesque.* Never before had she seen such a seductive female perform in high society while men and women alike appreciated the honest spectacle that even Old New York could not approach. *The essence of Paris.* She did not treat her sensuality like a plaything, and although still young, she exuded a mature and confident femininity and sensuality. She looked out at her audience with a frank and determined gaze and held them all in her thrall. At the end of the dance the audience jumped to their feet as one and applauded her over and over as she bowed in a gracious manner, Adelyn too, admiring, thirsting to see more.

"Come with me, Sugar." Howard had her hand as they stood in the darkness, waiters everywhere taking drink orders. One stopped to hand Howard a bottle of champagne that he must have ordered earlier. "Want you to see something." They took only three or four quick strides to the curtain and as she turned to go backstage, she saw Garnett in the distance, surrounded by his buddies. He saw her as well, his eyes tracing to the hand that Howard now held. Adelyn turned away as Howard made a sharp turn into a dressing room.

"Josephine, you inspire me. Meet my dear friend, Adelyn Crawford."

With shining dark eyes, Josephine looked deeply into Adelyn's face. "Thank you, Howard. So this is your friend?"

"What Howard said, Miss Baker, doesn't do justice to that marvelous performance." Adelyn stammered.

"Honey, I'm Josephine to almost everybody, and you'd be no exception. Where you from? I detect the South sliding into your accent." They shook hands, and Josephine held Adelyn's long enough for her to recall Momma Sorrow's powerful presence the few times she visited with her mother.

"Near Savannah, uh, Tulip Junction."

"My, she's pretty." Josephine turned to Howard, "Isn't she pretty?" Not waiting for his affirmation, "I can see why you so entranced Howard. There's mystery about you." Josephine breathed slowly, softly, "and there's sadness." Josephine sipped some of the champagne Howard had opened and poured.

"To your health, both of you." He touched Josephine's glass, muttering, "Enchanté," and turned to Adelyn, "Enchanté," touching her glass and sipping his wine. She sipped, looking over the brim of her glass and locked into Howard. The silence lasted a heartbeat but felt like eons had passed. She heard a guitar being strummed, a voice from out of the Delta.

"Well, honey, which is it? Savannah or Tulip...what? Junction? Sounds country to me."

"Just a small town, Tulip Junction. But near Savannah." Josephine pulled Adelyn to her like a magnet. "You looked so exciting up there tonight."

"Did I? Tell me, what did you like about the dance?" She sat on a lounge, and Howard poured another glass. Both still standing, he pressed himself against Adelyn's side.

"You were dangerous, like you could attack those men all hanging near the edge of the stage. As though you could tame them." Adelyn relived the power of the dance, felt it again in her soul.

Josephine closed her eyes while Adelyn spoke. "So you saw, then. I was not the animal; *they* were all animals?"

Adelyn nodded. "I have so much respect for what you did. What you do." Adelyn could hear her own voice, the vulnerability in it. *Am I this bruised?* She saw the expression on Josephine's face. *Yes, if she can see it.*

Josephine looked hard at Adelyn, from toes on up. "I'd say, if it's country, this Tulip whatever, it's not the same as country I know. You have people take care of you?" She reached again for Adelyn's hand and examined her perfect manicure. Her smile broadened her good-natured face.

Adelyn explained, "We have a farm, a great number of people to run it."

"Any 'aunties' on the place, in the kitchen?"

"Aunt May, ten years older than me, been with us most of my life." As she spoke of Aunt May, Adelyn saw Aunt May as Josephine meant, that she served. "She's not a servant the way you might think. I love her, we, my family, all respect her."

"How do you treat those people?"

"Aunt May is family to me, to all of us. She is wise,

smart." She felt the need to be understood. "The people who work there, we give to them, from the land. We're not rich because of this. And Aunt May has always been a counselor."

Josephine cocked her head to one side, listening. "Sort of reaping what they sowed, then?" She turned to look at Howard. "She is different, I'll give you that. I suppose that's why I asked, because I expected to hear one thing and not this. I didn't expect to hear this."

Josephine told them both to sit on the other lounge sofa. "What do you see when you look at me?" She walked to the table where Howard had placed the wine bottle and poured more champagne.

"I see a woman, a powerful woman." Adelyn held out her glass. "*Merci.*"

"Not a black woman, then?" Josephine sipped her wine.

"No." The emphatic negative rose from a deep place in her soul. "I would give anything to have your strength. You're young but mature at the same time. I'd like to have that kind of old. Experience, maybe."

"Girl, if you want it, you can. Ain't no one put you in a cage, have they?"

"Not one that I can't get out of. Thank you, Miss Baker."

"I'm Josephine. Come back to see me. When you've made sure that you toss the key to the open cage in the deepest ocean."

They all spoke together for a short while more, as the room filled and emptied like a tide coming in and out with admirers, men and women, though mostly men. Josephine's fatigue would also ebb and flow.

"Howard, we should go. She's tired." Adelyn whispered to Howard who had not left her side. Now he steered her with a gentle hold on her elbow. She saw Garnett as they entered through the stage curtains, the way they came in.

"Son, thank you for getting Adelyn safely here

tonight." He turned to Adelyn. "Did you like the show? Exciting?" Garnett embraced her, let go, and shook his friend's hand.

Howard found chairs for them at the table of some of the junior employees who cast a ring around Garnett. They all acknowledged him as the firm's crown prince, though little separated them except Garnett's exceptionalism. Adelyn saw the admiration from the young men who worked for him—the shadow he cast included the young women. *He cherishes what Innis had.* Adelyn and Howard sat to one side of Garnett who dominated the center. Adelyn knew Garnett's charisma charmed the people who surrounded him, but neither she nor Howard coveted it.

Garnett reached toward Adelyn, his concern traceable. "You having a good time, baby?"

"I'm okay, Garnett."

And she was. She was fine when he stood to toast one of the more senior men. She was fine and relieved to see Garnett stayed sober and in control. The crowd, his crowd, folded in on him, and she and Howard left. Her mind played over the evening, looked at it all, and left her satisfied. *Howard and Garnett.*

Howard said very little, waiting for the taxi, rattling the change in his pocket, which she took to be a nervous gesture. She did not want to break the spell, wanted this dream to be just that, so she kept silent as well.

"I am fine, Howard." She repeated this as they entered the taxi. "Thank you for all you've done tonight." As she spoke, he took her face in his hands, his lips covering hers, his passion met and given back to him. So much time had passed since the last time she had been with another man.

He pulled her along, gently, yet resolutely, and she understood the path they both trod. His breathing accelerated. He whispered to her, "I knew. I knew you'd be like this." The taxi stopped, the doorman opened a heavy glass door, crystal cut into the sides looked like shaved ice, filigreed nickel or chrome and highly polished to protect the glass from scratches. She felt herself gliding through it all. They embraced, and their mouths devoured one another in the taxi, in the lift, and as the lift door magically opened onto Howard's magical apartment.

The soft light from the outside lamps sent figures dancing on the walls as the butler opened the door to the apartment. *We cast those dancing shadows, Howard and me.* They stood in the center of the room, all silver and gold drapes, sofas and carpets. She tucked her arms inside his evening jacket and pressed herself closer to him. He reached for her face and ran his fingers down her chin to her neck but discreetly pulled back. She knew he restrained himself, his onslaught.

His butler discreetly held a silver tray out to them with two crystal glasses filled with a sweet aperitif. Howard pressed his cordial glass to her lips, tilting it slightly, and she did the same. They drank slowly, pressing their bodies full on into one another. Under their desire ran a current of subtle fear, both of them worried they would break the spell if their eyes did not remain locked onto one another. The tray mysteriously appeared again, and they set their glasses on it. He brushed his thumb over her lips and opened them, kissing her more fully.

"How I need you." His voice held a longing as spiritual as it was physical. *He needs to be loved.*

"Strange bed." Adelyn hears her own voice at a distance from the solid feel of the mattress, her tossing to settle in disturbed by a movement in the somewhere else where her voice has gone.

"You said you'd love me forever, Sugar." He cajoles her, less forgiving of what she has done.

Adelyn remembers this place. She brought newborn Trey here to show Sarah Crawford and Innis. *Innis had stepped away.* "Why did you move away from Trey?" She can see Innis, faintly, a scrim between them, between their two worlds.

"Best that way to protect him." A cool touch strokes her cheek. "But I can touch *you*."

Innis stands fully in front of her, the image of the back porch in Tulip Junction in the background behind him. This time he looks younger than when she last saw him in his world. He has some color in his face.

He reads her thoughts and touches her face again. "I'm just an earlier memory and with a tan, sweet girl, that's all."

"You're sad, Innis." Impossibly perfect grass covers the ground in that unusual place between real and imagined. A younger Innis means time ran backward, back to an earlier time; she feels her hair, checking that it is short, and he reaches out to her to touch a stray side curl.

Ignoring her question about Trey and her observation of his sadness, he says instead, "I like this style, Sugar."

She knows he does this to remind her that she lives in real time, and therefore she changes, not him. And with that she understands his sadness.

"You go forward, and I remain, but you give me such a priceless gift when you come to me. I can see the world changing through your eyes and thoughts." He hesitates, then, "A true gift." Another pause. "Now I want to give you something."

"I want peace of mind, nothing more." She looks into his face. He shakes his head 'no'. "Please, Innis, please. At least tell me how it will get better." She begins to sob, her heart aching with each exhale. "The hurt has to stop, Innis." Turning from him sharply, her voice becomes angry. "I know you betrayed me with that girl. I know all about Lucianne, that you must have loved her in some small place in your heart." The sobs between words grow harsh, intolerable; she can barely breathe. "Tell me."

"My sweet girl, I pledge that after our first time, I never touched another woman. Not anyone." His face grows dark, and he retreats from her. Adelyn suspects storms will be conjured at some later point, when they meet outside of her dreams, but for now he remains subdued.

"Not Lucianne?" She flings the name out to him again, this time watching him respond. But he stays still.

"No, never. Never after you." Then the quiet descends. "Isn't that enough, Sugar?"

Finding her legs bare, her body uncovered, Adelyn moved to retrieve the soft blanket, remembering Howard draping it across her legs and back. Tears dampened the pillow, her body quieting after deep sobbing and halted breathing.

"What was it Innis said?" She lay back, feeling the coldness creep into her in the darkness. Muffled sounds of a solitary passing automobile pulled Adelyn from the remains of her troubled sleep. *Dreaming of Innis?* Consciousness, though, wiped her memory clean of the disturbing dream. She could not enjoy a leisurely Sunday, knowing she must leave. She knew too, that Howard had her, and not one to play coy, she remembered it all, every caress, every exhale of his sincere caring for her, and she appreciated it all.

Inside the room a door opened onto a splendid bathroom, a small light inside. Quietly she bathed away the night, powdered her body, and dressed. Her skin tingled with sensation as she rolled her silk stockings up to her thighs and slid her shimmy down her lithe body. Speaking in a whisper to herself, she acknowledged it all. "A sweet young man."

Adelyn poked her head out of the room and noticed a light emanating from a room farther down the hall. Not surprisingly, it came from Howard's office, a desk lamp glowing, and Howard seated going over blueprints.

"Do you ever sleep?"

He concentrated intensely like he did everything else, but he looked up at her, a lazy smile playing on his lips.

"Girl, you are one overwhelming dream."

His shirt open, hastily put on to get on with the next thing. Adelyn knew this. She had no illusions, and she told him so. "So soon, and you've done with me?" her chiding seductive but good-natured.

A provocative widening of his eyes telegraphed the truth and, at the same time, the delight he experienced in her body. He began to take her in all over again; his eyes followed her inch by inch from her silk hose to her face, eyes caressing her along the way.

"My, you're practiced in your embraces." She keenly felt a need to congratulate him for this talent. Walking around the desk to him, he quickly pulled her to his lap.

"Thank you, thank you." He comfortably hugged her, and she felt the difference in the embrace.

"You're like a brother." She kissed his forehead.

"Well, girl, I hope not. I wouldn't want the responsibility for that biblical infraction."

"Howard. I meant to say there are two sides to us. This is the other, big sister, little brother." Adelyn watched him mulling the meanings while he nuzzled his face into her shoulder.

"Funny, I can accept that." His eyes widened with the epiphany, as her words sank in. "'Cause right now, I am sated, and I can love you like a brother might." He thinks some more, "Though I was an only child."

She heard something in his voice, a desire for intimacy replaced with a need to comfort him as she would her baby, Trey. "No kin, then?"

Howard stirred from the comfort, harshness in his throat. "Just a mother." A methodical clearing of his throat began, his body tightened.

Slowly she massaged his temples while he closed his eyes, she rubbed his shoulders where the tightness hurt him most. "Sweet, sweet boy, let me help you."

"You are a wonder." He looked up at her and fiercely held her.

They sat this way until the mood passed, and she felt him relax again. "Morning is almost here. I should go home. You going to be all right?" A shadow traced across his face, from immediate feelings replacing angry emotions about his early life to the affection he now held her in.

"As a matter of fact," the smile in his beautiful eyes returned, "can we meet again? I think I've found a good friend."

"You know we are, and we can."

While the world and Paris still slept, Adelyn taxied to her apartment, the lift glided to her floor unseen and unheard. Moments later, in her dressing gown, sipping her espresso, she read the London Times.

She heard the nanny with Trey, his diaper being changed, no doubt. Her eagerness for her son chased away the remaining crumbs of her recent life until that moment. No longer musing about a dream she couldn't remember, fairly certain nevertheless that Innis came to her. No trace other than a smile for Howard, her friend. The nanny carried Trey, bouncing him as he blew bubbles because he found that ability just now. His wet smile and his eyes lit up as he saw his mother. She pressed a handkerchief to his face and took him in her arms. His chubbiness from almost a year of breast milk had given him a good foundation. Though he fussed with new teeth coming in, the nanny had teething rings for him to chew to relieve the throbbing.

"I'll feed him his cereal." She mixed it with applesauce, which the nurse didn't approve of, saying in French, "He must learn to eat bland before sweet." Adelyn scooped her mixture onto the tiny baby spoon, and Trey's mouth popped open. "My little sparrow!" Adelyn exclaimed with joy at her baby's smacking lips—the sweet and sour of the applesauce blend on his tongue. Mother and son folded into one another in mutual love, reminding Adelyn of Howard as a child, unloved. The mother in her saw something missing. Reluctantly, Adelyn relinquished Trey over to his nurse's care.

Garnett appeared at the guest room door to see Adelyn folding her silk dress. She looked up to see him in his dressing gown, bare-chested, disheveled hair.

"I didn't want to disturb you, Addie." Sleep still lingered on him from his late-night carousing. She could feel his sudden hunger for her as he moved to embrace her. Until he took her into his arms, she did not sense the cool stillness that had stayed with her body that had returned after Garnett now, and Howard earlier, released her, having first infused her with their individual warmth. She didn't correct his assumption that she slept in the guest room, sensing he didn't check to see where she fell asleep last night. No one mentioned where he slept last night; no one asked whether he came home. Her not asking and not saying unraveled some of his good feelings.

"Still love me, Addie?" He held her at arm's length to appraise the measure of her giving, his voice tremulous.

"Sometimes, Garnett." But her genuine and caring smile removed some of the bite of her honesty.

"Only sometimes, then?" Her smile did not soften the unspoken meaning, the separation between them. In this one moment, he realized we always pay the price for everything we do or say in human terms. The steep price for his transgressions, her sometimes love, rattled his foundations. No matter how deep her love for him might go, it ran no longer constant. The universe shifted for them both.

## *Chapter Thirty-Three*
### *BEST FRIENDS*

"Why are you twitching?" Adelyn signaled the waiter and ordered in French. "*Deux cognacs, s'il vous plaît.*" Adelyn and Howard, seated outside at the *Café Trieunaux*, open air and flaunting convention. In Tulip Junction, this would never do, but the very sophisticated Parisian café became their customary meeting place. The brandies arrived quickly.

"What is it, Howard?" His repetitive motions betrayed his anxiety, especially the continuous clearing of his throat, trying to say something that wouldn't come out. Unaware of it, Adelyn looked for a trigger for this behavior. Her magic of changing subjects sometimes helped. For now, she held his hand, comforting him, speaking soothingly, and helping him sip his brandy.

"Not sure." Howard wiped his brow with the large napkin and placed it back on his lap. "I'm watching you watching me." He tightened his grip on her hand.

"You're quite strong for a rich boy from Texas. You out riding cattle herds to town?" She wanted to make light of his condition, because she felt and knew he did, too, that he would always have it.

"Don't know what I'd do without you." He leaned in closely to buss her cheek with a brotherly kiss. "To answer your nosy question about my so-called strength, I am the son of an oil man whose drills, thank God, keep me from oil rigs and such. But there was a time, when the old man was alive, that I had to sing for my supper like all the lackeys under his control." He expanded his chest a bit. "At this tender age, I run it or, as some down Texas way would say, I run it into the ground. You see, lots of people are not happy with my new-found independence to use the money the way I want." Looking at Adelyn, he felt her mind wandering.

"No, I heard you." She said, responding to his thought. "Just thinking there's this woman who works potions into magical cures. She lives down the lane from my friend, Delia, back home. All the Tulip Junction folk swear by her, my mama as well."

"How do you do that?" He slipped his arm around her chair, cozying up with his unspoken request for more of her than just time and attention. "You were in my mind, or at the very least, right next to my next thought."

"Now, sweet boy, you should know I have appointments this afternoon." She softens the rejection with a gentle tug to his chin, and a small fire ignites both of them.

"You really mystify me. That's twice in one moment where you answered me without me even asking. Y'all learn that in little ole' Tulip Junction? Can't be the answer to you reading my mind. And, no, I'm not interested in magic to fix my problem. Science is the thing. With science you can unlock it all." His speech pattern became staccato with a punch for every word he spoke. "And, baby, engineering is the way to make it all work." He nuzzled her shoulder just once. "Sure we can't find time today?" She had wandered again. "Now, darlin', you are not here with me." He feigned a crestfallen look.

"If I tell you, will you promise to keep this talk of 'magic' to yourself? Promise?"

While she roused his curiosity, he heard a desperate tremor in her voice, and wanted to help her.

"Without a thought, yes. If you killed someone, even, I am sworn. You know you mean that much to me."

"I was deep in love with Garnett's brother, back when I was just sixteen. Can you see how impossible that sounds?" She straightened the wrinkles out of her fashionable knee-length linen skirt, luxuriating in the warm breeze on her legs. "His name was Innis. Don't know if Garnett told you. Innis was studying law, and he consumed me." She quickly assessed Howard to see his frown lines signaling his complete attention. "He was tall, like you, though not as much now that I think of it. He was dark, and he had a dark soul, that I could tell on the first day. I was incapable of avoiding him, and he pursued me openly." She smiles, remembering. "I am sure that we were the town talk."

"Sweetheart, I could easily see why he would run after you. Sounds like he caught you, too." His face actually blushed at his own audacity.

"Yes to everything you so subtly suggest." She tugged on his finger to stop him from further insinuation. "I loved him, and then he died, killed when his car went out of control. From that day to this, I can't tell you what happened, how he died. I don't think Garnett knows, but maybe his daddy." Adelyn got caught up in images of places she and Innis secretly met, the furtive lovemaking, the fullness of her experience.

"Sometimes, Howard, I think he is still with me. I have dreams… I don't remember. When I wake up, there's this aftermath, silence as though my soul had taken a rest."

"And Garnett?" Howard whispered this to keep from breaking the spell. But wherever Adelyn's mind had wandered, she came back to him.

"He knows. Something. When we were at the university, he would chide me for keeping Innis inside myself. 'Course he had no idea of the dreams." She came fully back to the moment.

"And the magic?" Howard prompted her with a smile.

The words flowed. "From the day Innis died, I noticed I could read people's thoughts. I don't like to because some things should be sacred, but there are times with people closest to me that I can hear what they are thinking." She touched his hand. "Like you." She sighed. "Coming here, to Paris, was a break because it mostly stopped. Only now, I don't know. I know you're going back home soon. Before you do, I wanted to tell you that I am tired of this lunching and theater life. I talked to some women at the Sorbonne, and I am signing up for graduate work. I was happiest researching and using my mind for something real. I think I've got enough frocks and shoes and gloves."

"And silk hosiery." Howard touched her arm in a way that all Adelyn's magic mastery could not curtail. A bill of fare arrived, a short and very brisk walk ensued, and they entered his apartment after all.

Until Howard left by ship to America, with Garnett and Adelyn waving to him from the gangplank and he standing magnificently handsome on the windy deck, the not so unholy alliance served Adelyn well. She gained back her emotional equilibrium, filling her days and nights with good times. With peace once more reigning in her heart in those quiet late-night hours when the apartment slept, she began to think seriously about a future. But not before she caused something of an upheaval the day after her rather long Friday lunch with Howard. Saturday morning, as she and Garnett lounged through a very late brunch, she mused out loud.

"Guess I should call Elizabeth and Constanza." The words fell into the space between them and immediately she saw Garnett lower his newspaper.

"Who you talkin' about, Sugar?" He sipped his espresso and looked first at his son in a highchair banging his big wooden spoon and smiling his wet baby smile. Relaxed, he had not attended too deeply to Adelyn's remarks. He rested a casual arm on table, turning the pages of the London Times.

The sun shone full in the dining room, pouring through the tall windows that opened from the center in the French style in the high-ceilinged living room. A cool breeze slipped through. "I told you the other day. Elizabeth Berwick and Constanza Mariella." Despite Adelyn's concern that too many of the wrong questions might ensue, she stopped to note his young man's ruddy complexion as though he had just come off the football playing field.

"Told me what?" He still hadn't completely invested himself in this discussion.

"At lunch, about school. The Sorbonne?" Seeing her mistake, her face unmistakably reddened like a pomegranate. With nowhere to hide, she called out to the maid for diversion purposes. "Michelle, a Zwieback for Trey, *s'il vous plaît*." The maid reluctantly slid onto his tray a hard-toasted chewing food that no Frenchman would lift to his or her lips, so that she could never be blamed for introducing this food to a child. Trey grabbed it with his chubby hands and began to crunch down on the sides, the pressure on his gums providing sweet relief from the throb of his new teeth pushing through the delicate tissue.

"Sweetheart, I was with Bennett, our senior partner? Yesterday at lunch? I know I told you." It was one thing to exercise the unspoken and another to remind the offended party about it. Garnett suffered under a self-generated illusion that Adelyn's and Howard's attraction for one another expressed itself in mild and harmless flirtations. "Who else might you have told? Mistaken me for?" He expressed genuine curiosity without suspicion.

Adelyn knew not to let this cat out the bag. "You're

right; I am mistaken. Told Suzie and some of the others. I've been back to the Sorbonne a few weeks ago and was introduced to two people attending the graduate program for women. Of course, they have all those art programs, literature, and painting. I'm not one to disparage anyone's desire to learn anything of the arts. That's just not me. The people in administration introduced me to these remarkable women, soon to be my classmates in the history program."

"Back to the history of the Great War?" Garnett buried his nose in his newspaper, and Adelyn watched as the storm abated, yet a small cloud covered their sun. He looked up again after he had digested Adelyn's words much like the fragment of brioche that sat on the plate in front of him.

"You're excited. About all of this, aren't you? It puts me in mind of the Adelyn I used to know. Guess she's never far from me." He mused on this last morsel, and smiling, reached out for her hand. She still thrilled to his touch, the attraction latent and yet alive. They both felt it. His face took on a surprised expression as she climbed into his lap and touched his face. After a year of living with maids and nannies, they had thoroughly succumbed to the service and to the invisibility of the servers; Garnett had not expected Adelyn's spontaneity of affection.

"Do I? Remind you of that little ol' coed down at the University of Georgia? Seems like years, our baby growing so fast, you and me here in Paris."

"I miss that coed sometimes, when you were steeped in your history research, coming to New York City and then spending all that time at the World-Telegram & Sun, looking up war accounts. But I think I feel her here right now." His large warm hand seductively held one thigh and a smooth bottom. He nuzzled her neck, smirking so she could see. "You puttin' on weight, Sugar?" Then he braced himself for the several open-handed slaps he brought on himself.

All the good came back in moments like this and cemented them with fond memories and what they loved about one another, but it did not stop the changes taking place in each of them. Adelyn knew that Garnett had become more rakish, that he strayed. The swirl of his work blunted Garnett's awareness of Adelyn, making him blind to the person she was becoming.

Mostly she luxuriated in the excitement of learning more about the Great War, a time in her life she would embrace and explore for a long time.

# Chapter Thirty-Four
## *SORBONNE AND FRIENDS*

"But Adelyn, how can you support such a late entry into the War?" demanded Elizabeth Berwick, Adelyn's British friend, her eyes alight with a fire stoked from within. "And I am guessing that you'll refer to the fact that it all started with European royal houses." Elizabeth pushed away some loose strands of hair and emphasized, "And while that's all true, still we cannot forget the German aggressions."

Adelyn found it surprising that she rarely felt like rising to the occasion, taking the hard line. Elizabeth's position interested her far more. "Elizabeth. So many young men, a generation of English boys. That has to change England. I know you agree." She laid a gentle hand on her friend's throbbing wrist. So much passion, and from an English girl.

"Of course it must. Not just the famous among us. Not just the artists who came to Paris to learn from Cézanne or Pissarro." Elizabeth's blue eyes grew even rounder as she cupped her hand near her lips to block her words from all around them in the little café. "Many of whom were not accepted as they are today." A tall woman of thirty from Bloomsbury in London with long blonde hair wound up in an old-fashioned way, she regaled Adelyn with stories of the young and free sophisticates of Bloomsbury. Her clothes draped gracefully over her tall frame, and a small dusting of light freckles over the bridge of her nose relieved the impossible flawlessness of her English complexion. Like Adelyn, her family's affluence colored her perceptions, and the two women shared the love of owning and riding horses.

Adelyn bent her head closer. "I'm never far from the reality of my motherhood. I have a son, and I want him to grow strong, not so he can be shot and shattered all over creation by someone else's son." And there they forged their bond, striving to make a change, taking their newly won legal right to vote seriously—to protect their families. As a half thought, Adelyn sighed, "Thank God for women, and the vote!" Conspiratorially she bent closer and murmured, "I don't understand the French women. They seem so free, and yet how can they be? No rights under the law."

Simultaneously, the two looked at their watches. "*Mon Dieu! Au revoir.*" They bussed one another's cheeks and set off in opposite directions for classes that would further shape them into who they had already become.

Adelyn hurried along the halls filled with students passing, those going west traveling down the long hall on the left, and those traveling to the east on the right. Adelyn lifted her head to hear their voices, muffled by the heavy classroom doors that closed her off from their enthusiasm for discussion. Discussions took place often, animated, and heated, too, with so many international students holding closer to their own experience in Italy or Spain or England. She found it surprising how she and the others took positions favorable to their own land, and shrugged when she recalled some of her own very American values seeping in. Her constant conviction had woven itself now into a cloak she would wear forever: the futility of such a war where families lost sons, especially in Europe. She saw subtle changes to France and England, comparing these to America, through the eyes of the young men and women she met, and contemplated those no longer alive.

Other sensibilities asserted themselves. She longed for North America, the United States, and Georgia. She wanted to go back, so to move forward. Ideas, philosophies, and new knowledge took precedence over her own personal and private thoughts here at the Sorbonne. Her mind and emotions strayed from them while here. She gave this gift to herself, and she knew it would disappear as soon as she entered her apartment.

# Chapter Thirty-Five
## *THE INTERLUDE*

Adelyn and Garnett would experience unbroken emotional swings, she more aware of it than her husband. His career distracted him while Adelyn pursued a nameless foothold in the real world that would begin to mold her. She would not see it as seeking to define herself, she wouldn't use that language, yet if confronted with it, she would have emphatically nodded, yes! That!

Their Paris stay lasted two more years and their marriage suffered for it. For Garnett, far too many temptations to sample other women presented themselves to him. His work imbued him with purpose and his success confirmed the accolades the senior partners cloaked him with. He chose to work longer and longer hours away from Adelyn and Trey, bolstered by the praise from his superiors and colleagues, and by his desire to experience everything Paris had to offer, and that also meant many of the alluring, expensively perfumed Flappers. Their physical freedom, not specific personality quirks, enticed him.

But Adelyn knew better. The absence of Innis turned Garnett from the young man she traveled all this way with into someone she only intermittently recognized. Without the lingering memory assailing Garnett around every corner of Tulip Junction, he felt confident of his hold on Adelyn's love. His confidence would not always be this concrete, because nothing ever is. And now Howard left them. Garnett openly embraced and slapped Howard on the back.

"Well, son, it's going to be a helluva lot less fun without you. Sure you won't stay a little longer? We're goin' down to Nice and the Côte d'Azur. You could take that ship home from there. Right?"

Garnett let go of his friend and thanked God for a slight breeze that looked like it threw dust in his eye, as he quickly wiped a tear away. They huddled all together at the dock. Howard turned to Adelyn and saw what he wanted to see most of all, her honest caring and yes, maybe some real love.

"Let's get a kiss from you, girl. We won't be seeing you for some time, now."

She warmly hugged the brother he had become, the part-time lover she had needed, their kiss sufficiently unrestrained that Garnett for the first time took note of it. No instrument yet designed had a sophisticated enough sensor to compare the length of a kiss between friends and that between lovers, nor did Garnett need one. The gesture communicated to him their casual familiarity and intimacy, that each knew the other's body. Garnett watched as Howard took leave of Adelyn, his arm unwinding around her, and consciously, for the first time, Garnett thanked a distant god for the sea miles between France and America.

"Gotta go. California calls." Howard winked. "Got directors and such to deal with. Why don't you both take that boy of yours and come. Join me in California. It's all opening up. The movies are going to be the thing, you know." He reflected and then added, "And airplanes, son. Airplanes will make this little hop here so much easier.

Forget ships."

"You take special care now, Howard. We'll come back and maybe see you in California." Adelyn's arm and her voice released him. Then they both let go of Howard, their friend and lover, and watched him sprint up the gangplank, several men in livery carrying some additional luggage for him. They waved and he waved back, and they felt lost. Adelyn looked up soon enough to see Garnett's lingering knitted brow. Their eyes met, the thought shared; they both knew. The stillness remained as the chauffeur drove them back to their apartment. Adelyn's gaze followed the road back, and Garnett sat still, alternately tapping his finger on the leather armrest and touching his upper lip as though he remembered her lips on his. Garnett took hold of her soft hand, which seemed to him disconnected from him, attached to wherever she had just traveled in that fertile mind. He asked, "Where are you just now?"

"Oh, nowhere special. Just thinking some, of all the work ahead of us to get down to Nice before the winter sets in." She took a deep breath.

"I'm hoping to finalize everything now. But you have your research and such in order? Don't seem to even need to ask. Of course you would. That guest room has turned into a library." He bit his nail in contemplation, "Or maybe an office, with all the books and papers."

Adelyn roused herself from half listening, holding Garnett's hand more actively. "I think it was one of the better decisions I've made in my life. It will launch me into something substantial, maybe for when we finally go home." She pushed her hair back from her face and opened the car window to feel the cold and damp air. "It'll be good to feel warmer weather in November, more like home."

"Sorry you married me?" Garnett directed his attention more fully on the perfect ovals of her manicure, afraid to hear her response but suddenly desperate to know.

"Whatever made you ask such a thing?" She let go of his firm grip and touched his face, to pull his jaw up, leveling his eyes to hers.

His voice faltered. "Just, you know. I made you something of a gypsy, roaming the world. Trey doesn't even have real friends to play with, to learn from. Your mama and daddy sittin' in that big ole' house with just a few kin." Momentarily transporting himself to the south he grew up in, his voice and accent subsumed in the place and its people.

"Garnett, Mama and Daddy came over at least twice now, and we get to London to see them." She smiled a tentative smile. "Besides, I like being a gypsy. It's fun."

But she reflected about all of it, remembering her mother's recent letter, saying Captain Jackson ailed with a sore hip. "I'll be ready to go home." She knew her mother to exaggerate when it suited her, but not this time. And with Howard gone, she knew there would be a space left, formerly bright and colorful, that no one could fill. Remembering Howard, the night she met Josephine, she thought out loud, "That's what I'll do, I'll go visit with Josephine."

Garnett stirred from his own thoughts that, predictably, had traveled the same road to the same person, Howard. "What's that you just said?"

"Making a list of things to do before we leave. It's been some time since I visited with Josephine." Adelyn saw a flash of something remembered, an image crossing her mind, something she could see. "Have to tell her of my dream." She whispered this, knowing the dream had been of Innis.

Garnett interrupted her thoughts. "I don't understand your friendships. Suzie's from home, the women at the Sorbonne are both colleagues and students." It seemed he ticked off her life in a series of scenes and encounters instead of the solid base on which she had built her life. "What is Josephine to you, then, if not a dancer? Which I do not fault her or her talent."

Meaning to give it more thought, Adelyn responded abruptly. "Josephine and I share some experiences." Sensing

Garnett's awareness, he would connect it all to Howard, the person she hoped, today, would not be mentioned too often, at least not by her.

"You and Josephine. Surely the connection is not geography. Hell, she's from Missouri and that has to be as far away from Tulip Junction as New York is from Mississippi. What could you possibly have in common, then?"

"We're both women." Not wishing to encourage Garnett's response to the secret she just revealed, she peered out at the rainy streets of Paris on this quiet autumn Sunday. Passing roads made shiny black by the rain, she smiled at the sound of the tires shushing along. "We're home," she said gratefully.

# Chapter Thirty-Six
## JOSEPHINE AND ADELYN

Every time she visited her friend, Adelyn fell in love again with the seduction of art and music. Josephine's apartment, fresh in design and color, felt like a spring day. Sofas in soft colors of green and sometimes light blue arranged in groupings and along walls. The large grand piano occupied a place of prominence along the stretch of windows that opened to a small balcony. Charlene, Josephine's maid, opened the door. Instead of the traditional black silk dress with a crisp white heavily starched apron, she wore a slinky fabric of navy blue to mid-calf. Her dark hair, almost to black, lay on her shoulders in soft curls.

"*Bonjour, Madame,*" Charlene greeted Adelyn, and like close friends, they pecked a kiss to each side of the face. "Miss Josephine will greet you soon." Adelyn had deduced from her cadence and use of English words that the maid had a touch of Asian, which added greater mystery to her personality. *More like French than a French maid would be.*

Adelyn thanked her and accepted a tall glass of tea with lemon. Charlene had committed to memory the favorite drinks of every one of her mistress's friends. Her subtle perfume announced Josephine before she spoke or Adelyn saw her. The fragrance pervaded the room like a garden of roses warmed by a soft sun. Adelyn stood to greet her friend with an embrace. She held her friend's hands and stood back to admire her outfit. "You are exquisite, and that never surprises me." Her friend wore a kaftan robe of bright orange and red, the sash wound around her lithe body, accentuating her slim waist and hips.

"And how did our best friend Howard look as he left us?" Not waiting for an answer, she continued. "Sorry to see that lovely boy leave town. Wasn't it?"

"Well, things will not be as gay, surely." Adelyn felt an immediate pang of loss she knew she harbored in the inner reaches of her soul.

"Have you decided on another?" Josephine read Adelyn's emotions. "Or are we celibate?"

Shaking her head a bit more than casually, Adelyn responded. "Who could replace him? Celibate is not a question for this married lady. More like less lively?" She exaggerated her eyebrow and both women giggled like schoolgirls.

"I know he was that, lively I mean. He could charm a snake out of its skin. That boy is dangerously handsome." Josephine smoothed her hair, "More than a little lost. I'm going to turn serious and tell you what he said to me. He said he'd want you for his own if he could, but that his friendship with both you and Garnett stopped him."

Adelyn spoke to cover the flush of Howard's declaration, while thinking she should stay away from anything resembling extramarital liaisons. *Too complicated.* "My dear, dear friend. It has been far too long since we met, but still, I am glad it's just us for a change." She looked more closely at her friend. "I can see your mind working."

Josephine leaned forward from her seat. She pulled a

French cigarette from a blue box and lit it, blowing out the smoke. "She leaned slightly more toward the window. "I think of you often and wonder how you and your Garnett are."

"Trey and I don't see Garnett near as much as we used to. To be expected, I suppose." She heard a controlled sob in her voice and attempted to belie it with a frail smile.

"Maybe 'living hard' would be a better way to say it." Taking a deep breath, she nodded yes to Charlene's offer of a glass of champagne on a silver tray. "*Merci*, Charlene." She turned back to Josephine. "I am not an expert on marriage, but I would wager most have some falling down sides to them, when people are connected. Garnett and I are at that kind of impasse."

"Perhaps the trip to Provence will make the difference for you, until…," her friend wrapped her long and graceful fingers around the delicate glass stem and sipped, "until you go home?"

"We seem always preparing to leave Paris, yet something prevents us from getting there. We're both very eager. It will be good for Trey. He has one playmate, Monique's little girl, but now needs the company of other little boys."

"And the company of his father?" Josephine filled their glasses again from the bottle chilling in the silver ice bucket at her side. "That would be a very good change for both of them. What will you do in the Côte d'Azur? The weather alone will be a kind respite from the fog and dampness here. The North Sea asserts itself here, doesn't it?"

"Cold weather doesn't play well against the light colors I prefer." She spoke more to herself. "More than once Howard paid homage to my hosiery. I've spent days looking for dark blues and pale peach colors to make him notice…and he didn't disappoint me."

"*Ma chérie*, I'm afraid that would have been the only thing he wouldn't disappoint you with, because there were so many others, if you and he were to be together indefinitely. But I will say, he was steadfast about you, built his days and nights around your, uh, availability, shall we say? You haven't answered my question of your plans for your visit south."

"We are to visit with some of the artists. I am most excited about meeting the women. The Fitzgeralds will be there. Zelda is from over in Alabama, almost country cousins, she and I. The weather should resemble home; even winter in Tulip Junction is warmer and sultrier, not every day, but many." Josephine moved from her chair to sit at the other end of the sofa.

"What I am most interested in for you and for your little boy is that being might change Garnett? I know I speak out of turn, but we are both country girls and southern influenced. Men sometimes take greater precedence than we would like."

"My hope is for the same change in him. Yes, my dear friend, I am hoping it will." Their long afternoon wound down, the dull sky outside a contrast to the warm and summery feel in the grand apartment. Adelyn luxuriated in it, like a warm bath. And so she forgot to tell Josephine of the troubling dream, of Innis coming to her, and Adelyn waking with the memory because she usually didn't. She needed to share it for it to be real. But she needed to hear Josephine's thoughts even more. They said their goodbyes wondering when they would meet again.

Adelyn bundled herself in her heavy wool coat and hurried along the Champs-Élysées with cold rain slanting toward her cheeks, cutting her as it turned to ice. *The dream.* Curious how she remembered dreaming of Innis. "This is not the first time, only remembered moments." Innis acquainted her with his frequent visits when he stole into her mind and back into her heart. "What was it I wanted to say?" *We didn't imagine our happiness. We loved each other.* The wind reminded her of this cold world she wanted to escape. *Escaping to the Côte d'Azur.*

## Chapter Thirty-Seven
### *PARIS CHRISTMAS*

Early fall turned to winter in Paris, and business negotiations stalled Garnett's plans to extricate them to a warmer climate and eventually home. *Two whole years we've been here already.* Adelyn felt time slipping by, further underscored as she and three-year-old Trey decorated the Christmas tree.

"Trey, give Mommy the ball, and she will hang it on the tree for you." Adelyn looked for another, safer trinket for her toddler. She held out her hand, and he pulled his small hand back sharply. His brow creased, and his dark hair fell forward to cover his expression. Tall and slim, even now, she noticed, more like Innis than Garnett, but she judiciously avoided saying so.

When he frowned, like now, she saw Innis, and her heart opened to something warm and caring. *Would Innis still be that way, would he have changed over time, like Garnett?*

"You'll break that pretty ball and get a boo-boo. Give

it to Mommy, and you can put the tinsel on the tree. Look, how pretty." She shook the silvery strands in a bunch to entice him, and he relinquished the fragile red ball.

"Mommy, I want Daddy to come home." Trey danced around the tree that stood in the middle of the large living room, occasionally throwing the tinsel on the tree. "I'm hungry." He ran his fingers across his abdomen and repeated. "I'm hungry."

"Daddy will be home tonight. He'll come in to see you. Monique, please warm Trey's supper and ask cook to begin dinner. I'll eat with Trey in the dining room." Monique nodded and set a box of tree baubles made of painted tin down near Trey. "*Voici quelques babioles pour mon petit homme.*"

"*Merci*, Monique." He bowed to her and the nurse's smile glowed. "Mommy, I want to eat dinner with Daddy." Trey's face darkened with the oncoming storm of toddler tantrum, one a savvy mother who knew her boy could swiftly avert.

"Come to Mama, sweetheart." Adelyn smoothed his hair back and they sat on the sofa together watching the lights on the tree in a semi-dark room. "You'll have some dinner and then some chocolate pudding. Won't that be nice?" She left off her own loneliness in favor of assuaging his. And dinner with her boy concluded with watching him lick his lips after every spoon of his pudding, Adelyn feeling solitary, trapped in a swirl of love and hurt. Trey jumped down from his chair and reached to touch her face as he always did when he wanted her full attention.

"Mommy, don't be sad." He spoke with the precocious wisdom of an almost four-year-old, voicing his honest concern. She bent down so that he could reach her and placed his dimpled little hand on her cheek.

"Am I sad? No, baby boy, Mama's happy because you are her best ever boy and you ate a good dinner. That means you'll grow up big and strong." Her face beamed with love for him as much as it did from her effort to erase any evidence of depression. *God, Can't have my child feeling my emotions.*

Startled by her book slipping off her lap, she glanced over to the mantle where the clock told her what she'd already guessed. *Three o'clock.* Something about that hour brought her to a great unrest. *One o'clock, well, the group had a late dinner. Two o'clock, it took time to say good-bye to all and find a cab to come home. Three o'clock said it took an evening to complete the passion and find a way home.* Adelyn thought of all the words to use but none involved the word 'love'.

Garnett slept with another woman. *There, I've said it.*

A single little lamp at the end of the room provided a small halo of light. She heard a muffled bumping of the foyer door, a shoulder against the closet. She gently shook off the sleepiness to avoid the unpleasantness of shocking her system by moving too quickly.

"Garnett?" With great effort, more than he normally needed, Garnett fumbled with the buttons on his heavy woolen coat. "Here, let me." She pushed the buttons through the holes and slipped it off him, all the while smelling the heavy sweetness of the brandy.

"What time is it?" His voice came out furry and just slightly slurred. In another time, Adelyn might have found it amusing, yet she didn't resist her opportunity. "Three. You'd best not say too much, you're giving yourself away." She turned from him to see Monique outside the door leading to the servant rooms. "What is it, Monique? Everything is fine. You can go back to sleep." The maid had experienced scenarios like this before, and Adelyn didn't much care anymore about appearances.

Garnett steadied himself, gently pushing her away. "Don't need any help." He widened his eyes and took in a deep breath.

"Oxygen is good, clears the brain." She half smiled as

though dealing with an errant child. "Try to walk." She held him by the elbow and steered him to the couch.

"It's settled, tonight. We're going to the Côte d'Azur." He patted his hair down. "Next week."

She stood over him. "Did you say the Côte d'Azur? When did I hear that before?" She smirked. "Last week, yes, we were leaving last week. Or, was that last year?" She sat at the far end of the sofa. "Want some coffee? I can get you some espresso. Don't think it will wake you up too much." This last remark she said to herself more than him. She saw his eyes close, his head nod forward to his chest. "Or maybe sleep?"

Garnett's head jerked back, his eyes flew open. She held onto him and steered him toward the living room sofa. "No! Get the maid; that's what I pay them for. They can make espresso." Lunging for her, he roughly grabbed her arm. "Don't need to be waiting on everybody, friends, the maids, everybody." His eyes grew mean. "Howard."

"Stop it." She pulled her arm free without difficulty, and he slumped against the back of the sofa. She watched as he forced himself to focus on the room and then on her. *So, that's caused it. He's mired himself in pity.* "You listen to me, Garnett Crawford, and listen good. Don't search for too many reasons why it's okay to be drunk. I'm a helluva lot smarter than that."

"Don't have to fetch espresso. Maids do that." He repeated his earlier mantra, lost in it because he began sobering and knew he'd be safer insisting on that than going again where his words had just been.

Adelyn straightened her satin robe and bent down to pick up the book that had fallen, "that started me and this serious imbroglio." She smoothed his shirt. "I'm going to have some hot chocolate. Want some?" She placed the book on the sofa where she had sat. Her mind went back to the earlier remarks he'd made, and anger flowed. "Don't talk to me in that stupid, threatening tone. I'm not one of your secretaries." *So it begins, and this needs to be done.* Her face drained and so did her body; she grew lightheaded with her pent-up rage. "Is that the correct term for them, 'secretaries', or has that gone out of fashion? I'm sure it's more like 'whore' now."

Garnett by now had come fully awake, and halfway to sober. "How about you not talking to *me* like that either." He stood quickly, grabbing her arm again. He lost his footing when she pushed him away, falling once again on the sofa.

"At least you won't wake Trey, sleeping where you fall. He waited for you through his dinner, asking all the time, 'When's daddy coming home, Mama?'" Her voice came thick with emotion. "You're a fool." Adelyn turned away to hide her tears.

"What? You called me that?" A sickening silence stopped him. He saw himself for a moment, as she saw him.

"Just look at yourself, your clothes all mussed, your eyes bleary." She turned back. "Merry Christmas, Garnett."

Christmas, and Trey and the servants and a half dozen of their more genuine friends forced Garnett to retrieve good spirits without benefit of the alcohol kind. But before all that, Garnett's eyes opened slowly on a gray day with a dull headache. He lay in their bed. Near his head on the little lamp table was a glass of tomato juice with a large lemon wedge and two aspirin. Without raising his head from his pillow, he slid the glass carefully to him and drank down the aspirin. Turning to his left, he felt Adelyn's arm resting on his right thigh. His careful movements pushed her arm into his groin causing him to stir more than he wished. He looked directly at her as her eyes slowly opened. She smiled in the first blush of the day when memory fails and the honesty of the subconscious asserts itself. Certain she was not awake as she cuddled to his side, nuzzling her head near his chin, he took advantage of this heaven-sent miracle before it exploded and disintegrated. Carefully, he leaned into her affectionate claim on his body and claimed some of her for himself.

He laid back and concentrated on slow and easy breathing, his lips brushing the top of her head. And he waited as she fell back into sleep. His head clear, he saw the panorama of their marriage, where it had come to and felt a surprised and deeper love. He prayed with every ounce of his once avowed Catholicism for this to be the first day of his new life, and breathed out an imperceptible, "I love you with everything in me and pray forgiveness," which woke Adelyn.

Garnett watched her push her curls from her face, a smile playing on her lips. "Mmmmmm." She stretched her arms out, placed her hand on his face, caressing him. "You're warm." Her expert young mother's hands felt his forehead. He continued in this miracle of her love, hoping against hope that she would stay this way—forget last night, his drunkenness, and his sins. But it came as no surprise when her brow furrowed and her eyes grew dark with the memories he had prayed would not interrupt his new-found dedication to her. She pushed away from him and sat up. "I'm not happy with you."

Garnett winced. "I know." He took her arm and gently pulled her toward him. "Please, darlin', please." He felt her resist him and pulled her down on his chest, covering her face in kisses interspersed with pleading, "Forgive me; forgive me." And felt another miracle begin as she lay closer, gave in to his supplication, and began to paste her naked self against his naked skin.

Then, they were up like a shot, Garnett tugging on the new sweater Adelyn had one of the maids knit for him, wool and silk threads elegantly combined. Adelyn, her head bent down brushing the curl out of her hair and standing up to let it fall around her face. The nurse knocked gently on their door. "Madame, all is ready. The hour is two o'clock."

"Yes, Madeleine. *Merci*. We will be out presently." Adelyn tried to keep her vocabulary simple so as not to confuse the young woman. "Thank God I told them all near three. Do you notice how they all arrive on time? No one seems to want to be fashionably late."

Garnett grabbed her around the waist, his face flushed from sleep and sex and more of both. "That's 'cause they all can't wait to see you." He felt her try to move away and tightened his grasp. "No you don't, *ma chérie*." His breath came hot onto her cheek, and she reached her hand to his forehead. He answered her voiceless question. "Not sick, just love-sick."

The chimes could be heard as the first guest arrived. The maid took her time with the coats and Adelyn emerged to greet Delia and Cicely. "Thank God! Family!" She hugged them both and stanched a tear from gathering on her eyelid, knowing a flood would follow if she allowed even one. "I am so glad you're both here. Look at my boy." Adelyn took Trey's arm and brought him from behind her where he had planted himself, one of his legs between hers.

"*Bonjour, Tante Cicely et Mam'selle Delia.*" His soft, chirpy voice brought out sighs from them both. He switched to English to ask, "Mommy, is Tommy coming with Suzie?"

"Trey, you must remember to say *Missus Warren*, not *Suzie*. Okay? Tommy will be here soon. Don't fret. Tell Aunt Cicely about your new train."

Garnett circled Adelyn's waist while Cicely and Delia looked on. Smiles played on each of the women's faces as they drank in Garnett's good looks, his eyes pasted on Adelyn. They would never say it, nor admit it even to themselves, that they knew Adelyn and Garnett had, not too long ago today, made love. For his part, he couldn't get enough of her, nuzzled her neck with his nose, breathed her perfume behind her ear. Then he woke from his reverie and blushed wildly as he looked at his teenaged sister-in-law.

"You are becoming quite the young lady, Cicely. Breaking every heart in Tulip Junction?" He waited a beat and sipped his drink. "That is one big pink bow you're wearin', girl."

Cicely's red velvet dress complemented her dark eyes and fair skin, but the pink bow signaled her defiant fashion statement. "Garnett, you are always the most gracious host, aren't you?" The two of them had never lost their sparring over who would get Adelyn to confide most in each of them. They both felt the tension fully on, neither ever being quite sure who was winning. "Isn't he, Delia?" Suddenly they all laughed at the absurdity, and relaxed.

Throughout the day, the swirl of guests moved from one main room to the next—light flooded the living room and dining room with their high vaulted ceilings and light draperies, from candles and crystal chandeliers, and the beautiful Christmas tree stood as a centerpiece. Accustomed to the sophistication of their young and energy-filled parents, the children all played under the feet of the adults, looking up and seeing them like so many redwood trees, stretching toward the sky. Their attention centered around the train, little girls and boys alike, and the nurses and nannies took charge of their manners, so they would not jostle the parents and drinks would not spill on their little heads.

"Garnett never misses a beat." Delia whispered near Cicely and Adelyn. "You keepin' him on a leash?"

Adelyn reached over to her friend, affectionately touching her arm, while she straightened her flapper dress of red and green satin. Light shimmered off it as she moved.

She whispered a question to Garnett about his champagne glass. "What are you sipping there?" Garnett flirted with both women while still nuzzling Adelyn.

"No dog that bit me for today, Sugar." He turned his full attention to Adelyn. "You're my only form of intoxication." He handed the glass to her and she sipped the ginger ale that could easily have been the finest Moët. And so it all seemed that it would be good for them again, the joy and peace of Yuletide suffusing them—a fence mended, at least for the moment.

"Yes, it is ginger ale, for a change." She let him nuzzle. An intoxicant more insidious than alcohol drove their mutual addictions, one they acknowledged and even courted, yet never seemed to understand: conflict both created and imbued the magic of their world.

Delia lifted her glass in an intimate toast among them. "To your lovely boy and any other little ones that may accompany him." Her eyes lit up when she saw Adelyn's expression change.

The party went on and on. Chairs had been placed around several large tables to seat all, and Adelyn served her guests turkey and southern home-style foods, though no one could find grits anywhere.

And though the peace remained between them, Adelyn's dreams intensified and tore at her devotion to her husband. On waking in the morning and sometimes in the middle of the night when light hid from the world, she knew right away that Innis had beckoned her.

Fragments of words they spoke to one another would threaten to stay in her memory, and yet all faded even as they took shape on her lips. *What did you say? Love me?* Her whispers never woke Garnett, yet some of the words she spoke in her sleep seeped into him, disturbing his deep slumber. *He said that to you? Even now?* Neither one of them actually heard the other. At least, not yet.

The renewed stamina came with the bridge thrown across their differences, and parties kept them long into the nights between Christmas and the New Year; no time, then, to quarrel or look too closely from where their emotions had just come. December thirtieth found them crossing the channel to England, and Adelyn leaning over the side of the boat and into the choppy sea. She stepped back from the railing and wiped her lips with her handkerchief just in time to hear Garnett behind her.

"Well, Sugar, the ladies are waitin' on you down in the rooms for some fine wine and a little food. What are you doing up here?"

Adelyn recovered and marked the horizon to keep her level. "The air gets so stale inside. Thought I'd just catch a cool breeze." She stuffed her hanky into a coat pocket.

"Stale might not be so bad when freezing is your other option, baby. Come inside. Trey's lookin' for his mama."

They walked down the steps where she immediately felt the confinement and with it the sway of the boat. Her stomach growled with emptiness, and she tried for a wan smile at Garnett when she looked up to see he'd heard it, too. She fumbled in her pocket for some saltines to help fill the void. "Guess it's almost lunchtime. Trey will be hungry."

"Not to mention, your big boy here as well." He hugged her close. "You feeling sickly? A cold?"

She shrugged off his remark. "Fine, Garnett, honey. I'm just fine." Trey ran to them as they entered the small room of passengers in refined clothes and heavy wool coats. Cicely and Delia made room at the tiny table with hot coffee and tea service. Adelyn turned to the waiter, "I'd like some saltines if you have them, please." He nodded and pulled several cellophane packets from his apron pocket.

"Well, you all been behaving yourselves?" She turned to Trey, "Aunt Cicely and Miss Delia been good?" Trey giggled, "Mama, they don't make a fuss, they're old." They all laughed at his remark, Garnett the most. Adelyn congratulated herself at deflecting the attention away from her troublesome sickness as they all chatted, each remark bumping into another as their Sherry cordials infused them with merriment. But Adelyn knew their enjoyment had less to do with the sherry and more to do with their sincere care for one another. Her stomach began to quiet down as she surreptitiously wiped away some beads of perspiration from her upper lip.

*Soon. We'll be off this bucket soon.*

Tears seeped from the corners of Adelyn's eyes as she glimpsed her mother and father from the boat. For the first time since leaving Georgia, she longed for home. As they neared, she saw her mother frantically waving her lace handkerchief. The gate opened to the gangplank and the polite upper crust shoved and pushed their way forward, forgetting that their station obliged them to act better, live on a higher plane. Adelyn chuckled at the sight of them and Garnett held Trey back with a gentle tug to his slim wrist to keep him from being trampled.

Adelyn noticed her mother's face went from wide smile to pursed lips and a slight discerning wrinkle in her brow, and knew she caught Adelyn's pale face against all the complexions ruddy from wind and water surrounding her. Delia huffed up to Adelyn. "You must certainly be coming down with something, Addie. Here, let me help you." Adelyn didn't refuse as she held onto the railing.

"Come to your grandmama, little one!" Mary Jackson swooped Trey up and hugged him tight. "My, what are they feeding you?" She turned toward her daughters, alternately kissing Cicely's cool cheek and noticing the moistness on Adelyn's face. "You okay, sweet girl?"

"I'm fine, Mama. Just a little seasickness. The Channel was choppy today." She hugged her mother and moved on to her father. "How're you, Daddy?" She embraced him and felt the strong and warm of him and it comforted her. *Georgia.*

The day turned into a session of eating excursions because, after all, foreigners in a foreign land do just that. No house full of sofa cushions to plump up, no meals to plan, no social events to fit into a busy life of family and friends to otherwise distract them. So they floated from one restaurant to another, and stopped at the museum to talk while amid the art, half naked and fully naked sculpted figures, and rooms full of colorful paintings on walls. And the constant hum of their everyday voices because they were among their own, and 'everyday' spoke of intimacy and family and the best of themselves given to one another. Throughout Adelyn and her mother shared caring and compassion between them. Looking at Cézanne and the heaviness of his figures, the paint thick on them, Mrs. Jackson fretted. "I just want to be sure you're not coming down with some awful illness, darling." She slipped her arm around Adelyn's waist and Delia did the same from the other side.

"You're right about this, Missus Jackson. Adelyn just got thinner every year since she's been in Europe."

"Well, it's a wonder, because I certainly eat enough rich food. The cheeses alone are gloriously bad." Adelyn's last word brought the vision of all that food and the possibility of having another meal before they would end the evening.

"Forgive me; I'll be right back, Mama." She didn't need to look to see her mother's face with worry all over it.

"Go with her, will you, Delia?" Mary Jackson let go of Adelyn and took Trey's hand to walk back to Garnett, and the others pretending to look at a painting of a boat when they had just moments before stared for ten full minutes in front of a graceful nude. Delia casually took off in Adelyn's wake.

"Addie. You do look a bit green around the gills." Adelyn arrived at the luxurious restroom and dropped onto a sofa. "Can I get you anything?"

# Chapter Thirty-Eight
## *LA CÔTE D'AZUR*

The walls and railings all had an otherworldly look to them; the chipped stone reminded her of ancient stone statues, thousands of years under the sea. Adelyn decided the sun and constant salty ocean had made its mark on all that she touched. *Much like I'll be if I stay here too long.* The thought prompted her to ask herself the question she asked almost every day. *How long is too long?*

"You feel like kin already." Zelda reached out her hand to greet Adelyn, both women offering a dry palm and a firm grip. "Doesn't Adelyn look like Cousin Lucy?" Zelda turned to Scott, his eyebrows raised, appraising the simpatico that they and he could feel.

"It's good to hear the sounds of the south in your voice, Zelda." The handshake evolved into a quick hug. Friends.

She knew Zelda wanted them to stay. *The first Americans I know.* The pretty dark-haired woman said it almost daily, her loneliness putting a tinge to her words, even as she smiled while saying them. Adelyn wondered whether Zelda's sadness infused her own melancholy, stretching on daily with only briefer moments of delight for the place, its painted heavy cream-colored rooms with tall glass doors and a sun bursting onto walls and furniture, yet at the same time the glass doors kept the colder night sea winds from freezing them all.

She noticed the cold wind first, and yet, a warm sun. Still, the southern girl in her wore a big sun bonnet that cast a shadow on her face and wrapped her legs in beach towels to prevent freckles, as well as to wage war against the cold wind. She even shielded her eyes with sunglasses to see her son better. "Trey!" she called out and the four-year-old boy looked from his shovel and pail of sand to smile at her. "Just lookin' for my darling. Don't want any of those big fish to catch you."

Garnett turned on his chaise and opened one eye. "Sugar, you fairly startled me. No fish can catch him. You'll have the boy scared out of his wits about such nonsense."

"Did I wake you from your nap, Mister Crawford?" She smiled over her glass of lemonade, wishing for something stronger, and sighed heavily for Garnett to sit up and reach for her hand.

"Something on your mind? You've been restless since we got here." His green eyes under heavy lashes ran up and down her figure. "Must say, your appetite isn't suffering much." Realizing the violence of the movement of pulling her hand away, Adelyn feigned an interest in turning a page of her book. She spoke to soften her abrupt motion.

"Just that it's colder than I imagined. It's further north, I suppose that's why. Back in the Junction, we'd have some moisture to go along with the sun and things would steam a little." Her stomach roiled quietly so that he didn't notice. Careful to keep some saltines nearby for such an occasion, she nibbled on one now. *You've got to tell him today.* She thought back on their trip over to London last month and now she was three months gone. Last night when they were all bedded down, she wrote to Delia, then, instead of mailing the letter, walked into town and sent a telegram.

**You guessed right STOP Mama guessed too STOP We'll be coming back in late spring when I'm over the queasies STOP Love to all FULL STOP**

"Telegrams." She said this out loud as she walked back up the hill from town, mulling over all the things the telegram didn't say. "Garnett doesn't know STOP" She smiled at her own silliness but that faded away quickly when she thought of the tempest that might accompany her news. "Why, after all? Isn't this good news?" Adelyn knew it could be otherwise. She turned down a small path toward the side doors that led into the sitting room. Zelda had long gone to bed; Scott lingered in town with his writing cronies. Garnett sat in the big soft chair and turned on the light as Adelyn entered the room, startling her. "I thought you were asleep. You scared me."

"Why should that be?" He held a glass of whiskey, she knew, because often when he was restless he would settle into this chair with a book and wait out the nervous energy, and sometimes he would just sit with a drink. "You doin' something you're not supposed to?" His eyes were wary of her. "Where were you?"

Her nervousness matched his as she sat on the footstool, combing her lengthening hair with her fingers. "Walking. In town. It was quiet, away from the wind and the ocean sound."

"Why did you telegraph Delia in London?" He looked up from the ice cubes clinking in his glass and stood up so that she moved to give him room.

Before she could ask, he answered her question.

"The telegraph at the hotel phoned to say your message got through. Then they obliged me by reading it to me for any corrections I might have. Good thing I took those French lessons down there at our old Alma Mater." He poured another shot. "Course, you wrote it in English but the night desk didn't know so I heard it first in French." He gulped his drink. "All that 'guessing' in the telegram? You got a sick stomach."

"You're taking on over nothing." She hesitated. "No, that's not right. It's too important, not just nothing. I'm pregnant." The words rushed out of her while it seemed she stepped out of herself long enough to ponder it all. "We've been through so much; I wanted to wait to tell you."

"Not mine?" He put the glass down and slid forward in his chair, close to her on the foot stool.

And he said it, another of the occasional accusations that attended his whiskey drinking. She started to move, and he took her wrist, noticing its thinness, like Trey's. He became contrite. "No, sorry, don't. Please don't." And she surprised him by staying where she sat and by letting him hold her wrist.

"You're so damned sorry after you've hurt me." She heard his words like a phonograph needle lifted and then touching down again, repeating what should never have been said. "So, then, you've known, and that's what you thought? Not yours? Whose, then?" She realized he had to be far from sober to have said all this. But he said it, and now it lay between them. "Does this ever stop?" Adelyn pulled her skirt to cover her knees and stood. "The baby is yours, and you know it."

A vision came into their individual minds with those magical words, of the sweet smell of an infant and the beauty of that creation. They saw one another once again as the beginning of that life. He folded her into his arms, and he created a carapace around her, protecting her from all physical harm as she carried his child. The mood changed. *Until another time.*

## *Chapter Thirty-Nine*
### *ZELDA—ANOTHER WAY OF SEEING*

The late afternoon sun set the long living room awash with color and light, the room filled with young women in frothy tea-time dresses. "I see more damned flowers in here than out in that garden on a June day," Zelda Fitzgerald whispered in Adelyn's ear. Adelyn smiled broadly as her new friend continued a soft barrage of observations about the *petites fillettes françaises*—'little French girls'. One or another of the many intelligentsias that lined the Paris cafés traveled down to the Côte d'Azur to continue their espresso-and-brioche meetings with the writers *Américains*, and with them came their sweet young girls, all of them graceful, tall and willowy with sharp-etched coquettish faces, and exact and pure Parisian French. They sipped tea laced with liquor and threw long glances at Adelyn and Zelda who mostly ignored them.

Adelyn watched them now as they wove around one another, getting up from one place to greet and buss the cheeks of yet another one as she entered the room. She remembered them from Paris only two months ago, always looking languid and like they might soon fall asleep. *They are asleep.*

"Now tell me, because I know you're sitting there forming opinions." Zelda threw back her head, her fine Alabama accent permeating every word. "That is, one Southern girl to another." Adelyn and she burst into quiet laughter.

"Maybe later, after they retire." Adelyn observed the young women who knew much more English than they let on. She said as much to Zelda and added, "but our southern accents lend some camouflage."

"Adelyn, I don't quite have the energy to care. And Sugar, neither do you." The two young women lazed through the rest of the day discovering one another's history, the little towns they lived in, the young people they knew. They talked of best girlfriends and how they needed theirs. "As important for these girls to have one another."

Almost as one, the French girls began quietly to place their teacups and cake plates on the large tables draped in lace cloths. The sun dropped lower in the sky. They all would return to the hotels to bathe and dress for the evening. Zelda continued to sip her whiskey slowly as they all politely said good afternoon and melted through the tall glass doors. Adelyn settled into her chair, more relaxed.

Zelda breathed out a sigh. "Tell me what you're thinking."

Adelyn felt self-conscious as she picked at her lacy blouse with its full sleeves. "Those sweet and frothy things with their little-girl flat chests and hipless figures who spend their days deciding on which of the most expensive perfumes they'll let their lovers buy, they can't even vote in this country. And to be fair, I came to Paris to be one of them and was one of them, for a while." She said this contemptuously. "Not the many lovers buying perfume, never did that. And voting? Well, we're only just beginning to have a voice in our beloved country." She sat a little straighter. "But I ask myself, was I ever as young as they seem? Because I don't think so."

She noticed a jittery impatience in Zelda who stood to remove a long wraparound skirt, revealing her short ballerina skirt and her white leotard. Reaching under the skirt of the chair, she pulled her ballet shoes out and slipped her feet into them, carefully avoiding wrinkles that could later bruise and hurt her feet. She wrapped the long silk ribbons flat against her feet with a rhythmic motion, and they molded onto her feet, becoming one with them.

"Tell me what changed you, then." Zelda's deep eyes bored into her.

"I had something of a vision. Remembered the university and how fulfillment came while I studied."

Adelyn listened for a heartbeat of a moment for Garnett and Trey. *They must be in town still.*

She brought herself back to the moment. "At the Sorbonne, and even earlier when I was at the University, I was just me, not anyone's at that point. I belonged to me."

Zelda lifted her head, her feet and legs done up. "What does that mean, 'anyone's'?"

"At Georgia U, and before I was married, of course, at school, I wasn't my mother's daughter, my friend's confidante." Adelyn hesitated, "not even my beau's to do with, though, truth be told, I was on fire when he was there, couldn't hold back from touching him. Caused his brother, Garnett, many a fierce temper when he saw us, because he knew from the start."

"How is it that he knew? His brother, what was his name, Innis? So much older, they wouldn't travel in the same circles, would they?"

"Because there was always honesty between Garnett and me, back then." She saw an image of them in the barn after Innis's funeral, and remembered the magic of them reading one another's thoughts. *Not something we've done in a long time.*

Adelyn continued. "I never denied it when he challenged me that I was Innis's." She stopped for a second, recalling how the two brothers had been when she first met them. "They were close, but Garnett almost hated us both for it, yet never quite damned me."

All this talk conjured a score of images long forgotten, and she fell into a reverie of emotions from the time.

"Garnett accepted it, I think. Somewhere along the way I actually hoped I would grow out of my need for Innis. Or he would find someone else."

Adelyn conjured a flash, thinking she saw the sun moving across the sky, a momentary vision. Several dreams of Innis, she reckoned them as dreams now, where a girl in a white dress stood so very close to Innis, their bodies almost melding into one. Images so disquieting, Adelyn retreated from them and turned back to Zelda. "Tell me why dance has so intensely captured your interest."

Zelda smiled, "You heard us arguing last night? Hell, every night, it seems. I am so very tired of the same lament." She blew smoke from a cigarette in a long, ivory holder, and the two women watched the smoke billow and fall from an unseen draft of an open window.

"You ask me about dance, why am I obsessed with it? Dancing takes the place of writing. That's what we really argue about. His temper is ferocious—the only word for it. Enough to scare me."

"What does he say?" Adelyn leaned forward to capture Zelda's words as they began to fade into a whisper.

The quiet space between them became interminable as Adelyn watched her friend struggle with whatever demons captured and held her. "That I was stealing his stories. But, Addie, he froze when I told him he was stealing my life with his writing. Because every story was me." She swallowed the sob in her voice as she stood and opened the wide doors into her studio.

And Adelyn knew and felt grateful for her life and how it had come to be.

After Zelda's sad recounting of her dilemma with Scott, she retreated into herself through her dance, spending more and more time in her studio. Adelyn understood, relieved just to take walks on the beach with Trey, where his observations of the world made her feel younger and older at the same time. And Garnett, when he strolled with them, managed to express that center-of-power part of his persona.

"Watch now, Trey. See how the waves crash in and then go back out?" His voice sounded harsh against the sound of the sea that threatened to mute him. "Be careful! Don't get too close." He lifted the boy away from the edge as the undertow produced yet another danger.

Adelyn walked behind but came quickly up to them as a nubile young woman in a one-piece revealing bathing suit approached from the opposite direction, all smiles and coquetry; Garnett, tipping his hat to reveal his blond-streaked reddish hair. Adelyn saw the woman's eyes on him, and sadly his expression, forgetting for that moment those who loved him.

"Come here, Trey." Adelyn brushed hard past Garnett on the water side and took gentle hold of the boy still bound to test the strength of the waves. She swooped him toward the rush of waves and dipped his legs and bottom in for him to feel the coldness of the water. Trey squealed and she hugged him to her as she walked fast and away on the hard sand.

"Now wait, you two." Garnett breathed heavily as his feet sank into the softer sand farther away from the water. He came up to her, shyly looked down, avoiding her eyes.

"You bastard." She formed the words without saying them so her son would not hear. "Well, now, you're out of breath, son." She knew using this language would evoke Howard. "Must be you're gettin' older, need to have a nurse to help you along." Her smug voice and sharp smile revealed the taunt.

"Baby." Garnett stopped in front of her. "Let's try that little café down the way." He pointed to a building a half mile away. "If it's not too far."

"Not for Trey and me, but we're not sure about you, ol' man." She rushed along, finding new energy through her anger at him.

They sat in the outdoor café, Garnett all hail-fellow-well-met, doing his best to be more to her, kindly, stroking her hand, winking at his son who giggled when his father made funny faces.

She wished for home. For the familiar and comfortable and the piece of her she used to be, wondering whether she had changed so much that going back home would not be the same. And in that thought, something happened. Her mind and something else took her inward where images of Tulip Junction heaped on her in pieces. She saw Innis, in a summer white linen suit, walking toward her, his beautiful shining dark eyes embracing her. She closed her eyes, felt his hand on her cheek. She said his name and heard him say hers. Opening her eyes she saw Garnett's face, white under a tan. *Did he hear me? Calling you?* And back came the answer, unmistakably, *Why, yes, Sugar, he knows.*

# *PART IV*
## *JOURNEY HOME*

## *Chapter Fourty*
### *THE VOYAGE*

The ocean's turbulence made a fitting metaphor for Adelyn's emotions. She counted her spiraling up and down as part of her delicate and very pregnant condition. The baby seemed to grow despite her roiling stomach and frequent nausea. In London, before they left, Mrs. Jackson filled her daughter's make-up case with tonics 'from home' with explicit instructions.

"Now you listen to me, Missy. I know you've become an expert in all things, but these potions with the red stopper are going to get you through this trip. If you'll just do as I say."

Her mother held up a hand and continued before Adelyn could object. "I've written everything down. When you find the time, you sit long enough to read each one."

Not wishing to end their days in a snit, Adelyn nodded, taking the little notebook and leafing through it, recognizing her mother's neat handwriting on page after page. Headings topped with heavily underlined labels identified each little bottle of potion and what it magically cured: "<u>Headache</u>", or "<u>Heart Burn</u>", and lastly, "<u>Upset and Nausea</u>". She tucked them all away inside the big steamer trunk but neglected to take them out when the maids were packing. Now, stowed below in the ship's hold somewhere, she suffered with each of these symptoms, more than she cared to think about. *Not going to ask someone to dig through god knows how much luggage to find mine.*

Nauseated in the state room, Adelyn lay on her bed, cold damp cloth on her forehead, forcing herself to breathe slowly and deeply. The door to the room opened.

"Trey's asleep. Took some time, though." Garnett sat down carefully, fearful of jarring motions that would send Adelyn back into the lavatory. "You okay, Sugar?"

"It's slowed down some." She reached for a package of saltines. "Cicely and Delia up on deck?"

"Here. Let me." He tore open the cellophane and handed her one cracker at a time as she munched and swallowed. "Delia's back in the cabin watching over Trey, and Cicely is on the indoor deck watching some young men playing backgammon. Or, they're watching her watching them, not sure which is the most accurate."

Her dizziness dissipated. "Think I'll try to sit up. Sick of lying about like an invalid."

"Shouldn't this be gone now, this morning sickness?"

Adelyn laughed, "Morning? Haven't recollected the time much, but I'd say it was an all-day affair."

He smiled at her wit and then they smiled at one another as he took her hand and stroked it. "So sorry, baby. Wish this were over." He looked at his watch and she asked him the time.

"Almost dinner." Whether she would sit alone in their room and eat the plainest of foods as she had done for the last three days went unasked.

"Nope." She sat up slowly, and he put his arm around her.

"No about what, precisely?" He waited and, seeing her steady, moved off the bed to reach into the bathroom and start the shower.

"Just sayin', not addressing anyone in particular. *No* to being an invalid. Think I'll try on that new dress, see if it still fits." Her words came back at her like a wind had blown them. *This bulge is a beautiful reminder.* She slipped the dress over her head, a dark wool usually fitted at the waist. At the last minute, before they left the Côte d'Azur, the seamstress let it out to accommodate her midsection growth. Mentally, she scolded herself for her vanity about her bulging abdomen, recalling how thrilled she'd been when she carried Trey. Yet she knew everything had changed about her, about pregnancy, about Garnett. *Almost five years ago.* Garnett stood facing her, gently pulling her to him. He felt the bulge of their tiny addition and rubbed her belly protectively. "Thinking on any names yet?"

She dropped the dress to the floor, and he bent to pick it up. And as people who share a life of intimacy, she stripped to her unselfconscious nakedness. He reached behind him to turn off the shower, cupped her, and felt the warmth, thinking for a moment of the miracle that would spread her and be born of her. She moved in his hand and his pulse quickened. They made love in a slow and languorous way, and he filled her with himself.

Adelyn turned over on her belly. "Tyler. I thought the name Tyler, after my cousin. That I loved that boy. Such a pity to lose him in a stupid war."

Garnett nuzzled her breasts; she smelled of flowers the way that only French perfume can capture. "Tyler's nice. Bet he'll have red hair." He covered her legs with the light blanket that lay on their feet. "Listen to us, taking on this way. Could be a girl."

Adelyn propped herself up on her arm. "No. I don't make girls. Only boys." She raised her brow to make the point, and he laughed, shaking his head. *She probably knows that for sure.*

"I'll go warn everyone that you'll be having dinner upstairs. Good thing, too, 'cause we're at the Captain's table tonight." He quickly hitched up his trousers, one suspender at a time, and threw on his blazer. "Now, don't take too long fussing with your hair and such."

Adelyn showered in the tiny cubicle of their bathroom, first carefully covering her hair in a shower cap. The water glanced down her face and she held a cloth to it, keeping in the steam, remembering someone – her mother? – telling her how the steam kept the face clear. She wrapped up in a thick robe and dotted her face with a Parisian cream, softly rubbing her neck and face. The cream absorbed, and she examined her eyes, green and amber, the irises ringed with black, making them appear darker than they really were. *So like Innis's.*

She conjured images of them together, remembered how he held her—how different his lovemaking from Garnett's. Her heart beat faster again. *Stop!* Then, continuing to think out loud, "What is wrong with me? Why is he still so alive to me?" Her mind flooded with every dream she'd ever had and never recalled, though each time she held just a little piece of the memory. Most of it would be gone immediately after she saw the dream in her mind's eye, she would feel the loss, though not understand why.

Her eyes flitted back and forth, watching the images, walking with him, talking with him. *Go away, Innis.*

Rapidly and looking each way around her for him, Adelyn dressed, pulling on stockings, gliding lipstick faintly on her lips, brushing and shaping her hair to frame her face. She stepped into the green dress that still lay on the floor framing the slip inside it, dashed some perfume on her wrists, and without looking around, switched off the lamp, and bolted out the door and up the stairs to her husband and the others. Yet all the while, Innis stayed in front of her eyes, his long fingers reaching for her arm, his whispered breath on her earlobe. She could hear him. *"Adelyn, sweetheart. You're coming home. I feel you nearer every day."*

# *Chapter Forty-One*
## *SUSPICION*

"What is taking her so long?" Garnett groused to Cicely and Delia, but neither paid him any mind. He turned directly to Delia. "The nurse is with Trey?"

Delia took a small gulp of her champagne. "Not to worry, dear. That nurse is fine. I'll be taking her from you one day." Garnett smiled at that. *She will marry late, and may not have need of a nurse or nanny.*

Finally, at the edge of the large banquet room, he saw Adelyn enter, the green dress disguising her changing form. He began to smile, but something about her expression stopped him. Later he would reflect that she closed him off, the way she acted when Innis courted her, and Garnett felt a metal gate and lock kept him from her. The sound around him muffled—no longer did the high ceilings create a great echo in the ballroom. He heard no silverware against china, nor voices soft or loud. His mind traced the last days of Paris with memories of slights and hurts. *Does she hold memories of Howard?* He wondered at these thoughts; why they should bedevil him now?

Garnett watched Adelyn move fast toward him, not running, but skimming the ground, floating as her spirit ran ahead of her. *The magic lies not just being back home; it lies in going home.* Garnett knows this, has seen this before, all those years ago.

As quickly as they were shut out of sound and air, and only them, it all came back, the room, the noise of a hundred voices in conversations at all the tables. All waited and then a hush. The Captain arrived and traced his way to the table. Garnett felt the cooler air coming back into the room, into his lungs. Adelyn stood by him and placed her champagne glass on the table in front of her seat.

*"Bonsoir, madame et monsieur."* The captain lifted Adelyn's hand, and though it took only a moment, he paused as his lips kissed her hand, making it a caress. He smiled while replacing it with its owner. The moment did not get past Adelyn, or Garnett, who looked more closely at Captain Heller. Tall, with soft dark hair falling a little onto his forehead, dark eyes, and a smile Garnett remembered as familiar. The resemblance to Innis suddenly jolted him.

"Good evening, Captain." The words came out in bites. Garnett dropped the solid handshake before it squeezed into an unfriendly crush. The moment stretched long enough for them to seek one another's souls, and an advantage over the other's weakness. Garnett's athletic strength won out as the Captain remembered his position and relented.

All at the table had been seated except for Heller who raised his glass and saluted Adelyn, then the other women and men, and then the ballroom in general. "Our voyage is now closer to home for some of us, and farther away for those who come to visit our great country." He replaced his glass on the table, and still standing, bowed his head gracefully to offer a prayer. "God, keep us safe now and wherever we travel." All around, soft murmurs of *Amen*, a synchronized chorus sounding as one voice.

"Mrs. Crawford, I've had the pleasure of meeting your mother and father in Portsmouth before we departed."

Adelyn sipped from her glass. "How is it that you know them, Captain Heller? Surely, you don't know Tulip Junction?" Her eyes never left his face.

"Captain Heller has kin in our county, Sugar." Garnett's voice smoothed to a sultry lilt, something Adelyn hadn't heard so much while in Paris.

Adelyn pulled her gaze from Heller's eyes and looked deeply into Garnett's. "A small world for all of us, then." She leaned into his side and felt him relax with her warmth.

"Your husband tells me you all traveled quite a bit in a short time. Paris, London. You've been to New York as well. Impressive for one so young."

Reflecting on his remark, Adelyn sipped some more of her champagne. Something turned in her, a moment of ascending the ladder one step more toward maturity, and awareness of the way of the world. "Why Captain Heller, I didn't know extensive travel was a benchmark for anything impressive. I'm just grateful to the powers that be for being born a Jackson, married to a Crawford."

Garnett heard her through all the din of the grand dining room, and in turn, found himself more fully aware of her outside of her roles of his wife, the mother of his son, pregnant again. He loved this girl, now a woman, maybe he always had. One other thought came niggling into his consciousness. *Maybe Innis saw her this way, and how she would grow.*

Garnett squeezed her hand in affection and in desperation, holding on to her. Understanding the rage he experienced when she stood up against him at Christmas; she cajoling better behavior out of him; he knew she meant it for his benefit, and yet he hated it at the same time. She had become more precious than ever to him.

Dinner arrived and Adelyn forestalled further response, grateful for the chance to examine the swirl of the others at their table—Delia smiling broadly at her and Cicely making moon eyes at the young man to her right. *This does feel like a magical night, more like Tulip Junction than a ship at sea.*

Jealousy, though, came in as green as the turbulent ocean as Garnett listened to the Captain straining to make an impression, outright flirting with Adelyn. *Does it ever change, can I expect this always, even at home?* Raising his fork to enjoy the most lavish of foods served to him, he decided to stay sober and be watchful. Heller played his role as host impeccably, sitting between Adelyn and Garnett, turning alternately to one and then to the other.

"Mr. Crawford, I understand your work involves law?"

Garnett put his fork down, having just swallowed a bite of sumptuous gratinéed potato laced with grated cheese. Sipping from his wine glass, he replied, "We work in international law really, much of it in corporations establishing themselves in other countries."

"Paris, then, would be one such place?" Heller adjusted his immaculate white jacket, his muscles bulging slightly.

"Paris, yes." Garnett smiled to himself, reasoning that the captain should either give up his rowing machine or risk splitting a seam. "We're in Belgium and as far away as India."

Heller nodded, ruminating over his filet mignon Béarnaise. "And you negotiate the contracts as far away as India? That must entail travel as well."

"We send mid-level attorneys accompanied by some senior people. I spend most of my time drawing up the conditions and finalizing after the negotiations."

"Well, my best negotiation is done on the waves of this ocean and the elements frequently call the shots for us. Nature can be a humbling experience." He turned toward Adelyn, "Mrs. Crawford, in all that travel, do you accompany your husband?"

Garnett watched Adelyn with fresh eyes. Her color high from the wine and the company, Garnett knew Heller's attention wore on her. She much preferred the moving crowd of a salon where two or three exchanges occurred before she moved on, only to come around again an hour later with some witticism that closed the discussion or lent it new perspectives. He watched her with a heart exploding in love and appreciation as she made short work of the captain's fawning.

"We spent most of our time in Paris, Captain Heller. India doesn't appeal to me, so thank goodness Garnett's business didn't require us to travel there." Delia signaled Adelyn to join her. "Excuse me, gentlemen."

Garnett watched her graceful movement as she floated out of the grand ballroom with Delia. His thoughts sought release from a maze of conflict, remembering her on campus, Innis's funeral, all of it. His heart beat a little faster as he thought of her reaction when he revealed he would be traveling to New York almost as soon as they arrived home. He could not resist a smirk with the thought that no one in Tulip Junction would turn her head. *With Innis gone now.* The smugness of his thinking evaporated, as if his brother waited at home for their return. He shrugged away the thought. *Don't believe in ghosts.*

Adelyn and Delia stopped to talk with Cicely and curtail her gin and tonic consumption. Hugging her friend and her sister, Adelyn made her way back to Garnett, curious about the expression playing on his lips. *A smile? Rare for him.* She sat down like a whisper into her chair. "My, darling, you look like a Cheshire cat with cream on your mind, and on your lips."

His muscles went from coiled to relaxed as she leaned into him. She heard his breathing change and luxuriated knowing that she could still reach him this way. "What's on your mind, Sugar?"

"Thinking on our trip home. Before he started making his other rounds, the captain said we're in for some more storm." He played with her fingers, opening her palm and kissing it.

"Garnett, honey. Not in public like this." She squeezed her palm shut and nuzzled him to lighten her scold. "More storm? And I just began to feel a little better. I wish I had not sent Mama's parcel of potions down in the hold with our other stuff." A change took over him and she watched as it pulled him into himself, reminiscent of their lives when they were apart in Paris.

"Something troubles you." She looked around at the half-eaten desserts and the espresso growing colder in their tiny cups. "Let's go back to our room."

And his body shifted once again as he stood and offered his hand to help her rise, pressing her toward him; for an instant she felt his warmth, his solidness, and hoped that this worry he carried would float away.

# Chapter Forty-Two
## *TULIP JUNCTION*

As they inched forward toward home, Adelyn wished for calmer seas. The trouble in Garnett's eyes increased. Several nights on this long journey she woke to find him absent from their bed, and more than once she threw a heavy coat over her silk nightgown to search for and find him on the upper decks, walking or just sitting in one of the lounge chairs. They argued between moments of caring gestures, he protective of her and their unborn child, she listening to his concerns about work over the companies he needed to protect.

"Why are you out here in this cold?" She threw a lap robe over his legs and sat along his side, feeling his shivers. When he failed to respond, she threw angry words at him. "Sorry you left your little mademoiselles back there, are you?" As her belly grew, so did her petulance.

"Why do you say that?" Puzzled by what he considered sudden anger in her voice, he would come back to her from his own thoughts, see her again. "Did I say something? Do something? To warrant this?" They retreated from one another finding refuge in silence; avoidance became their solution. Late in the night when their physical need of one another asserted itself, they found unhindered honesty. Garnett loved Adelyn and she loved him. And Trey, he brought out their best with one another and with him.

"Sweet girl. You're almost home and back to me."

"Innis? How can this be? You're gone." No ocean's steady motion; Adelyn stands on hard ground in her dream, dusk and Tulip Junction and the gravel road in front of the great house.

"Can you see? You're home. Right now, in your heart. Tell me you still love me."

The gravel feels real as it pushes against the thin leather soles of her shoes. Innis's warm breath tickles her bare neck.

"Everything looks like spring, Innis. Young and clean."

Her hand travels to her belly, but it is flat.

"Tyler's not there." Innis's warm hand on her shoulder steadies her, calms her.

Alarmed, she asks him, "Did you take him?" She turns to see his face as he shakes his head.

"No, Sugar. I don't have those powers, and I wouldn't want them. He's safe inside you right now."

"Then why is it? There's no place for reality here? Just a dream?"

She sees emotion in his otherwise serene face. Darkness, sadness. "Because I want to see you as you were with me."

"Adelyn, wake up, baby. Wake up." Garnett's warm hand on her shoulder held her against him. She remembered the dream. How Innis touched her but she never touched him back.

"Nightmare last night?" Compelled to ask yet wary of her, of what she would tell him. Garnett stirred his coffee, waiting, while she stared deeply into her espresso as if to find the answer there.

"Was that what happened? I'm not sure. I thought it was a dream about Tulip Junction. Everything as I remembered it." She laid her hand on his arm to stop his stirring. "Garnett, you'll stir the heat right out of your espresso."

"It was a dream, Sugar. Maybe wrapped up in a nightmare. You were talking out loud, sounding disturbed by something." She bided her time and he bit down hard on his lip to keep from screaming in frustration. "Are you still asleep, or daydreaming? Didn't you hear my question?"

"I don't know how to answer you." Searching, she fell back inside herself again and then as quickly spoke. "I had a dream about Innis. Only it wasn't a dream, it was real. I know from the look on your face what this is doing to you, but I made a decision and now I'm going to say it. He was courting me, like back when I was just a girl." Hesitating, she stopped Garnett from the torrent of his rage. "I know how you feel because...."

"Stop it, Adelyn!" His words came out whispering yet staccato and biting. "Trey is in the next room and finally, Lord knows, down for his nap. I'm trying not to blame you because reason says you don't control a dream, yet there's this unnatural sense of it, like you're saying it was real. How? How can it be real? Innis was real? You were with him and knew he was real? Do you have any idea how ridiculous this all sounds? What did he want?"

"Yet you ask me what he wanted. He wanted me." Her voice barely a whisper.

"We all know that. He's always wanted you. What did he say he wanted?" He pulled her to her feet. "Because whatever you say he wanted is really what you want. If he's in your dream telling you he wants you, then you're wanting him. Do you see how unnatural that is? And you, you are pregnant."

"Can I be hung for a dream?" She loosely embraced him, out of her desire to comfort him, not out of desperation. Garnett picked up the phone on the first ring. "'Yes. I'll be up now. Thank you.' Addie, they have a telegraph message for me from New York." Grabbing a sweater, he told her, "I won't be long. Call the nurse to sit with Trey while he naps so you can rest."

# Chapter Forty-Three
## *SPIRITS BECKON*

Wishing for a moment of his father's time to gain perspective and realizing how childish that must sound, Garnett took the steps two at a time to the telegraph office. Two stodgy old men with objectionable cigars stood in front of him, blocking him from the only reality he'd felt on this damn boat.

*With the exception of Adelyn and Trey.* He thought this like a *mea culpa* in the priest's confessional. Yet truthfully, the desire for solid land under his feet paled next to his desire to talk with his father, Will Crawford. He always helped his son see the farther shore of things where a stronger truth held sway.

The cigar smoke set everyone in the office coughing.

"Sirs, would you kindly divert the smoke? The ladies here would certainly appreciate it."

Garnett cleared his throat more emphatically to drive home his point. The men harrumphed a few times, one of them picking up his telegraph message, and left the office. Garnett presented his passport to the young man behind the teller's cage. The boy sifted through a thick pile of papers to find the right one, took Garnett's signature, and handed him the telegram.

*Hope sailing weather is good STOP See you in Southampton Sunday next STOP Good news on the Irvington Account STOP Boston for you following week FULL STOP J Tinker*

Garnett knew before he'd read it. He knew before he climbed the stairs, before he got those two old blowhards out of the way with their cigars. He knew his company had planned this, prepared him for this. Walking slowly on the upper deck, he forced himself to luxuriate in the sun behind a pale cloud, the cold air of the sea. He plotted out how it would go and headed back to the telegraph office. This time no one waited.

"I'd like to send a telegram."

The boy shoved a form out to him. "You can fill it out right here." He handed Garnett a pencil. "Usually quiet when we're closer to home."

Quickly, before he changed his mind, Garnett wrote hurriedly and shoved it back. The boy counted the words, lips moving as he read. Garnett thought he saw an eyebrow raise when he saw the word 'Dad'. He shrugged; it didn't matter. The form fluttered from the boy to yet another young boy who's thin and long fingers typed out the words onto the Morse machine. The message went back through the ranks to Garnett as the boy handed him the copy. Garnett walked down the steps, and like the boy, read with his lips forming every word.

*Almost home STOP Adelyn Trey and all are well STOP Want to spend some time with you before we get too busy STOP Love you Dad FULL STOP Garnett*

He checked his first impulse to hurry back to the stateroom and Adelyn. With a measured step, Garnett climbed to the upper deck, the place she found him late at night. He asked himself what he expected his father to say to make his world better. Could he be that honest, to say he's worried about his marriage? He remembered his younger years when Innis courted Adelyn, how he sought his father's opinion about her because he loved her even while Innis loved her.

*Are you sure Dad didn't just make himself available?* He shrugged in answer to an unasked question and decided a crazy magic surrounded him, Adelyn, and the Jackson family where thoughts flew one to the other, and it had all started with his wife.

No, he would not tell Adelyn about the telegram and New York. He would call Tinker, maybe meet up with him in Washington, and try to stall on New York until the baby came. He knew he could do that. His step came lighter with this decision. But halfway around the great ocean liner's deck, he became morose again. *When, though? When should I tell her that I'm leaving? That she'll have to weather all of it, living with her mother and father? Adelyn and Trey and the baby. I'll tell her. But not now.*

"Cicely, honey, hold onto Trey for a bit while I get these clothes separated." Adelyn surveyed the stateroom—every surface, every chair, the beds and sofas, strewn with her clothes, Garnett's suits and such, and Trey's little sweaters, pants, and blankets, so she could hardly see the furniture. Shoes formed a long train from the door to the adjoining rooms.

"Sure thing, Addie. Will the shoes go in first?" She had Trey's hand and bent to him to say, "Now sugar, you and I'll walk upstairs to watch the big ocean water."

"Aunt Cis, I saw that ole' ocean. I want to see something else." His face brightened at a thought. "Maybe we'll see seagulls. And you could help me find a cookie." He twisted toward Adelyn, "Mama, I'm hungry."

"You're always hungry, little man. Let's see what we

can find up on deck." Cicely swooped him up and carried him out to the hall. "Delia said she'd come by in a bit."

Absently, Adelyn nodded to Cicely. "Sure thing. Now, where did I put that fur jacket?"

Though the bustle had kept her occupied, Adelyn felt a lingering nagging at the back of mind. Something had changed in Garnett yesterday. Nothing important, he had said, just some business to tend to at the New York office when they disembarked. They would be staying a few days and then traveling down to Savannah by train. While her mind flew, so did her hands, as she folded and packed clothing, all the lightweight things at the bottom of suitcases, or in the lower drawers of the steam trunk. Finally, the late winter-weight clothing for New York. The shoes went in a separate smaller case, lined up much as they had been on the floor.

"Some fresh air for now," she decided. Feeling the perspiration run from her hairline down her neck, she closed the last of the cases and threw on her heavy sweater.

Absentmindedly, she pushed the lift button to find herself on the second floor. Halfway down the wide halls she looked up out of her reverie to see an arrow pointing to the Grand Ballroom. "There's a service elevator in here I'll use, 'cause I won't trace my steps all the way back to where I started." Careful not to strain herself, she found the door heavy, yet it swung open easily enough. The sound of it echoed down the vast wood dance floor and up into the rafters of the stage where the orchestra entertained them through dinners and events.

She noticed a faint sound of instruments, muffled but clear enough to recognize—music from a time back in her memory. *The Christmas party at Delia's when I first danced with Innis.* She feels something graze her shoulder and looks into the dim haze of the room. People move around the floor in their formal dance steps, faint, like the music, in old-style ball gowns, women with long gloves and long strands of pearls. Diamond clips sparkle on white satin. A couple brushes against her as they slowly waltz past. *What'll I do when you are far away, and I'm so blue, what'll I do?* An arm surrounds her waist; she looks to see Innis.

"How?" She barely speaks the word because she knows she walks in the waking world. He doesn't speak, just holds her close and she remembers it all. The dance, his body, his legs pressing against hers suggestively. "I saw these people, Innis. Back then. They danced around us, with you and me, but they do not dwell in this world. Did they follow you then, knowing you would join them?" She looks up to see his expressionless face fall sad around his lips, and then they all disappear, and so does he.

"No, no. Can't be." Her voice rang louder than any of the sounds she'd just heard. A live voice, she decided. She walked quickly, though her feet felt as though she walked through water, and she felt herself shake all over. She turned and screamed at the empty room that seemed to be beckoning her back. "No! Go back, all of you!" Running through the opened door, she found the hall she needed in a series of right turns, saying out loud, "I came in making left turns. This way, then." A stairway appeared she hadn't seen earlier, and fresh air and light flooded the hall. She ran up toward the air like someone swimming up toward the water's surface. The sun almost crushed her eyes as it burst on her after so much dimness. She merged onto the deck and into Garnett's arms.

"Addie, sweetheart. You look sick. Why did you take the stairs?" He smoothed her hair and kissed her face. And she felt alive again. *None of this happened. None of it.*

# *Chapter Forty-Four*
## *NOW WE ARE FOUR*

Her nightmare stretched out in front of her. Adelyn felt chained to New York City, yet for all its bustle and excitement, it increased her restlessness. Even with Trey in tow, she felt alone; with Delia meeting her new beau and Cicely back at college, the hotel room lost its charm. She found the park difficult to navigate, and she really just wanted to feel the warmer Georgia breezes, and to see her family.

"You've been either down in that lobby meeting a bunch of cigar-smoking Neanderthals or up here on the phone. I'm going home."

"That's right, Mr. Sandwell. We'll be there tomorrow at nine sharp." Distracted, Garnett only heard her irritation, not the content. He reached out to take her hand where he shared the spacious couch. "Don't you like this suite, honey? The luxury of it…"

"Hush, luxury. I booked our car on the train to Savannah for tomorrow." Adelyn surprised herself as she took a deep breath and slowly breathed out a more patient tone. "I know you can't help being busy. I want to get settled at home."

Everything reminded her of Paris; she thought New York made a poor substitute. Her pregnancy stretched her clothes tightly around her midsection. "If I'm to be this ungainly, I'd rather be in Tulip Junction."

She bit her tongue against her thoughts spilling out how the mirrors in the hotel didn't always reflect her image. On one or two occasions, she thought she saw something fleeting behind her, something in white. The specters in the ballroom as the ship neared New York's harbor became a faded memory until she and Garnett saw land. Then the ghosts dancing to old tunes came sharply to her and refused to leave. *And now these mirrors.* Adelyn began to remember. Remember dreams with Innis, and how she spoke to him. She recalled him pulling her into somewhere.

"Just a dream." She chided herself out loud, and as she did, her words fell like leaves off a tree in cold weather. *Just dreams?* She questioned herself, and then knew.

Deliberating on her words, Garnett pulled her back from her increasingly sullen moods, telling himself her pregnancy triggered her moodiness.

"I want you near me, but maybe it's better for Trey as well. They'll be other children to play with back home." He got closer and laid his cheek against her neck and she let herself be comforted. She left the next day; only the porter saw her and Trey off.

"Miz Crawford, wake now." The voice whispered. "I don't like it. Call Doctor Harris. She's not responding quick enough." A cool hand at Adelyn's wrist. "Miz Crawford? Adelyn?"

Turning on her side, Adelyn winced. *How could it be so easy the first time and so difficult now?* A breeze freshened her face, or did it come from the fan Garnett brought down from New York? Or was it Boston? She gave up trying to recall yet her body wouldn't let her rest; the stitches pinching her reminded her.

A strong hand covered her own, pressing into her. "Sugar. Can you open your eyes for me?"

Adelyn blinked. "Get something to wipe my eyes, they're closed shut." A cool wet gauze swept over her lashes and she blinked to see the worried face of her husband. "Baby." His lips touched her forehead. "Sweetheart." He smiled and kissed her face and her lips. "How're you feeling?"

Adelyn struggled with the sheet laying over her legs and tried to pull up, wincing again. "Help me sit up some, Garnett."

The nurse appeared on the other side, with Garnett lifted Adelyn gently, and propped pillows behind her. She felt how sitting on a comfortable mattress took the strain off her back, and thankfully deadened the nerves where the pain would be coming from. She took cool sips of water followed by some lemonade.

"Thank you, Jesus." Still befuddled by the anesthesia, Adelyn exclaimed at the chicken dinner placed in front of her. With knife and fork in hand, she ate while Garnett chatted.

"You were late." She sipped the last of the lemonade and checked the clock on the wall. 4:15. The late August sun slanted toward the west and away from her window, as a breeze pulled the warm air around.

"And thank you for the fan." Turning toward Garnett, she raised a brow. "Have you seen Tyler yet?"

Closing the *Tulip Tribune*, Garnett inched his chair closer to the bed. "Now, you know that the first thing was to see that little fella. The nurses say he sleeps any chance he gets." Lowering his voice, he whispered, "Brought Trey over to see his little brother. I know what you're going to say, Trey carrying germs and such. The boy was looking at him through the glass window." Then Garnett admitted, "I know I was late. Boston took much longer than New York.

I'll be here now for the month, promise."

He was gone two days later, before she completed her lying in, something about New York and Wall Street. Adelyn tried to keep up but it always came down to the greater world. From her arrival, homecoming had a false ring of celebration, with her mother making a fuss, Trey wanting to claim her for himself, and everyone filling the void made by Garnett's absence.

# Chapter Forty-Five
## ALL THE PIECES

*This accordion.* That's what she called it. Pressing in, when everyone came home and Garnett down from New York or Boston then stretching out when he left. The days and weeks turned faster now, years passing without their notice. Love and affection flowed when Garnett returned; she felt his struggle, finding it harder to leave them as the boys grew. But an estrangement of the heart dogged Adelyn, though she hid it from herself.

In the first year back home, she would remember only the vividness and color of her dreams. Then she woke one day, her consciousness asserting that Innis filled her dream. One morning she felt his hand on the top of her legs. She began to sleep-walk, first waking in the kitchen or on the side porch, and finally at the stables to fetch her horse. Captain Jackson caught her as she tried to lift the saddle onto Ramses, calling him Pharaoh.

"You're scaring your daddy, little girl. Pharaoh passed

the year you left for Paris." She heard his voice as she woke from a trance to see herself in her nightgown, her father's worried face. She told herself she should be frightened, but she felt exhilarated, secretly coveting Innis's sexual energy. Worst, though, she craved her gin drinks more and more.

"Sister, you are too thin." Adelyn decided her mother meant for her to have one less gin drink and one more serving of meat and potatoes. She sipped her drink slowly and forced a few more tiny mouthfuls of Aunt May's roast and gravy.

"I'm fine, Mama." She picked a bit more at her dinner. "Remember Tyler in that little makeshift crib Garnett made for him?" She went on before her mother spoke. "Him, asleep in the alcove after his dinner and a bath. That child is a miracle. Keeps on growing, though, so I guess we're doing it right."

"Won't you try some of this coconut cake? A little sweet won't hurt, you know. You don't have to keep that figure so flat."

Adelyn smiled more inwardly than what her mother could see. She could hear the words her mother didn't say, 'you're not in Paris anymore.' "Oh, Mama. I like this look. Think I'll take Ramses for a run along the big pasture after Trey and Tyler settle in." The rush of gin rose to the top of her head though she had stood slowly. "Here, let me help." Starting for the kitchen, she carried her plate and glass. Aunt May met her halfway in, knitting her brow. "Not you, too, Aunt May," Adelyn whispered.

"I'm not saying much though I'm seein' more than I care to." Aunt May bustled the dishes into the sudsy water, rinsed, and placed them on the rack. The older woman took Adelyn's elbow, as she had so often in Adelyn's early teens. A flood of memories swamped Adelyn and a contrite tear fell. "You have everyone worrying on you, girl. Cicely took the boys up right after their supper and got them washed up. They're up there now, waitin' on you."

"I'll go up now, then." Adelyn straightened her dress and wiped her eyes with the back of her hand. "Unless you have something for me to help you with here."

"Just go on, then." Aunt May's pinch to her elbow turned into an affectionate squeeze.

"One more thing. Don't break your mama's heart with hard drinking. It's that prohibition that's driving people up in the cities, and you too, crazy. That gin is poison. It will take your looks."

Aunt May's words fell hard on Adelyn, losing looks from gin being the top of her list of things she would war against. She took the steps to the boys' room quietly and two at a time. Cicely caught her doing that and laughed. "You haven't changed big sister. Not at all."

Adelyn inched into the boys' room. A breeze blew from the east bringing with it the promise of sea air. She bent down to her first-born and gently brushed his hair off his brow, pressing her lips to his forehead. "I believe you need a trip to the barber, child." Trey turned restlessly toward her and smiled in his dreams. "Baby boy," he mumbled in his sleep. To her the truth of his love for Tyler showed when he said so in that world of dreams, with no one there to impress. She stood and carefully walked back out, closing the door to just an inch to draw the breeze into and through the room. "I love them so much." She said this to Cicely and anyone who might have ears close enough to hear. She looked toward the attic.

Adelyn slipped into riding boots and silently laughed at the spectacle of heavy boots and a thin summer dress. September almost gone, she ticked off her fingers. *Fall season upon us, baby two years old today.* She grabbed her riding gloves and left by the back stairs, heading out into a cricket-filled night. The light from the barn's open door trailed a path though Adelyn swore she'd have no difficulty finding her beautiful horse even if she'd gone blind. Grabbing his mane for stability, she swung up onto his bare back. Startled for a moment when she thought she'd felt a hand on her arm hoisting her, she remembered Innis at the Howards when she was sixteen, how he had helped her up and called her 'little girl', and how indignant she felt.

"Let's get to Delia's 'cause she's waiting on me." Ramses heard the words he'd heard a hundred times and headed toward the open pasture for the welcomed leg-stretching gallop. The horse moved as though buoyed up by a substantial wind, and she let him have his lead, holding onto his thick mane, and with her head pressed into it, smelling his heavy animal musk.

Relieved to see lights on, she neared Delia and the Howard homestead. The early moon lighted their way. She released the tension in her shoulders, as she became more herself, though she didn't know who that was anymore. A shadow crossed the dirt path and without a bridle, she hugged into Ramses's flanks. The great horse pulled up, coming into a trot. "Good boy." She whispered into his ear as he rounded the corner to the back door. "No one there." She wondered where the shadow had gone, knew she'd seen it. Watching them approach, Adelyn jumped down, tied Ramses to the post, and saw Delia just inside the porch.

Delia lifted her arm to wave. *She always knows when I'll be here.*

Delia hugged her friend close. "You certainly keep that figure." She stretched Adelyn out at arm's length and squinted between the light of house and moon to delight in her friend's resilience in bouncing back. "I know you haven't had your coffee. Come in and visit and we'll see if I can find a bit of cake to go with it."

Sitting in a back parlor that her father had fashioned for "just us folks" and not the fancy and cavernous living room, they drank their coffee strong and black. "I like it black and sweet." Adelyn poured them each another cup.

"You'll sleep tonight?" Delia knitted her brow, then smoothed it out when Adelyn assured her.

"Mama thought I was being presumptuous coming over like this."

"You're family, no announcement needed. How are the boys?" Something soft and silver caught the light of the lamp. Delia lifted Adelyn's wrist to look at a bracelet on her slim wrist.

"Now is this some bauble from your Mr. Crawford?" she teased.

Adelyn gently pried her arm away to look at the delicate filigree. "No such thing. I found it in my drawer when I shook out my nightgown. Somehow, it had been sitting far back, and I guess with all the unpacking when we first got back, it was shoved down into a crevice. Almost hiding in there." She shook her wrist and the silver chain shimmered in the light. "I don't think it's Italian, maybe made here in the South."

Delia settled reading glasses onto her face and looked more closely. "Very old-timey, like some I saw when we were girls in high school."

"I've been finding all sorts of old things, pieces of lace from dresses I know I never wore, and such. Yet they seem familiar. Sometimes it makes me shiver 'cause I keep thinking there's some surprise just around the corner."

Both young women fell silent into a reverie of images conjured out of memories or created anew. "Stop it with your stories. You're part witch, I've always known it." This time Delia visibly shivered. "Addie, why did you come over tonight? Is it this?" She gestured toward the bracelet.

"Maybe. I feel so alone sometimes. I'm in a house full of people and of new life with Trey and Tyler. Yet there's something…"

Delia fanned herself. "I'm just glad Garnett is back with you all. But when I think on it, I've never known you two to be separate at holiday time, though dead summer is not a holiday 'round here."

Adelyn knew this to be true. Garnett always made sure to be home for Christmas and New Year, as though to protect them all from harbingers bearing evil messages. *How could that be?* Adelyn said as much to Delia, "What could it be about the holidays? That he finds his way home?" Delia raised an eyebrow signaling Adelyn some magic surrounded them.

"Sugar, those are special dates. Innis was in your life and you were in his. Garnett remembers that sharply, mind you, quite sharply. It cuts into him to this day. Innis was on fire for you then. Lord, I remember how he was when you took sick." Delia stopped fanning herself and poured more coffee. She continued then she picked at her cake. "Don't be making faces, Miss Thing. I'm afraid I'll be eating less of this with Lyle in my life." She dropped back to a quiet space.

"Delia. Did you fall off somewhere else? Is it all those séances with Momma Sorrow that have you confused?" Adelyn saw her friend's eyes light up and knew she'd have Delia's real intent soon enough.

"What did Innis say to you alone that day when everyone was everywhere else? The boys were all playing pool or backgammon, and I had gone into the kitchen to ask Miss Lily for some tea and cake."

Not expecting this, Adelyn's head shot up with Delia's question. *All these years later. No one had ever asked.* She prepared to make light of the event. Adelyn reminisced on how Innis sat and talked to her about Jane Eyre, asking what she liked most about Jane.

"He asked about my studies at school and picked up my copy of Jane Eyre, wanting to know if I liked the story and why people thought Mr. Rochester was so attractive. I told him I thought Mr. Rochester's rough looks were an aphrodisiac. Innis was surprised by that."

She smirked and Delia noticed. "You tell me what that smile means, Adelyn Jackson…uh, Crawford. Damnation, it's easy to fall back on old habits when we look back at old times, isn't it? But I know what you're doing and you're not going to get away with it."

Looking down at her hands, Adelyn saw the events of that time play in front of her, her feelings that day she rode to Delia's house, proclaiming then and now that she should make a rule to always wear her riding gloves.

"Get away with...? What? You mean Innis and me? I suppose as young women, I can tell what Innis said that day." She felt the air leave her lungs without any replacing it and thought she might choke, knowing Innis troubled her. She berated him. *These words will get out no matter.* Shaking her head, clearing a path to the past, Adelyn looked in the direction of Delia's grand sitting room.

"He was surprised when I spoke of Mr. Rochester and the passion I felt from Miss Brontë's writing. He sat down close and asked me if I felt passion that deeply, because I was so young. Before I could answer he had my hand. Innis said, 'Adelyn, you're like no one I ever met. Something modern and fresh and informed and even mature.' He despaired. It was a torment that even sixteen-year-old me could recognize. He repeated himself over and over. 'I have no right to say these things, I need...'"

"What did he need? Lord, Adelyn, his torment could have been that he was overstepping a boundary."

"He said as much, that he was old enough to know his feelings were wrong. And his voice caught in something near a sob. He held my hand; he pressed it to him. He lost all his flirtation and I knew he was speaking from his heart. He begged me, 'Adelyn, you have got to let me see you, be with you,' but then he added, 'even though there is someone.'"

"Someone else? Not any one of us here in Tulip Junction. Or we would have known." Delia folded her arms, making a stand, ready to demand. "Well? Did he tell you her name?"

Adelyn looked at her friend as if seeing her for the first time, the strawberry blonde hair and blue-green eyes. "You are such a picture. I'm so glad Lyle Spencer found you. Just don't wait too long to marry." She caught Delia's exasperation at Adelyn's stalling for time.

Adelyn continued, "You know, I fell ill with the fever. In truth I'd been sick all day, gradually weaker and the fever was coming over me. Honestly, Innis's declaration seemed to forestall the illness. And I was battling it. That was when I lost the battle." She turned to Delia. "I got chills, and you fetched blankets and then Garnett was carrying me upstairs to the guest room."

Delia listened very hard, stayed quiet for a space of time. The clock in the front hall, a distance away, sounded muted but the tick-tock reached them, comforting them. "You were mumbling and tossing about with the fever. Innis stayed by your side until your mama and daddy came by with Doctor Fanning."

Somewhere in all this talk, Adelyn felt steeped in that time and a part of it more than the moment she lived in. "It could have been yesterday. I felt my body burning, my lungs filling, and then I was lifted up."

"You talk nonsense. You were in that bed a week."

"No, Delia. I remember it, and I even told you when Garnett and I got married, how there was this girl and I took her place, somehow, when she died." Adelyn's heart quickened, as did her breathing. She felt her heart beating against her chest in painful stops and starts. "Delia, I remember it all."

"You frighten me, Adelyn. You're so pale." She took her friend's hand and held tight to it, fearing if she didn't Adelyn would be taken from her. "So cold, your hand is like death." Delia hugged Adelyn to her. "Wake up, sugar, you're slipping away. Slipping."

"I'm here, I'm here. Don't be afraid, Delia." Adelyn took large gulps of air. "You're right. It was as though I was being taken somewhere. Just now, I wanted to go."

They sat a long time, not talking, Delia waiting for Adelyn's breathing to go back to normal. Quietly, she held her friend's wrist and took her pulse, feeling for it to slow. "Adelyn. I'm going in to Papa and get his car keys. Ramses can stay here for the night. You can come by tomorrow. You're not riding that beast home tonight." And Adelyn had the good sense to agree.

The two friends spoke very little most of the way back to the Jackson farm. The moon hid behind a cloud, making the dark road even darker, and hard to navigate. Adelyn broke the silence first.

"It almost feels deliberate, this clear night turning so dark."

"Adelyn, thank goodness you're telling *me* your feelings, and not someone else. Yes, it does feel that way." Looking over at her friend's beautiful profile, she frankly asked. "Do you know who could do this?"

"Innis. He could make some magic. When he was crazy with jealousy, while I was on campus the first semester, he would send little messages to me." She paused, then answered Delia who had not yet asked. "He would send images of us walking together, of that first night... The night we…"

"Hush, Adelyn, you don't have to say."

Almost speaking just to herself, she went on. "I was too young to know what it all meant and how it would end. Lately, I've been so lonely and it's been for Innis. I need something from him."

Turning onto the circular gravel drive in front of the Jackson home, Delia stopped the car and pulled up on the brake. "From Innis, not Garnett? Why is that, Addie?"

"Unfinished. Something is unfinished between us. Innis had called the night his car crashed. He left a message for me at the dorm, saying he was coming down, needed to talk to me. The message sounded different. When he had his green-eyed devil of jealousy chasing him down, he would signal me by reminding me, saying 'you're the one' and other nonsense. It was always left unsaid, the 'or else.' Like, 'you best do as I say'. The darkness coming after us tonight, that was deliberate, Delia. Like that moon's shining on us, now that you got me safely home."

Hugging Delia, Adelyn asked. "Do you want to stay?"

"No such thing, honey. Innis isn't after me. I'm safe." She waved goodbye as they both laughed at Innis, and the magic. They laughed uneasily.

# Chapter Forty-Six
## *INNIS, ADELYN, AND GARNETT*

And the hammock swung many times before Innis visited Adelyn with his body on top of hers, his hands caressing her like he had in 1918. This time he made love to the woman, Trey's mother, Tyler's mother. This time Garnett came back for good; his strong, young man's body full of life, ready to redeem himself with his wife, and to face his brother, something that he guessed at instead of really knowing.

Now with Tyler, four years old, and his brother eight years old, Adelyn had some rest from toddlers and babies. Her mind forming around ideas now kept her restless.

She endured sleepless nights for weeks before her séances with Momma Sorrow. Each day of Innis's unseen visits enhanced her senses to hear more distinctly, see farther away, be mindful of others approaching long before they knew they would.

"When will you be going north?" Adelyn had just dusted off Garnett's largest valise and thought she should purchase a new one.

"Sugar, you must be feeble-minded for sure." He took her wrist and drew her closer to him, their bodies complementing the bulk of him against her legs. "After that parade of evil you described outside of the light the other night, I'm not going anywhere. Whatever is visiting you, I'm here to challenge it."

"And work?" Adelyn stalwartly refused to hint to him the measure of her happiness. He believed what she saw, giving her a curious feeling of his protection enveloping her. She didn't question his change. In a moment of quiet after a storm of passion, she had told him about Momma's séance, and finally that yes, she saw Innis in the shadows beyond the light from the veranda. Her eyebrow lifted slightly, enough to catch his attention.

"What's that silly bauble on your wrist? I know I didn't buy that nonsense for you."

"You do know how to avoid a subject, Mr. Crawford. Are you taking time to be with us?"

Looking at the bracelet, she twisted her arm this way and that for the silver to send off sharp points of light. "This? I don't know. Delia asked me, too. It was in the back of my drawer. Delia thought it looked like something for a much younger person."

Her memory wandered back to a small pile of things she'd been collecting for weeks, since Garnett got back, and Innis's making love to her. Little lacey handkerchiefs, some with embroidery, tiny stitches a girl would make in the outline of a violet, sewn with purple silk thread. Another, a lace veil for church, yellow from age. *And then this bracelet.* She knew. *Innis.*

Before Garnett asked again, Adelyn turned her arm behind her and shuffled off the flimsy piece of jewelry. Mentally she spoke out to Innis. *You took this from that girl and gave it to me. Shame, Innis.* Placing it in a pocket of her skirt, she felt a breeze, a warm breath at her neck, and then gone. The floorboards in the attic above her head creaked. A *reckoning looms, Innis.*

"Adelyn, I invited my daddy over tonight." Garnett's eyes watched the strange happenings, although if asked, he could not fit them precisely to Innis.

His voice fidgeted as he continued. "Mentioned inviting my father to your mama and she was delighted. It'll be nice for the boys as they're staying up to be with everyone." He drew her near him again, murmuring in her ear, "I've got a new project here in Tulip Junction and down in Savannah. We'll all talk tonight."

Adelyn saw all these things happening simultaneously, throwing an uneasiness into her voice. "I've missed your daddy these many months. Such a great idea for him to be here."

She pressed her cheek to his ear and slid her lips down to his neck at his open collar. Their bedroom door ajar, Cicely tapped lightly. They pulled back and beckoned her in with a dress on her arm.

"Would this be nice for tonight?" She held up a dress and smiled as Garnett mumbled something about seeing about supplies for a summer wine punch he wanted to make and left the two sisters to share their secrets.

Taking the dress from Cicely, Adelyn admired the light green color. "No sleeves, that's good. Lord knows it'll be warm in the dining room." As a heavy humidity settled, Adelyn opened her chifforobe wide to find a proper dress that would keep her cool. "Now, this is strange indeed. I swear this was way in the back." She held the dress up to herself.

"Why not that one?" Cicely stretched out her hand to touch the gossamer thin white cotton dress with short, capped sleeves, woven for the air to pass easily through. "Just the thing, Addie." Cicely fanned her face with her hand, the perspiration beading on her lip.

Adelyn admired the fine stitching of white flowers on the white dress. *Have I really gotten this thin?* She shrugged with relief to think she maintained such a lithe figure after two babies. "Yes, this is perfect, thank you for saying so, Cicely."

Captain Jackson rose out of his seat. "A toast before we begin. Welcome back, Garnett, and happy to know you'll be here most days, and welcome to your daddy. Will Crawford, we're hoping you'll be no stranger to our table."

"It's nice to have family all at the same table." Mary Jackson lifted her glass to her husband's toast. She wore her lacy dress she considered special, for no specific occasion but for every celebration, from christenings to dances.

Happy to see her mother so relaxed, Adelyn looked toward Garnett's father with warm eyes as he sat as a special guest at the other end of the table, senior to all except his host, Captain Jackson. The boys, Trey and Tyler, sat on either side of him, and Garnett, usually at Adelyn's side, seated himself across the table and next to Tyler. The table fairly groaned with food, serving dishes, and glassware.

"Will, would you start with the blessing tonight?" Captain Jackson hiked up the side where his bad hip needed easing, and Adelyn winced in sympathy. *Momma Sorrow surely has a potion to relieve his pain.*

Nodding to Adelyn's father, Will Crawford folded his hands in prayer. "Bless us, O Lord, and these, Thy gifts, which we are about to receive from Thy bounty, through Christ, our Lord. Amen." All said a quiet "Amen" and crossed themselves. Lifting his eyes, Adelyn watched Garnett's father rapidly search each face, and she felt the sincere blessing of this kind and gentle man.

In that quiet space, Adelyn noticed the constant whirring buzz of the fans, set out in the hall to soften the noise, yet close enough to cool the great room. She felt Garnett looking straight into her heart, saw that it skipped a beat. *I know you fight a horrible battle. Soon it will stop.* She lowered her gaze as his message seized her and looked up to answer him. *Please. Just wait for me.*

And all the while the clatter of forks and knives on china, and the conversations spiraling up from the warm, beating hearts in the room masked the conflict, that two of their family fought a war between two worlds, a war of Innis's power. Trey's questions for his Grandpa Will about the best flies to use on a fishing pole distracted Garnett for a moment.

A loud knock at the front door reverberated like thunder and halted their familial chorus. Nearest to the front hall, Garnett jumped up with Trey and the ever-curious Tyler, who grabbed at his father's hand. Adelyn could see the boy tremble with fear. Tyler, she decided, had the gift, attuned to the spirits around every corner tonight. She rushed after them while Garnett barred her and the boys to keep them behind his imaginary safe zone.

"Hold up now. Stand back some," he admonished in a low voice. "All kin came here tonight, but it may just be one of the neighbors." He turned to Adelyn. "There may be some strangers on the roads."

Garnett voiced what Captain Jackson and others thought—in the midst of the Depression, hobo camps along the railroad tracks and deeper into the countryside posed a subtle threat to the safety of the homes in their area. The large door opened, emitting a creaking sound that echoed through the hall. "Mama's great granddaddy fashioned this door in 1844." Adelyn said absently to her boys.

"Well, it sure sounds like it." Garnett's face flushed as he felt her body pressing hard against the back of him. He recognized two men's faces from such a long time ago. "I've seen you before."

"Yessir." Their hats came off simultaneously. The fairer of the two cleared his throat. "I'm Kendall Bonet from down near the end of the Junction. And this here's my cousin, Louis." Kendall pronounced the name as the French would, *Louee*.

Garnett and Adelyn saw two thin and wiry men several inches shorter than Garnett. Garnett extended his hand and shook first Kendall's hand, then Louis's.

"What can I do for you?" He stopped short of saying "boys" in deference to their age, several years senior to him. "I remember you both. I met you near winter while I still attended college." *When Adelyn almost died.* He repeated himself, "Is there something I can do for you?"

Kendall stepped forward. "Mister Garnett, I've come upon some things of Lucianne's that I thought you might want to see." The young man's thin cheek bones stood out when he spoke. Kendall held out a small diary, the kind a young girl might keep, covered with a checked red and white napkin.

Adelyn reached out to touch the diary and found herself hesitating. She turned to Garnett. "I'll take the boys back to finish their dinner." She thanked whatever heavenly spirit for the dessert of apple pie set on the table that tempted Trey and Tyler to return without a fuss.

"Excuse me, Mama, and everyone." She said this while quickly settling the two boys in front of their desserts, and left, eager to hear more of the Bonets.

The two men had their heads close together speaking, one, and then the other, to Garnett. As they looked toward her, she sensed they saw her for the first time. A change arose in Kendall Bonet who stared hard at Adelyn. He handed the diary to her.

"Lucianne?" Adelyn's enhanced senses watched the sound as Kendall's voice echoed off the walls and the high ceilings stretching to the second floor, and beyond, to the attic.

The thin, blond Kendall reached out, beyond Garnett and his cousin Louis. "Lucianne, girl. How can this be?" His voice held ten years of sorrow, of longing for his dead little sister and a strange hope to be given this gift, to have her hear him one last time.

As a man who worked the earth, he sensed he would not possess time and good health for long. The heavy heat and dampness of the country air clung to the trees, grass, and earth, seeming to suffocate them all.

Adelyn looked toward Kendall's outstretched hand and held the warm and heavily callused palm against her own. "Kendall?" she spoke with another's voice. Adelyn closed her eyes, feeling her body lift above them all, heard strained voices, Garnett, her mother, and Cicely, all calling to her as she left them all, the diary falling from her hands.

A woman's voice, deeper than Lucianne's, speaks to Adelyn. *"You can open your eyes, now. No fear, Adelyn."* Sarah Crawford appears in Adelyn's mind; still young, close to Adelyn's current age, sitting on a rocking chair on the wide porch of her home, her hair dark and sleek and falling down her back.

"Sarah?" Adelyn now in Sideways, opens her eyes to the still clouds, the green grass that does not move in a place that has no wind or breeze or storm. Peacefulness, though, moves, descending on the troubled mind that wants to understand. *You brought me here.* Adelyn's thought travels to Innis and Garnett's mother, and sees Sarah look out toward the eastern sky where no sun appears. Two figures move toward them from a long distance.

"They don't seem in a hurry," Adelyn murmurs to Sarah.

"No, *chère*, there's time for them to come." Momma Sorrow's warm scent of French perfume gives freshness to this other world. She responds to Adelyn's thoughts. *"Chère*, I am outside this place, just to guide you through. Just stay, stay there for now."

Adelyn no longer feels the pull on her body and mind to leave, as she sees Innis and Lucianne approach.

"Stand with me." Sarah places herself in front of Adelyn. Innis reaches the porch and stops, angry. "Why? Mother? I thought you loved me."

Adelyn flies back home—raises her head from a pillow to see Sarah and Innis at the foot of her bed. *Come to me now?* Adelyn hears Innis but feels some other strength pull her away from Innis's will.

Worried faces— Garnett, her mother, and Momma Sorrow—looked down at her where she lays on the sofa. "She's back." Garnett's voice choked a jubilant sob.

"I'm sorry, Lucianne. I didn't know." Adelyn's voice became her own again as she felt her spirit in pieces throughout the room, squeezing Garnett's hand while searching Momma Sorrow's face, wanting to know but afraid to ask. None could see Innis standing behind them all.

*Momma knows you're here, Innis.* Strong arms, Garnett's, lifted her. *The way you did all those years ago.* She moved in and out of a deep sleep.

"Mr. Garnett, let's everyone leave her to rest. I'll stay with Adelyn." Momma said this in a rush to avoid argument and to empty the bedroom.

Adelyn wondered whether Momma Sorrow hypnotized them because they all left together except Momma and Kendall.

"Little sister." Though Kendall whispers from the farthest side of the room, yet she hears him.

"Confusing changes," Adelyn said out loud. "Kendall, your sister needs to speak." Her voice changes, "I love you, Kendall." Tears wash Adelyn's face as Lucianne's spirit moves inside her. Lucianne cries out. "I'm sorry I hurt you, my dear brother! I disappointed you. You had all your own dreams, threw them away on me. I didn't...."

She released a heavy sigh as Kendall came closer to Adelyn, reached his hand out to her. "No, no, hush, girl. All I ever wanted was a better life for you."

Adelyn's body moved, thrashing left and right, pushing the covers away. She settled with a gentle touch from Momma Sorrow. "They're making me leave, Kendall, I have to go with them, go back. But I'll come to you again; look for me in dreams."

Her voice broke off, and Adelyn's eyes closed and reopened as she sat up, wiping tears from her face, startled to see Kendall in her room.

"*Ma chère*, don't fret." Momma calmed her with a

touch. Kendall nodded to Momma and left the room. Adelyn saw a sliver of light, though the heavy drapes and large hurricane shutters pulled to darken the room. "It's already day." Sounds of movement in the attic awakened her further. "Innis still here, up to no good."

"He moved about all night without stopping." Momma pushed out on the shutter to lighten the room. "He's angry, that one is. He's stuck, or he'd be down here bedeviling you, he would."

Jamming the pillows behind her to sit better, Adelyn unbuttoned her white dress. "What is keeping him up there, Momma?"

Momma Sorrow straightened the blanket across Adelyn's legs. "There's been a moral reckoning, and you are almost free, child."

Adelyn knew there was more—power she gained from Sarah and Lucianne holding Innis away from her. She pushed the covers off her legs.

"I'm the only one to end this. You know it's true." A mix of sorrow in her voice—Sarah and Lucianne on the other side, calm with one another. They had formed a bond.

"Tell me now, *chère*, what you learned over there." Momma unwound her bright blue and orange turban on the bed, and carefully flattened and then folded it, winding it without benefit of a mirror snugly around her head. Just so, in that special way she had. Time spent in winding and unwinding as she sorted thoughts; her hands busy while her mind worked. They did not speak for Innis to hear but spoke from their hearts to one another.

*I learned about Innis's love for me.* Adelyn waited until Momma came to the best conclusions from her thoughts. *He planned to use my love.*

The sounds of the attic grew quieter, Innis, biding his time, sure that he would win Adelyn back. She slipped off the white dress and wrapped her summer robe around her, tying it loosely. She experienced a moment of lightheadedness. She stilled, getting her bearings, letting the blood settle in her. *Hungry.*

They left the room and climbed the narrow steps to the attic. Momma opened a deep pocket in her full and long skirt, handing Adelyn a sweet cake of raisins and nuts wrapped in a dinner napkin. "Lots of energy," she whispered in Adelyn's ear. Adelyn chewed it slowly and swallowed, and Momma passed her a small flask. The cork popped, emitting a flowery fragrance tasting mildly of licorice. Refreshed with these two small works of magic, Adelyn silently opened the door, walked in a deliberate fashion. *The time had come.*

"*Chère*, you must know all these years, why you never saw Lucianne long enough to remember. He kept you two separated from one another, kept you from the truth. Your own magic flew you into her when she died."

"I went into her body in her coffin. I saw Granny, Kendall, and the family all around her, weeping." Adelyn saw movement and heard Innis stirring again, yet he waited.

"There was talk back then that women carrying life inside them weakened and perished from the influenza easier than most. All that strength to make the baby left none for the mother," Momma said. "*Chère*, Lucianne was the victim."

"Stop. Stop." Innis implores them. Adelyn sees first his white summer shoes, then the razor-sharp pleat on his white summer slacks, as Innis moves out of the shadow to where they could see him. He hesitates to approach them and does not touch her. Turning to Momma, his words bite. "You, you. If you had stayed away."

A veil of serenity envelops Momma Sorrow. Adelyn has seen all in the month since Innis had her on the hammock. "If I had stayed away, you would have taken her where you live. Look at you now, you are as you were then, when she, a girl of sixteen…when you took her." Momma's stern words held a purity, a truth.

"A man in love?" He sneers at Momma. "I was a hardly a man, twenty-one. And my love was real. You can't question that. There was no motive except love." He covers his face as tears form in his eyes and run down his cheeks.

"When you held my hand the first time, Innis – you're like that young man you were." She turns to Momma and looks at both of them. "That was the truth then, Momma, Innis. I don't doubt it. We both felt it. You have to go back to the other side, to Lucianne, the young woman you loved first, and who died with your baby in her. "

Adelyn leans against the older woman, gathering the strength she will need. "Help him, Momma, because for a very short time he loved me, mourned me, when he thought I was dying."

"He had already gone to one funeral, Adelyn. Sarah learned and knew all these things, died to keep him from taking your happiness…and Garnett's." Momma's words were like ice water in a desert.

Anguished, Innis cries, "Can't you see? I wanted to build the bridge, yes. I wanted to come back to live it over, and over, and…." A light from inside Innis shines out, but it is not a soft light, instead a harsh light that needs softening.

"I have Garnett and Trey and Tyler. You have to go, Innis, my sweet Innis."

He fades, his fist up against his mouth, an unutterable sadness enveloping him. No longer can she see him as she had at sixteen, her gallant knight, and at eighteen, her strong young man who took her to young womanhood. He's gone.

The pieces fell into place. "When I visited their world this last time, Innis was exposed by Lucianne and Sarah. The unborn child had moved on. That is Lucianne's sorrow to endure. Innis spoke of breaking the bond, saying he will come into this world again, threatening, saying he would rock me like he did in that hammock."

"But this time, Momma, you heard his thoughts, sent them to Sarah." Adelyn squeezed Momma's hand. "And Sarah rose up and advised Innis his evil desires to abandon Lucianne were not possible. Sarah embraced Lucianne; the bond broke for us. If he could finally join me here, he would change all of it for all of us."

It was Momma's turn to ask, "Why did he come back then?"

Adelyn held out her hand to Momma. "He had to hear me say no."

## Chapter Forty-Seven
### THE AFTERMATH

Life continued below while Momma and Adelyn helped Innis back to his proper world, the world he'd created and hoped to join with Adelyn's world. With each step descended, Adelyn knew it could never be, knew most when she saw the life all around her, her family gathered on that bright Saturday in 1931, Cicely and Trey with their heads together reading *Black Beauty*, so like Adleyn and her love of Pharaoh and then Rameses.

Adelyn glanced at Tyler with Garnett's father, learning how to tie a fly, the fishing tackle box all scattered on the floor and the kitchen table full of feathers and the special string used to wrap flies.

Then Garnett, off in the corner of the living room in the big overstuffed chair, ruminating over a law book on land grants, occupied with title searches of Tulip Junction, drew her full attention. He lifted his handsome head and met her eyes the instant she sought him out. And they knew true and magical love once again.

# *Epilogue 1947*

She caught herself daydreaming about all of it, how it all happened, and remembered it vividly, full of color, emotion, and romanticism. *Yes, it had all happened because the magic stayed; it didn't wear out over time.* Adelyn got up from her desk and straightened the long skirt. "Skirt lengths have gone up and down so many times." She says this out loud and shakes her head at her own peculiar ways, talking aloud as if to ghosts.

She passed the mirror that reflected back the image of her university office, and saw first the young girl she'd been, then the young mother. And now?

"Well," she fussed with her hair and drew closer to the mirror, "yes, some gray strands stand out." When she frets over them, Garnett reminds her silver must be found among the gold. "Foolish man." She says this kindly with a soft smile forming on her lips.

"We all were so young." Adelyn pulls back a hairsbreadth from the mirror. *Sometimes too close is not a good thing.* Then she scrutinizes the subtle lines near the corners of her eyes, and sees movement behind her, someone wearing white. She turns abruptly. *Enough.*

A knock on the door. "Must be Trey, he said he wanted to see me today while he was on campus." She hesitates. "Come in."

Trey opens the door, swinging it wide to let himself and a young woman enter together, side by side. "Mama, I'd like you to meet someone."

Adelyn's heart skips at the sight of her first-born, beautiful son. His longish hair flops over his brow, a sleek and shiny dark brown, his eyes the same color of his uncle.

He shoots a nervous hand up to push the hair to the side, a gesture she has seen before. *Where?* She notices he holds the girl's hand, a beautiful girl, long blonde hair caught behind the ears with combs on each side. Adelyn recalls seeing a movie star with those same combs and wonders at the way young people find such objects to invite into their own world. She recalls seeing the girl on campus.

"This is Lucianne Bonet, Mama. She's from up our way in Tulip Junction."